The Block

Peter Vollmer

First published in 2018 by Endeavour Media Ltd.

Table of Contents

CHAPTER 1   9

CHAPTER 2   20

CHAPTER 3   23

CHAPTER 4   33

CHAPTER 5   40

CHAPTER 6   46

CHAPTER 7   50

CHAPTER 8   60

CHAPTER 9   70

CHAPTER 10   78

CHAPTER 11   81

CHAPTER 12   83

CHAPTER 13   85

CHAPTER 14   97

CHAPTER 15   108

CHAPTER 16   110

CHAPTER 17   114

CHAPTER 18   119

CHAPTER 19   123

CHAPTER 20   128

CHAPTER 21   132

CHAPTER 22   136

CHAPTER 23   138

CHAPTER 24   144

CHAPTER 25   152
CHAPTER 26   154
CHAPTER 27   158
CHAPTER 28   163
CHAPTER 29   173
CHAPTER 30   175
CHAPTER 31   176
CHAPTER 32   179
CHAPTER 33   181
CHAPTER 34   186
CHAPTER 35   188
CHAPTER 36   190
CHAPTER 37   192
CHAPTER 38   193
CHAPTER 39   196
CHAPTER 40   197
CHAPTER 41   199
CHAPTER 42   203
CHAPTER 43   206
CHAPTER 44   209
CHAPTER 45   212
CHAPTER 46   213
CHAPTER 47   214
CHAPTER 48   216
CHAPTER 49   220
CHAPTER 50   222
CHAPTER 51   223
CHAPTER 52   225
CHAPTER 53   227

CHAPTER 54   231

CHAPTER 55   236

CHAPTER 56   241

CHAPTER 57   246

CHAPTER 58   251

CHAPTER 59   253

CHAPTER 60   256

CHAPTER 61   263

CHAPTER 62   266

CHAPTER 63   268

CHAPTER 64   270

CHAPTER 65   272

CHAPTER 66   283

CHAPTER 67   285

CHAPTER 68   290

CHAPTER 69   294

CHAPTER 70   297

CHAPTER 71   304

About the author   310

Acknowledgement

Firstly, I wish to thank my copy editor, David Baclaski. He worked his usual magic while interacting with me until we both were satisfied with the result. He has done a splendid job. Secondly, my agent in London, Thomas J. Cull, who was always there when needed unrelentingly works hard at getting my work published. Finally, my daughter, Dr Lindi Murray, who was always willing and ready to lend her support.

CHAPTER 1

David returned the security guard's greeting with a nod. He strode through the opened steel security door and entered the rear of the main banking hall. It was only eight o'clock but already a few of the early birds had arrived. This was not unusual. These people drove in by car, some from afar, and wanted to miss the morning rush hour traffic. He, as usual, had caught the commuter train. From Park Station, he had walked the six blocks to the main branch of the Republic Bank, which took up the ground and mezzanine floors of the fourteen-storey building.

David was in his early thirties, six foot two in his socks, and broad shouldered. His chiselled features and square jaw complemented his rugged looks. He had an unruly mop of black hair, which required copious amounts of hair conditioner to maintain some degree of control, which belied his career as a banker.

He lived in the sprawling Witwatersrand Metropolitan complex. This megacity with Johannesburg at its centre was similar to any other major urban sprawl in the world, one city adjoining another as they expanded over time.

His apartment overlooked a lake with a golf course on the opposite shore but, unfortunately, the building's proximity to a major feeder thoroughfare did not qualify it for the degree of elitism he had sought. Had the highway not passed below his sixth-floor balcony, the apartment's price would have been almost double.

David had chosen banking as his career, but only after common sense prevailed. Compulsory military training after school saw him opt for the Air Force, signing on for a seven-year stint, which included the conflict in Angola. He did well, emerging as a captain with wings and getting time on a host of different aircraft. He also qualified as a helicopter pilot. Once this was over, he gave up everything to acquire the necessary academic qualifications, including drinking and women, except for the occasional one-night stand. The sacrifice paid off and he graduated with a degree in accounting and a good, if boring, job in banking.

Huge armoured glass panels surrounded the banking hall on three sides, stretching from floor to ceiling, on the mezzanine floor. The building took up half a block, with the bank's executive and administrative head office occupying the remaining floors.

As usual, he bought the morning paper, the *Rand Daily Mail*, from the corner newsvendor on his way in to work and then ducked into a small coffee shop he religiously visited before starting his working day.

He nursed a cup of tea and scanned the headlines. The confrontation between the British government and Ian Smith's Rhodesian Front in Southern Rhodesia was intensifying. He skimmed the article. Smith was adamant that majority rule in his country would not occur during his lifetime, irrespective of what others demanded. David sighed. Such a statement was tantamount to throwing down a gauntlet. The British Prime Minister, Harold Wilson, demanded inflexibly that Smith's government consider an immediate move away from the current representation disparity in the country, where whites had 95% of the votes in national elections although they represented only 5% of the population. The political situation was volatile. The pressure from the Commonwealth countries was intense. Certain recently fully-independent African countries demanded Britain resort to military intervention, threatening to break away from the Commonwealth if she did not. David wondered what the outcome would be. It seemed that Ian Smith's Rhodesian Front party was not about to capitulate but would stand its ground. What would Smith do – break away from Britain as he threatened?

Wilson was correct morally, of course. But how often do morals play a role in political power games? Those holding power invariably have a problem relinquishing it. Eventually the will of the majority would prevail and history would repeat itself. David was comfortable with the way things were. The concept of power-sharing with blacks left him with a feeling of unease. He enjoyed his privileged life and hoped that the whites would remain in power in Southern Africa. He preferred not to see a change in his lifetime. Worry about any disproportion later was his attitude.

Most whites in both Rhodesia and South Africa shared these sentiments.

Every day at nine sharp, the bank's doors opened to the public. Upstairs on the first floor, the foreign exchange dealers sat hunched over their adding machines, out of the public's eye, forever poring over incoming telexes, which revealed the slightest fluctuations in exchange rates, and drafting new messages to be dispatched urgently. Their continuous striving to improve and secure the bank's financial lot was a quotidian paper war.

David had recently been appointed the sub-accountant of the Foreign Department and was responsible for its activities and the performance of his fifty-six staff members and senior clerks. This was the bank's biggest branch.

He settled himself into his accountant's box. This was wood-panelled, slightly raised on a platform about a foot higher than the general banking floor, the top half of the glass allowing him unfettered vision. It contained a low, highly polished wooden cabinet, executive desk and three chairs; and, giving evidence of his status, carpet. It was only the more important clients who would be directed to his box and then take a seat opposite his desk.

He poured his own tea. Everyone else had to collect his from an urn on a trolley. David's was brought to him on a silver tray with a teapot, milk jug and bowl; and three cups made of fine porcelain. This, even more than carpeting, gave him intra-office cachet.

It was four-thirty and David had just finished signing his name to a host of documents when an accountant approached and, without invitation, pulled out a chair and sat down opposite him.

'David, they want to see you on the fourteenth floor.'

The statement caught him by surprise.

'What on earth for?'

'They didn't say, just that they wanted to see you.'

'Well, I'll have to wear my best suit tomorrow, won't I?' After the sarcasm, he smiled to mask his concern.

'Sorry friend, it's now. Immediately. Not tomorrow,' the accountant said. He leaned back in the chair, a grim expression on his face.

'Know any reason why?'

'No.'

'Christ. That's serious. Okay, I'm on my way.'

'Done anything wrong lately? Not another air hostess, I hope. God, the lengths a man will go just for a piece of skirt,' the accountant sneered with a lecherous grin.

'Not unless it's that piece of fluff I took home Friday night.'

'Could be. I hear she was a screamer. Maybe somebody complained.'

'Fuck off, will you?' David grimaced and rushed off to the men's room to check his appearance.

A letter invariably advised a promotion in the bank and documents setting out revised scales of remuneration and benefits. Dismissals were different. You were summoned. But that was to a lower floor, the domain of the Personnel Department. He was puzzled. With a sense of foreboding, he entered the lift and requested the fourteenth floor from the operator.

David had been summoned to the top floor once before during The Infamous Airhostess Hubbub. Just thinking about that now made him cringe. He had noticed her in the banking hall, standing at the Information counter, dressed in an air hostess uniform. That she was beautiful was undeniable. His hormones reacted instantly. He just had to have her; she was an opportunity not to be missed. After she conducted her business and left, he requested her signature card from the junior clerk behind the counter. Using these details, he contacted her and soon he persuaded her to have dinner with him. One thing led to another and a short, but passionate, affair followed. When he dumped her some months later, she had gone to Head Office and reported that he had used the personal details from her account opening form to trace and contact her, a serious breach of information and confidentiality.

Fortunately, the General Manager – Personnel did not consider his actions serious and merely verbally admonished him. No letter of reprimand followed and nothing appeared on his file. Maybe, he thought, they realised they had already invested heavily in him and probably believed there would be no repetition of romantic relationships based on information gleaned from the bank's records. Of course, the story leaked out, and he was labelled as quite a ladies' man, not true really, but now there was little he could do about it. He was sure that whenever he walked into the Waste Department, where scores of young women sorted the host of cheques that passed through the bank daily, the women pulled their short mini-skirts down, an involuntary reaction when confronted by a womaniser, and were probably convinced he was a voyeur or some other rake.

As the elevator doors slid open, David stepped out into the vast, opulent reception area. The wall-to-wall carpets were deep and dark green, the walls wood-panelled, and the reception area taken up by two clusters of leather sofas, armchairs and coffee tables. The two large paintings adorning the walls were by a renowned South African artist, worth a fortune, befitting the executive division of the bank. A few discreet flower arrangements were the only other decoration.

Margaret Stewart, private secretary to Robert Muller, the managing director, sat behind her desk. She was in her mid-thirties, a tall beautiful blonde with legs that seemed to go on forever. She always dressed in a dark suit and matching shoes. In the banking hall, she was known as Miss Stewart. Rumour had it that she was more than just a secretary to the MD, but no one knew whether this was true or said out of spite. This had given rise to a number of jokes and every time David saw her the best came to mind. Once, the bank was held up and the robbers forced management to render themselves starkers and lie on their stomachs. Miss Stewart, returning from lunch, walked in on the scene and, without any prompting, stripped and lay down on her back next to the MD.

'This is a hold-up, not a staff party,' Muller deadpanned.

David suppressed a laugh and smiled.

She returned his smile.

'Good afternoon, Mr Tusk. You seem in good spirits. Just a moment please.' She winked and he wondered about its significance. She always seemed to play him. Maybe she also knew about the air hostess contretemps.

She disappeared through a door marked 'Boardroom' in some fancy script. She reappeared, holding the door open for him.

'You can go in now,' she said and gave him another wink.

David stepped through the door and halted, surprised. He quickly got a hold of himself. Every chair in the boardroom was taken. The MD sat at the head of the table, the rest of the executives seated along both sides. Clearly, they had been there for a while as papers, files, cups and glasses littered the table. Some had even removed their jackets. This had obviously been an all-day session.

'Good afternoon,' he croaked.

'Come in, Tusk. Take a seat. Somebody please find the man a chair,' Robert Muller said, 'Coffee or tea?'

'Tea, please,' David stammered.

Muller waited until David was brought a cup of tea and then made himself comfortable, not that David felt comfortable. His sense of foreboding was strong.

'I take it you have heard Rhodesia proposes to announce a unilateral declaration of independence and Britain will not recognise it. Let me rephrase that. We believe this is about to happen and that there is no saving the situation between the two countries,' Robert Muller said quietly. He stopped, waiting for a comment from David, his fingers tapping the table.

'Well, it would seem to be highly probable. Or so the papers say.'

'Have you a personal view on this?' Muller raised his eyebrows.

Was this a trick question? Why would they ask me this? Best take a neutral stance, he thought. He knew the Bank's board and general management tended to lean to the right.

'I'm a South African. They're doing no more than we did in 1961, when we declared a republic and broke away from the Commonwealth. There was no way then that we would accept majority rule and we were not about to let anybody coerce us into it. In retrospect, it would seem the government foresaw what would eventually occur. Although belated, Rhodesia appears to be following the same logic we chose. I suppose I'm comfortable with that.'

The Human Resources Director gave him the faintest of nods, indicating David said the right thing. It was he who got him off the hook with the neurotic air hostess.

Muller did not respond but glanced around the table, a meaningful look, which was acknowledged and returned by a few. He picked up a file from the table and opened it.

'You speak four languages. That's impressive. I see that you spent time in England and France?'

'Yes. I'm actually of German extraction. My mother's second marriage was to an Englishman. They live in Paris. I spent time with them and went to the Alliance Française for about a year.'

'A seven-year stretch in the Air Force. You're a captain and you do your annual stints to maintain your reserve status?'

'Yes, I'm a captain,' he replied and grew puzzled by the direction of Muller's questioning.

There was a lot more to it. His Air Force training had been comprehensive and, while never in command, he had co-piloted clandestine flights into Cabinda and Angola. This information was top secret and would remain so.

'It says here that you are a helicopter pilot.'

'That's correct.'

'But as an officer, you are bound by your secrecy oath? You attended the Air Force College?'

What was this man getting at?

'Yes, sir, that's right.'

'Good,' Muller said, 'Now, Tusk, listen carefully. All the other commercial banks of note in South Africa have British shareholders. In fact, Great Britain itself holds substantial shares in these banks. This is not the case as far as we are concerned. We are truly a South African bank.

'A unilateral declaration of independence by the Rhodesian government will have severe consequences for their country. Their assets will be seized. Their foreign currency reserves, if any, will be frozen. Although I'm sure the Rhodesians would have foreseen this and cleaned out the foreign accounts.' He paused to allow the subdued laughter from the table to die.

'Rhodesia needs to continue to function as a country. British-controlled banks in South Africa and Rhodesia would have to abide by their majority shareholders' directives and would not be able to assist the Rhodesian government to circumvent the financial sanctions the British will impose. We propose to be Rhodesia's banking ally. What do you say to that?'

'You want my opinion?' David was surprised.

'Yes.'

He thought for a few seconds, wanting to say the correct thing.

'Well, we are already represented in their country as the Rhodesian Commercial Bank which, I understand, is wholly owned by us and which we manage as an extension of our bank here. In fact, we run their branches as if these were branches of our division. Staff transfers and all loan and overdraft facilities are approved from here, that sort of thing. During my stint in the Advance Department in Head Office, I dealt with large Rhodesian overdraft applications, all approved in Johannesburg. They're really no different from any other branch, other than by name.'

'Impressive. You seem to be well informed. Well, we wish to put you in charge of a new division whose main function would be to keep the doors of trade open, allowing Rhodesian goods to be exported and enabling them to buy and import essential goods on the world markets. We believe it's a foregone conclusion that a trade embargo will be slapped on their country by the British as well as the United Nations. How this will eventually relate to the rest of the world, we don't know; but we propose to be ready for this. As far as your banking activities are concerned, you will report directly to Mr de Groot, our general manager in charge of our Foreign Department, and to Mr Butler, the Rhodesian Minister of Trade and Industries. Of course, not directly to him, but you would follow prescribed protocol. As you adjust, you will become a Rhodesian operative as it were, but ultimately you are still in our employ and whenever this mess is resolved, you would return to the fold.'

'I'm going to be working for the Rhodesians?' His voice rose in inflection.

The first hint of irritation appeared on Muller's face.

'Yes and no. Primarily, you will still be working for us. Anything to do with Rhodesia will be handled by your special department. However, the interaction necessary between you and the Rhodesians, in particular the Rhodesian Central Intelligence Organisation, requires that you be given some military status. I'm told that you are to be seconded to the Rhodesian Air Force as a Flight Lieutenant. There is no intention that you should fly their aircraft or participate in any military manœuvres. This is merely to facilitate interaction with their various undercover divisions, which are run on military lines, as is their police force.'

David was astounded. 'But I don't know any of these people. I'm not even a Rhodesian. I've never even been there.'

This did not seem to perturb the MD.

'You will be introduced to those that I've mentioned. You're an essential part of a team that Butler is assembling, but more of that later.' He paused. 'This will entail a good deal of travel on both of your passports. We know that besides your South African passport, you hold a German passport as well. You will halt all your activities with the South African Air Force. Don't concern yourself; we have already been in touch with them. I might add that the Air Force has sanctioned this 'somewhat unorthodox transfer', as they put it, and they will accept your resignation and confirm that on application at some later stage you will be accepted back with your previous rank at least. The South African government considers Rhodesia an ally and what you will be doing is indirectly of strategic importance to South Africa. Do you accept?'

He was stuck dumb. The entire room looked at him and waited for his reply.

Finally, he spoke.

'Just a question or two, if I may. Why's this being done through the bank and not directly by the government? And why my resignation?'

'The government intends to keep a very low profile. They wish to create the impression that they have no knowledge of this and that you are acting on your own initiative. It would be embarrassing if it were to be discovered that a South African military officer was in any way involved in a sanctions-busting exercise. They will also add a Rhodesian passport to your collection.'

'Acting on my own initiative?'

Muller sighed. 'Calm down, Tusk. Sometime in the future, this will stand you in good stead. We just want to know whether you are prepared to accept.'

Good God, he was well aware that were he to refuse, he would be shooting himself in the foot and throwing his career out the window. This sounded like a Mafia option. They weren't asking him. They were telling him. But then, why not? He wasn't married. He had no real relationships. It was all a bit of a Hobson's choice, wasn't it?

'It sounds attractive, but it won't harm my banking career if the British get to know of me?'

Hell, had he actually said it sounded attractive?

'Tusk, let me personally assure you – how do I put it? It will definitely lend your career tremendous impetus.' Robert Muller emphasised the last two words and leant over him with raised eyebrows and a smile revealing his top four incisors as well as both canines.

David hesitated and then threw caution to the wind.

'I'll do it.'

'Good man.'

'Hear, hear,' was murmured around the table.

'I need not say you appreciate the need for utmost secrecy. Not a word to anyone. This is serious. The British will not take kindly to what you will be doing. We don't quite know yet how we will go about things, but meanwhile just carry on with what you have been doing. You do have an understudy, don't you?'

'Yes, sir, a Mr Hartman.'

'Good. A capable man, I presume?'

'Yes, very capable, in fact.'

'Rest assured that should your new duties take you elsewhere, your position will not be given to another, and Hartman will merely stand in for you. Thank you. You may go now.' Muller rose from his chair. 'Not a word.' He came round the table to shake David's hand. 'Oh, by the way, others will want to know why you were here. Just say that we are investigating a foreign exchange fraud at one of our branches and that, at this stage, you are not allowed to disclose any details.'

It was well after six when he left the bank.

The usual late-afternoon thundershower for which Johannesburg is renowned had come and gone. The streets were still wet, the gutters washed clean, the smog gone. He hardly noticed what was going on around him, his thought absorbed by the afternoon's developments.

He realised that the bank had a predicament. Whilst he was a South African, many of the newly recruited bankers were British. It seemed unwise to inform them that the bank proposed to assist the Rhodesians. Surely, their allegiances would lie with Great Britain.

The board obviously considered that he spoke perfect English with the right upper-class accent, a consequence of the private schools he had attended. His stepfather had been a student at Oxford and was a stickler for the proper use of the Queen's English. Even family correspondence was duly corrected in red ink and returned if it contained errors. You chose your words and pronunciation carefully in his presence as he would interrupt any misuse of the mother tongue. This was just one of his stepfather's many idiosyncrasies.

Years before, being only twenty-two and just out of university after four gruelling years, he needed to let his hair down and decided to travel Europe. His sojourn was brief and it ended on his mother's Parisian doorstep with nary a sou.

His relationship with his stepfather had always been untenable and, finally ignoring his mother's pleas to stay, he left. Other than the little money his mother had surreptitiously slipped him, he arrived in London nearly destitute. Without a work permit, he was fortunate enough to find illegal employment as a bookkeeper with a firm of leather merchants who paid him the princely sum of £14/10/- per week. Being an illegal employee, they deducted no tax from his earnings.

The owner of the company, Lionel Harris, was a kind, compassionate man who treated David as his own, even inviting him to his home in Hampstead for the festive season. The Harris family were distinguished members of North London's Jewish community, originally from Germany, and still able to speak Yiddish. Lionel had lost many of his family to the Holocaust, leaving David with an undeserved sense of guilt brought on by his German origins. They certainly did not celebrate Christmas, which he did not miss, but made up for it with sumptuous meals. They doted upon him and went out of their way to make his stay pleasant.

There he had met Joanna, Lionel's eldest daughter, a twenty-year-old dark-haired beauty. At the time, she was besotted with an Israeli she met when spending a year on a kibbutz, adamant that she would return permanently to Tel Aviv. Her father, afraid that she would be caught up in the ever-threatening Arab-Israeli conflicts, was desperately trying to stop her.

Out of courtesy, David invited her to a Saturday night party he and his flatmates in Hampstead had organised. To his surprise, she arrived. His good sense diluted by too many beers, he recklessly made a play for her and she responded. This led to greater things and, initially, Lionel encouraged what he saw as a romance, hoping she would decide that she no longer had any interest in Israel or the chap she had met there. As their relationship intensified however, religion began to rear its head. It all came to a boil when her mother demanded outright whether they were sleeping together. Her parents' support evaporated overnight and when the relationship continued, they shipped her off to an uncle in Manila in desperation. They even phoned David's mother, an ardent Catholic, in Paris, who was equally opposed to his relationship with a Jewess.

One day, in the *Evening Standard*, he noticed the Republic Bank in South Africa was advertising for staff.

His banking experience and language skills, which included fluent Afrikaans, his possession of a South African passport, and a full head of steam, found him on a plane to Bloemfontein, South Africa, with two months' salary in his pocket, paid as a settling-in allowance.

He and Joanna had had a close and vibrant relationship. With her no longer there and he unable to communicate with her left him lonely and frustrated. Also, as he was ever so often reminded that at stage, if he were to return to South Africa, a two-year military stint was in the cards. When a bout of homesickness added to his feelings of misery, he decided it was time to go home.

A month later he arrived in Johannesburg. The military authorities would soon seek him out, so he reported to the South African Air Force recruitment authorities at Waterkloof, Pretoria.

CHAPTER 2

The few months after the boardroom meeting saw dramatic changes. Rhodesia still dominated the headlines. Ian Smith unilaterally declared independence, quickly dubbed 'UDI' by the newspapers.

This had not surprised David.

The British government, pressurised by the black African countries becoming newly independent, did not hesitate to rope in the support of the United Nations, which imposed a worldwide embargo on Rhodesia. The Rhodesian dollar was a banned currency and could no longer find any takers in the financial world. South African was to play an important role here. With her positive balance of payments, including her gold sales, she could support Rhodesia by converting the Rhodesian currency necessary to pay for imports. It was a foregone conclusion that the South African Nationalist government, with its apartheid policy, would support Rhodesia. What was surprising was that South Africa failed to recognise the new state officially, yet openly resisted the embargo.

David realised that were he on British soil, he would be breaking the law; but as a South African, he felt a kinship with his neighbours.

The extraordinary fact of his being singled out imbued him with a degree of importance. This was what he wanted to do. Once the furore was over, his future was guaranteed.

If he could pull this off.

Like most, he believed the Rhodesian problem would soon be resolved. It was the Labour government and Harold Wilson who were the problem.

David handed his department over to Hartman, a Dutch national also recruited abroad, who would be working closely with him. They had an excellent rapport, strengthened by the fact that Hartman knew his advancement was due to David's support. David, in turn, moved to the sixth floor, to an executive office, with a private secretary and two assistants. The true symbol of his ascent was his own underground parking spot in the executive section. Now a member of the inner circle, senior colleagues embraced him as one of their own.

Over a few beers after work, a friend and former colleague said, 'Your eyes have suddenly become very blue. Better watch out you don't get too infatuated with your own importance.'

David soon learnt that the business world did not care for embargoes. They impacted negatively on their ability to make money. Embargoes are the work of politicians who are reliant on the vote of the man on the street; yet, they bow to pressure from their electorate simply to mollify their supporters and gain additional support.

There was any number of businesses still ready to sell their goods and even buy Rhodesia's exports, provided there was a way to do it. Selling goods to these countries carried a premium. The pariah nations were prepared to pay handsomely, guaranteeing excellent profits.

Individual Rhodesians lost no time setting up mechanisms enabling them to continue to do business with the world. Shippers with quickly registered South African shadow companies arranged finance for their Rhodesian clients. These companies acted as South African confirming houses and shippers and, with the full knowledge of the bank, applied for letters of credit, arranged for import bills of exchange, and dealt in foreign currencies. Goods were imported through South African ports, all the documentation indicating that these were intended for internal consumption within South Africa. Once unloaded in South African ports, these goods moved on to Rhodesia by train and road. Similarly, Rhodesian tobacco, chrome, platinum and other goods were issued with fictitious South African certificates of origin and shipped as South African exports from Durban and Cape Town, often on British-registered ships. Most goods still stemmed from the United Kingdom, where the industrialists were well aware of their final destination but provided documentation showed that these were destined for South Africa anyhow.

In other words, business as usual.

This attitude frustrated the British government no end. Their industrialists did not give a damn, ever-ready to earn a quick buck and to hell with sanctions. Many were Conservatives and unready to support a Labour government decree that they opposed. Money talked and anything could be bought, albeit at a price.

Within a month, David's department was humming like a well-oiled machine. His hand-picked staff supported Rhodesia and knew the importance of what they what they were doing.

There were only three items that Rhodesians had difficulty acquiring: money, other than Rhodesian dollars; arms; and oil. As for the rest, their ingenuity knew no bounds.

South Africa was itself still an importer of fuel and other petroleum products. Because of her apartheid policies, many oil-producing countries conformed to an international request that South Africa be embargoed, although the United Nations had yet to endorse this. The South African government lived in fear that if it were discovered they were passing on petroleum products to Rhodesia, she would also find herself a victim of a UN fuel embargo.

A way around this problem had to be found, and rapidly.

CHAPTER 3

David's arrival in Salisbury was anticipated and he was whisked through customs with no undue scrutiny. When the Rhodesians heard him speak, they became suspicious of him. He was not a resident, his Oxford accent was too British; there was no way he was South African. The rumour mills were rife with stories of British undercover agents and some mistook David for the same.

'Mr Tusk, welcome to Rhodesia.'

The young man who shook David's hand was dressed in khaki shorts and shirt with long socks that reached to just below the knee, typical civilian attire of the Rhodesian police.

'Please follow me.'

A nondescript, grey Peugeot 404 waited at the main exit to the airport. David climbed into the rear seat, the young man sitting in beside him. The black driver drove off. Nobody spoke. The young man kept turning around to look through the rear window.

'Is there a problem?' David finally asked.

'No, not really. Just checking whether we are being followed.'

'You can't be serious,' David exclaimed.

'Mr Tusk, these are strange times and while you may not realise it, you are rapidly becoming a man to be watched. I wouldn't be surprised if the Brits haven't started wondering who you are. There must be at least one individual in your bank who is passing information.'

David was shocked. He had not thought of that.

The car took them to the centre of a city bustling with activity. Cars filled the streets and people, predominantly black, thronged the pavements. There was no indication here that the country had been ostracised. Rhodesians, both black and white, were renowned for their friendliness and nothing appeared to have changed. The Peugeot came to a halt in front of an imperious building, obviously housing some governmental department since the new Rhodesian coat-of-arms already emblazoned the main entrance.

They entered the lift after passing thought stringent security checks.

'Where am I?' David asked.

'This is the Department of Trade and Industries.'

A receptionist led them down a long carpeted corridor into a boardroom where three men were already seated. One was dressed in a dark suit and David realised that this had to be Mr Lionel Butler, the Rhodesian Minister of Trade and Industries. The other two were dressed in beige trousers with matching bush jackets.

All rose when he entered.

'Good to finally meet you, Mr Tusk. This is John Taylor and Michael Read,' the minister said as he indicated them with a wave of his hand.

They shook hands.

'Please make yourself comfortable and use Christian names. We don't stand on formality here,' the minister said and chuckled, 'This is Africa. John is an officer in the British South Africa Police and attached to our Central Intelligence Organisation, and Michael is the Coordinator for Petroleum Products, a new section within my department.'

After some small talk centring on sport, they got down to business.

'Oil. That's our problem and you chaps don't appear to want to help. By that, I mean your government. Sure, we understand why, but we're not here to discuss that problem. We need to find out how we can ship our own oil purchases into our country. I understand that you have already been involved in discussions?'

'Yes. I have and have twice been abroad investigating possibilities. I travelled on my German passport.'

'Convenient?'

'Very. The problem is not getting the oil. The problem is getting it here. The British truly believe the oil embargo will break your back. It's a serious problem and not to be taken lightly. Scuttlebutt in the crude industry is that if caught, there will be severe ramifications for the seller. It's not auto spares or typewriters we're talking of smuggling.'

'You're right, the bloody Brits know what without oil, our economy will grind to a halt in no time,' the minister interjected.

David continued, 'An oil tanker discharging in Beira means only one thing: the oil is intended for the Rhodesian pipeline. There's no way you can pretend that it's going anywhere else. The Portuguese have no refining facilities in Beira, so why ship it there?'

'What do you propose?'

'The way to do it is become crude brokers ourselves. Buy the oil once it is already in a tanker on the high seas, that's common practice. It's not unusual for a shipment of oil to be bought and sold a few times while still at sea. We can then divert the tanker to whatever port we may nominate. The country of origin is then superfluous. They would have no idea where the crude would eventually land up and cannot be held accountable. If anything goes wrong, we're involving individuals. It's like playing the commodities market. Of course, it would be best not to buy oil that originated from a country with British connections or British investment in the petroleum industry or any country closely affiliated with Britain, just to be on the safe side. The rest of the world really couldn't give a damn, provided they are not directly involved.'

'But that still doesn't get it here.'

'That's right, but I've found two tankers we can buy. Obviously, we use bogus companies and ensure that they fly the flags of a neutral country or country not sympathetic to the British. We crew them with officers from countries who are not partial to the British. I believe the French are not a bad idea.' David smiled. The French dislike for the British was legend. 'De Gaulle has never liked the British and, remember, he sanctioned the Berzack deal. The British are still pissed off about that but can't do a thing.'

'Couldn't you do another Berzack deal?' the minister asked.

David chuckled.

'Absolutely not. That was a barter deal. As you know, the tobacco industry is government-controlled in France, so it was easy. Rhodesian tobacco for French textiles. A swap, no money changing hands. Nobody could point a finger. Oil is different.'

Michael Read had been listening intently. He now intervened.

'We need to get the oil to Beira, then from Beira to Umtali, through the Rholon pipeline. Sure, Rholon is a British-owned company but what can the British do? This is Africa and they're not boss here.'

'Simple, the tanker runs the British blockade,' David said with a shrug of the shoulders.

'Hell, simply runs the blockade? What makes you think we could get away with that?'

'Hopefully, it will be flying the French tricolour. Any British Navy captain is going to think twice before he engages a French vessel. He'll ask for written confirmation from Wilson himself before he opens fire.'

25

David's smile hinted at a growing smugness. He modulated his voice to sound serious once again. 'You are assuming that the British will let Rholon use the pipeline. While you may not agree with me, I believe the Brits will intervene and stop that. The British government made the money available when the pipeline was originally built. I believe you'll find they think they have a vested interest. They're not about to let Rholon forget that. Don't forget, Beira is on Portuguese soil.'

Butler grinned from ear to ear. 'Christ! I'd love to see Wilson's face when he's asked to authorise a British Navy frigate to open fire on a French vessel. Don't worry about the pipeline. Bully Rowman, Rholon's chief exec, is very favourably disposed towards our cause and he is a personal friend of Jack Howman, our Minister of Defence.'

David knew the minister, an impeccably-dressed man, pompous but shrewd, whose accent was more British than the BBC's. It was said that he loved everything British except the Labour government.

Silence followed.

'Can you do this?' Michael Read asked.

David thought. Getting oil into Rhodesia past a British blockade would never be easy.

'Yes. I believe so. But I need you to give an undercover operative. I heard what happened to Bertie,' he said.

'I know, bloody freak accident. Poor Bertie. I'm still not convinced it was an accident. I think MI6 took him out,' Michael Read said.

'Perhaps. God, I can't believe they would stoop to killing your operatives. Christ, the man was from British stock. I think he still has a brother and sister in England,' David muttered.

Bertie had died in a motorcar accident in Germany, apparently while drunk. The problem was that Bertie had never been known to touch a drop of alcohol.

'What about this operative I want? For God's sake, don't give me a Rhodesian. They stick out like sore thumbs,' David said.

John Taylor pursed his lips and then made a triangle with his fingers below his nose, his elbows resting on his lap. 'I've a new operative. Funnily enough, she's from East Germany. She escaped a few years ago, met a Rhodesian in Europe, married him, and came here. She's a Rhodesian now, but has not been here long enough to acquire any Rhodesian quirks, if you know what I mean. She can easily pass as a Brit or German. They had a farm here. Unfortunately, he died and, what with this damn business and her fluency in languages, she landed up here in my division. However, she's an excellent undercover agent,' he said.

David shook his head. 'I don't know. A woman? I don't think that's a good idea, if could get rough out there.'

'Meet her first. I guarantee she'll knock your socks off. She should be okay, it's not like we're at war with the Brits.'

David did not ask him to explain the remark, but he agreed to reserve judgment.

The men got down to serious business. David was to put the deals together. The oil would be bought on the high seas and shipped in their newly- acquired tankers, flying either French or Panamanian flags. The cargoes would be diverted to Beira where David would deal with the commodity brokers, arrange for payment, and ensure that the documentation was good enough to pass scrutiny.

'John, just remember, my job is to get the crude into Beira. From there, it's your problem,' David said.

'Don't worry, my people will handle Beira.'

As their discussions ended, Lionel Butler drew David aside. 'Look, you're only due to fly back tomorrow. Why don't you join us for a barbecue? I've a few people coming around. I'll invite Michael and your new prospective operative as well. You can them make a judgment. Who knows, maybe you'll be pleasantly surprised.'

'Sounds fine. Thank you, sir. Where is this dinner?'

'Don't worry. I'll have you picked up at the hotel by the same driver and car. Incidentally, dress is casual. And when I say "casual", I mean casual. Some people will even come in shorts. This is Rhodesia.'

David laughed. There certainly was nothing stuffy about these people when it came to dress.

The Peugeot 404 collected him from the hotel and, a short while later, they drove into the entrance of the property. It wasn't a house, it was a mansion. Butler was situated in Highlands, the Salisbury suburb was where most of the upper echelon of society was to be found. A black servant came down the stairs from the porch to open the car door.

He had decided that shorts would be taking it to the extreme, so he chose to wear casual beige cotton trousers and an open-neck shirt, slim cut, so that it hugged his torso in the latest fashion, and tan slip-on Brook's Brothers-inspired loafers. David was proud he carried no hint of paunch. He regularly worked out, played golf and squash, and considered himself in fair shape for his mid-thirties. His dark hair was cut in typical English style, a parting on the left side, the hair on the right brushed sideways just touching his ears. It had just begun to recede and he fancied this gave him a distinguished air. He had brown eyes, with the first sign of crow's feet accentuated by a golfer's tan.

Both Butlers received him through the front door under a huge veranda. Edith was a typical colonial wife. They just have something different about them, he thought. You realised immediately they were colonials. It probably came from having so many servants at their beck and call, coupled with excellent schooling and an upbringing which gave them a very clear perception of what was done and not done. Christ, it's an enigma, he thought, they're straight out of Kipling. I didn't know that still went on.

'How do you do? I'm so glad to meet you,' Edith said. He guessed her to be in her forties. The harsh African sun had left its mark with her dry, tanned features, but she still was a pleasant and attractive woman. He noted with pleasure that she was not one inclined to excessive jewellery and make-up as he often found with women d'un certain âge in Rhodesia.

'My son is a rancher nearby and is an officer in the Rhodesian Air Force,' she said with pride. There were about twenty guests, mostly civil servants and their wives. None volunteered any information as to what they did for a living. If this was cocktail hour, it should have been renamed: the men predominantly drank beer and only a few of the women drank gin and tonics or pink gins.

David accepted a beer from a passing waiter. It was ice cold. Others introduced themselves, but none asked what he did.

About a half an hour later, he heard the sound of gravel crunching. He looked through the bay windows to see an archaic Land Rover, open to the elements with only a canvas canopy, one of those with the twin headlights still in front of the radiator. A tall, blonde woman, her hair tied in a ponytail, jumped out. She wore a sleeveless blouse tucked into a pair of cotton Bermudas, showing off her beautifully tanned legs. A wide red belt matching her pumps split the white of her top and shorts. He was struck by her beauty. She climbed the stairs appearing not to notice the furtive glances she received from the men.

It was obvious she and Edith were acquainted as they were already deep in conversation. Lionel Butler said something and the women turned and appraised David for a few seconds. Then she and Butler broke away and walked over to him.

'David, may I introduce you to Gisela Mentz. She is the lady Mike Taylor was telling you about.'

She was even better close up. Her eyes were light blue, her lips full. When she smiled, he saw she had perfect white teeth. She took his proffered hand.

'I imagine you must be Tusk,' she said in perfect English. He thought he could detect the slightest hint of a German accent, but it might have only been noticeable because he knew of her origins, others would not discern it.

'Hi,' he replied in typical South African fashion.

'Listen, you good people, could I leave you alone? I'm the host, I've things to do,' Butler said. He left them and headed to the barbecue, which was manned by two servants.

As Butler turned to walk away, David said with a broad smile, 'Incidentally, you were right. I lost my socks.'

The minister just laughed.

David turned to face her, still smiling.

'Excuse me if I sound blunt, he introduced you as "Mentz". I thought you had married a Rhodesian.'

'I am Mentz. My married name is Roberts, but after my husband's death, I reverted to my maiden name. My German passport is still in my maiden name. It just made things easier. There are no children and no in-laws, so it really doesn't make any difference. And you, Mr Tusk, are you married?' she asked with a quizzical expression on her face. 'Incidentally, you lost your socks?'

He chuckled, somewhat embarrassed. 'Oh, just a figure of speech, a private joke. No, I've never been married and this job doesn't make marriage a good idea. Too much running around and subterfuge.'

She laughed. It was a beautiful sound. 'Don't tell me. I know.'

He stopped a passing waiter and asked for another beer. She asked for the same, surprising him. They found themselves a corner on the veranda out of earshot of the others.

'Look, I'll be blunt,' David said, 'I'm sure you are well qualified, but you're a woman. This could be dangerous. I'm concerned.'

She stared at him for a few seconds. 'What did John Taylor tell you about me?'

'Not much, he hardly said anything.'

'Typical. Well, then I'll have to tell you myself. I'm originally from East Germany. I escaped.'

'When was that?' he asked. He sipped from his beer glass.

'About six years ago. Before that, I worked for the Stasi.'

David was dumbstruck. The Stasi, Ministerium für Staatssicherheit. They were the East German equivalent of the KGB.

She read his reaction. 'Surprised?'

'Yes, I am. What did you do there?'

'I was recruited while still at school. As a child, I was tutored in languages – those that my father considered important. His connections ensured me a place at a very young age in the basic Stasi training program. The Stasi is a lifetime career. My fluency in languages assured the rest. Anyway, the reason I'm telling you this is to assure you I can look after myself.'

'I don't doubt it. So, if you were privileged, I'm assuming that Stasi members were privileged, why did you leave?'

'Do you have any idea what they do to people? I was never a Communist. My father was, and a party member to boot. He died and they assumed I held the same convictions he did. Not true. I fled.'

'May I call you Gisela?'

She nodded.

'Where did you learn to speak English so well?'

'My father's fault. As I said, he always believed that it would be an asset. So from a very early age, I was exposed to the language every day. In fact, I went to a special school. Do you know what a sleeper is?'

'Yes,' he said, 'it's somebody infiltrated into a country and only activated when he's needed. He just pretends to be a normal inhabitant. Wife, child, house, job.'

'That was one of the things they trained me to be.'

'Well, you're certainly qualified.' He hesitated for a moment. 'Gisela, I think you'll do,' he said, adding a dash of humour.

She laughed, pleased by his decision. '"I'll do?" Is that how you put it? God, only a man could put it that way,' she said. She shook her head in mock disbelief.

The ice broken, they spent the next few hours talking about themselves, where they had lived, and what they had done. They both knew Europe well, particularly England and France, and swopped languages easily, speaking English, then German, and then French. She spoke the languages extremely well.

They agreed that within the next few days she would come to South Africa and take up 'employment' with the Republic Bank.

John Taylor would make all the necessary arrangements and ensure that his South African counterparts were made aware of her new status. Gisela would be issued with a South African passport to use while in South Africa, to avoid any entries in her German passport that show when she had been to Africa.

David turned to Gisela.

'I better talk to Butler and arrange to get back to the hotel,' he said.

'No, wait. I can take you, or rather drop you off. I'm going in that direction. That's if you don't mind a bit of fresh air while you're out on a drive. And if you want to speak, you have to shout.' She had a look of contained amusement on her face.

He laughed, seeing the fun in the situation. It was a pleasant evening; the threatening rain had vanished. And, God, she was beautiful.

'Okay, let me tell Butler.'

David found Butler on the porch. Whisky soda in hand, talking to one of the guests he had been introduced to who was about to leave with his wife. He remembered the man, Reynecke was his name.'

'Do you want to go?' Butler asked.

'Yes, but Miss Mentz has offered to drop me off. If it's all right with you, and if you have finished discussing what was to be said, I think I'd like to take her up on the offer.'

'Sure, she's going to be working closely with you anyway,' he replied. He pulled David to one side. 'Just to let you know. On Monday, I'll be putting wheels in motion authorising you to go ahead and acquire the two tankers. Meanwhile, you need to find a commodities broker, preferably a European, maybe Dutch or Belgian, through whom we can buy the tankers and the crude. Just tread warily, we don't need the British getting wind of this too early?' He paused. 'Okay?'

'I'll remember. I'll speak to you when I get back to Johannesburg.'

The Land Rover was meticulously maintained. It fired up at the first push of the starter button next to the clutch on the floor. The seats were covered in leather, the zebra fur with its white and black stripes lending the vehicle a safari air. All it was needed was the rack holding the rifles. She seemed to read his mind.

'The rifles actually fit into the rack behind us, but I thought it wouldn't do to be seen riding around town with them.' She laughed, enjoying his appraisal of her vehicle. 'Next, you're going to ask why I'm driving this vehicle. Because I love it! My husband used to say it was a piece of junk. I had it rebuilt. I go everywhere with it. Sure, she's sprung like an ox-wagon, heavy to drive, but I like it.'

He feigned surprise. 'Please, I had no intention of questioning your choice of vehicle. It's fun,' he shouted above the roar of the engine. They were moving at a good clip, the wind rushing through the cab.

She drove well, in total command of the vehicle. Everything worked but, yes, it was archaic.

He began to feel comfortable with having woman as an operative assistant. She appeared to be competent and in full control of herself, striking him as one of those straight-down-the-middle types. She'd tell you the truth and not pull her punches. It was the only attitude that could win this game. Bad news must be told immediately and quick reactions were essential. If she didn't like something, he was sure he would know soon enough. To top it all, he found her beauty captivating.

She dropped him off at his hotel.

'I hope you're not proposing to motor down to South Africa in this,' he said.

'No. I'll leave my beloved here and find something that tickles my fancy in Johannesburg.'

'Well, let's see, maybe I can help. Until next Friday then. I'll collect you at the airport if you let me know when you're flying down.'

'I don't know my plans yet, but I'll let you know. Anyway, thanks.'

'Thanks for what? It's going to be tough. You may get to think it wasn't such a good idea after all,' he warned. His face was guileless.

She just smiled, putting the vehicle in gear. She waved as she drove off.

CHAPTER 4

It was a typical winter's day in Rotterdam. A bitter, cold wind blew off the North Sea over the Schelde, driving the rain before it, buffeting the DAF Daffodil they had hired. The little car was ideal. It negotiated the narrow streets easily and, with its ingenious gearbox, requiring no gear-change, was a pleasure to drive. He drove while she navigated to the offices of René Oosterwijk, the broker through whom David proposed to route all the crude transactions. The man's background had been scrutinised and his credentials appeared impeccable.

More to the point, he had done this before.

The British and Dutch governments had worked closely together to close all oil loopholes. This did not seem to deter Oosterwijk. He knew the ramifications if his government ever got to know that he had assisted in busting the embargo, though still agreeing to act on their behalf. The fee he was offered and the added incentive of making a profit on the oil was attractive, although it did not appear he needed the money. He thought it abhorrent that some European countries now turned on their colonies and its white colonists – the English, Dutch, Belgians and French. Oosterwijk's family were not newcomers to conflict and adversity. They were colonists in Indonesia who lost everything. In Indonesia, his brother had been a POW in a Japanese camp during WWII. He had not survived the ordeal. The loss of his only brother devastated René. He was sympathetic to the Rhodesians. They, as the Dutch colonists in Indonesia, risked losing everything, their home governments no longer supportive of their previous colonies.

'Stop here,' Gisela said.

They were in front of a tall, modern building, all concrete, aluminium and glass. The Rotterdam Bank NV

'We can't stop here,' David said, 'Jump out and I'll go and find parking somewhere.'

She walked to the main entrance to get out of the rain. He drove around and finally found parking, initially baulking at the ridiculously high hourly rate. Real estate was obviously at a premium in this city. He walked back the two blocks to the bank building.

They met in the foyer. Gisela was studying the large glass-encased board and found that Oosterwijk's offices were on the seventh floor. 'De Mescht Markelaars NV', he recognised the name.

They stepped out of the lift and followed the arrow to the reception area. 'We have an appointment with Mr Oosterwijk,' David announced in German.

A few minutes later, a tall, white-haired man appeared from a passageway. David thought him to be in his mid-fifties. He was thin and at least six foot three. He wore modish, rimless glasses with large lenses and was immaculately dressed in a silver-grey sharkskin suit. He exuded an air of opulence, affirmed by the gold Rolex on his wrist and the Gucci loafers on his feet.

'Goede dag.' He greeted them in Dutch.

They followed him into a large office which overlooked Rotterdam harbour in the distance. The office was wall-to-wall carpeted; the furniture was modern Swedish. A few chairs surrounded a coffee table while his desk and cabinets in matching wood took up the other side. Paintings of ships at sea adorned the walls.

David studied him as Oosterwijk ordered coffee to be brought in.

Rhodesian Intelligence had researched Oosterwijk. He was a member of the Dutch nouveau riche which had emerged after the Second World War. While Holland was occupied by Germany and his brother held by the Japanese, he had been part of the Dutch underground and heavily involved in the black market. When the war ended, he had surfaced as a small commodities broker who appeared to be reasonably well financed and soon gained a reputation for good business ethics and prompt payment. His war activities opened a few doors in the newly-appointed Dutch government. As time passed, he spread his business wings by going international. He had a reputation for looking at anything that had money in it. He lived with his wife in an apartment which overlooked the Nieuwe Maas Canal in the Hillegersberg suburb of Rotterdam. His children had already left home.

His secretary came in carrying a tray of coffee, leaving it on the coffee table as everyone got down to business.

'I bought the ship as instructed, the *Georgio V*. Currently, she flies a Greek flag, but we'll change her registration within the next few days. It would be best to get her registered out of Panama.' Oosterwijk spoke

34

quickly, 'She's heading for Bandar Mashur in the Persian Gulf where she'll load 16,000 tonnes of crude. The documentation shows that a commodities company, fictitious of course, has bought the crude shipment from the Iranians. The whole transaction was routed through a South African entrepreneur, a Mr Michael Rafael. He has excellent connections with the Iranians.'

'As I thought, the Iranians never ask where or what, they just want to sell their crude,' David said.

Oosterwijk looked at David.

'Well, the fact that everything is being paid up front worked miracles. It's a lot easier to confuse the paper trail. The Iranians were very keen to do the deals, especially with immediate payment and no questions. Now, currently the ship's officers are all Greek. Once we re-register the ships, we'll replace the crew and re-issue cargo papers and certificates. I've a French crew on stand-by. We couldn't have chosen any better. De Gaulle has been re-elected in France. Rest assured, Anglo-French relations are not about to improve.' The Dutchman smiled. 'De Gaulle's dislike of the English is notorious. Also, he was involved in a colonial war in Algeria and, whilst not openly admitting it, he admires Ian Smith. Of course, he would abide by a United Nations directive if necessary, or at the very least, go through the motions.'

'I think the use of a French crew is an excellent idea.'

Oosterwijk nodded.

'The captain is paid for taking the ship from point A to point B, that's from the Persian Gulf to Beira. According to the documents, the crude is destined for a company situated in Beira, a Portuguese company in fact. What happens to the crude thereafter is not his concern. Therefore he is in the clear.'

'The English will know it is a ruse, but once the ship's in the harbour and discharges its cargo into the tank farm, what can they do? Sure, they'll be obstreperous, but that's it. Also, the Portuguese will endeavour to help without being too obvious,' David confirmed.

Oosterwijk leant back in his Jacobsen Swan Chair. 'Well, all I've got to do is see to it that the ship is loaded and sell the cargo while it's on the high seas. After that, it's your concern. You do agree, don't you?'

'Of course, Minjheer Oosterwijk,' David replied.

Gisela looked at David, 'What are you going to do if the British blockade stops your ship?'

'When it's flying its new flag? They would not dare.'

'With a United Nations oil embargo in force? Don't be so sure. I believe you can expect a lot of trouble,' Oosterwijk warned.

David ignored the warning. 'What other progress have we made?'

'Well, we bought another ship, the *Deborah*. She is also en route to take on her cargo of crude, but that will be a little later.'

They rehashed a few other less important items for the next half hour before David rose from his seat and proffered his hand, which René took.

'Thank you. We are on our way to Germany and London. We should see you again within the next fortnight.'

****

They had planned to cross to England using the ferry services but Gisela said that flying was better.

'There's more pressure on immigration officials at airports. On ferries, the pace is sedate. They are more thorough with people trying to covertly enter a country, usually lacking funds, choosing the cheapest option – either rail or ferry. I learnt this during my stint with the Stasi,' she said.

Producing their German passports, they passed through HM Customs at Gatwick without incident. They booked separately into the Belleclaire Hotel, a nondescript but good hotel in Knightsbridge, London, as they did not want to create the impression that they knew each other. Gisela had a few other duties to perform for Rhodesian Intelligence, which she had not divulged to David.

David, on the other hand, needed to visit Industrial Confirming's London offices. This would have to be done clandestinely. It was known that MI6 had it and its personnel under observation.

The employees in London were all British nationals and most had never been to Rhodesia. Virtually all Rhodesians had strong family ties with Great Britain. The colony was not even seventy years old and many in Britain believed what Ian Smith said about the British government working against their own 'kith and kin'. Aghast at the Labour government's attitude, they were supportive of Rhodesia.

David had hired a Morris Minor from Avis, which he left parked in the street nearby. In the hotel, he went to the public phones in the foyer and dialled a number from memory.

'Hello, Mallory and Sons,' a female voice replied.

'Mr John Davidson, please.'

'John Davidson? We don't have anybody by that name here. You must have a wrong number,' the receptionist said.

'I dialled Swiss Cottage 0371, my apologies.' David put the phone down.

The receptionist would tell Mallory that he had phoned, mentioning the digits 0371. This meant they were to meet that afternoon at 17.30, five thirty. Both knew where and would spend part of the afternoon losing any tails they might have collected.

That afternoon, David rode the Underground, climbing into and then deserting coaches as the doors were about to close, hopping on or off buses and ensuring that he was not followed. At five twenty-five, he walked into The Bohemian, a crowded pub near Belsize Park. He ordered a pint of bitter at the bar. As he strode through the haze of cigarette smoke, he espied a pillar around which a chest-height table had been constructed for those patrons forced to stand. Most of the clientele was office staff: the men in suits, the office's women clearly single, judging by the interaction amongst them.

David kept a sharp lookout and, precisely at five thirty, he saw Doyle enter while removing his bowler. There was no missing his six foot two height. He was dressed in a dark, pinstriped suit and waistcoat, wearing his regimental tie. Doyle was in his mid-thirties, with a mop of ginger hair and a slightly ruddy complexion. He saw David but moved towards the bar and waited until he got the beer he had ordered. Then he looked round as if he were looking for a place to stand, finally sidling over to the pillar where David was.

They stood in silence as they scrutinised the patrons. Only when satisfied nobody appeared suspicious or was watching them did David speak.

'Abominable weather, what?'

'Absolutely,' the freckled-faced man replied while smiling, 'but what can you do, this is England.'

They made small talk, like strangers in a bar. Once they finished their beers, they left and entered a small, nondescript Chinese restaurant, still deserted at this hour. They were the only occupants. They took a table facing the door. Doyle knew the owner, who produced two bottles of Yangtze Chinese beer which David sipped while they waited for their light meal.

'So, how are my aircraft and radio spares coming along?'

'The radios aren't a problem, but those spares for your Hawker Hunters and Canberras, that's another story,' Doyle replied while scanning the empty restaurant. 'I've got somebody within the Force who'll help. He's connected to the logistics side of the maintenance division, but he's looking for a hefty price. He's legit all right. His folks are in our country, but he says he has to pay handsomely to get his hands on these.'

'I can believe that. How are we going to get them out of the country?'

'Boldly. We are going to ship them as aircraft and radio spares right under their bloody noses, to National Airways, Rand Airport, Johannesburg, as spares for Hawker Siddeleys and Vickers Viscount Rolls-Royce jet engine parts. It'll take a bloody expert to realise what they really are. Ship them conspicuously. They'll never expect that. I suppose you will be able to intercept these once they arrive at Rand Airport?'

'I can arrange that. We'll have to be careful. The South African Customs will be really pissed off if we smuggle spare parts for military use. Remember, South Africa is also contending with an international arms embargo. Christ, when they get involved, things are tied up for months while they debate whether they should or shouldn't release the stuff to us. We call them draadsitters.'

'What's that?'

'Guys who sit on the fuckin' fence,' David said.

'What else is new? South Africa is just looking after itself. Watch, if the shit hits the fan, they won't be there for us. They've got their own lot to attend to.'

'How are things in London?'

'Not too good. The British are wising up. They know we're buying stuff for you but they can't prove it. They're always sniffing around on some pretext. If it isn't the fuckin' tax people, then it's Customs. The phones are tapped and we are followed. Be careful they don't follow you now,' Doyle said. He improvised a smile to emphasise his point. 'I personally believe we should close this office down and reopen elsewhere with new staff. It's easy enough.'

'Okay, come up with a proposal and let's look at it. Maybe put the main office in France and just keep a guy and a girl here. The British are very careful about upsetting the French. If British Intelligence were to send operatives into France to harass your chaps, that'd create a fuckin' furore, especially if we tip off the French Sûreté. They hate British undercover operatives.'

David, absorbed by his thoughts, stared out of the restaurant's entrance at the people passing by outside. He woke from his reverie.

'What about the spares? What have we got to do to get those?'

'I've got a Bedford in RAF colours. My contact tells me we must get the truck to RAF Brize Norton. He'll see to it that it's cleared through the base's security checkpoints. Once inside, we drive it to the maintenance and spares depot. The driver and assistant do nothing other than produce documentation, which my contact will give us. We merely go through the motions of being RAF personnel there to collect the consignment. The documentation will indicate that this is an urgent collection. Our contact will load the crates, produce the papers, and we're gone.'

'Well, if it's as simple as it sounds, do it.'

'I can't.' His irritation showed.

David swivelled his chair to face Doyle. 'Why not?' He paused. 'What about MacTavish? I thought he did all this undercover stuff with you?'

'MacTavish, our illustrious Scot, is in hospital, in St Mary's in fact, having his bloody appendix plucked from his bowels. Actually, it's worse than that. The damn thing burst and now he's fighting peritonitis, or whatever it's called. I understand he'll be out of action for weeks.'

'Fuck. Well, use somebody else.'

'You don't get it, do you? I don't have the people. Nobody wants to take the chance. If arrested as British subjects, they'd be up for bloody treason,' Doyle retorted.

'You're shitting me. I don't like what I'm hearing.'

'You're right, David. It's just fuckin' you and me, friend.' His lips stretched into a sarcastic smile.

'Don't call me David. I'm Gunther Wohlhuter.'

'Christ! And a German, too.' Doyle shook his head. He didn't like David's attitude.

'Listen, I can't get involved. I'm not a spook. I'm a bloody financial sanctions buster. I work for a bank.'

'Sssh. Not so loud. That's not quite correct. You have affiliations with a bank, but you work for us now. Everybody believes you're one of us. You're Rhodesian CIO.'

'God Almightly! You've got a cheek asking me,' David replied. He was unable to veil his feelings of irritation.

'I need somebody who can pass himself off as an officer. With that toffee mouth of yours, you're a sure thing.'

'Let me get back to you on that,' he muttered.

CHAPTER 5

Bruce Doyle drove. Thank God it was raining, David thought. That meant any security people would be in slickers, keen to get out of the weather again. He hoped to avoid a jobsworth who wasted too much time inspecting the contents of the vehicle instead of just relying on their papers for veracity.

The Bedford truck had its home base, Northolt, stencilled on the door; its Royal Air Force lineage clearly displayed. This was the main staging point, the logistics centre from where the forces airlifted all material to its overseas bases. Doyle was dressed in a sergeant's uniform while David was a flying officer. They were on the access road that led to Brize Norton. As far as David was concerned, this was madness, whereas Doyle thought it was, as he put it, a piece of cake. Christ! This was ridiculous. If they caught you doing this during WWII, they hanged you, no questions asked.

The documentation was perfect. The goods were intended for onward distribution. Who would believe otherwise? David didn't know whether he was perspiring out of fear or because Doyle had the heater on.

'Turn that bloody heater off,' he said.

Doyle looked at him for a moment. The tension on his face was obvious.

'Just relax,' he said, but he turned the heater off.

They rounded a corner. In the distance, down the tree-lined road, he could see a huge signboard proclaiming the base. The base was surrounded by a double fence of barbed wire, patrolled by a security detachment with dogs. Sliding gates sealed the entrances and exits. These were open but sturdy booms across the entrance barred any vehicle access or departure. Next to the gate, a brick, window-lined building had been erected. From its roof, radio aerials and a radio dish sprouted. Lights glowed in the interior of the building. At regular intervals around the perimeter fence as well as the building, additional security lights could be seen.

As they neared the boom, the knot in his stomach began to take hold. He made a supreme effort to exude total boredom.

A corporal, wearing a slicker, came out of the building. He carried a clipboard which was covered by a flimsy piece of transparent plastic. He looked down at the name stencilled on the door of the truck and then into the cab. Seeing an officer in the vehicle, he came to attention and saluted, which David nonchalantly returned. Doyle opened his window and handed the corporal a sheaf of documents in a blue plastic folder. He studied these.

'Northolt, huh. What you're fetching, Sarge?' he asked.

'Spares that everybody's screaming for. We've got a Beverly on the apron waiting to fly these out,' Doyle replied in a broad Yorkshire accent that surprised David, no doubt put on especially for this performance.

'I know, the brass're always screaming for something.' The corporal chuckled before remembering an officer was present. 'Sorry, sir.'

'Don't worry, Corporal, you're right. They're always screaming,' David replied. The corner of his mouth turned upward indicating that he was enjoying the impromptu humour, the attempt at kinship.

The corporal smiled in return, handed the documents back to Doyle, and then walked forward to the boom, which he unclipped and raised. They drove through.

David exhaled a long sigh of relief. 'For fuck's sake, I don't want to go through that again,' he said quietly.

'Contain yourself, my friend. We'll be back at the gate within an hour to do the same again. This was nothing.'

David shook his head and mentally prepared himself for what was next.

Doyle had been given a map of the base's layout, which he had memorised. He knew exactly where he was to take the truck, thus not having to stop or ask for directions. As Doyle drove, he talked to himself, 'Left here, left again, right here.'

David realised that he was not the only one scared shitless.

They drew up alongside a huge warehouse. Doyle stopped the truck and went to its rear to lower the loading body flap. Above the roller shutter warehouse door, a huge D was painted. Doyle reversed the truck right up to the dock-leveller. David remained seated. Doyle climbed out again and walked to the door through the receiving door. He pressed the red button marked Press for attention"'. They heard the shrill ringing of the bell inside. A minute later, a chain rattled and the roller shutter door rose. David was standing on the platform, having been told by Doyle to get out of the truck.

Once the door was up, a warrant officer stepped out and saluted David.

Doyle handed the man the blue file. They were out of the rain, the loading dock covered by a large overhead canopy. The WO was obviously a career soldier, in his mid-forties, probably with years of experience in logistics. They were dealing with a man who prided himself in the manner in which he did his job. He would be meticulous. This man had to realise something was wrong? The officer examined the document and then turned to Doyle.

'This is urgent, right?'

'Yes, sir. There's a transport aircraft on the apron waiting for this stuff.'

The officer looked at David, who just nodded. He was terrified to say anything, fearing his voice would croak.

'Okay, just wait here. This will take a minute or two.' The WO walked into the warehouse and left them standing on the ramp.

'God, what's he gone to do? Check our papers or what?' David whispered to Doyle. He did his best not to move his lips.

'I don't know. Just hang on.'

They waited for a few minutes of electric tension. Finally, they were greeted by the sound of an approaching electric forklift. A young corporal in overalls drove this, balancing two wooden crates on its forks. He drove the forklift into the truck and deposited the crates next to the headboard.

'Hang on there, there are another four. The WO will be back in a moment. Ah, he said I should ask whether you would like a cuppa.'

Both realised it would give the game away if they refused. In this weather and cold, a cup of tea would never be refused, and certainly not by military men. Their apprehension rose as they followed the forklift into the interior.

The warehouse consisted of a multitude of fenced-off areas. Nothing stood free anywhere. All goods and equipment were behind a fence. They saw through an enclosure with its wire-mesh sliding-gate open the forklift in the interior loading another two crates. Two other men stood with clipboards in their hands. One was the warrant officer, the other a flight lieutenant.

From an office in the middle of the warehouse, a person gave that unmistakable 'come-hither' wave. They knew their tea was about to be served and walked toward the office, relieved to discover only one man there. He saluted them and then proceeded to pour the tea, it strong with lots of milk and a generous helping of sugar.

David wasn't going to speak to the man. He left that to Doyle, who engaged him in conversation in his thick Yorkshire accent. David, exuding an air of boredom, stared dully out of the window into the warehouse watching the activities below. Again, the forklift drove to the truck and deposited another two crates, returning for the last two. Once these were loaded, the cage was locked by the WO and flight lieutenant and they walked towards the office.

Doyle and David came to attention and saluted the flight lieutenant smartly. He glanced down to read the nameplate on David's chest.

'Lieutenant Bathingswaithe, glad to meet you,' he said. He proffered his hand, which David shook, sure that the man would realise he was perspiring. 'You've certainly chosen the worst weather to be driving around the countryside. However, the papers say this stuff is urgent.'

'Sir, we've a plane on the apron waiting for it. They asked me to accompany the driver just to ensure all went smoothly,' David croaked.

The officer looked at him. David didn't know what he was thinking but felt compelled to say something to divert whatever it may be.

'I've a bit of a cold coming on, sir. It's this confounded weather.'

The officer ignored the remark.

'They don't normally use officers for this,' the flight lieutenant said.

'I was bored stiff.'

David did not want to pick up his mug from the table, frightened that the officer would notice him shaking.

'I've been in this game a long time. I've never seen you before. Where are you based?' the officer asked. His tone was friendly as he pointed to David's wings above his left pocket, signifying that he was a pilot.

David had been carefully primed on how to reply if asked certain questions. This was one of them. The wings had been added as this placed him amongst the elite of the force, a glory boy, ensuring him a good degree of respect.

'I've just returned from a long stint in Germany. I'm with 18 Squadron in Gütersloh.'

'You chaps are converting from Hunters to the Lightning now, aren't you? Once that's done, they'll probably send your squadron back to Germany again. Keep the Reds in check, what?'

'Probably.'

David hoped that his short supply would suffice. It did. He remained silent, lifting his cup to take a swallow of tea, pleased to note that the shakes had disappeared.

Doyle signed all the necessary documentation. Copies were detached and retained and the remainder handed back to him. They thanked the men for their hospitality and the WO led them to the loading dock where they climbed back into the cab and drove off. At the exit to the base, the vehicle's contents were inspected and verified against the documentation. David's heart was in his mouth, waiting for the telephone in the small security building to ring. He imagined the men charging out, weapons unslung, demanding that they climb out of the truck.

Finally, the corporal was satisfied. He made a notation on his clipboard and waved them off.

David felt drained. He swore never to do this again.

About a mile or two from the base, he slapped the dashboard with the flat of his hand.

'Stop the truck!' He was already gripping the lever to open the door.

Doyle looked at him.

'I said, stop the damn truck. Stop it now!'

The truck stopped. David flung the door open, leapt out, and dove into the bushes. He bent over and vomited. Wiping his face and mouth with his handkerchief, he returned without speaking, his face ashen.

'It only happens the first time,' Doyle said after a minute or so. He never looked at David, only staring ahead through the windscreen.

Near the outskirts of London, they entered an industrial area where Doyle swung the vehicle into a factory yard housing a small warehouse. The doors were already open and he drove straight inside. The doors closed behind them.

'For a first timer, I must admit you did very well,' Doyle said.

'Not the first time, the only time. I'm not a fuckin' Rhodesian. You can do this shit yourselves,' David replied.

Doyle laughed.

By the time they changed out of their uniforms, two men had already removed the crates and were using crowbars to split them open and remove the contents. These would be repacked in the new crates standing ready alongside. The old crates would be fed to the boiler on the premises, as the stencil markings were a definite giveaway. Another man was removing the RAF identification marks from the truck as well as the frame and canvas canopy. The vehicle was quickly transformed. It no longer resembled anything in use by the military. However, with the South Devon Chicken Farms boards attached to the doors, it looked like any other everyday commercial vehicle.

'What's going to happen now?' David asked.

'As I said, these are now innocuous radio and commercial aircraft spares destined for South Africa. National Airways will buy these against a letter of credit from one of the companies we have registered here in the UK. In fact, the money will actually be used to pay for these. We can always use the money here again for other purchases. These will now be shipped or air freighted to South Africa as standard imports. All the necessary documentation and certificates of origin, duly stamped, will accompany the consignment, lending authenticity to the deal.'

'Quite impressive.'

'Yes, but in this case, as you know, it was dangerous acquiring the goods. Usually, we simply purchase them.'

'Well, don't count on my services again.'

Doyle chuckled. 'Come on, let me take you back to your hotel.'

CHAPTER 6

Doyle dropped off David a few blocks from the hotel, allowing him to approach the hotel on foot. He browsed in a few shops along the way and checked that he was not being followed.

At the hotel's reception desk, the concierge handed him his key and a folded note.

'The Usual – take care!' Gisela's message read.

He was to meet her at the pub around the corner. The 'take care' was ominous. It meant he had to make sure he wasn't followed. He looked at his watch. It was eight thirty. He spent an hour trying to lose any tail he might have, again jumping on and off buses, finally taking a taxi.

He walked into the pub and saw her sitting at a table, nursing a gin and tonic. He went to the bar, got himself a scotch, then slid into the chair opposite her.

'Cheers! Damn Rhodesians, you won't believe what I've just been through. I really need this drink,' he said. He raised he glass and exhaled a long sigh.

She returned the toast. 'I was just about to ask you how your day's been.'

'You really don't want to know. You Rhodesians are insane.'

She half-smiled.

'Well, I've bad news for you. When I returned to the hotel, there were two men in suits in front of me at the concierge's desk. They were describing a man. I thought it was you. It certainly matched you. Maybe it was my imagination, but I think I'm right. You recognise this type of thing when you see it again. I used to do it for the Stasi.'

'And what did they find out?'

'Not much. They porter said that there were too many guests. Without a name, he could not help them.'

David looked at her. She resembled a junior executive. She was smartly dressed in a dark two-piece suit, the lapel and cuffs edged with some lighter material. Under that, she had a white lace-frilled blouse and her feet were tucked into black, square-toed, mid-heeled shoes. She wore her blonde hair swept high on her head, which emphasised her height. Tiny earrings glinted in the light.

'You can be sure they're watching the hotel. They obviously don't know under which name you have registered. If they did, then why the description? God only knows how they find these things out. We must have a leak somewhere.'

'I think I'm just going to go back to the hotel and play the innocent guest. Revert to being German, only able to speak broken English. That'll confuse them. I'm here on business. They may think what they like but I've a genuine German passport. They'll be careful.' He smiled at her.

She returned the smile. 'That's actually quite clever. I'll be your girlfriend, we'll be visiting England together.'

He looked at her high cheekbones, the slight, aquiline nose; and the thrust of her breasts, taut under her white blouse. He felt an involuntary stirring.

David and Gisela walked back to the hotel, her arm in his, chatting in German. Fortunately the rain had stopped. He quipped he was sure that they lost any tail they may have had.

'Did they teach you that in the RAF?' Her tone was not flippant.

She led him past the hotel, the epitome of a happy couple on holiday or on business in London. They stopped at various storefronts and then walked what seemed aimlessly, using passing buses and lorries for cover while surveying their environs. Satisfied, they doubled back and then split up before the hotel so they could enter separately.

He checked his room carefully. Nothing appeared to have been tampered with. Now in shirtsleeves, he poured himself a drink from the diminutive fridge under the dressing table when there was a knock on the door. David opened the door to find two men in overcoats, their hats in their hands.

'Mr Wohlhuter? Mr Gunter Wohlhuter?' the one on the left asked. He looked like a police officer. His English was not quite cultured, a trace of some country accent discernible. He held a piece of paper.

'Jawohl, ich bin Wohlhuter. Was wollen Sie mit mir?'

David could see this threw them.

'Ein bischen,' he replied in heavily-accented German, just a little.

The two men looked at each other. 'I apologise, sir. Sorry, we've made a mistake.'

'Aber, ich bin Wohlhunter.' He implied that he wanted to know why they came.

That confused them even further. Shaking his head, holding out a hand as if to ward off David, the taller of the two repeated that they were sorry and they backed away, putting on their hats. David caught a glimpse of the piece of paper. There were several names written one below the other on it. They must have copied these from the reception desk. He retained his bewildered expression and repeated his name as the men disappeared down the passage.

He phoned Gisela. He spoke in German.

'They were here. Police, by the look of things. They asked for Wohlhuter, obviously not yet associating the name with a face. My apparent inability to speak English confused them further. They're probably checking on the other names they got from the register.'

'Well, we know they're up to something. Come on up, you know the number. They won't be confused for long.'

She was right. Play the boy-and-girl bit, just for show.

'Okay.'

Gisela opened the door for him. It was nearly eleven and she was in a white terry gown, her feet bare. She had removed her makeup and seemed quite at home.

Without asking, she bent and removed a miniature bottle of whisky from the fridge and poured this into a glass for him. She poured herself a gin and tonic and added some ice from a nearby bucket. She then sat down on the couch next to him, her gown splitting to reveal her leg and a short expanse of thigh.

She giggled when David described the confusion on the faces of the men.

'Still, I think we need to book out tomorrow. Stay elsewhere,' she said.

'Yes, we'll do that. They obviously have something, a sniff in the nose. Why are they fishing around here? Maybe they'll be back. It's possible they just wanted to verify something.'

'Why don't you move your stuff in here? We'll leave together in the morning. Is your account paid?' she asked.

'Yes, I paid up front.'

'So is mine. We can leave well before dawn.'

She rose from the couch. He was unable to ignore the quick flash of thigh.

'Quick, go pack your things and bring them from here before they get back. If MI6 is able to give them a description of you, it won't take them long to realise who Wohlhuter really is. They might already have a description of you.'

He realised that her proposal was only intended to ensure his safety and therefore quite innocuous. He found himself feeling slightly sorry. He used the fire escape stairs, making sure no on one was loitering in the passageway leading from the elevators and stairwell to his room. It took him a few minutes to pack his things. He wiped all the surfaces of fingerprints. Was that necessary, he wondered, or would it only serve to make things more suspicious to them? Too late now. Making sure that nothing was left behind, he grabbed his travelling bag and returned to her room.

They shared another drink. After, he went to the bathroom, changed into a sweatshirt and sleeping shorts and climbed into the three-quarter bed next to hers. A large bedside table split the beds. Gisela had already retired, sliding into her bed while he was still in the bathroom.

CHAPTER 7

He woke to somebody shaking him. He opened his eyes. The lights were on, the curtains were still drawn, and Gisela was bending over him.

'David, come on, wake up. It's nearly morning.'

Still groggy, he got out of bed.

'I've already bathed. Get into the shower. We have to leave here before the hotel's morning staff arrives for work. We'll use the back entrance,' she said. She, already dressed, applied her makeup in front of the dressing table mirror.

Within half an hour, dressed in the same suit he had worn the day before, he was ready. He reached for a valise.

'Leave it in the room,' she said.

He stopped. His expression was quizzical.

'In case we have to move quickly. We'll telephone the hotel and have it secured later.'

David understood.

It was still dark when they left the room. They had some items from the bar fridge but proposed to settle these later. They took the fire escape stairway and emerged at the back of the foyer where various doors led either to the kitchen, administration, or staff changing rooms. Unable to find a door that led to the back of the hotel, although they realised there had to be such an exit, they opened a door that led to the kitchen. A notice stated, 'Kitchen – Staff Only'. These were not the doors that gave access to the dining rooms, but were side entrances.

The kitchen was huge. Opening the doors revealed a long, narrow room done in white tiles and row upon row of basins, stoves, and open, stainless-steel shelving, with just a few dim night lights on. It was still deserted. They walked down a long aisle between the equipment and exited through what was obviously where they received their produce. This led directly to a large courtyard. A few dumpsters, a small van, and some large four-wheeled trolleys lined the inner walls.

'Stay here,' Gisela whispered, unclasping his hand. She was dressed in the same business suit she had worn the day before; the skirt was short, the hem a hand or two above her knees. She crossed the courtyard towards the gate and peered through a gap between the two doors. He saw her quickly draw her head back. She returned, walking quickly, an expression on her face.

'There's a car parked outside with middle-aged guy in a suit sitting in it.' She paused. 'At this time of the morning? We can't go out there. I'm sure he has the rear entrance under surveillance.'

Damn. He was surprised about how seriously they were looking out for him.

'How are going to get out of here? Surely they have the front under observation as well.'

A bell rang in the kitchen. They jerked around to face the noise, looking at each other in confusion.

'Quick, inside,' Gisela said.

They returned to the kitchen, closing the door, but leaving a slight gap to see through. They could hear footsteps on the concrete from outside the kitchen. Gisela peeked around the door. The night porter was walking towards the gates. She did not know from where he had come. He opened the gates and drove a large electric cart into the yard. They could hear the clattering of milk cans. It was the morning milk van.

They heard the porter greet the milkman. They obviously knew each other well.

'I'll be back before you get this lot off-loaded,' the porter said and they heard his footsteps as he walked away.

'I've got an idea,' David said. He walked out of the kitchen and approached the milkman. The man was clearly surprised at encountering a man clad in a suit, clearly a guest, at this early hour.

'Good morning, guv,' the milkman said.

'Morning. I've a spot of bother, I wonder if you can help.' David smiled, pulling his wallet from his pocket. 'There's ten pounds in it for you, but if anybody should ask, you know nothing. That's important.'

'Well, that depends, doesn't it?' the milkman replied. He was obviously wary.

'My girlfriend and I would like you to smuggle us out to the street in your cart. It's just down the road, maybe a block or so.'

David saw the man's face change as he became more suspicious.

'Hang on, we've paid our hotel bills,' he added. He still held his wallet out. The fact that it was bulging with banknotes was not lost on the milkman. 'We're not trying to bilk. If you look out of the gate, you'll see a guy in a car.'

'Yes, I saw him, guv.'

'Right, he's the chap we are trying to avoid.'

'Are you sure it's okay, I'm not about to land myself in the shit, guv?'

'No, the girlfriend and I need to get away without being seen.'

'Oh, I understand!' the milkman said while tipping the side of his nose. A lecherous grin of understanding appeared on his face.

'Okay, guv, let me unload this; it'll make room for you. The porter will come back to check the goods so you best disappear. I'll make a plan to get him to go back inside so that you can come out and board. You'll have to squeeze in and hunker down behind this panel here.'

The space looked minute to David. He slipped back into the kitchen, hiding just behind the door. They heard the milkman unloading the van, packing the goods on the small platform before the door. Within minutes, the porter again appeared and diligently began to check the delivered goods against a document in his hand: milk cans, orange juice, yoghurts and various other items. Once done, the porter disappeared.

As soon as he was out of sight, the milkman beckoned to them and they climbed into the rear of the cart. The milkman placed a few cans in front of them.

Gisela and David sat with their knees drawn up against their stomachs, their faces only inches apart, their heads lowered. He could not but notice the considerable amount of thigh Gisela displayed, so much her suspenders were visible.

The cart jerked into motion and they were flung together. He could smell the fragrance of her perfume and feel her warm breath on his cheek. He was acutely aware of her nearness.

'Close your eyes. You're not supposed to look,' she whispered. She must be embarrassed, he thought. He didn't know whether she was serious or whether this was just in jest.

He heard the gates being closed. He did not dare look up, knowing that they were close to the car in the street. A minute later, the cart bumped slightly. It now ran over cobblestone, with its unmistakable slight rumble. Out of the corner of his eye, he could see the walls of high-rise buildings on both sides. The trolley slowly stopped in the alleyway.

'Guv, you can get out now. It's safe. We're about a block away from the car.'

They were relieved to uncurl themselves from their cramped positions. Gisela pulled her skirt down.

'Who's that guy in the car, guv?' the curious milkman could not help asking.

David jerked his thumb in Gisela's direction, saying nothing. Again, he pulled his wallet from his pocket.

'Thanks, we appreciate this. Please not a word to anyone. Here's another ten.'

The milkman's eyes widened. Two weeks' wages for a short ride?

'Guv, if you are ever around here again, just let me know.' He beamed as he pocketed the banknote.

They walked the length of the alley until it exited into the main road. It took a while before they found a passing cab. The driver was surprised to be flagged down at this hour by a well-dressed man and woman carrying their bags, but nodded when David gave him the name of a large, well-known hotel adjoining Heathrow Airport.

'Let's lose ourselves in the crowd,' he said to Gisela.

She smiled. 'You know, you don't smell bad at all.'

He realised she was referring to the ride in the milk cart. He laughed. 'You've great legs.'

They both laughed, evaporating the tension.

She opened her handbag and withdrew two passports. They were olive drab and embossed with Bundesrepublik Deutschland. He recognised them immediately.

'I came prepared. You are now Werner Seidlitz and I am Vera Wagner, just two ordinary Germans; tourists, in fact. I think we need to change clothes to play the part, something less smart and conspicuous.'

He became aware that the relationship had subtly changed during the past few minutes, triggered by their shared danger.

'You're quite an operative. I'm impressed. Of course, you realise that if you had been searched, you would've given the game away.' David grinned at her.

'They aren't after me. They're after you.'

'I suppose you're right, but be careful,' he replied, unconsciously patting her hand on the seat next to him. She never removed it or showed any sign of surprise.

The cab stopped in the driveway of the hotel opposite the main entrance. The hotel was grotesque. Designed to hold as many guests as possible, it resembled a white brick wall, an assembly of cubes randomly stacked one on top of the other, an edifice of concrete, chrome, and white paint. It lacked character, modelled on the enormous hotel chains springing up all over cities – merely a place to sleep, devoid of all frills. Coffee, tea, sugar, and milk powder were all in little packets in the rooms, the only meal available being breakfast, and at an extra cost if you took it. However, the one upside was that these hotels, while sterile, were squeaky clean.

Two clerks manned the reception desk. 'A double room, please,' Gisela said. She slid an American Express card over the counter.

This surprised him. Sure, the previous night they had shared a room, but that had been out of necessity to avoid the black-suited spooks who had visited him. But now?

They had the elevator to themselves. Neither spoke. If she thought he would say something about the room they were about to share, she was mistaken. He was not about to make a fool of himself. Was this to confuse the enemy or had she some other motive? If he queried her reasons, he could leave her with the impression that he thought she had designs on him. If she countered saying that she did it to throw the English, he'd look like a bloody fool, embarrassed. She would not have to say it, but the message would be clear: hey, don't flatter yourself.

Since the unexpected intimacy of the milk cart, he'd felt like a voyeur. He remembered her legs and hoping her skirt would ride up higher. Was he a latent deviant? Though his mind had been taken up with escaping the detection of the man in the car, he still got aroused.

The hotel room was clinical and clean with two three-quarter beds pushed together. Beside them were nightstands with lamps. A large dressing table stood against the wall opposite the beds. Above this, a large mirror took up most of the wall. Leading off the room was a fully-equipped modern bathroom. There was no under-counter fridge with drinks. These had to be collected from a dispenser down the passage, which required coinage to operate. Another machine provided free ice.

'The first thing we need to do is change our backgrounds. That will require a drastic change in clothing. I suggest we go shopping.' Gisela opened her suitcase on the bed.

'Christ, I'm starving. Can't we go and find breakfast first?'

'No, first the clothes, then the breakfast. I'm going to make you look like a college student. You look young enough to still be a student.' She eyed him. 'I need you to look like one of those permanent students you find in

Germany, needing years to get their degrees. A career student. Let's keep the British guessing.'

'That's really not flattering.'

'Wait, you haven't seen your girlfriend yet.' She laughed.

They left the hotel and walked to a brand new mall, one of those clusters of shops of every description interlaced with a few fast food outlets that seemed to be springing up wherever huge numbers of people gathered, such as airports and central points in suburbia. This was a new shopping concept to him, obviously, something imported from the Americans. It hadn't arrived in South Africa yet.

She dragged him into a young man's clothing shop. If you were looking for a suit or tie, this was not a shop to frequent. It sold only sweatshirts, T-shirts, jeans, and assorted paraphernalia, all casual wear.

'You're a thirty-four?'

He nodded. She removed a few hangers with jeans and shirts. She handed him the jeans.

'Try these on.'

He emerged from the change-rooms and she nodded.

'We'll take them,' she said without consulting him.

They left the shop with a few packages containing enough clothing to give him a few changes. Next, they entered a women's boutique. This took longer, as she often tried something on and then discarded it for something else. Of course, he was constantly asked for his opinion, which didn't matter as she ignored it anyway.

They returned to the hotel to change. David emerged from the bathroom in jeans and a sweatshirt over which he wore an unbuttoned shirt. He had never worn a shirt unbuttoned before. It felt strange. Against the cold, he had a kapok duffel coat in a khaki material. It had a small West German black, gold, and red flag on each upper arm, a copy of the jackets issued to the German military, which had become fashionable. To cover his head, he had a navy blue German ski-cap, one of those where you could fold the sides down to protect your ears. The flaps were up, buckled together above the visor. David thought it was hideous and lost no time saying so.

'Wear it. It's the perfect disguise. German students don't have any dress sense. Just remember, speak only German, okay?'

He nodded. She was the boss when it came to espionage.

Her transformation was amazing. Gone was the makeup and her hair was now done in a simple ponytail. Dressed in blue jeans and a loose, bulky, red pullover with a wide roll neck, she looked like a teenager.

'Do you like?' she asked. She pirouetted in the room and smiled at his look of surprise.

'I do. You look as if you're still at uni – or haven't even got there yet.'

They were both wearing sturdy black boots, styled after the German military. They were quite fashionable and commonly sold as 'Wehrmacht boots'. He thought the name apt.

They breakfasted at a Lyons Tea House, one of the many fast food outlets in the mall, both having the full breakfast. David felt better after his and even ate a portion of hers. Once again, he went through the ritual of contacting Doyle, providing a meeting time. They met at the Chinese restaurant, but this time David had Gisela in tow.

Doyle confirmed that the *Georgio V* was in Bandar Mashur. She would leave the harbour some time the next day for Marseilles with her new cargo of crude. Engine trouble would develop before leaving the Persian Gulf and her crew would carry out repairs while she was anchored off the coast. This would be entered into the log as an overheating propeller shaft requiring a few days to rectify. In reality, nothing would be wrong. However, it would enable the complete contingent of officers, currently all Greek nationals, to be replaced with a French command of officers and engineers who were standing by in Kuwait City. The deckhands, most of whom were Koreans, would remain on board. Once in international waters, a company especially created for this purpose would purchase her complete cargo and the ship would be redirected to Beira. Currently, her cargo manifest gave Rotterdam as her port of destination.

Doyle seemed taken with Gisela and was intrigued by their relationship, not knowing whether this was simply a business relationship and platonic or not. Gisela also noticed Doyle's interest, but she kept her mien professional.

When opportunity knocked, David whispered, 'I think our mutual friend is developing the hots for you.'

She smiled and then replied, 'It's not him. It's his damn pecker.'

David thought her response hilarious.

There was more to this woman than he had thought.

****

'The *Deborah* will dock in Bandar Mashur about a week later, going through the same process,' said Doyle. 'However, in this case, we have a different intermediary shelf company. The crude will be shipped to Genoa. At least that's what the documentation will say. We'll let the tanker pass through the Suez Canal, then redirect the ship and change the crew.'

'When will the *Georgio V* get to Beira?' David asked.

'In about five weeks.'

'And the *Deborah*?'

'That'll take about five or six weeks at least,' Doyle replied.

David turned to Gisela. 'I was going to suggest that we accompany the tanker, boarding her at Kuwait City, but I don't think our presence would help if things go wrong. We would both be directly associated with this escapade and it would elevate us to public figures. Do you agree?'

She thought about it. 'You're right. I think we should be in Beira to meet the ship. That's where the fun will start. The British might attempt to stop her off the Mozambique coast.'

'I agree,' Doyle said. 'It's already common knowledge that they have a frigate stationed off the coast for precisely that purpose. I understand it's the HMS *Bristow*.'

'Christ, I should've stayed with my knitting. My father used to say, "Schuster, bleib bei deinem Leisten," David muttered. He realised how far removed he was from the real world. Oh, this was real all right. Too damned read and too dangerous and not his forte. He was a banker, not an undercover agent.

'What's that?' Doyle did not understand what David had been getting at.

'Nothing – just a stupid remark. Something about not straying from your area of expertise,' David replied. He dismissed the question with a wave of his hand. Gisela looked at him, but did not comment.

****

They spent the next three weeks moving around Great Britain and Europe, sometimes together, often separately, retaining Frankfurt as their base.

Rhodesia's huge textile industry demanded fabrics. David pulled off a good deal with Société Abelon, one of the largest textile manufacturers in southern France. The French company was happy to do business, their prices high but not as exorbitant as others he had obtained. A deal was struck. The French would ship these as exports to South Africa through Durban. Payment would be effected in French francs against a letter of credit drawn on the Société Générale Banque in Paris, the drawee bank being the Republic Bank in Johannesburg.

Gisela had learned quickly and was already an astute sanctions buster. Her German background enabled her to approach German manufacturers, who didn't give a hoot about the British embargo provided they could not be directly implicated. Household appliances, motorcars and trucks, machinery and electronics, all from Germany, had become her specialty. Pharmaceutical requirements and other medical needs were also in continuous demand.

David concentrated on the military requirements. This was a great deal more difficult as very few wanted to take a chance. Spare parts for various pieces of military equipment remained a headache.

The irony was that while the United Nations could announce an embargo, it did not possess the ability to enforce it. If countries like Germany and France only went through the motions, without any real intent, the UN was powerless.

David found himself becoming more and more attracted to Gisela, continuously thinking of her, particularly at night. They still shared hotel rooms and he would lie in bed unable to sleep, highly aware of her in the bed alongside him. She made no move. She was always friendly and polite, treating him as a good friend. She would on occasion touch his hand or arm to make a point, but it was not a come-on touch. She occasionally questioned his judgement but ultimately would allow him his way in a manner which led him to believe that she thought his judgement of the situation to be better. As far as any subterfuge was concerned, he never tried to compete. He accepted that she was the expert. She had after all been trained by the best in the world.

They had been busy for over two weeks, working at least ten or more hours a day, from hotel to hotel and country to country. David decided it was time for a rest. It seemed their changes of identity had completely thrown British Intelligence.

'Come on, it's Friday. Let's take a full-blown holiday, courtesy of the Rhodesian government. Where would you like to go?' David asked.

Her surprise was evident. The offer was completely out of character for the David she thought she knew.

'And where would you suggest?' She lifted her eyebrows.

'I'll leave it to you. Anywhere, within reason, of course.'

'That's extremely generous.'

'I know.' He smiled. 'But then, I'm not paying, am I?' He sighed. I just have to get away. What I'm doing now is as far removed from banking as ice is from the Sahara, and I'm not adjusting very well. I'm mentally buggered. I've not been sleeping well at night.'

She rested her head on her hands; her elbows propped on the table and she stared at him from under her lowered brow.

'Is that because…' She was about to ask whether his insomnia was a result of her close proximity but then thought the better of it. 'Okay, let's get out of the cold and at least go to where it's hot.' She laughed.

'You were about to say something else?'

'No, no, forget it. Will we be coming back here?'

'No, we're done here for a while.' Still, he was curious, wondering what she had been about to say.

Her face lit up.

'Cape Town! That's it. It's autumn there. It never rains in the autumn. We eventually have to go south anyway, you know, to Beira.'

CHAPTER 8

David got in touch with Doyle and it was agreed that from Cape Town they would fly to Beira via Lourenco Marques in Mozambique.

'But there's no hurry, the *Georgio V* is still on the high seas. Extend your stay if you wish,' he said magnanimously. 'I'll clear it with Salisbury.'

They found seats on a virtually non-stop South African Airways flight out of Frankfurt the next day.

It was a long, cramped flight in economy class, with a refuelling stop at Ilha do Sal. Then, it was non-stop to Johannesburg for the Cape Town connection. At least they caught up on some sleep.

They arrived in Cape Town on a Sunday afternoon. It was hot and they were welcomed by the Cape Doctor, a southeast wind of considerable strength. It was so strong, it was said to blow all germs and viruses out to sea. They checked into the Ambassador Hotel in Cape Town, which overlooked Clifton Beach, South Africa's own bikini beach, the home of the young and nubile females keen to wear as little as possible. While David was speaking to the reception clerk, Gisela interrupted.

'Why two rooms? Why the change?'

'Well, this is a holiday, not business – you know,' he replied.

'What's the difference? I am all right with it. We've shared rooms for a few weeks now. Tell them to change it. We're not in each other's way. Just get the largest room they have. Remember, this hasn't been sanctioned yet; maybe we'll have to pay for this sudden bit of luxury ourselves.'

'Christ, I hope not. That would be damn unfair. We've been working our arses off. Sure, they pay all expenses, but our salaries are nothing to write home about. The bastards need to be a little flexible. We're out on a limb here.' David's stern voice was just above a whisper. 'It would be a bastard if we had to pay.'

'It could happen, so one room's the way to go,' she retorted.

He did as she had asked, quietly elated at the arrangement, wondering if he should read something into it. Not once had she shown or implied that anything had changed. He knew that if he made a move and it backfired, the situation would become untenable; they would no longer be able to work as a team. James Bond, England's mythical spy, the lucky bastard, did his job and grabbed arse all the time and still managed to retain a working relationship with the women he bedded. In real life, it was different. But he still saw those suspenders and stocking'd legs in the milk cart. What a turn-on they were. Just thinking about them made him harden. He had a problem; this woman was getting to him. He grinned.

'What's so funny?'

'You wouldn't understand.'

She shrugged.

****

The hotel's claim to fame was its attached restaurant which more outsiders frequented than hotel guests. Seafood was their specialty. Of course, if weather permitted and the awnings were up, the panoramic view of the bay under a crepuscular sky did much to enhance its reputation. He had booked a table for eight o'clock that evening.

He dispensed with a tie, content with an open-necked shirt and a dark blazer. She was radiant in a while floral dress, which displayed some cleavage, no stockings, slingback flats and a white, lightweight evening jacket that was sufficient to ward off an evening chill should it materialise. They sauntered into the restaurant, situated on the top floor overlooking Table Bay, just as the last of the day's sunlight faded on the horizon. Table Mountain loomed behind them. The usual wind had abated, allowing the awnings on the leeward side to be opened.

She took him by the arm, momentarily pressing herself against him. 'Come on, David, get that stick out of your arse, please. Relax, let's enjoy ourselves. God, you're impossible. It's not really your war and you carry on as if you're the last bloody Mohican. Let's have a wonderful supper and lots of wine – we're on holiday!' She squeezed his arm, but stayed close.

He chose a Backsberg Sauvignon Blanc, a true cultivar of the Cape, ice cold. They both opted for grilled calamari with lemon for starters. The succulent squid melted in their mouths. For their main course, they selected Cape lobsters, grilled over an open fire and served on a bed of rice and a fish sauce with a touch of lemon and garlic, a sauce only the Portuguese can prepare. They finished another bottle of wine, she matching him glass for glass.

Decidedly mellow, their relationship was taking on a degree of conspiracy. The main course plates were removed and they washed their fingers in the finger bowls. For the first time, they had shed some of the shackles of decorum and reached the stage where they were prepared to be honest with each other. They might rue this the next day, but that was tomorrow. Tonight, they were not giving it a thought.

Gisela insisted on Crêpes Suzettes for dessert. They drank more wine while watching the waiter go through the whole flambé ritual.

Irish coffees topped off their meal. The table was small. Gisela had shed her flats and he was aware of her bare feet under the table. Every now and then, she would run her toe up his shin, seemingly free from all inhibitions. Her eyes shone. There was a slight smile on her face. She lapsed into German.

'Here before me sits a man who looks an opportunity in the eye and does nothing about it,' she announced with the solemnity of one reading a heavy German poem, again rubbing her foot against his. She half-rose from her chair, leaned over the small table, and touched his face slightly with her fingertips. Then she kissed him on the lips. As she drew away, he looked down her dress and saw that she wore no brassiere. He could taste her lipstick and the Irish coffee.

She sat down again and reverted to English.

'He looks down my dress and now the young man's really confused.' From under the table, she pushed her bare foot into his crotch.

He was speechless and could only sit there grinning.

Christ, he thought, I'm being seduced. Sure, he had been seduced before, but never so overtly. God, he had to do something about this. Her bare foot was still on his groin. He was so damned hard he thought he'd snap.

'Oh, my goodness. He's human after all.' She giggled, feigning surprise as her toes walked over his erection.

He groaned and beckoned the waiter. Scribbling their room number and adding a huge tip, he grabbed her hand and hauled her out of the dining room.

'I think I'm drunk,' he said.

'I hope not, I'll never forgive you,' she whispered as she caressed him with her hand in his pocket.

He had barely closed the room door when she pushed herself against him, drawing his head down, kissing him deeply and passionately. He ran his hands down her back and drew her buttocks closer, grinding himself against her. She worked his shirt buttons, finally just ripping his shirt off his shoulders to kiss his chest, her lips tracing a path down to his navel. He unzipped the back of her dress and it fell from her shoulders. She stepped out of it, now only in a pair of white panties.

He picked her up in his arms and carried her across the room, doing a two-foot hop to shed his pants as he went.

'God, I've wanted you for so long, what kept you?' she whispered in his ear as they fell onto the bed together.

Spent, he lay on his back and she on her side, cuddled into his shoulder, her head on his chest. They were both slick with perspiration.

'You must know that since I lost my husband, you are the first man in my life again.'

'I know.' Somehow he knew this to be true.

When he awoke the next morning, she was still in bed. They made love again, quieter and gentler this time, only getting up when the sun streamed into the room, forcing them to move. The rest of the day they were on the beach, covered in suntan lotion, amongst the huge boulders and sheltered from the wind. He had brought a cooler bag with ice and wine from the hotel, taking two wine glasses from the room. For lunch, he bought a large piece of smoked snoek, similar in taste to mackerel. They ate this with fresh buttered rolls and a salad.

By the late afternoon, they made their way back to the hotel. He ached for her again. The moment they got back into the hotel, they both got into the shower and one thing led to another.

It was a sultry, sexy two days.

Then the holiday was over and they were flying to Johannesburg.
****

Everything had progressed smoothly. The *Georgio V* had departed the Persian Gulf with her new crew of officers aboard and had travelled without incident, now entering the Mozambique Strait off of Madagascar. The master was a Captain Le Clercq, who had been properly briefed and was comfortable with the risk. Naturally, the officers would be paid an above-average remuneration with a promise of a substantial bonus if they were successful. Word was that the British frigate was stationed off of Beira. Whether the British were aware of the approaching tanker was not known, but they were sure to spot her well before Beira and realise what her intentions were.

Captain Le Clercq had been adamant that he was not going to yield to British threats.

The *Georgio V* now flew the French Tricolour. How Oosterwijk had managed to pull that off must surely be remarkable. To top it all, the officers were also French. Britain would have to tread wearily if they proposed to pressurise the French.

The question was how they would react.

****

The shrill ringing of the telephone attached to the bulkhead above his bunk woke Captain Le Clercq immediately.

'What is it?' he asked. The chronometer above his desk said three in the morning.

'Captain,' the first officer said, 'we have picked up a blip on radar, steaming towards us on an intercept course. She's doing nearly twenty-five knots. It's got to be a warship.'

'Merde! It's the British. I'll be up in a minute or two.'

The captain appeared on deck a few minutes later.

'I'll take over,' he said.

Captain Le Clercq stuck his head up against the hood over the radar display, and quickly found what the first officer had. It was closing rapidly. At that speed, there was no doubt she was a warship, and she was no more than fifteen miles away.

'Let's adopt a wait-and-see attitude. Hold your course. Do not attempt contact. Let them make the first move. Just see to it that we have an Aldis lamp up here. If the captain starts something, I'll need to communicate with him. There's to be no radio traffic, is that clear?' he barked to the first officer.

'Yes, sir.'

A stiff wind blew from the stern, the ship in a following sea. She was fully laden but still rode the sea well. Her bulbous bow ploughed through the water, easily managing fourteen knots. It was still dark, but the ship was clearly visible, lit up like a Christmas tree.

The warship closed the distance and when a mile or directly abeam, she turned sharply to port, doing a complete about-turn, and started to approach the tanker from the stern on the starboard side. She was well lit and, as she advanced, the officers recognised her as a frigate, not missing the helicopter deck on her stern. Once abeam and no more than a half mile from the *Georgio V*, the frigate slowed to match the tanker's speed.

The first officer had his binoculars clamped to his eyes. 'It's HMS *Bristow*, sir,' he confirmed.

'What are her gun turrets doing?' Captain Le Clercq asked.

'These are still facing for'ard, sir.'

Le Clercq stepped closer to the first officer, not wanting the coxswain to overhear him.

'Tell our radio operator to inform us the moment the ship attempts contact. Under no circumstances is he to respond. You got that?'

'Yessir.'

The first officer disappeared.

The British ship held station. It would be at least nine to ten hours before they had Beira in sight. The frigate would have identified their ship by now and probably were babbling to their Admiralty trying to establish to whom she belonged and under what flag she sailed. It was still dark and no flag fluttered from her stern. Le Clercq mentally corrected himself – he was sure they already had the current information about the ship and possibly even more. They must have already realised that she was French-owned and that this could create a sticky political situation.

Captain Le Clercq chuckled. This was difficult for all. Nobody was actually at war and no one wanted to upset the other.

The first signs of dawn appeared on the horizon when the first officer returned to the bridge. The captain looked at him and the officer grinned.

****

'Sir, the shit is hitting the proverbial fan. The British have obviously been in touch with the French, who are desperately trying to contact us. We have no responded to any messages. May I confirm that is what you want?'

'Don't worry. It won't take long before our good British captain starts trying to contact us on the Aldis.'

The captain was quite pleased with himself. The British would never fire on his ship. Either way, he and his officers were guaranteed their exceptional salaries, even if they did not make Beira.

The bridge phone rang. The captain picked it up and listened, the others on the bridge watching him with apprehension. His face broke into a grin as he replaced the phone.

'That was our wireless operator. He says all hell's breaking loose on the airwaves because we are not replying. Everybody's calling us.'

The first flashes of an Aldis spat out from the British warship, the Morse coming across in double-quick time. Operators always tried to impress their recipients.

'What's he saying?'

'First he introduced himself as the HMS *Bristow* and then asked our destination,' the first officer replied.

'Let's give the fucker something to think about. Send, but send very slowly, as if we are having difficulty sending Morse, "Cannot read you, send again slowly."'

Le Clercq was sure the speed at which they were operating the Aldis lamp would drive the British captain to distraction. It took a good while to get the message completed and it even contained a few transmission errors. There was a minute or two's delay before the frigate responded, this time irritatingly slowly. It was a repeat of the first message.

On the bridge, the first officer handed Le Clercq a piece of paper.

'You don't have to do that. Of course, I can read what he's saying, at that speed my grandchild could read it.' Le Clercq said. 'Okay, send, "Who are you?" That should give the bastard apoplexy.'

Again, this was laboriously transmitted.

****

Captain John Reynolds RN, KFC, DSO was livid.

The ratings and junior officers on the bridge of the HMS *Bristow* did not dare look at their commanding officer.

The first officer handed the captain a piece of paper.

'For fuck's sake, Number One, scrap the bits of paper! I can read that.' He gestured towards the tanker's flashing Aldis lamp as he crumbled the message into a ball and threw it onto the deck. 'That bloody frog captain's playing games with us. Are they still not responding to any radio messages?'

'No, sir.'

'All right, Number One, let's play his game. Send, "British Navy ship HMS *Bristow*. What is your destination?" Christ, he's probably going to need fifteen minutes to formulate the reply,' the captain said.

The captain was wrong. The reply took no longer than a minute.

'Why?'

Captain Reynolds wasn't enjoying this, aware that the tanker captain was playing the indignant and wronged victim of a British bullying tactic. The man was smart. Reynolds withdrew a piece of paper from his pocket, smoothing it out on the bridge map table.

'Send this: "Your cargo of crude oil is intended for Rhodesia. You are in breach of United Nations Resolution 221. We are enforcing an embargo on all ships. Heave to. Failing to do will force us to fire on you." Let's see what the bastard does now.'

'Captain, you don't propose to fire on him, do you?' the first officer asked.

'Number One, in terms of the United Nations decree, we are entitled to use force.'

It took fifteen minutes before the tanker replied. The message was terse. 'This cargo is intended for the Portuguese company Galp in Beira, Mozambique. Our documentation clearly states: final destination Beira.'

Captain Reynolds ran his hand over the stubble on his face. He had not yet had time to duck away and shave. The Admiralty had authorised him to shoot a warning shot across the tanker's bows, provided he had prior permission from them to do so. In terms of the UN resolution, force had been approved. Even a warning shot would be cutting the legalities of his action very fine.

'Number One, you realise, of course, that if the Conservatives were in power we would not be here making bloody fools of ourselves. This is a typical Labour cock-up, no doubt sanctioned by Wilson. The Conservatives would have solved this round a table; we would never have even got to enforcing embargoes. Christ! We've a ship owned by the French with a French crew thumbing its nose at the British Navy. It's fuckin' ridiculous.'

'Sir, what do you want me to do now?' the first officer asked.

'Immediately signal them to heave to. A simple "Heave to" should suffice. They'll ignore it anyway.'

****

Thirty minutes passed. There was no response from the tanker. Captain Reynolds sat in his bridge chair staring out of over the foredeck and the ship's bow.

'Number One, call the crew to stations. I hope that French bastard hears the bells – he'll know what's happening. Have the for'ard turret to bear ahead of the tanker.'

The harsh shrill of the station bells reverberated through the ship, the crew running to take up their stations, the men disappearing from the deck. The tanker would realise that the ship was preparing for action. How would they interpret this?

A minute later, the first officer confirmed the ship at battle stations.

'Okay, Number One, send a repeat of the "heave to" message.'

The captain lifted a phone from the bulkhead next to his chair. This connected him to the frigate's gunnery officer.

'Guns, prepare a shot across the tanker's bows. Not too close, mind you. Wait for my signal.'

The first officer overheard the captain's conversation with the gunnery officer.

'With respect, Captain, we could create an incident.'

'I know, but that's Wilson's bloody problem, not mine. We've got our orders.'

****

Captain Le Clercq deciphered the next message as the Aldis flashed from the frigate. He kept a constant vigil while trying to fathom the frigate's next actions. Again, he ignored the frigate's second request that he heave to.

'Don't reply, ignore the message. Hold your course. Let's see what he does now,' he ordered the men on the bridge.

The atmosphere on the bridge had changed. The tension ratcheted up a notch.

A few minutes later, the frigate's call could be heard across the water.

'Captain, he's going to battle stations,' the first officer said. All were aware of the officer's heightened apprehension in his voice.

Le Clercq nodded, watching the tanker through his binoculars. He wondered whether the British captain could see him on the tanker's bridge. They both knew they were playing a game, and that they were only the pawns. He saw the frigate's men disappearing from the deck, the hatches being secured. He realised that they were now about to move to the next phase.

He was right. The frigate's Aldis flashed another 'heave to' request. Again, he ignored it. A minute later, the for'ard turret swung towards the tanker. This did not go unnoticed. The other officers and crew were all staring at him, fear etched on their faces. A few seconds later, the turret belched smoke. A huge fountain of water erupted a half mile in front of the tanker's bow as they heard the boom of her turret gun.

The agitated first officer turned to Le Clercq.

'Captain, what must we do now?'

'Ignore the shot. Maintain your course and speed.' He expected to be obeyed without question.

He turned to the officer. 'Send another message, "I wonder what President de Gaulle will have to say about this. You are threatening to fire upon a French crew in international waters."'

The first officer stared.

'Dammit, send it,' Le Clercq shouted.

****

Reynolds read the message as the Aldis slowly flashed it letter by letter. He had to smile.

'Touché,' he said. His number one had read it as well and appreciated his captain's remark, a hint of a smile on his lips.

'Number One, transmit the tanker's last message verbatim to the Admiralty. I want to see how they respond. Christ, I hope the First Sea Lord has to have Wilson woken for a response. How on earth did we get ourselves into this? That man's political intellect can't even be measured even with a bloody micrometer.'

'Aye, aye, sir.'

'Oh, Number One, have the men stand down. No more messages. Just keep station and leave the tanker more than enough room to manœuvre in.

****

'You know, I have to admire the man,' Le Clercq said to his first officer. 'He knows this is not our fight, and he knows we know it. Let the politicians fight it out. He'll want a coded message from the top authorising him to fire again, even if it's just another shot across our bows. Maintain course and speed. Wake me when you're ready to drop anchor outside Beira.'

'Oui, mon capitaine.'

CHAPTER 9

Beira sits on a low-lying flood plain the northern coast of Mozambique. This is the convergence of a number of rivers so intertwined you never know which is which. These all discharge into the sea creating a three-mile wide river mouth, part of it tidal. Beira is situated on the north side of the river on a small peninsula. The harbour lies just within the river on the northern bank and is the terminus for the rail line from Rhodesia. It is land-locked Rhodesia's lifeline, through which all her imports and exports are routed.

It was here that the tank farm had been built to store the crude oil imported into Rhodesia. The tank farm complex was surrounded by an enormous earth wall, which was intended to contain the crude in the event of any breach in the tanks. As is usual, it was surrounded by high-security fencing, and the perimeter was floodlit and patrolled at night. A nearly two hundred-mile pipeline joined Beira with the town of Umtali across the border in Rhodesia.

The moment they stepped out of the turboprop Fokker Friendship, David and Gisela hit a wall of heat and humidity. Within minutes, they were both perspiring profusely. Of course, they had known what to expect. Gisela had been to Beira before on vacation, this was Rhodesia's nearest holiday resort on the sea. The town boasted a number of decent hotels, most with their own private pristine beaches, primarily built to provide holiday facilities for the Rhodesians who annually flocked in droves to the coast.

David had left accommodation arrangements to Gisela. She preferred not to consider a hotel in the city, but instead chose a holiday place about twelve miles further up the coast, secluded and, hopefully, not known to too many outsiders. In a small seaside hamlet called João Bandeira, it sat on a small peninsula along the pristine coast, with white sands and palm trees. The resort was a cluster of thatched bungalows built on the white sands of the beach just beyond the high-water mark. Although spartan, the bungalows contained all basic amenities and the linen was spotless.

The resort was run by the de Alveras, a middle-aged Portuguese couple. They were assisted by a few local blacks who went out of their way to

70

make their guests' stay as pleasant as possible. The clientele was mostly Rhodesian tourists. Anybody not Rhodesian would be conspicuous.

David and Gisela collected their Mercedes 250SE from the car rental, one of the few cars with air conditioning. They planned to masquerade as tourists. Before leaving the airport for the resort, David phoned a number he had been given in Johannesburg. A male voice answered in Portuguese.

'Mr Sardinha, please,' David asked.

'Who's speaking?'

'Martinez from Johannesburg.'

'Ah, yes senhor, your package will arrive tomorrow morning. There are a number of your friends already in town staying at the Hotel Tivoli.'

The man put down the phone. This meant that the *Georgio V* would arrive off Beira harbour tomorrow morning sometime. The friends Sardinha had referred to were British. MI6. Christ, the bastards are already here and waiting, he thought.

They spent a pleasant evening at the quiet resort. The de Alveras served a splendid meal of endless grilled prawns accompanied by savoury rice. They washed it all down with copious quantities of Lagosta wine, a crisp, dry import from Portugal, served well chilled. They retired early.

The next morning, they left for Beira to meet other operatives at an undercover Portuguese-registered company near the docklands. It was in a better part of the town, in a new multi-storied building, which leased space to doctors, lawyers, manufacturers' agents, as well a host of other professions.

The offices of the Silva Costa Import Company took up an entire floor. They were staffed by Portuguese, all of whom held Portuguese passports but were affiliated with Rhodesia. Goods labelled as local imports were off-loaded in Beira and these offices re-consigned them for Rhodesia. They were usually restricted to textiles, motor oils, spare parts, and other consumable items assumed for local use. Since they were imported by the Portuguese as well, anyone nosing around would find it difficult to prove they were destined for Rhodesia. Items labelled of strategic importance were invariably imported through South Africa.

Crude oil was something else. There was no way that its destination could be disguised.

Access to these offices was through a locked grille-door. Any person other than an employee had to be identified and signed in. John Taylor came through to authorise their entrance. He shook hands with them and led them through to a small conference room.

'My God, what a relief,' David said, already drenched. 'This aircon is a bloody Godsend.' He slumped down in a chair next to the table, wiping his forehead with a handkerchief.

A black woman brought in a tray with glasses and an enormous jug of lemon juice, its ice cubes clinking. They all helped themselves gratefully.

'Well,' Taylor said with a smug smile on his face, 'the fun is about to begin. The *Georgio V* is just off Beira ready to drop anchor. The British frigate is lying just outside the twelve-mile limit. Rest assured, diplomatic messages between the English ambassador and the colonial Portuguese government in Laurence Marques must be flying. Our captain remains adamant that his instructions are to discharge his cargo in Beira, and he proposes to do just that. However, as you know, the only place the crude can go is into the Rhodesian storage tanks. He says that's no concern of his, and he's quite right.'

David stared out of the window. He could see the harbour and the tank farm. If he looked out towards the right, or east, he could see the ships anchored out in the bay. There was only one tanker. He realised that this must be the *Georgio V*.

David looked at the man opposite him. Taylor had given him the rundown. Senhor de Mello was a senior member of the Portuguese government, a thickset swarthy man with a mop of black curly hair, a thin moustache below a slightly bulbous nose, and thick lips. David knew him to be a member of the Portuguese PIDE – the Policia Internacional e de Defesa do Estado, the secret police and henchmen of the Portuguese dictator Salazar, and not an organisation to be trifled with. The South African intelligence service BOSS, the Rhodesian CIO, and PIDE worked closely together, sharing a common enemy: the communists in their countries and those engaged in subversive activities against their governments. The emerging black nationalists in the three countries usually had communist affiliations, not out of ideology but rather because only communist countries were prepared to assist these subversive movements.

'Senhor Taylor, you know that there's nothing I would like more than to allow your ship to enter the harbour. You will appreciate that we are sympathetic towards your cause. However, we are enduring considerable pressure from the British. Their ambassador is virtually encamped at the offices of our Governor-General. Plus, I need to mention the pressure from the United Nations. They maintain that we are in violation of their resolutions. Of course, we refute that.'

'Senhor de Mello, please just let our ship enter the harbour. At least let's get it to tie-up alongside the quay. Not to start discharging. We can wait for the furore to die down. Of course, we'd have to get the British agents to leave. I don't know how many you know of, but I know of at least six agents running round here in Beira masquerading as tourists and businessmen,' Taylor said.

'I know, we know who they are and we are watching, but Senhor Taylor, I must warn you – and this comes from the top: you dare not make a move against them. Is that clearly understood?'

David ventured a question, interrupting the two. 'What if they move against us?'

De Mello laughed. 'That would be different, but of course, they would be fools to do that. There is to be no shooting.'

'So you're saying that if they in any way attempt force and place us in danger, we may defend ourselves?'

'Of course, but be certain that you can prove that they initiated it and that you were merely defending yourselves. I can assure you, if MI6 – and we all know they are MI6 – behave in anyway threatening, my people will retaliate. Rather we do so, not you.' De Mello stressed the final word.

John Taylor smiled. 'That's good to know. We are going to tell the captain of the ship to raise anchor and bring his ship to the harbour mouth. We'll also instruct the harbour services to assist the ship to come alongside. We'll wait for a British reaction.'

De Mello shrugged his shoulders. 'I can't stop you, but don't be surprised if the harbour authorities refuse to co-operate. Our government may tell them not to co-operate. They have yet to make a decision. It all depends on what results from the discussions between the British government and us.' He paused. 'Anything can happen,' he added as an afterthought.

'We'll take our chances,' John Taylor said.

There was a knock on the door and a woman clerk entered, handing a note to John Taylor.

Dismissing her, he glanced at the note and then turned to those round the table. 'The French consul is on the quayside looking for a boat to take him out to the *Georgio V*,' he said, looking at David and Gisela.

David laughed.

'No doubt the British have put pressure on the poor bastards. He's probably here to lift the captain's papers. That's not going to help. Knowing Captain Le Clercq, he'll probably tell him to fuck off,' David said.

He looked at Gisela. She didn't bat an eyelid.

'Well, we won't interrupt normal commerce in our ports, that's the stance Portugal proposes to adopt. The English can go to hell,' de Mello said.

Taylor offered his thanks to de Mello. De Mello stood up and shrugged, for no reason apparently, and exited the conference room.

John Taylor sighed. 'Of course, most believe there's a Greek crew aboard. They are probably wondering why he is not replying to their communications. You should read what's being said in the international press, it's a laugh a minute. Wilson's in a flap and he has his Under Secretary for Foreign Affairs running around in Portugal, only to find they are uncooperative and that they are stonewalling him. Wilson called for a meeting of the UN Security Council to further clarify the use of force but bloody U Thant refused. The blacks who are supporting the president of the council – I believe he is from Nigeria – seem to have some other agenda, and are vying for outright military intervention. They are trying to buy time and so garner more support from other countries to demand direct military intervention. Meanwhile Wilson can't shoot and could lose the advantage he now holds. Fuckin' Brits.'

Gisela suddenly sputtered. David started laughing too.

Taylor looked them sternly. 'That's not funny. Okay, listen up. While all this is going on, our ship lies out there just waiting for the Brits to mount some raiding party to board her. They could hold the crew captive and move the ship out into international waters. If they do that, we're stuffed. So, we need to reinforce the crew. De Mello says he'll look the other way. I'm taking twelve men out there armed to the teeth with automatic weapons and bazookas. David, I want you and Gisela to stay here and keep an eye on things around the harbour, especially on those British agents.'

That night, under cover of darkness, a large fishing vessel moored alongside the fishing jetty was prepared. Twelve Rhodesian Special Forces scouts would board her, suitably armed with assault rifles and bazookas and clearly ready for a fight. On instructions from de Mello, John Taylor was to issue John and Gisela with automatics and spare magazines.

They now stood on the jetty and watched the fishing boat prepared for departure.

'I've also left two R1 automatic rifles and two handguns in your car's boot. Use them if you have too. De Mello will back you – this is war, you know. You do realise that, don't you? It has become a war.' John patted David on the back in encouragement.

David was appalled. He had never intended to get into any shooting match.

'I'm not going after the British! De Mello was emphatic – we're not to shoot!'

'I know. This is simply to protect you if they come after you. Remember, they know who you are and where you two fit into things. Be careful, but if you have to shoot be assured we will support your actions.'

With that, Taylor turned on his heel and stepped off the jetty onto the fishing vessel. It slowly backed away, its propeller churning the muddy water.

They stood on the jetty and watched the fishing boat depart.

David and Gisela drove off and headed for the main road that would take them to the restaurants that thronged the sea. They decided to eat out as the evening was still young.

They left the restaurant after eleven. David drove. After a few miles, Gisela tapped him on the arm.

'I think we're being followed.'

He looked in the rear-view mirror. There certainly was a set of lights behind them. He had seen them a while back, but they had not come any nearer.

'You could be wrong, you know.'

'I don't think so. Even at the fishing harbour, I had the distinct feeling we were being watched.'

He switched off the lights and let the car coast to a stop alongside the road. There were no streetlights as they were already beyond the harbour town. Suddenly, the other car's lights also disappeared.

'Shit. Something's up.'

'I don't think they know where we're staying,' Gisela said, 'That's why they're following.'

'Okay, about a mile or so ahead is a roadside garage with an all-night convenience store and coffee bar. We'll stop there but not go in. We'll hide, leaving the car in a conspicuous position. They're bound to see it. Let's see what they do and who they are.'

She agreed.

Soon he swung the car off the main road and stopped in the park space next to the pumps. They climbed out and walked toward the store. There appeared to be nobody else around. Instead of entering, they swung left and then hid behind a large storeroom that was part of the garage. It was merely a corrugated roof supported by pillars joined by mesh-wire. The enclosure was packed with paraffin drums and gas bottles.

They did not have long to wait. A few minutes later, a large Chevrolet sedan swept into the parking lot, its headlights sweeping the walls and store as it entered the forecourt. Three men alighted, dressed as tourists in long pants with their cotton shirts hanging out, no doubt to conceal their weapons. Two of the men were young, maybe in their late twenties, the third older and obviously the man in charge. Their pale complexions gave them away as new arrivals from Europe. David wondered whether they spoke Portuguese. They looked around the parking lot and when they saw David's car, a short discussion followed. They slowly made their way to the store, two of them disappearing through the doorway, the third remaining outside. Within a few minutes the two re-emerged, clearly agitated. It was evident that not all was well and their frantic conversation was accompanied by gesticulations. The three spread out.

'Christ! What are they going to do when they find us? Start a gunfight?' David whispered.

'Don't be ridiculous.'

David wasn't taking a chance. He drew the automatic from his belt. It was a Swiss SIG P210 automatic with a sixteen-shot magazine. He flipped the safety off and held the weapon alongside his leg, pointing at the ground. He watched the man approach. The man's hands were empty. When he was three or four yards away, David stepped out from behind the storeroom, his automatic levelled at the man's chest.

'You're looking for me?' His voice was barely above a whisper.

The man stopped, his head snapping back. He stared at the gun in David's hand. Gisela then also emerged from behind the building with gun in hand. The man raised his arms above his head, an automatic reflex.

'I was looking for somewhere to piss,' he said.

David didn't move. 'Really? Why are you following us?'

He could see the other two opposite the property.

The man sighed probably realising that bluffing was pointless. 'We were sent to warn you of the consequences of what you are doing.'

'Who wants to warn us?'

'The British government.'

'Really? Well, I've an answer for you. You said you wanted to piss. Well, you've come to the right place. You can start pissing in your pants right now.'

'I can't do that,' the man said.

'Oh, I think you are going to. I'm sure you're armed and I will shoot you, in self-defence of course. Your knees first. So, I suggest you start pissing now. I'm going to count to five. One … two … three …'

'Oh, shit!' was all the man said, the front of his pants revealing an expanding wet spot. Aggrieved, he added, 'For fuck's sake, you bastards.'

'Good boy. No need to get nasty. Now, go back to your friends and leave. If anybody makes a move in this direction, we'll shoot. Know something else: the PIDE know who we are and that you are following us. So, should anything go wrong you'll land up without your nuts. I'm sure you know about the PIDE, they're worse than the KGB and you're British agents in this country under false pretences, aren't you?' David asked. His automatic never wavered.

The man nodded and slowly backed off, his shoes squishing. The other two realised there was something wrong as their partner walked backwards, his hands still in the air. When he reached them, there was a quick flurry of conversation and then they all climbed into the car and drove back towards Beira.

Gisela watched the tail-lights fading into the distance.

'Piss in your pants, hey! That's original, I must say. Not bad, maybe banking is not your forte. Intelligent, hot in bed, hot with a gun, what else?' She laughed, putting her arms round his neck and kissing him full on the lips.

That took him by complete surprise. 'They'll be back,' he said.

'I know, but not tonight.'

CHAPTER 10

Captain Le Clercq was expecting John Taylor and his men. He had received a coded radio communication.

The fishing vessel drew alongside as it rose and fell in the slight swell. A pilot's ladder was dropped from the tanker's deck above and the men, encumbered by their weapons, scrambled up onto the steel deck.

'Quite a force you have brought with you. Are you expecting the British to try something?' The captain raised his eyebrows.

'You're damn right! They're not about to give up. If this crude gets through to the tank farm, they're going to look pretty ineffective in the eyes of the world. If you only knew what has been going on behind the scenes. They've gone to the UN to get permission to use force. They're still pressurising the Portuguese who, thankfully, just shrug their shoulders with a 'business as usual' attitude, even with the Britain's Under Secretary for Foreign Affairs paying Portugal urgent visits trying to twist their arms. I understand you are now a ship without a flag and a captain without papers?'

The captain laughed. 'Do I look concerned?'

'Where's the *Bristow*?'

'She's lying just outside the harbour in international waters. They've got their glasses trained on us most of the time.'

'Good, I want them to see that we have heavily armed men patrolling your decks. That should deter any attempt at boarding.'

Taylor withdrew a packet of cigarettes and put one in his mouth.

'I wouldn't light that if I were you. You're standing on 16,000 tonnes of crude. Please ensure that your men know they're not to smoke except in designated areas. I must insist that they hand in all lighters and matches,' Le Clercq said.

Taylor widened his eyes. 'God yes, I understand. I'll make sure this happens right away. We wouldn't want to help the British get rid of this crude, do we?'

Taylor knew that if the British attempted an assault on the tanker it would have to be at night. Any approaching crafts' intentions would be too obvious during daylight, the element of surprise not there.

He decided not to retire for the night, although Le Clercq had assigned a cabin to him and his second-in-command.

Around three in the morning, a lookout alerted him to four inflatable boats approaching, Zodiacs, powered by large outboard engines. British Marines, eight in each boat, recognised to be formidable foes anywhere in the world, came alongside the tanker.

Taylor's men remained hidden behind the high gunwales of the tanker. The soldiers in the dinghies immediately started to fire grappling lines across the tanker's deck preparing to board.

'Ahoy! *Georgio V*, we represent the British government and in terms of UN Resolution 221, we are boarding you. Any resistance will be met with force. If you do not resist, you will come to no harm.'

Taylor looked over the gunwale and saw a Marine officer standing in the foremost Zodiac, a megaphone in his hand. Out of the corner of his eye, he saw Captain Le Clercq walk up next to him. He also had a megaphone in his hand.

'What do you want me to do?' he whispered.

'It's your ship, but if you agree, I'll speak to them.'

Without a word, Le Clercq handed Taylor the megaphone.

He brought the megaphone to his mouth.

'This ship and its cargo is the property of the French government. Any attempt by an armed force to board will be considered an act of piracy and will be met with force,' he said, his voice amplified. 'Secondly, you appear to need reminding that this vessel is anchored in Portuguese waters,' he added.

As he spoke, he signalled his men, who rose as one from behind the steel gunwales, their automatic weapons and bazookas at the ready. They were backlit by the numerous lights that illuminated the tanker's bridge and deck. There would be no mistaking that they were armed.

Taylor signalled again and this was followed by the sound of rifle and machine gun breeches being cocked.

'Your move,' Taylor said through the hailer.

Each party stared the other down. Nothing further was said.

The officer in the Zodiac spoke into a walkie-talkie. They turned round and roared off in the direction of HMS *Bristow*, abandoning their grappling lines.

'Phew, that was close.' Taylor's voice was a breathless, husky sound. 'Not often do you get to out-think the British.'

'Clearly, the British are serious about avoiding any armed conflicted,' Le Clercq said.

Taylor had to agree with the captain.

Both men watched the departing dinghies.

'Merde, de Gaulle would have considered this something to see, the British returning with the tail between the legs. That stupid Prime Minister, he makes his navy fight one-handed. We are lucky. Of course, you realise they could have destroyed our cargo long ago with the firepower they have at their disposal. But no, the politicians make them play their stupid games. Trust me when I say I have tremendous respect for the British Navy.'

Taylor wiped his face with his handkerchief.

'God yes, they're certainly in a tizzy. Doing what they did is so stupid. They must have realised we would protect the ship. I'm not going to make an incident out of this – I don't want to embarrass the British Navy. Hopefully, they don't want to mention this either. It would not bode well for us to antagonise them. The American press, who have not been very supportive of Wilson, will make mincemeat out of them.'

CHAPTER 11

David tossed and turned. The woven bamboo shutters of the bungalow windows were tied in the open position, allowing a slight sea breeze to waft through the room. They were both naked.

He slid from the bed and groped through the clothing draped over a chair next to the bed looking for a pair of shorts. He pulled these on quietly. Taking binoculars, cigarettes and a lighter from the bedside table, he tiptoed out of the room on bare feet.

The beach sand underfoot was cool. He walked along a well-worn path, which wound its way through the palm trees interspersed between the bungalows towards the beach, where he could hear the sounds of the surf. The sky was free of clouds, a half moon rippling its reflection on the water. Towards the south, he could see the lights of Beira and, out to sea, the lights of the ships anchored in the bay.

The events of the last twenty-four hours had his mind in turmoil. When he took on this job, he never for a moment believed it could lead to the possible use of weapons. He was no more than a glorified bank clerk, not an undercover agent. Yes, he had no problem sourcing goods for Rhodesia or establishing letters of credit or anything else which would assist the country, but he drew the line at violence. If breaking the embargo demanded that he look the other way, he would do that too. Drawing a weapon on somebody else, well, that was an entirely different matter. What made it worse was that he had done this without thought. He had acted out of pure reflex. This must have sent a definite message. The British would now consider him dangerous.

He lit a cigarette, drawing the smoke deep into his lungs. He could see the small fishing boats anchored just beyond the shoreline through his binoculars, the fishermen after line fish in the shallows.

He knew it would be difficult to extract himself from where he now was in this operation. Any attempt to do so would be misinterpreted and affect his career. All he could do was to try to separate his operation from that of John Taylor and his minions and, at all costs, avoid direct confrontation with the British.

He heard a soft footfall behind him and turned to see Gisela. She was dressed in a long, collarless cotton T-shirt that reached to just above her knees. Her hair was loose and cascaded to her shoulders, blowing in the light sea breeze. She stopped alongside him and lowered herself cross-legged to the sand.

'What ails thee, Jock?' she asked, laying her head on his shoulder. He caught her smell.

'I just couldn't sleep. What happened in the car park was bad. I've never pulled a gun on anybody before.' He paused. 'Christ, I've never even walked around with a revolver except as a showpiece while in uniform.'

'David, you must believe that they had something in mind. They were also armed. Yes, maybe they didn't want to harm us, but you'll never be sure. You had to take the initiative, you had no choice.'

'What if the man had done something threatening? Was I supposed to shoot him?'

She ran her fingers through his hair, not immediately replying. 'Rather shoot him before he shoots you. We're at war,' she finally said.

'Uh-uh, you're at war, not me. There's a difference.'

'Not true, you're a mercenary paid by the Rhodesian government. You're now committed.'

'Bullshit. I am not paid to shoot people.'

She turned towards him, her face inches from his.

'Listen, just take this a step at a time. That's all we can do. Hopefully this will all be resolved in a couple of months.' She leant forward and kissed him softly on the mouth, her tongue probing his tongue. She took his hand and placed it on her breast. He could feel her hard erect nipple. She slid her other hand down the front of his shorts, closing her fingers around him.

They made love on the beach under the stars, the palm trees rustling, accompanied by the intermittent thud as the breaking waves crested and toppled over on the sand, oblivious for a few moments to the world around them.

The two British agents sat on the sand in the shadow of a tamarisk thicket no more than forty yards away. They made no move. They had returned to Beira only to be sent out again to check every holiday cottage complex along this stretch of coast. They had found the Mercedes and thus knew were the two were holed up.

CHAPTER 12

The *Georgio V* slowly entered the harbour. Two tugs nudged her alongside the oil terminus quay. Surprisingly, there were several people on the quayside awaiting her arrival. David had no doubt that these included one or two British agents. The Portuguese had resisted pressure from the British government and ignored their request that the ship be barred from entry.

Discharging the crude oil would be an entirely different matter, as the tank farm and its facilities were the property of Rholon, a British-registered company. No doubt, they were now feeling the heat. God knows what Wilson would threaten them with if they dared receive the crude in their tanks and attempt to pump this through the pipeline to Umtali.

David looked at the others on the quay, hoping to recognise the three he and Gisela had encountered in the car park a few nights ago. If they were here, they must be watching from a distance.

The first to disembark was John Taylor and his men, now unarmed. He approached David and Gisela with a contented grin on his face. They shook hands.

'Well, that'll teach the bastards. They sent a raiding party the first night we were out there. Thank God, we didn't wait until the next day. Can you believe it? The bloody Marines had to back off.' Taylor grinned from ear to ear, quite pleased with what had been achieved.

'You were just lucky,' Gisela murmured.

'What do you mean … lucky?'

'They're British, you should know, if they really wanted to take you on, they could've. It's all bloody politics. Some damn politicians are making all the decisions. Don't forget, you were anchored in Portuguese waters. The Portuguese would've had every right to intervene,' David said in support of Gisela's statement.

'I suppose you're right, but as sure as shit, if they had tried anything I would've opened fire,' Taylor said, intent on displaying his stance on the subject.

'Where's the frigate now?' David asked.

'Left the moment they realised the Portuguese were letting us enter the harbour.'

'Well, there's not much else I can do here. It's now a matter between Rholon and London and yourselves. What are we to do now?'

The discharge of the crude oil was indeed a serious problem. However, this was not to be handled locally, but rather from Salisbury at a very high level. Meanwhile, the *Georgio V* would remain alongside the tank farm with its crew aboard indefinitely.

John Taylor addressed Gisela and David. 'I've been advised that both of you need to return to Salisbury. There is a Rhodesian government aircraft at the airport here in Beira. I'll take you out there after you've collected all your clobber from your beach bungalow. All I may say is that you are to leave for France. David, whether Gisela will accompany you, I've no idea and what is all about, I don't know either.'

CHAPTER 13

Ian Hewlett, a colonel in the Rhodesian Army yet commander of the CIO, sat at the head of the table. There were a number of notable others: two men from the Rhodesian Air Force; the Minister of Trade and Industries, Lionel Butler; and a high-up official from the Rhodesian Treasury.

'As you probably know, the black nationalists have decided that because the British will not consider military intervention, the Zimbabwe African National Liberation Army will initiate their own military incursions into the country. At the moment, these do not pose a serious threat. However, we believe with the support of other nations sympathetic to their cause and not forgetting the Russians and the Chinese, it's going to escalate. We need to acquire specialised equipment to counter these terrorist incursions and this means buying weapons and aircraft from those countries that will still clandestinely assist us or alternatively deal with arms dealers. I think Air Marshal Hartley should address you.'

He was dressed in a khaki uniform. Other than his shoulder boards and ribbons, he looked like any other enlisted personnel.

'The best weapons against insurgents are helicopters. Yes, we have a few but certainly not enough. We desperately need to acquire them. The French are not against supplying us but we will have to ensure that we acquire these in a manner which will not bring them face-to-face with the UN for sanctions busting. Now, I understand that this is a tall order, with the British watching everybody's moves.' He looked at David. 'Mr Tusk, I hear that British Intelligence has a special interest in you. Apparently you had an incident in Mozambique?'

'Well, I suppose I'm just one of a few that they are watching, primarily because they associate us with sanctions busting,' David replied.

'I agree, but we require your expertise and language skills. I've had discussions with the French and will provide you with the names of my contacts. However, we are relying on you to get these helicopters to Rhodesia. We have one or two ideas which we will impart to you, but you may have something better.'

'Personally, I believe that we would need to route any such transactions through the Middle East. All the arms dealers seem to be congregated in Lebanon. There are a number of them and provided we break the deal up, giving each a slice of the action, we just may pull it off.'

'Have you anybody in mind?' Butler asked.

'Yes, from others in your CIO1, there's a chap by the name of Hussein Hiram in Lebanon. Said to be a discreet but unsavoury character. 'Suppose he will never let out who the real purchasers are. He is also capable of sowing so much disinformation and creating so many red herrings that the British will never tie it together until it is too late. Also, we will have to fly these helicopters in as cargo. We dare not transport these by ship.'

'Can it be done?' The man from the treasury spoke for the first time.

'I believe so, but it'll cost.'

'Well, that's my department, not that I want to imply that you have carte blanche but I believe we have a lot of leeway,' the Rhodesian bank executive said while smiling.

'In broad terms I just want to tell you what we are after. We need to purchase twelve Aérospatiale Alouette III helicopters fitted with Turbomeca Astazou engines. In principle, we can get them, provided we pay and, of course, know how to get them here. That's your job,' the air marshal said.

'I'm going to need assistance.'

'Well, we wanted to give you Miss Mentz. I hear that you work well together as a team. However, she may be a bit of a hindrance in the Middle East. You know what the Moslems are like,' Ian Hewlett said.

'Still, I would prefer her as I've worked with her before. She's a good operative.'

'I know.' It was all Ian Hewlett said. David wasn't sure whether he should have read anything else in that remark. Did they know that the relationship had gone beyond that of business?

'Mr Tusk, as the man responsible for the money, I've one concern. You had better make sure you've secured the items before you request payment to some arms dealer in the Middle East. I'd hate to pay and not receive the goods. I mean, this will involve millions,' the treasury executive said.

'I realise that.' David's irritation was audible. Christ! All the man did was worry about the money. Well, what about the logistics?

'All right, gents, that's it. David, you can liaise with my department with regard to your arrangements, okay?' Ian Hewlett said, getting up from his chair.

'Miss Mentz?' David again asked.

'She's yours,' Hewlett replied.

David had found himself a furnished, two-bedroom apartment in the city, belonging to a Rhodesian who had taken a prolonged leave of absence from the country. The rent was reasonable and the apartment was tastefully furnished with everything he needed down to the linen and cutlery. The Rhodesian government made a handsome contribution to the rent. He had also bought himself a car, a Hillman Minx, used but in excellent condition.
****

David and Gisela were leaving by air early the next morning for Johannesburg. They decided to go out to dinner and chose the Cattleman, famous in the capital for its excellent service and steaks.

Rhodesia was no longer a tourist haven and most of the patrons were locals, not that there were many, but they had opted for an early evening and, no doubt, others would arrive later. David ordered an exquisite South African cabernet from which they now sipped, discussing their forthcoming trip. They would spend a few days in Johannesburg before leaving on a TAP flight to Lisbon.

'I take it you'll be able to rustle up two German passports. Christ, I don't know how you do it but they're definitely a Godsend. Have you thought who I'm going to impersonate this time?' David asked.

She reached over and took his hand. 'I've decided that you should be an electrical engineer employed by Siemens. That company is so huge it could confuse anybody what with all their branches and departments. In particular, they are well represented in the Middle East, in Lebanon to be precise.' She continued while smiling, 'Your new name is Hugo Ostendorf and you are originally from Kiel. They speak High German in Schleswig-Holstein, so Kiel is appropriate. You speak a cultured German.'

'How did you know that my family was originally from Kiel? My father actually went to some naval academy type school, you know, where they wear military instead of school uniforms.'

'I know, it's ridiculous, schools making soldiers out of children before they grow up. But, they can't help it, it's their Prussian heritage,' she said.

'And you, my sweet, what are you going as?' he asked.

She pondered this for a moment and then laughed. 'As your sex slave.'

'Well, I couldn't think of anything better.'

'But I do that after hours, otherwise I'm Frau Dokter Gisela Hoppe from Berlin, a specialist gynæcologist. All men are afraid of gynæcologists, didn't you know?' She giggled, squeezing his hand.

'Clever. You mention that to any Moslem and he's bound to treat you with the greatest of respect.'

'Precisely.'

She had been staying out at her ranch. She spent as much time there as possible. Because of her prolonged absences, she employed a farm manager and his wife, letting them to graze their herd of cattle on her property rent-free, allowing her to reduce their salary. They both thought it an amicable arrangement. Nonetheless, she spent every free moment on the farm.

'Are you staying with me tonight?' he asked.

'No, I've got to go back and collect my things. Kallie will drive me to the airport tomorrow morning where I'll meet you. Is that okay?'

'Sure, I'll be seeing quite a lot of you, won't I?'

Back in Johannesburg, they stayed at his apartment. Most days were spent at the bank ensuring the purchases they made during their last trip were being handled correctly. Letters of credit needed to be issued. Meanwhile, South African Import Permits needed to be obtained then and cross-referenced to ensure every document listed them, lending further authenticity if scrutinised.

The bank provided them both with a substantial amount of American Express traveller cheques in US dollars as well as bank notes in dollars and German marks, all from the account of the Rhodesian government.

Preparing for the trip abroad was difficult. Every item was checked before it was packed. Anything originating from South Africa or Rhodesia had to be left behind. Two days before their departure, they left his apartment in the very early hours of the morning using a hired car parked a short distance away at an overnight travel lodge. His car was left in the apartment building's underground parking garage, hopefully creating the impression that they were still at home. He was convinced that the British had set up a surveillance team watching his movements around the clock.

He was convinced they had evaded the British. While both were at work yesterday and their presumed surveillance was thus concentrating on the bank, others removed their luggage from the apartment and moved it to the hotel. In the early hours, they sneaked out of his apartment via delivery entrance after ascertaining it was clear. Finally, they boarded the aircraft separately and were reunited only through persuading others to swap seats.

The plane arrived in Lisbon at ten at night. They booked separately into an airport hotel and avoided any contact. The next morning, Gisela sought out an out-of-the-way hair salon where she had her hair cut and then dyed black. She changed her makeup as well. The transformation was incredible. Replacing her Nordic look with a definite Mediterranean appearance of heavy, black eyebrows and mascara ringing the eyes, she was absolutely striking. Her pale blue eyes pierced her now slightly swarthy look, assisted by her African suntan.

They departed on separate flights for Le Bourget Airport in Paris. Gisela booked into an obscure hotel on the Rue de Montpensier near the Louvre. Meanwhile, David decided to visit his mother at her apartment in the nearby Palais Royal. He had phoned first and when he learnt that his stepfather was in Scotland, he asked whether he could stay. She was delighted to have him.

Maintaining the guise of a German, he took the bus from the airport to the city terminal from where he boarded the Métro to the Palais Royal station, only a few hundred yards' walk to her apartment. His mother was overjoyed, shedding a few tears as they hugged each other, saying 'mon fils, mon fils' repeatedly. The apartment's opulence amazed him. It was as if one returned to the time of Cardinal Richelieu. The doors were still fitted with a latticework of mirrors and the walls were white with a light blue border and a gilded, patterned outline painted thereon. His stepfather had acquired the furniture to go with the apartment, all Louis XIV. Even the table and bed linen was monogrammed with his stepfather's family's coat-of-arms.

His mother was taken aback by his appearance.

'My God, what is wrong? I thought you are a banker and now you are dressed like a Schlumpf,' she said, reverting to her German origins.

'Mother, don't let it worry you. I chose to dress like this, there is a good reason.'

'Bankers wear dark suits and waistcoats. You're not running away from something?'

He laughed. 'No, no. This is by choice, nothing's wrong.'

'Well, sit down. Let me get you something to eat. I've prepared your favourite room. You must tell me everything. How are you doing in South Africa?' she said, leading him to the dining room where a place had already been laid next to an opened bottle of vin rouge. She spent a short while in the kitchen and then returned with a huge mushroom omelette and a baguette.

'Please, you must eat.'

He had to smile; mothers never changed, always worried whether you were eating enough even after an absence of a few years.

She sat down at the table opposite him.

'How is Diarmid?' he asked, referring to his stepfather.

'He's fine, though still disappointed that you took off like that. He's actually very fond of you.'

'Mother, let's not go into that. You know my reasons. Anyway, I'm now quite settled and if I don't see him, I really don't mind.'

He saw the disappointment register on her face.

'It's such a pity. He could do so much for you with his connections,' she said.

He sighed. His mother believed that connections were essential in life. Whom you knew was most important. He wondered how she would react if she discovered what he was actually doing.

'Please, I just want to stay here for a few days. Let's leave the past behind. I've quite a lot to do here.'

'All right, if that's what you want. Let's enjoy each other's company.' Her disappointment was apparent in her voice.

His mother hadn't changed. She still wore her hair short, though now streaked with grey. Her dress was typically French and she still donned a beret whenever she left the apartment to go shopping. It was winter, so whenever she went out, she wore one of those new-fangled double-lined black plastic Mackintoshes, which crackled with every movement.

'Have you got a car I can use?' he asked.

'You can use the DC, nobody's using that.'

'Excellent, that's just what I need; I won't be travelling far, just around Paris.'

The deux chevaux, the 'DC' his mother referred to, was the ideal car for driving around Paris. If anybody were to attempt to follow him, of course assuming that they found him in the first place, then following a deux chevaux in the Paris traffic could be a near-impossible task. DCs were as numerous as yellow taxi cabs in New York.

From the apartment, he phoned Aérospatiale, asking for Monsieur Devereux. They spoke in French, David requesting a meeting. Devereux mentioned an obscure bistro near the Comédie-Française, which suited David well, not too far away. It adjoined the Palais Royal complex, certainly within walking distance, which would allow him to lose any possible tails. There was nothing out of the ordinary about the bistro, just one of many dotted all over the city. He entered and ordered a café blanc taking a seat at a small table as far away from the counter as possible. Within ten minutes, a man dressed in a dark business suit entered. He looked around, his eyes falling on David, who nodded. The man walked over and sat down, taking David's hand in greeting. Devereux gestured the waiter over and ordered a café noir. For a few minutes, they discussed Paris, the French Algerians, and then the infamous OAS, who would awaken Parisians with a well-placed bomb to remind France of their hatred for a government who were, in their opinion, abandoning them to the Arabs and other unimportant denizens.

Devereux withdrew a packet of foul-smelling Gauloise cigarettes from his inner pocket and proceeded to light one, staring intently at David. He exhaled, blowing smoke at the ceiling, his eyes again falling on the young man opposite him.

'I have been expecting you, Monsieur. I have already started arrangements for the manufacture and delivery of the items for which you are looking. You will appreciate that this cannot be done as a single order. That would be too obvious. We have similar orders from Argentina and Indonesia. What we have done is simply increased their orders to make up your numbers. Your items are to be shipped in a disassembled form and will not be part of the final assembly line. That makes it difficult for anybody to make a count. Or let me put it this way, at least it is not blatantly obvious.'

'Monsieur Devereux, we are extremely grateful. I believe it was mentioned to you that you would receive payment via Lebanon. I will be leaving Paris within the week to make suitable arrangements. Our party in Lebanon will contact you and make sure that you receive payment up front.'

'Who is it? Not Monsieur Hussein Hiram?'

'I'm afraid so. He was the only one prepared to do this and knows how to get the items to us.'

'Too true. He is the only one who gets away with it. At the moment, the British are particularly observant. I believe that they know that you wish to purchase Alouettes.'

'I suppose it's obvious, we're already using them.'

Devereux finished his coffee and then rose, taking David's hand.

'Well, there not much else to discuss. We will wait for Hiram. Once he pays us, we will ship as instructed. Au revoir, Monsieur.'

David watched Devereux leave.

The helicopters would leave the Aérospatiale factory piecemeal – two or four completely disassembled helicopters at a time, destined for the military in Lebanon. There would be no legal paperwork, the transaction untraceable. These would be loaded on a ship owned by an anonymous South African entrepreneur. In Beirut, the cargo would be re-crated and issued with new documentation to a large company which had been granted a massive contract for the construction of an international airport and hotel complex in the Comoros.

These crates would be shipped as elevator and escalator parts. The airport had yet to be commissioned despite its being nearly finished. In the interim, cargo aircraft flew equipment and staff in from South Africa.

The crates would be loaded on the aircraft for the return flight to South Africa, flying via Rhodesia, landing at Thornhill Air Force base, near Gwelo. David thought the plan ingenious, although it was a provisional plan and could be changed at a moment's notice. Still, a good plan provided the British did not find out.

Gisela had gone to see Berzack, one of France's largest textile manufacturers. She was to meet him after her appointment. They had agreed to meet at eleven at the George V station on the Line 1 platform. David was a few minutes early and stood on the platform awaiting her arrival, knowing that she would have to come down the escalator stairs. Precisely on time, he saw her. She did not join him but stood on the platform like any other commuter waiting for the Métro. When the subway train arrived, they both stepped into the same carriage, remaining apart, no sign of recognition passing between them, both carefully checking who else stepped aboard. David was convinced that they were not followed. He doubted whether the British had tracked them down yet.

He walked over to her. 'How did your morning go?' he asked.

'Doing business with the French is easy. They're not concerned about the British and the UN, provided we pay. And you? How were your arrangements?'

'I've got it in hand, but will have to go to Lebanon and see Hiram. I'm not looking forward to that. Devereux was very accommodating. They'll ship the items two or more at a time as elevator and escalator parts. It looks like the French have this wrapped-up tight and their security is just about impenetrable. I don't think the British would ever get an inkling … What I mean, they've probably guessed but haven't a clue how we propose to get them to Rhodesia. However, where it could go wrong is in the Middle East. British Intelligence is pretty jacked up there and they can rely on the assistance of the CIA, or so I hear.'

They stepped off at the next stop where they returned along the same line, getting off at the Palais Royal Métro station.

'I'm sure we're not being followed. Let me take you to lunch. It's the least I can do seeing that I'm not going to get any nearer to you for the next few days,' he said.

'Sorry, can't do. I've an appointment with some electronics people. I've got to go, but let's arrange for tomorrow. Better still, why don't you come round to the hotel tonight? I'm sure that the Brits have no any idea where I'm staying.'

He glanced at his watch, 'We've still got a few minutes. Let's have a cup of coffee or something.'

They found a sidewalk bistro where they sat down. He ordered a beer and she a café noir.

'When we leave here, I'm going back to my mother's apartment and try to phone Lebanon and South Africa. I've got to arrange for the first payment to Hiram for the first few Alouettes. According to Devereux, these will be ready to leave in the next few days. Hiram's got to pay the French. We owe him twenty per cent of the value for his troubles. That's bloody steep, but that's the deal, so what can we do?'

'How are you going to do this?' she asked

'We've an undercover office in Beirut. I'll have the funds transferred to their banking account with the Byblos Bank in Beirut. I'll effect a US dollar transfer from South Africa.'

'God, won't such a large amount make someone suspicious?' she asked.

He smiled. 'I doubt it, they so used to getting large transfers. Beirut's one of the money capitals of the world. I don't think there will be any reaction at all.'

'I hope you're right,' she said, finding the concept implausible.

She finished the last of her coffee and rose from her chair.

'I've got to go, I'll see you later. You know where I am. I'll be waiting,' she said with a mischievous smile as she walked off towards the Métro stairs, her beautiful legs drawing the attention of a few customers.

David returned to his mother's apartment. It was situated on the Rue de Montpensier, a one-way street that bordered the side of the Palais Royal building. Those apartments were considered to be the best in Paris, especially those situated on the second floor. Some ambassadors resided on the Rue de Montpensier and chauffeured cars were not uncommon. However, parking was impossible, the street continuously patrolled by gendarmes.

He approached the apartment from the Comédie-Française end, walking on the pavement facing the oncoming traffic and able to peer into the windscreens of the cars parked on the nearside of the road. He immediately became aware of two men in suits seated in the front of a dark Citroën parked a few yards away from No. 32. They seemed not to have noticed him yet. He turned away and gazed into the window of a small shop, the place of business of a renowned philatelist, staring intently at the exhibition of, to him, ridiculously priced rare stamps on display. He turned his back to the car, looking at the shop's glass window, hoping to see some reflection of what was happening around the car.

He did not doubt the identity of the occupants. They had to be British agents. Christ! How had the British cottoned on to his movements? Surely, the Rhodesian Intelligence Service had not been compromised in any way. Although most were originally of British descent, they had all been carefully screened and only a few knew of the impending helicopter deal. It astounded him that the British knew him to be in Paris and that they even knew of his mother. Her surname was now Charlton-Johnston and he had not seen her for years. Did they know that Gisela was in Paris? The one Godsend he could rely on was that the French Sûreté was not about to assist the British. They would take strong exception to British agents on French soil involved in an operation indirectly targeting the French arms industry. The French were fiercely independent, even maintaining the own nuclear force, the Force de dissuasion. They shunned NATO membership and were totally independent of the British and Americans.

He spent a few minutes in front of the shop and then entered. An assistant approached to help, David saying that his younger brother was an ardent stamp collector and that he was looking for something. The assistant realised that he was not about to spend a large amount and guided him to a table which contained stamps in profusion, all in envelopes with a cellophane window and sorted by country and denominations. From where he stood perusing the envelopes, he could just see the car and its occupants. He doubted whether the occupants of the car could see into the darker interior of the shop.

The minutes ticked by. He began to feel that he was overstaying his welcome and felt compelled to make a purchase. He scanned the contents of the display cabinet again and was about to make a choice of purchase – a collection of brightly-coloured stamps of some obscure country – when he saw a third man in a suit emerge from the building with his mother. Christ! What the hell was going on? She seemed in deep conversation with the man, gesticulating and then pointing in the direction of the Comédie-Française and the Louvre with an outstretched arm. This was also the direction of the one-way street. The third man then got into the rear of the car, which drove off. His mother watched it leave and then walked in the same direction. As she got to the entrance of the philatelist's shop, she stuck her head into the entrance door.

'Follow me,' she said, looking directly at him and then continued walking. He emerged, following a good ten yards behind.

She walked a good ten minutes to beyond the Louvre and into a bistro, taking a seat just within the enclosed area, avoiding the tables directly on the pavement. He followed and sat down at the same table, both facing outward.

Her countenance was one of distress and concern.

'I may be old, but I'm not stupid. I know when something is going on. Those men were looking for you. They were English and I'm damned sure they're government employees. They just seemed too official, you know, like police. What is going on? They just about third degree-ed me, saying that you were in serious trouble and that it was imperative that I told them where you were. You're fortunate. I spotted you as I was about the pass the stamp collector. I always say hello to him,' she said.

Clearly, she was upset. She took a pack of mild French cigarettes from her bag and lit one, which she fitted to a cigarette holder.

'What did you say?' he asked, his voice just above a whisper, furtively looking around the bistro at the other customers.

She blew blue smoke to the side. With every movement, the synthetic black Mackintosh of hers crackled, irritating him. 'That you were in trouble, well … I instinctively knew that.' She paused. 'I lied. I said you had visited but had left, giving no indication when you would return. I said you had gone to meet someone and I gave him the name of a restaurant on the Champs Élysée. I don't think they believed me. I'm a bad liar. I told the man that I was on my way out. That's why I came down with him.'

'Thanks mother, I'm glad you lied,' he replied with relief.

'What is going on?'

'Mother, it's complicated. I can't and I'm not allowed to say, but rest assured, if you knew you would approve.'

'Have you got huge debts?' she asked. All her life she had been horrified at the thought of huge debt.

He laughed. His mother read too many thrillers.

'No. Nothing like that. I still work for the bank.'

'Okay, I won't ask, but what to do now?' she asked resignedly.

The waiter approached, they ordered coffee.

'Never give anybody any indication as to where I am. I'm certainly not going to return to your apartment. Please, the few things that are there, can you bring these to the Hotel Tivoli? Leave them with the concierge. Just make sure you're not followed.'

His mother just stared at him. She knew the hotel well. It was nearby and we had once slept the night there when, years ago, she had accidentally locked us out of the apartment.

'Can you not at least give me some indication what this is all about?' she insisted.

'Look, all I can say that it is of national importance. I've had to sign all sorts of documents related to secrecy, so whatever I've said is not to be repeated.'

This seemed to satisfy her. They parted, he promising to be in touch but not indicating how he would do this. She returned to the apartment while he made his way to the hotel.

He spent the night with Gisela, their passion possessed of urgency, the threat of the British operatives never quite leaving his mind.

96

CHAPTER 14

They arrived at Beirut Airport on a direct Air France flight to be greeted by a cloudless sky. A slight breeze blew off the Mediterranean, sufficient to take the edge off the intense heat. Beirut International Airport was a mass of people. They were just a couple of the many tourists arriving in the Lebanese capital, allowing them to lose themselves in the crowd. After all, this was the height of the tourist season. Of course, the same could be said for any others who were following them or any who anticipated their arrival. They had given the British the slip. David found it difficult to believe that the British could have tailed them from Paris. Of course, if MI6 had anybody on the inside in Rhodesia, all this subterfuge would be in vain.

After clearing customs, which was a rapid affair, a taxi whisked them off to Le Royal Hotel, a large, upmarket tourist hotel directly on the beach road overlooking the Mediterranean on the way to Dbayeh, an adjoining holiday town just up the coast. The sun was still high so they decided to spend the remaining hours on the beach soaking it up. Hiram could wait. David would contact him during the evening.

Wheels had already been put in motion and Hiram was expecting his call. Of course, he only knew him by name and was not aware of David's real identity. Arrangements had been made through the banks to ensure that an initial amount of seven million dollars was available which, if necessary, could be withdrawn from the Byblos Bank SAL. For this purpose, David and Gisela had been provided with specific codes which would enable them to have these funds released in US dollars. However, it was hoped that would be unnecessary and Hiram would accept transfer of the funds, although there was a danger that this could leave a trail. Two other agents based in the Far East – an Indian, Faizal Bhayat, and an Iranian, Abdul Joussof, who had assisted the Rhodesian government in the past – were available if needed. David was to contact them if he thought their services necessary – he definitely needed them! He was not about to part with seven million without some backup. You would have thought the Rhodesian government would dedicate a few more men to an undercover operation of this financial magnitude. What if the operation was hijacked? Certainly they could not look to Gisela and him alone.

Before going down to dinner, they strolled to another hotel a few hundred yards further along the beach road. David found a row of telephone booths next to the reception and chose one at random.

The phone only rang a few times before it was answered in Arabic. In French, David asked to speak to Hussein Hiram. He was asked his name and to phone back in ten minutes. This he did and again was asked to wait. From the background noise on the phone, he realised that this had to be some sort of public place – a bistro or restaurant – the noise, a cacophony of voices and music. He waited quite a while.

'Hussein Hiram,' he heard on the phone.

'Monsieur Hiram, this is Michael Delport from Monoprix Investments. Bonjour,' David said. My God, real cloak and dagger stuff, David thought, Sometimes these games are ludicrous with all those damn passwords and names.

'Bonjour, Monsieur.'

Hiram knew what the call was about, the reference to Monoprix Investments the opening code word.

'I'm in Beirut with my partner. Could we meet?'

'But of course. It's still early. Why don't you and your lady join me for dinner here?'

'Sounds good. Where is that?'

Hiram gave him the name and address of a restaurant in Beirut, which David scribbled on a piece of paper. He phoned Faizal Bhayat asking whether he knew of the place.

'But of course, Monsieur. This is a famous restaurant in Beirut frequented only by the rich. A dark suit at least, this is essential. Others still consider it a black tie affair. Yes, I'll ensure that Abdul and I are there in the background. When do you want us there?'

David had no idea who this Faizal and Abdul were but knew they had been briefed and would surreptitiously make themselves known. David gave him a time and a brief description of himself and Gisela.

Gisela was dazzling in a low-cut burgundy cocktail dress, which contrasted well with her black hair piled high. Small earrings glittered on her ears and matched a silver chain necklace. David wondered where she had conjured the dress. Surely she had not brought this with her. He made a point of asking her about it later. He wore his best dark suit. Black tie was just not going to be possible.

For an additional fee and the promise of an extravagant tip, the hotel concierge arranged a taxi. The driver, to his amusement, was persuaded to wait the evening out and return them to the hotel. David found his mirth odd.

The doorman of the Al Murjan Palace Restaurant opened the taxi door and assisted Gisela.

The place was huge, with oriental decor and opulent gold drapes and chair coverings. A number of big brass chandeliers hung from the high ceiling. Every available space contained a table with four to six chairs and the occasional larger table between but not all were occupied as Beirut only started to hum from ten on.

Most attention was drawn to a pair of belly dancers who had just taken up position on a now-cleared dance floor. One cued the band to start their number and the musicians in Lebanese cultural dress taking up a corner played soft music with a distinct Arabian flavour.

David gave his alias to the maître d'hôtel, who guided them to a table. It was already occupied by a man dressed in a white dinner jacket seated with two women. David could not but notice that they both were beautiful. The man rose upon seeing David and Gisela approach.

'Mr Ostendorf, it's a pleasure to meet you. Please, may I introduce my wife, Nadia, and my daughter, Layla,' the man said, flashing a friendly smile. He was in his late forties, his black hair slicked back, with flecks of grey visible at the temples. Though fair-skinned, his eyes were black and his black eyebrows were quite pronounced. He had a Roman nose and thin lips. Hussein Hiram was tall and slim and struck an imposing figure in his dinner suit. They shook hands. David introduced Gisela. The Hirams spoke impeccable French, as did Gisela; only David stumbled along in his badly practised French. He sat next to Hiram at the round table, permitting them to converse quietly. Gisela joined the women on the opposite side.

They discussed generalities: the threatening civil war between Moslem and Christian; the tourists; and the attempts on President de Gaulle's life in France. It was only after the main course had been removed did Hiram broach the subject of business.

They all refused dessert, instead opting for coffee. Hiram produced a box of cheroots and, having offered them, lit his own, blowing a cloud of blue smoke towards the ceiling. It was obvious that the two belly dancers were close to the finale of their number and most of the patrons were giving them their undivided attention.

'Are you ready to make payment?' His tone was casual whilst not looking at David but rather across the room at the dancers.

'We are, but need to know how you wish be to be paid; this such a large sum.'

Hiram never hesitated. 'In cash. In US dollars. No note to exceed one hundred dollars.'

This was not what David wanted. It was too dangerous.

'That's a large amount of cash which would have to be carried around in a large suitcase. A briefcase would be too small,' David protested weakly.

'I know, but like you, I'm under close scrutiny. Any other way will leave a trail and clues. You probably already know that you are being watched.' He paused, pursing his lips, making a triangle with his fingers in front of his face. 'Don't look around but there are two British agents in the restaurant. There could be more. They've been here since early evening, arriving very soon after you. They look jovial enough and appear to have drunk too much. Don't believe it. They're watching.'

David could not contain the shock he felt. British agents in the restaurant? That could not be possible, they had been so careful. Nobody could have followed them.

'You can't be serious?'

'Oh yes, I am. They've watched you since your flight landed. They've obviously been tipped off. Your organisation must have a leak,' he said, leaning back laughing, creating the impression that their discussion was no more than light-hearted banter and some ribald remark about the belly dancers had passed between them.

David laughed. What else to do but not let on.

'I have to throw them before we can even think of cash,' Hiram said with a chuckle. 'I've planned a diversion. I'm constantly under surveillance. Somebody's always watching,' he smiled, 'This should be fun. Get ready to move in about five minutes. Incidentally, your two operatives have already been briefed and know what to expect. During the diversion, you are to leave immediately. Both of you – just get into the car. Your taxi driver is actually one of my men. Be fast about it; he will take you to a new rendezvous.'

David was aghast. What kind of diversion did this man have in mind? Hopefully, nobody would get hurt, but these were professionals.

A few minutes later, the two belly dancers vacated the dance floor amid loud applause, signalling the waiters to resume their duties. They emerged from the kitchen through swinging doors carrying large trays of plates and dishes while others balanced laden plates on their arms.

There was a loud thud and crash. Everyone swung round to look. A waiter had gone sprawling. He landed, plates and all, on a table occupied by two men in dark suits, the ones that Hiram referred to as agents. The piping hot plates had splashed across them. They jumped up and tried to brush the food off with their napkins as they howled in pain. The waiter slid from the table onto the floor with all its crockery and cutlery smashing. It was an awful mess.

'Go.'

David and Gisela never hesitated. They were out of their seats and made their way to the exit. Their departure went unnoticed given the two men's plight. The taxi was waiting with its door open and the moment they slid on to the seats, the vehicle was in motion, swinging out of the parking lot with a squeal of tyres.

'Christ, these people are insane,' David said to Gisela in a loud whisper.

'It was necessary,' she replied, her voice quite level, showing no emotion.

'Necessary? Dammit! I don't think we were even being followed. Who says those men were British agents?'

'Who do you think is in the car following us?' Gisela said.

David swung his head around. Sure enough, about a hundred yards back a car followed, its headlights stabbing the darkness.

'The lady is right. That car left the restaurant just behind us. There were more than just those two in the restaurant,' the taxi driver said in strongly accented French. With that, the taxi surged forward as the driver floored the accelerator. It was a large American sedan with soft suspension. The car pitched and swayed as he negotiated the many bends in the road. They were now in the mountains winding their way through throngs of cedars. The other car tenaciously clung to their rear.

David swung round again to look if the other car was gaining.

'There's another car,' he said.

'Probably Hiram or his men,' the driver replied, concentrating on his driving.

'They're gaining on us,' Gisela said.

The driver swung into another sharp bend with a squeal of tyres, causing them to fishtail.

'I know. Theirs is a Mercedes. It handles these curves a lot better. The suspension is firmer.'

Again, the tyres squealed.

'Christ! We've got to do something!' David was frantic, looking back and forth from their driver to their pursuers.

A moment later, the driver dangled his arm over the front seat, in his hand was a SIG 9mm automatic.

'Use this. It should scare them off. C'mon, take it!'

David hesitated. Gisela leant forward and took the automatic.

'You're not going to shoot at those agents, are you?'

'Well, if you don't then I will.'

'For fuck's sake, this is madness.' He grabbed the automatic from Gisela.

The Mercedes was right on their tail, its driver attempting to come alongside. David was certain they were about sideswipe them and force them off the road.

With an oath, he jabbed at the window button. He slipped the safety catch on the SIG and pulled the hammer back. The Mercedes was only yards away. He leant out and took aim. The automatic bucked in his hand. A star-shaped bullet hole appeared in the Mercedes' windscreen. The car swayed as its driver strove to take evasive action. This spoilt his aim and his second shot went wild. By now the other car had moved up on the Mercedes and David heard two distinct shots over the roar of their engines. The Mercedes veered across the road and collided with the rear of their car, slewing it sideways. The driver battled to regain control as it skidded towards the verge and a deep drainage ditch which had been dug parallel to the road.

The taxi driver was not going to manœuvre his way out this one. The car was going into the ditch.

'Duck!'

He pulled her down into the well between the rear and front seats, throwing his body on top of hers.

The car was still at high speed as the right front tyre clipped the ditch. Its front bumper threw up a shower of gravel and stone which clattered on the windscreen and the side of the car.

Inertia landed them against the back of the front seat. The car swung broadside and as the wheels dug into the soft ground, it started to upend.

The car flipped. It hit the ground with a bone-jarring crash. Inside, they were thrown around like rag-dolls. It went over and over until it finally toppled back on its wheels. The lights still shone and a loud hiss emanated from the engine.

Despite being dazed, David's first concern was for Gisela.

'Are you okay?'

He heard her moan. She lied crumbled in the well between the seats.

'I think so,' she said, groaning again.

The driver had disappeared. The stress on the car's body had forced his door open, spilling him.

David tried opening the rear door and then tried the others. They would not budge. He lifted Gisela carefully. She seemed to be okay.

'Come on, we have to get out of here,' he said. He helped her over the backrest and then slid her out through the driver's side door.

'Where the hell are they?' he said to no one in particular.

He then saw the car which had followed the Mercedes. It had stopped behind them. The car's headlights silhouetted its two occupants who now stood in the road, their hands, carrying pistols, by their sides. They looked in the direction they had all been travelling. David turned to see what they were looking at. He winced. He saw the Mercedes bathed in the light from the stationary car. It had left the road and collided head-on with a massive cedar. The impact pressed the engine into the passenger compartment, driving the firewall and dashboard backwards, and pinned the occupants to the back of their seats. He could vaguely see the two men. He realised that they would not have survived. He turned away, a biliousness rising in his throat.

'God Almighty.'

Gisela had sunk to her haunches with her head in her hands.

The two men approached.

'Are you all right? You'd better come with us. This place will soon be swarming with gendarmes,' one said.

 He realised that these men must work for Hiram.

'Who were those men in the Mercedes?'

'They're English spies,' one of them replied. He spat on the ground, clearly despising them. 'We are sure they were after you. Better it happened this way, we would have had to kill them anyway. We couldn't let them spoil a deal like this,' he said with a nonchalant shrug of his shoulders. 'Come. We must hurry.'

'What about our taxi driver?' David asked.

'He's dead – broke his neck,' the other replied.

'And those?' he asked, pointing at the wrecked Mercedes.

'We leave all. We've got to get out of here now! Please come immediately.'

He knew the man was right. What a shambles, he thought. They could've been killed.

David was forced to clamber back into the car to retrieve the SIG. Hopefully the spent cartridges had ejected in the road during the chase. He found the automatic lying on the floor.

They continued on the road into the mountains. Now that the shock and adrenalin were wearing off, he became aware of the bruises and aches he had sustained. He was cold and shivered. He realised it was shock. His suit was torn and both he and Gisela were covered in dust. He tried to brush himself off.

'You can't return to your hotel. I've arranged to have your belongings collected. This will not arouse any suspicions. Your bill will be paid.'

David knew that the latest events would galvanise the English into action. With two men dead, although not his fault, he was sure MI6 would extract vengeance. The gloves were off. No more pussyfooting around.

He laid his head back against the seat, Gisela resting her head on his shoulder. They had been lucky to get away with their lives.

David's head swam. Two dead agents. Christ! Nobody was supposed to die. And the taxi-driver …?

About twenty miles on, the car swung off the asphalt onto a track, its lights tunnelling through the towering cedars.

They had climbed steadily all the way from the coast, the road winding through the mountains, now much higher, manifested by the light fog that clung to the trees. It was also now much colder.

Finally, the car swung into a wide clearing dominated by an expansive, low-roofed bungalow with an enormous porch. In the centre was a crystal clear swimming pool, lit from below the waterline. Deck chairs and recliners with large beach umbrellas surrounded the sparkling blue water. The bungalow was modern, all steel and aluminium. The lounge inside was roomy with chrome and plastic furniture scattered. Plate glass windows and sliding glass doors stretched from floor to ceiling, permitting a panoramic view from the pool to the valley below.

The two henchmen ushered them inside and showed them to separate bathrooms where they could clean up and attend to their bruises and scratches. They had barely returned to the lounge when they heard the sound of a car stopping in the parking area in front of the bungalow. The sound of car doors slamming was followed by footsteps on the patio. Hiram entered with another two men behind. He moved to where Gisela and David were sitting.

'I truly regret was has occurred. But, this is a dangerous game. Buying arms on the black market brings enemies and sometimes death with it. That's why I employ these men,' he said with a sweep of an arm indicating those in his employ, 'It is unfortunate that the two British officials lost their lives. This was not intended – truly, it was an accident. Nevertheless, have no doubt, the British government won't see it that way.'

'Of course they won't. For Chrissake, we fired shots at them. Maybe we hit the driver which led to the accident,' David complained.

'What were they trying to do?' Her face still reflected the shock of the past hour.

'The British know you are trying to buy weapons and helicopters. It's impossible to go around buying Oerlikon rapid fire cannons, Aérospatiale helicopters, and the like without people finding out, no matter who you are,' he replied. 'Although we don't know what information the British really have, it certainly looks like they've got something on you two. They're smart. They pay informers big money. They have to. Like the Americans, they have too many enemies. They know they have to stay a step ahead.' Hiram sighed. 'Of course, your association with me is old news now. They're not going to be easy to surprise. Those men, well, they were trying to stop you. That's all.'

'Stop us from what?' David asked.

'From paying me, of course. That could be the only reason. After all, I'm known to be an arms dealer who sells to the highest bidder.'

A well-stocked bar took up one corner of the room. Hiram walked over, taking down a few glasses. He turned to face them.

'A drink?'

Both David and Gisela settled for a scotch on the rocks.

Hiram raised his glass in salute.

'You know, your Rhodesian problem is rather unique. You're actually outlaws, free game if you like. Any action against you sanctioned by a UN Resolution allows for harsher action to be taken against you. That's why they were prepared to force you off the road. Normally, they would never have tried that. I believe they were prepared to kill you. Best you remember that.'

'What are we to do now? We're in a foreign country. The local police must be going fucking ape by now.' David said.

'Well, you need to pay me and soon. I want that money before the British gets it. Next, you need to get out of the country.'

'I realise that.'

'The money, how are you going to get it to me? It has to be in bank notes, especially after what has happened this evening.'

He had given the money a lot of thought because Hiram insisted it be paid in cash. Firstly, it had to be removed from the bank and then somehow stored without raising suspicion, it also had to be easily portable. Suitcases were definitely not the right thing.

'I've an idea. Do you play golf?'

'Yes, in fact, I'm a member of the Golf Club of Lebanon.'

He had heard about it. It was exclusive. Very.

'Okay. Arrange a game for the day after tomorrow. Phone me and give me a tee time. We'll meet you there and make payment. You're going to lose your golf bag and clubs so don't take your best. Just be ready to inadvertently swap golf bags.'

Hiram smiled, it dawning on him what David proposed to do.

'Quite clever, I must say. Meanwhile, where do you propose to stay?'

'We'll assume new identities. These should hold for a day or two. The place is full of tourists. I'm sure the Lebanese police have not yet associated us with the death of the two British operatives, let alone the taxi driver. Rest assured, the British will say nothing to the Lebanese Police.' David looked questioningly at Hiram as if he wanted him to confirm his thoughts on the matter.

'You're right. Things don't happen too fast here.' Hiram confirmed.

Silence followed.

Hiram sighed, slapped his thigh and rose from his chair, evident that he wished to terminate the conversation.

'All right, we've removed your belongings from your hotel. Forget about making reservations elsewhere. I've booked you into a resort hotel in the mountains. My people will take you there. In addition, I've arranged that a car be placed at your disposal, not one traceable to me. Just leave it at the airport when you eventually fly out. My people will take you to the hotel tonight. I'll stay in touch. Just remember, keep a low profile. The British will be looking for you.'

The trip to the resort hotel was uneventful. They were both in pain, their limbs aching, displaying a few bruises along with having headaches. As soon as they got into their room, they showered and then took barbiturates.

Both utterly exhausted, it was with relief they slid under the sheets.

He pulled her close to him.

'God, had I known where this was going to lead to – spies, guns, car crashes, people killed – I would never have accepted this. It's fuckin' crazy and it has only just begun. The fucking bank coerced me into this. I doubt whether the bank's board even has an inkling of what's going on. People are trying to kill us while they sleep safely in their beds dreaming up the next scheme to capitalise on somebody else's misfortune.'

She snuggled into the hollow of his shoulder. 'Don't worry, I'm sure the worst is over. You've got to remember that we are really on a war footing. The Brits are out to destroy us. There will be casualties and we could be next.'

He was not convinced, still overcome with a sense of foreboding.

CHAPTER 15

The next day, the promised hired car arrived and they drove to Beirut. David asked the driver to find a lesser-known golf club. There he bought the largest golf bag and a decent set of clubs at the pro shop. It was large and brightly coloured, with a host of zippered compartments on the outside and a manufacturer's logo emblazoned across it. He then visited a hardware shop and exited with an assortment of tools.

He slid the ne pas déranger sign over the doorknob. Inside, he removed the boards that compartmentalised the golf bag and otherwise stripped it of its innards.

He fashioned a pre-drilled board to fit snugly into the top and glued it into place. Using a hacksaw, he cut the golf clubs about a foot from their club end. These were inserted and glued into the holes. He also clipped a towel, ball cleaner, and a brush to the bag.

He admired his handiwork and smiled. From any angle, the bag looked ready for a game of golf. As it quite light, being largely empty, and he hoped once the banknotes were added, it would be near the right weight.

They contacted the manager of the Byblos Bank with the name and number they had been given in Rhodesia. Codes and signatures were exchanged and, eventually, two medium-sized leather suitcases were produced containing the seven million dollars. They were assured that no note exceeded one hundred dollars in value. The most dangerous part of the operation was removing the suitcases from the bank without drawing attention. In the end, they simply decided to walk out, one suitcase at a time. Nobody even gave them a glance.

Inside a large Mercury station wagon, David proceeded to transfer the money to the golf bag. Fortunately, it was large enough to accommodate all of the bills.

Back at the hotel, they simply left the golf bag and the suitcases with the porter. He carried them to an ornate luggage trolley in the foyer, which he pushed to the elevator and on to their room. The porter was none the wiser, believing it to be no more than a golf bag. As Gisela said, if only he knew!

David smiled. If it could fool the porter, it certainly would fool the British. It looked authentic.

Two days later, the swap of the golf bags went without a hitch in the parking lot of The Golf Club of Lebanon. Hiram had arrived with a number of golf bags, bringing two of his associates in order to make up a four-ball, adding to the confusion for any interested onlookers. Hiram had his money and it was up to him to ensure that Aérospatiale received payment for the first consignment of helicopters. The balance was to follow later when the next consignment of knockdown helicopters was due for release. Of course, by then, a different method of payment and delivery might have to be found. As for the game itself, well, David was paired with one of Hiram's friends, who played superbly. Still, they were no match for Hiram and his partner. They played a well-managed game exploiting each other's strengths, beating him 3-2. David had to part with a hundred dollars as did his partner, this being the bet. Insignificant when compared to the purchase price of the Alouettes, but still a hard pill to swallow. Hiram's smile just said it all.

He took the hundred dollar bills.

'It's been a pleasure doing business with you.'

All laughed, the comment not lost on them.

CHAPTER 16

On the Air France flight back to Paris, they sat in adjoining seats and decided that the best course of action would be to split up again once in France. They would avoid each other and assume new identities. Although he understood that Doyle had arrived in France from London primarily to ensure that the departure of the knockdown helicopters proceeded without a hitch, he was to assist the Rhodesian in that regard. They were to meet at some obscure bistro near the Air France city terminal in Paris. Gisela would continue to source goods in Europe urgently needed in Rhodesia. David was to retain a German identity and continue to masquerade as a lifetime student-lecturer.

They had heard nothing regarding the status of the tankers.

They left the aircraft separately at Orly. David entered the men's room on the concourse where removed his clothing and donned his student's garb. From the lining of his bag, he produced a new German passport, courtesy of Gisela. He was now Helmuth Baumbach, lecturer at Cologne University, his speciality, electronics. Gone was the suit, now jeans and windbreaker, his head covered by a beanie to protect him from the weather.

With his personal belongings and few items of clothing stuffed into a duffel bag, he caught the bus to the terminus in the city. There, he phoned Doyle, who was already in Paris and had installed himself in a dingy hotel near Sacré-Coeur. The terminus was crowded. Doyle was nowhere to be seen. He waited about ten minutes and then sauntered to the bistro he had been given as the rendezvous point.

He ordered a café noir and, taking it from the barman, sat down at one of the nearby tables. The bistro was a typical worker's bar, nothing fancy about it.

'Jetzt sieh mal an, was wir da haben,' someone said. David turned to look. At first glance, he did not recognise him. It was Doyle. Look what the cat dragged in, indeed. He seemed to have aged considerably: his hair and eyebrows were grey; he sported a moustache, also grey; on his nose was perched a pair of large square, rimless glasses. David smiled, glad to see the man.

'You did a brilliant job in Lebanon.' Doyle said staying with German. They shook hands.

'A few people died. I'm worried.' David said.

'So I've heard, well, that's par for the course in this game. This is a bad business but it has to be done. Christ, we're actually paid to do these things. You better get used to it,' Doyle replied with a shrug. The loss of life left him unmoved it seemed.

David looked around to ensure that they could not be overheard.

'What's happening with the helicopters?' he asked, his voice low.

'You won't believe it. The bloody South Africans are fucking us around. The crates are standing in a warehouse on an airfield near Toulouse, which Aérospatiale uses for test flights. It's pretty well guarded. A Safair Hercules C130 was supposed to have collected these. Now the South African government has refused to do so, afraid that this could implicate them. Jesus Christ, implicate them. Can you believe that? What a bunch of arseholes.'

'So what are you going to do now?' an astounded David asked.

'Oh, my dear friend, you've got it wrong. It's what are *you* going to do.'

A real bastard, David thought. He wasn't sure whether he liked or disliked the man.

'Forget it. I'm not masquerading as any officer or whatever. Once was enough,' David said. He wasn't going to be caught up in another of Doyle's plans.

'Nothing like that. I've leased an aircraft, a DC-7B cargo plane from a Luxembourg crowd. They have a shady reputation, you know, involved in smuggling and similar activities, which suits me. Actually, they're rather well-known in Africa. They did a lot of flying in the Congo hauling all sorts of shit around. Cash upfront of course, nearly enough to buy the bloody plane, I might add. Anyway, I've also found a pilot. May be a bit old but with over 10,000 hours to his name.'

'So, where do I fit in?'

Doyle smiled sadistically.

'You're the co-pilot.'

'Oh, no! Fuck off. I want nothing to do with this.'

'You have no choice. You do as ordered, Captain. Remember, I can't fly an aircraft that size and a two-man crew is compulsory,' Doyle countered with a smirk.

He stared at Doyle, unable to conceal his malice.

'I take it that that's now settled,' Doyle said, his eyebrows raised questioningly, a trace of a smile on his face. 'Incidentally, I'll be coming with you as the engineer. Not that I know much about the plane.'

'It's not quite that simple,' David said.

Doyle knew nothing about commercial aircraft. David thought he had him. This was Europe, the authorities checked everything. Without proper papers, you don't get anywhere near a cockpit. 'I've no papers, licence, logbooks, etcetera. They'll never let me fly. And as for you masquerading as a flight engineer, well?' David said, rolling his eyes.

'Ah, but you're wrong, I've everything. Airline Transport Pilot Licence—'

'Jesus Christ! You're bastards.'

'You bet! Airline Transport Pilot Licence, authentic logbooks and certification, the whole damn lot, some it compliments of the British,' Doyle said with a smug expression on his face. 'Oh, incidentally, you're about to undergo a name change again,' he added.

****

The airfield was in Blagnac, near Toulouse. It was a commercial field but was also used by the French Armée de l'Air as a test base for new aircraft. Their area was fenced off and subject to close security. It had an eleven thousand-foot runaway, just right for heavily laden transport aircraft. Doyle had found discreet accommodation in a nearby village, often used by aspiring flight students who trained at the various flight schools on the airport.

The Douglas DC-7B had arrived the previous day. This was a four-engine, propeller-driven cargo plane. It was not a particularly well-known or well-liked aircraft as it was prone to re-occurring engine problems. The aircraft news industry referred to it as the last of the large piston-engine aircraft. It was devoid of any livery, only displaying its registration number which confirmed that it was based in Luxembourg. Surprisingly, it had been flown solo from Luxembourg, unique for an aircraft this size – what had Doyle said? – owned by a shady setup? The operating manuals stipulated a minimum crew of three: two pilots and a flight engineer. No wonder, David thought; those engines needed a lot of attention.

Doyle introduced him to the pilot. A bit old, as Doyle had said. Well, he thought the man close to sixty. He was tall and thin, with a mop of white hair hidden beneath an old airline captain's cap with a faded insignia. David was unable to recognise the airline. The man's eyes were blue, but a

112

watery blue, and David thought he caught the faint smell of liquor. Hopefully the remnants of last night's sojourn and not today's, he thought.

They shook hands.

'Gainsborough,' the man said, 'but call me Tony, everybody does. Would you like an inspection of the aircraft?'

'Sure.'

For about forty-five minutes, they carefully inspected every nook and cranny. The aircraft was not very old, only about eight years, and was well maintained.

'Number four engine is a bit dicey,' the old man remarked.

'Dicey? What do you mean?'

'Well, she's runs rough, especially on start-up. The plugs foul. She may have a broken piston ring. However, she always clears after a few minutes. We'll have to watch her though.'

'Well, that's a comforting thought,' David said softly to himself. Gainsborough gave him a look.

CHAPTER 17

It took four days to get the aircraft loaded and refuelled. The paperwork caused most of the delay as a completely new set of papers were necessary. The crates had arrived by truck and were loaded with difficulty through the large double doors in the fuselage. Once inside the fuselage, they were manhandled with straps and ratchets until the load was properly distributed. None of the crates were weighed.

'We haven't weighed the crates. There seems to be a helluva lot of them for just a few helicopters.' David said.

'Not necessary, the manufacturer supplied the weights.'

David lowered his voice. 'I hope these aren't fictitious.'

'Why should they be?' Doyle asked.

'Is there any other stuff besides the helicopters?'

'Only a few items that the country urgently needs,' Doyle replied.

They were due to take-off at ten in the morning. To the surprise of all, Gainsborough insisted that David take the left-hand seat, theoretically putting him in command of the aircraft. Doyle just shrugged his shoulders with a 'why not?' expression. He believed both were competent pilots.

David was unhappy. The load concerned him; the aircraft was too heavy. It moved ponderously from the loading dock, trundling slowly along the apron. To crown it all, the tanks were full, far more than was necessary for the first hop to Frankfurt in Germany. Doyle refused to listen to him, dismissing his objections; Gainsborough made no comment. Finally, they were lined up, the aircraft cleared for takeoff. David eased the four throttles forward to their stop, the four engines thundering, the aircraft laboriously starting its take-off run.

The acceleration was not dynamic. It was downright sluggish.

'Thank God for eleven thousand feet,' David said with reference to the long runway.

A few seconds later, he added, 'Christ! She's fuckin' heavy.'

'That she is,' Tony replied.

The aircraft was rapidly approaching V1, the point when the pilot is committed to fly, unable to abort the takeoff.

'V1 coming up,' Tony remarked.

David's hand was still on the throttle quadrant. Out of the corner of his eye, he saw Doyle lean over from the back, placing his hand over David's, firmly holding his hand forward. If David proposed to yank the throttles back, aborting the take off, well, he would not have been able to do so.

They passed V1, the aircraft still accelerating. Without a word, Doyle removed his hand, as did David. The parallel white lines in the runway demarcating its rapidly approaching end came into view. Still they rolled. They were running out of runway. It was time to fly. David eased back on the stick, lifting the aircraft's nose, the nose-wheel free of the ground. The main gear still rumbled, the wheels still on the asphalt. Suddenly, the rumble ceased as they came unstuck, the aircraft flying, the airfield perimeter fence flashing past just feet below them.

'Come, baby, fly,' he whispered, as if calling on the angels to help. The heavily laden aircraft staggered through the air as it tried to build up speed. Slowly the airspeed indicator moved up, gaining another ten knots. David jabbed the toe-brakes to stop the wheels spinning.

'Wheels up,' he said.

Tony activated the undercarriage lever and the wheels disappeared with a thump into their wheel wells.

David let his pent up breath out with a whoosh.

'Holy Mary, Mother of God, that was close,' a white-faced Doyle whispered.

David was livid. They had nearly died. The aircraft was grossly over-loaded. Had the tanks been half full, they would've been okay. David directed his venom at Doyle.

'You fuckin' idiot. You had better pray that number four engine doesn't decide to start missing. You could've killed us all. That could still happen.'

Tony said nothing. His face was pale. It was obvious that he, too, had been frightened. Once they cleared a thousand feet, David gave control to him.

David turned to face Doyle. He was surprised. Doyle's face was a picture of abject fear.

'I'm sorry,' Doyle stammered, 'I thought you were being overly cautious and that you would yank the throttles back and abort the take-off. I'm sorry, I should have let you.'

He said nothing. What good would it do. He merely shook his head in disgust. He heard Gainsborough softly saying to himself, 'Jesus Christ. Fuckin' Rhodesians. God help us.'

David had wanted to give Frankfurt a miss. They had more than sufficient fuel to make Grande Comoros but Doyle insisted that they land, not providing a reason. Making a stop in Frankfurt had necessitated a great deal of preparation, the Germans insistent that all pilots be familiar with their approach procedures, airport layout, runway and taxiway usage and parking slot designation. They had been given Parking Slot 159. This was all done in the Operations Room at Toulouse Airport when they were in contact with Frankfurt Airport filing their flight plan. Doyle took charge of all cargo documentation.

As they approached Frankfurt Flight Control Perimeter, Tony was flying.

By this time David realised the man had an alcohol problem: the ruddy complexion, the continuous dry lips, and his licking them. The other giveaway was the smell. It was as if this seeped through his very skin. Still, he piloted the plane expertly, in total control of the situation. Eventually, they turned on final, clearing the fence, the wheels touching down with a mere kiss notwithstanding the fact the plane was only marginally below the maximum weight for landing. Frankfurt Tower was impatient for him to clear the runway. Soon they were on the taxiway approaching a crowded apron of aircraft clustered in profusion. Tony rummaged in a briefcase between the seat and console.

'What are looking for?' David asked.

'The bloody airport map showing where our parking bay is. I know it is number 159 but how do I get there? I don't think I'm going the right way.'

It was as if the flight controller in the tower read his mind.

'XD-one niner-niner-two, where are you going?'

'Frankfurt Control, I'm looking for Parking Slot 159.'

'XD-one niner-niner-two, don't you know where that is?' the tower asked, obviously exasperated, and impatient, 'Have you not been to Frankfurt before?' This asked in a clipped strongly accented German.

Tony turned briefly to look at David, clearly annoyed, and then a mischievous grin split the old man's lips. Tony responded putting on his best attempt at upper class Queen's English.

'Frankfurt Tower, yes, I've been here before, but unfortunately that was in 1944.'

There was no response from the tower. Both David and Doyle broke down in fits of laughter.

'Fuckin' Krauts. I was flying a Lancaster bomber then and these guys were trying to shoot my bloody arse off,' Tony remarked, obviously pleased with his one-upmanship.

It was with relief that they saw the traffic controller waving his illuminated paddles guiding them to the parking lot.

Doyle still had not explained the need for the stopover in Frankfurt. They did not have long to wait. With typical German efficiency, a tractor appeared pulling a few pallet trucks, which stopped next to the aircraft. Following it was an airport forklift.

'What's all this?' David asked.

Doyle stared at the pallets, his hands on his hips unable to hide his expression of self-satisfaction.' Second-hand Turbomeca turbine engines for helicopters. I found them. We bought them from the Arabs, they didn't even ask who we were and what we proposed doing with these and, above all, they were cheap. They've been lying in the sand in the desert for a while though. It's quite amazing what you can find lying around.'

The crates were soon loaded, David taking careful note of the weights as these appeared on the manifest.

Gainsborough stared at the crates. 'This take-off is going to be worse than Toulouse. Be grateful that the runway's longer and that the damn wind is blowing hard. We're going to need it. I'll fly and you can start with, "Our Father,"' he remarked to David.

A Lufthansa minivan drew up and, to their surprise, Gisela alighted. She quickly climbed the flight stairs with satchel in hand. Everyone was glad to see her, especially David. She gave him a shy hug. He held her close. An indescribable feeling overcame him as he realised how much she meant to him.

'Where did you spring from? I missed you,' a surprised David asked in a low voice.

He again realised how beautiful she was. It was naturally so, none of it was put on. It was in her gestures, in her smile, and the way she moved. Her black hair cascaded down the side of her face, accentuating her blue eyes. Her lipstick was subdued, one of those lighter colours currently fashionable. She was appropriately dressed in jeans, near-calf-high boots and a sweater with a roll-neck top.

'Our bosses thought you would need me, especially with my impeccable French.' She laughed. 'Where are we going?' she asked, more seriously.

Doyle interrupted.

'From here we fly straight to Mayotte, an island in the Comoros still governed by France. Ask no more.'

She stared at the crates in the cargo section of the aircraft. 'I'm impressed, whose idea was this?' she asked.

'Mine,' replied Doyle, 'but we haven't got there yet. These goods are disguised as elevator parts. The documents are impeccable and should pass scrutiny by the best. Fortunately, since you got back from Lebanon, we have not seen or heard from the British. It seems that we have thrown them.'

The flight to Mayotte was long and dull. The aircraft carried sufficient fuel for a non-stop flight.

CHAPTER 18

London was bleak and dreary, the rain threatening to fall. Another cold front had edged in from the Atlantic, sliding over Ireland and then England.

The porter greeted him with the customary 'Morning, guv,' Nonetheless, recognised as he was, he still had to produce identification, which was meticulously perused for its authenticity and whether the mug shot contained therein actually matched him.

The morning had started badly. It had been his first night alone. His live-in girlfriend had walked out on him. Over the last few months, her ardour had cooled appreciably. He knew the main reason, it was his lack of commitment to a long-term relationship. She was bothered by having turned thirty and this, combined with being childless, drove the relationship over the edge. Yes, he loved her and she him, but this was not a recipe sufficient to sustain a long-term relationship.

His phone had rang at an ungodly hour in the morning. His departmental head, Sir Harry Monterey, was on the line demanding that he present himself particularly early at Century House for a meeting of national importance. Century House, well, that spelt trouble. This was the main offices of MI6.

The porter handed the card back. 'Third floor, guv, they're expecting you and you are a tad late. I would hurry if I were you.'

He was only a few minutes late but Sir Harry's look conveyed his disapproval. Christian Seymour apologised.

MI6 was an apolitical organisation or, certainly, it was supposed to be. A glance around the room would have immediately revealed that if the occupants had any political affiliation at all, these would tend to lean heavily towards to the right, most being supporters of the Conservative Party. All were from public schools and old money. The dark suits and waistcoats, the black brogue shoes, and regimental ties were a definite giveaway.

Sir Harry was seated behind his desk. A long table also occupied the room, abutting the desk. Four other men were seated at the table. Sir Harry indicated that Seymour should sit.

'Gentlemen, I've just been lambasted by the Home Secretary; believe me, an unpleasant experience. In fact, he phoned me last night. It is the Rhodesians and the bloody French who've got his wind up. Nobody seems to know, but somehow the Rhodesians have got their hands on few new helicopters, French Allouettes if you must know. The Prime Minister is furious.'

What a fiasco, Christian Seymour thought. Going up against the Rhodesians did not sit well with him and nor with a number of his colleagues. He had gone to school and university with Rhodesians. Even at Sandhurst, Rhodesians were to be found. Ex-Rhodesian officers were amongst the best of the British Army and now were at war, or at least a near war – fighting kith and kin, as it were!

'Gibson, what do we know about this?' Sir Harry asked, looking at the man seated next to Seymour, the current divisional head of a recently created Rhodesia desk.

'Well, we do know they've made some deal with the French. Our source tells us that an order for Aérospatiale Alouettes from South America, thought to be Argentina, is actually intended for Rhodesia. Part of the order, maybe three or four, has been loaded onto a Luxembourg-registered cargo plane at Toulouse Airport which departed from there yesterday.'

'Have you any idea of the identity of the crew?'

'Believe or not, one of our own, a retired RAF pilot. That fellow, Tusk, you and I discussed is apparently also on board.'

'You mean that banker masquerading as who knows what? He's the one who organised payment, isn't he? Well, we need to deal with him.'

'Yes, it's him.'

'This RAF fellow, who is he?' Sir Harry then demanded.

'Squadron Leader Anthony Gainsborough, DSO.'

'Can't we solicit his assistance, you know, Queen and country and all that?'

Gibson contemplated the director's question before replying. 'I truly doubt it. To be blunt, he is more inclined to give us the finger, if you know what I mean.'

'Well, short of actually shooting people, I'm instructed to stop this aircraft – what is it? – a DC-7B, I understand, before it gets to Rhodesia.'

'Sir Harry, the problem is that neither the French nor Germans seemed to want to help. They're just turning a blind eye,' Christian ventured.

'I know, I know,' Sir Harry said impatiently, with a wave of a hand, 'The Germans don't want to get involved with anything with an international flavour or which is subject UN directives, while the French, well, it's de Gaulle, that should tell you all. He'll never forgive Montgomery. I think he actually hates the man.'

Gibson interrupted, 'What we did find out from the Germans was the destination of the aircraft. Our people managed to get sight of the filed flight plan handed in at Frankfurt. It landed at Frankfurt after taking off from Toulouse. Mayotte in the Comoros is its final destination. It's due to take off from Frankfurt at three this afternoon.'

'Mayotte. The bloody French again,' Sir Harry said exasperatedly, smacking the desktop with the flat of his hand. 'I'll bet my boots that it's only heading there to refuel. From there, it will be either South Africa or Rhodesia. Who's there to stop them? Come on, gentlemen! My head's on a block here. I need some ideas.'

Nobody seemed to have any ideas, some squirmed in their chairs, their discomfort apparent.

'How about forcing it ...' one of those at the table with Christian ventured.

'Forget it. At the moment, the Middle East is a powder keg. We can't send up fighter aircraft. That option has already been considered and dismissed.'

Christian racked his brains trying to remember whether there was anybody he could recall who was sufficiently qualified or in the right place to be of assistance. If the aircraft was to be stopped, this probably was going to be a wet affair. Somebody was bound to be killed. Whoever they found would have to be the type that did not shirk away from anything messy. Killing people was always messy. They had to destroy the aircraft. Revolt threatened in the Seychelles and the British had sent a couple of Royal Marines to support the High Commissioner. He thought for a moment. Could they not use these men to sabotage the aircraft? He put this to Sir Harry who believed it to be the only alternative, time being of the essence.

It was incredible how fast a plan seemed to materialise and be put into motion. A flurry of radio signals and telexes followed and, within hours, two Royal Marines disguised as tourists boarded an Air Seychelles Fokker

Friendship flight bound for the Grand Comoros, winging their way over the Indian Ocean. Their luggage contained no firearms, only timers, detonators, and Semtex explosives. No attempt was made to hide them. There were no customs searches or luggage screening on these inter-island flights. In fact, there never had been. Life was laid back. Most travellers were tourists and the occasional bit of political upheaval or readjustment was merely an irritant to them. Never had any subversive activity ever been encountered.

CHAPTER 19

Anthony had flown the DC-7B from Frankfurt, which had left as scheduled just after three in the afternoon. It made its way across southern Europe and the Mediterranean, Malta visible on the right, then it crossed into Libya during the first hours of darkness, the Sahara sixteen thousand feet below them.

Behind the cockpit bulkhead was an area with an access hatch to the outside. From this area, another door opened to a galley, which contained a small fridge and food warmer. Another door allowed entrance to a toilet while another opened to another cabin containing four bunks. Courtesy of the aircraft owners, these were made up with pillows, sheets and blankets. The fridge was well stocked. Doyle had seen to this.

While crossing the Mediterranean, David relieved Anthony, piloting the aircraft until midnight. The aircraft flew below its optimal cruising speed, primarily to save fuel, as no fuel would be available before Mayotte. The pilots shared the navigational task, taking turns to shoot the stars, doing the computations and listening out for the various radio beacons, intersecting each other on the chart indicating as to exactly where the aircraft was.

At midnight, Anthony again relieved David, the aircraft high above the Ethiopian Highlands, shrouded in cloud and no lights to be seen. The flight progressed smoothly except for a few minutes of concern when ice began to build up on the aircraft's wing leading edges and propellers, making the aircraft sluggish. David shone a torch through a window, the beam revealing the ice build-up on the wing and the accumulation on the propeller bosses. The de-icing equipment was activated which soon cleared the ice.

With things back to normal and Anthony flying the aircraft, David passed through from the cockpit into the small central cabin. Nobody was to be seen. He opened the door to the cargo hold only to find Doyle sprawled in one of the seats, fast asleep, the backrest reclined as far back as it would go. He had an open paperback lying face down on his chest. He entered the galley to find the light on and Gisela busy preparing coffee.

'Hi, I was about to make you some coffee. I need a cup myself,' she said.

He nodded. She probably had been asleep, he thought. She had removed her jeans and now wore a pair of loose shorts and slip-on sandals, her painted toenails visible. She wore a loose-fitting white cotton top of thin material, buttoned down the front, the swell of her breasts distinct, evidence that she wore nothing beneath. She had removed her lipstick and her hair was still tousled from her sleep.

He stepped close to her and placed an arm on her shoulder. He caught her distinct aroma, an arresting mix of perfume and lotion combined with her natural scent which he found arousing. She laid her neck to one side, her head pressing against him. Finding her nearness electrifying, he turned his head, placing his lips on hers and kissing her passionately, his need a demanding throb. Her tongue probed his. He pressed her pelvis against him, acutely aware of his rampant arousal.

She broke away from him and, without a word, led him through the bulkhead door past where Doyle still slept sprawled in his seat, his mouth open, snoring.

There was a narrow passageway between the crates packed on each side, which led to the rear of the aircraft. The crates were lashed to the floor with straps that criss-crossed the fuselage. Halfway down the aisle, there was a gap of about fifteen feet where no crates had been placed. Here, folded cargo mats lay on the floor, also strapped down. She sat, pulling him down with her. She crouched forward, her shirt spilling open, allowing him to see her breasts and erect nipples.

'Oh, I missed you so,' she said, kissing him. She lay back on the cargo net, both of them oblivious to the grime. He bent over her, undoing the few buttons still closed on the blouse. He kissed her breasts, his lips closing over her nipple. She moaned as she arched her back. Her hands roamed over his body until they found his belt buckle, unclasping it.

His whole being centred on his arousal. He ached for her.

He stripped off her shorts and his trousers and entered her. In what seemed a moment, his world exploded. He was unaware of his surroundings. The monotonous drone of the aircraft engines, the dim string of ceiling lights in the cargo hold, the dirty cargo mats, all he was aware of was her loud shrieks in his ear and his total surrender.

Spent, they lay for a good quarter-hour, she with her eyes closed, their legs intertwined.

'You've got to get out of this. It's too dangerous, especially your being a woman,' he said.

124

Her eyes were still closed. 'I can't,' she whispered, 'I was a person without a country when I fled East Germany and the Stasi. Rhodesia gave me everything: a country, a home, and a husband. How can I abandon her now?' she replied, her head still on his chest.

'That type of loyalty is not expected of you.' He was adamant.

'My love, you don't understand. That's exactly what is expected from all of us. For you, it's different. Rhodesia is not your home.'

'Christ, you're obstinate,' he said.

After dressing and brushing themselves off, they returned to the cockpit. Doyle still slept. Tony was in the cockpit monitoring the autopilot. He gave David a thumbs-up sign. All was well. For somebody said to be an alcoholic, David thought the man's behaviour had been exemplary. He was sure the man had not touched any alcohol since they first met. However, it was clear he was fighting his own inner battle. The slight tremor in the hands as these moved forward to grasp the control yoke, the copious cups of coffee, the screwing up of his face and eyes as he fought the demons within were a definite giveaway. At one stage, he had ventured to ask Tony whether he was ill. The man had dismissed the question with a wave of hand muttering something to the effect that he never felt better.

Gisela made coffee and handed the pilot a cup, more out of a need to keep herself busy. David took the left-hand seat and thus command of the aircraft. It was now two in the morning. The aircraft crossed the coastline in the vicinity of the Kenya-Somalia border. The engines droned in the darkness with rings of blue exhaust flame around the engine nacelles clearly visible.

Finding a suitable refuelling point for the aircraft had posed a problem. Even if the British had wind of the aircraft and its cargo, it was essential that any attempt by them to intercept the aircraft had to be stopped. This was a cat and mouse game. Most countries in Africa were hostile towards the newly independent Rhodesia. The last leg of the flight would be crucial. Mayotte seemed to be the best option. Firstly, it was not on a direct track from Europe to Rhodesia. No one would believe that an aircraft on track for the island would have Rhodesia as its final destination, or so Doyle believed. A flight from Mayotte Island to Rhodesia would take the aircraft over a desolate area of Mozambique and Zambia, an area with virtually no air traffic control and certainly no radar. Also, the intention was to fly this leg at night. Last but not least, Mayotte was part of France and administered accordingly, not that the Grand Comoros government agreed. They disputed France's rights and had already taken the matter to the United Nations. France exercised her veto and created a deadlock. Should the British ask the French to intervene and seize the aircraft, they probably would do so, albeit reluctantly. Hopefully the process would be so slow that it would afford them a window in which to fly the aircraft out of French-controlled airspace. Again, this is what Doyle assumed. Everyone was aware that matters could turn out quite differently.

The dawn was a mere streak of pink on the eastern horizon, the volcanic peaks on Mayotte already visible when the DC-7B turned on long final for its descent. Tony again piloted the aircraft. The runway at Dzaoudzi was built on a peninsula which had not been long enough to accommodate the full length of the runway, forcing the French to build a causeway which extended into the ocean and stuck out like a finger. The tower directed them to park on the edge of the apron close to the perimeter fence a fair distance from the tower and administrative buildings. Maintenance men brought a set of flight stairs, which they adjusted to allow those on board to disembark.

David stood on the top of the stairs and took in the surroundings. They were now in the tropics. Full daylight was only minutes away, the sun ready to peek over the horizon. In the distance on the other side of the aircraft apron, a group of men dressed in green camouflage uniforms mustered. There were a few hundred of them. David realised that they must be the detachment of French Foreign Legion soldiers deployed to deal with any problem in the Indian Ocean. The continuous discord between the Comoros and Mayotte had left the French with little choice but to create a military presence in order to dissuade the government of the Comoros from taking matters into their own hands and unilaterally annexing Mayotte.

The air terminal was deserted. They presented their passports to a lone customs official who perused them with little interest. No one intended to leave the confines of the airport. Doyle had indicated that they would take off just before dark, completing the last leg of the flight during the night. This was an international airport and, provided they did not leave the terminal, the customs official saw no reason to restrict their movements. Gisela mumbled something about looking for a shower, the other two men thinking this a great idea. They agreed to meet in the cafeteria for breakfast. David saw that a tanker had already drawn up to the aircraft where two men were attaching fuel hoses. He realised that Doyle must have arranged this. He did not know whether Doyle proposed to pay with a fuel carnet or with cash. Presumably, the aircraft was supplied with an international fuel card.

They sat down to a continental breakfast a half hour later. Doyle had yet to join them. The coffee was good, as were the croissants. David and Tony ordered omelettes.

David sat facing the entrance to the cafeteria and was the first to see Doyle approaching. There was no mistaking the concerned expression on his face. He swept to a stop next to the table not bothering to sit.

'We've got a problem,' he said quietly.

This news hit David with a jolt, his muscles momentarily contracting, his body jerking. This had to be bad. He could see that Doyle was agitated.

'What's wrong?'

'Air Traffic Control is closing the airport in half an hour. A tropical weather front driven by a cyclone is about to sweep over the island. No aircraft movements will be permitted until tomorrow morning. They forecast gale-strength winds and rain within a short while.'

'Christ, we didn't know about this. The bloody sun's still up,' Tony blurted.

'I know, that's because we didn't bother to ask or listen. This warning has been on their radio for hours.' Doyle looked down at the floor, 'I tried to persuade them to allow us to leave, but they would not hear of it. It would be stupid to press them.'

A Fokker Friendship could be seen taxiing towards the apron in front of the terminal building.

Doyle indicated the aircraft. 'That's the last aircraft that's been permitted to land. It's from the Seychelles.'

'This is a stuff-up, isn't it?' David said.

'We're only going to be able to leave tomorrow night. There's nothing we can do, so I suggest we have a bit of fun. We've all got passports so a razzle at the local tourist hotel should be fun.' Doyle smiled. 'Compliments of the Rhodesian government. This place is bloody expensive as you will soon learn.'

Only then, did Doyle sit down and busy himself with his coffee and breakfast.

CHAPTER 20

By the time the two Marines had disembarked, the wind had increased significantly, whipping their clothes. Already the sky was darkening and the first rain was moments away. Lieutenant Hawthorne had noticed the DC-7B backed up to the perimeter in the corner of the apron. He saw that a set of flight stairs had been placed against the aircraft, although the cargo hatch was closed. Probably because of the weather, he thought.

'See what I see?' Hawthorne said.

'Yes.' His companion, Sergeant McCleary, replied, his rich Scottish accent unmistakable. 'The weather seems favourable as well. Just right for a walk at night.'

'Well, let's hope the local legionnaires don't pose a problem.'

For the last two days, Anthony Gainsborough fought an inner battle. His need for alcohol was overpowering. Constantly aware of this, he worked his mind ceaselessly trying to keep the craving under control. Continuous tremors flowed through his body, occasionally so severe they were akin to a fever bout. These only lasted for a minute or so, by which time he managed to get them under control, dewy sweat on his brow, his shirt clinging to his body. If the others noticed, they did not say. Sleep was out of the question. He merely tossed and turned. Still, he remained resolute: this time he was going to dry out.

The unforeseen delay brought about by the weather and the prospect of spending a night on the plane with nothing to do persuaded the group to book into a hotel and sample the best cuisine Mayotte could offer. Doyle made the arrangements. He booked them into a decent tourist hotel in Mamoudzou, the island capital. This was on an adjoining island, accessible by a ferry which crossed every hour.

Anthony politely refused to accompany them saying that he would sleep aboard the aircraft. They knew better than to press him. He did not need them to help fight his demons. On hearing that he was not sleeping well, Gisela parted with a few of her sleeping pills, they quite strong but leaving no after-effects. Anthony proposed to take two of these hoping to sleep through the night.

They were not concerned for the safety of their aircraft. Three teams of two local legionnaires patrolled the perimeter of the airfield with dogs from sunset to midnight when they were relieved by a fresh troop who continued until sunrise. The French government considered this precaution necessary. The airfield was, in fact, a military base, in full view of the neighbouring Comoros islands, with whom they shared a strained relationship.

Captain Hawthorne thought the wind was gusting in excess of forty miles per hour. This was a blessing in disguise and a distraction to the legionnaires patrolling the perimeter. They'd probably keep their heads down. Both he and McCleary lay in the undergrowth alongside the perimeter, the DC-7B looming in front of them in the darkness. Small branches and leaves wiping above camouflaged them with the whistle and moan of the wind disguising all other sounds. They did not wear uniforms, nor were they armed. They had dressed in whatever civilian clothes they could find which allowed them to blend in with the terrain. Both wore green shirts and trousers and, on their feet, brown brushed leather hiking boots. Each carried a small rucksack. McCleary's contained the detonators and Semtex. Hawthorne carried the timers and the other two items considered essential: a large pair of pliers and a pair of wire cutters. They agreed to make their move before midnight.

The weaving beams of two torches warned them of the guards' approach. As they neared, they saw the Alsatian on a leash, trotting between the two soldiers. Fortunately, the wind blew any scent the marines may have had away from the field and the dog. The guards were unconcerned and conversing loudly in German. The two Marines hugged the ground until the soldiers and dog had passed.

Certain that the legionnaires were out of earshot and lost in the darkness, they jumped to their feet and cautiously approached the fence. Within seconds, McCleary had cut through the close-knit steel mesh, bending the cut squares backwards affixing them to the fence with a piece of wire. Crouched over to avoid presenting a silhouette, they scrambled through and quickly made their way to the aircraft. The timers had been pre-set. Hawthorne inserted the timers into the Semtex. Standing on McCleary's shoulders and steadying himself with a hand on the aircraft's stationary propeller, he inserted the explosive into the front of the outer starboard engine nacelle. The curled front section of the cowling prevented the explosive from falling out. There was no need to affix it to anything. It could not fall out and would just lie in the nacelle. The whole procedure did not take a minute. The next patrol, according to observations they had made of the guards movement, would pass here in ten minutes' time. The legionnaires' torches were a giveaway. The two men would have ample warning of any approach.

'For fuck sake, get down!' McCleary whispered. Hawthorne never hesitated. He just let himself drop from the Marine's shoulders, executing a classic parachutist roll as he struck the ground.

'A light's just gone on in the cockpit,' McCleary again whispered.

The two men quickly moved to the starboard undercarriage leg, moulding their bodies to it so as to present as small a target as possible. Through the undercarriage struts, they could feel the wind, which drove showers of rain before it, buffeting the plane. Here under the wing, it was relatively dry. The strong smell of hydraulic fluid assaulted Hawthorne's nose. He dared not move. He thought he heard the faint screech of metal and then footsteps on the steel flight steps. His blood hammered in his temples. He saw McCleary's face inches away, his teeth clenched.

'Oh fuck,' McCleary whispered, hardly hearing the expletive over the wind and rain, craning his neck around. A legionnaire patrol approached along the perimeter fence, their torches dancing in the dark.

McCleary saw the man who stood looking towards the approaching legionnaires who, having seen him descend the stairs, veered towards the plane. They clutched their automatic carbines across their chests in proper military fashion, their camouflage-imprinted ponchos whipping around their bodies in the strong wind. The man at the bottom of the stairs seemed oblivious to the weather, his wet clothes clinging to his body.

At first, they conversed in French and then switched to German.

What the hell was going on? Hawthorne wondered, watching the trio intently.

After about a minute, the legionnaires turned away walking towards the perimeter fence, heads down against the wind. The other man turned and retraced his steps and disappeared through the hatch, which he closed because of the wind and rain.

'Maybe we're going to get away with this?' McCleary whispered to Hawthorne, the prospect of spending a while in the French army's brig beginning to fade away.

'Maybe.'

The soldiers had resumed their patrol, now following the perimeter fence and walking away from the aircraft.

'Okay, let's make our way back to the fence but walk directly under the fuselage towards the tail. Nobody should be able to see us,' Hawthorne said.

Soon they reached the fence, scrambling through the hole they had cut. The cockpit light was still on. McCleary, using a pair pliers and soft wire, proceeded to mend the hole. When he had finished, Hawthorne inspected the man's handiwork.

'Excellent. They're not going to find this for a while unless they've taken that bloke's concerns seriously. It certainly didn't seem as if those legionnaires thought something was amiss.'

The two men disappeared into the wet brush.

CHAPTER 21

Anthony was not happy. He was sure he had seen two figures in the darkness approach the aircraft. The gendarmes had assured him that they had been keeping an eye on the fence as this was one of their duties. Nobody made it through, they were sure about that. Anthony could see that the guards were sceptical about his insistence that he had seen something. They promised to keep a special lookout.

His intense need for alcohol was driving him crazy. It was difficult to breath, his skin crawled and he constantly wanted to scratch himself. The violent tremors intermittently racking his body left him mentally shattered and exhausted and caused him to black out for a few moments.

Maybe his mind was paying tricks on him. A few times he had nearly succumbed to the hallucinations which crept up on him and he had to grit his teeth in an effort to resist them.

He returned to the galley and threw the two sleeping tablets into his mouth, washing them down with a cup of tea. He lay down on the bunk, leaving the cockpit light on. Fifteen minutes later, he was dead to the world, his breathing regular, his features relaxed.

Throughout the night, the wind howled, at first blowing from the east and, as the cyclone traversed the islands, then swinging and blowing from the west. Every now and then, the wind would buffet the aircraft. As the first light of the morning slowly illuminated their surroundings, the destruction the airfield had sustained during the night became apparent. Part of the air terminal's roof had been ripped off and a few large windows were broken, allowing the rain to flood the ground floor. Continuous banks of dark cloud still scudded across the sky, subjecting the airfield to torrents of rain. Every few minutes the showers would lift only to resume as soon as another cloud front raced in from the sea.

Anthony awoke, feeling listless, his mouth dry as if stuffed with cotton wool. At least the tremors had disappeared, as had his headache. He stumbled out of the bunk into the galley and switched on the spill-proof urn, coffee foremost in his mind. A look out of the cockpit screen revealed the wind-bent trees and the driving rain. He realised that the weather still did not permit a take-off.

At about midday the others returned from their night out. They were drenched by the time they entered the aircraft. The wind no longer blew a gale and, although the rain still fell, it had decreased in force, now no more than a normal thunder shower.

'I believe that by early evening we may be able to get away from here, God willing,' Doyle remarked, helping himself to hot water, which he added to a large cup containing instant coffee and sugar.

'I'm sure I saw two men approaching the aircraft from the fence late last night. I stepped out into the rain to tell those legionnaires that I'd seen them but they did not appear to take me seriously. I had the impression that they thought I was seeing things,' Anthony said, feeling compelled to tell the others.

'People out there in this shitty weather?' David's surprise was evident.

'Christ, I saw them,' Anthony replied with conviction, clearly unhappy that they should question him. 'You chaps left me here to look after the plane. Well, that's exactly what I did!'

'Okay, we'll wait until the rain lets up. We'll give the aircraft a thorough going over, see if everything's all right, both inside and outside.' Doyle said with condescension.

By early afternoon the weather had abated. The wind now only a strong breeze and although it was still overcast, the rain had been reduced to patches of drizzle.

From the maintenance hangar, David had been able to scrounge a mobile mechanic's stairway with an elevated platform specifically designed for working on aircraft, which they now used to carefully inspect the plane, starting at the nose wheel and then moved slowly clockwise around the aircraft.

David climbed the stairs to the propeller hub of the starboard outer engine. Bits of branch, bark and leaves had lodged in the nacelle and cooling fins of one of the engine cylinders. He removed some twigs and then looked into the bottom of the nacelle, immediately seeing a square black satchel no larger than a small shoebox. He knew that this had not been lodged there by the wind.

'Doyle! Come and look at this.'

Doyle stood on the apron next to the aircraft. From David's animated gestures, he realised that something significant was going on. As he approached the bottom of the ladder and saw what David held in his hands, he felt a shudder pass through him.

'Fuckin' hell! That's an explosives satchel. It's the damn British. They must be here. How's that possible? Just be bloody careful with that. Who knows when it's due to go up.'

Gingerly, David descended the ladder. He knew little about explosives. Doyle took it from him and opened the satchel, seeing the timer was wired to the detonator which had been inserted in the Semtex. He saw that the timer still had eight hours to run.

'Christ!' he whispered. 'Those bloody bastards. They were planning to blow us up while we were in the air. Probably hoped this would have been over the bloody ocean. No evidence. Victims of the cyclone or something.'

By this time, Gisela and Anthony had arrived, curious as to the commotion.

Gisela saw the satchel. She squinted at them, angry, in recognition of the possible danger.

'We would have all died,' Gisela whispered.

'Even if we had managed to ditch the aircraft, nobody would have found us, what with the false flight plan that's been filed. We would've been shark bait,' David said.

Everyone realised that this was no longer a game or a gentleman's war. It was a serious business and the British were about to stop the Rhodesians no matter what it took.

Gisela put her hand out. 'Give me the explosives.'

David did so. She carefully opened the satchel and removed the primer from the Semtex. Then she removed the timer. David watched her studied nonchalance. Finished, she handed the putty-like lump of explosive to him.

'Gently break it up and strew it in the grass. Without a primer, it cannot explode, even if a flame is applied. We'll have to keep the timer. It is too large.'

'What are you going to do about this?' a distraught Anthony asked.

'What do you think? Nothing.' David continued, 'I can't go to the French. This will become an incident, and all that will happen is that they'll hold the aircraft and its cargo, including us, until they've got some clarity. That'll be the least that could happen; it could be worse. Keep searching. We fly out of here on schedule. We don't say a word. Do you hear?'

They agreed.

As soon as it was dark, the aircraft took off heading in a southerly direction towards Madagascar and Antanerivo. About fifty miles from the island, it turned west, heading towards the African continent. They had searched the aircraft thoroughly but still a slight feeling of apprehension remained, unsure if they had missed something. They maintained radio silence crossing into Mozambique and then Zambia, maintaining a height of ten thousand feet. Only in Rhodesian airspace did they contact Salisbury on the special frequency Doyle provided.

The aircraft touched down just after three in the morning. A small reception party awaited them, a selected few aware of the purchase of the helicopters and the significance of what had been achieved. This was the first arms airlift of significance that had been undertaken. Many would follow.

CHAPTER 22

With a slight nod and subdued wave of her hand, Sir Harry's secretary indicated to Seymour that he could enter the office.

It was a dull day and although the curtains were open, Sir Harry had a desk light on, casting its pale light over his desk and illuminating his face in a manner, which made him look older than he was.

'Ah, Seymour, what can you tell me?' he said, laying down his pen and leaning back against the chair's backrest, his glasses perched on the bottom of his nose, squinting over the top.

'I'm afraid I've bad news. They got away. We planted a device on the plane but they must have discovered it. The chaps we sent from the Comoros reported that they were spotted, the legionnaires investigating. The plane flew out of Mayotte last night. Our agents tell me it has already landed in Salisbury. I'm sorry,' Seymour said, still standing in front of Sir Harry's desk.

'The Prime Minister will be unhappy. This damn Rhodesian business. Who'd ever have thought we would land up fighting our own kind again? Just keep the lid on the Mayotte incident. We don't want the French getting shirty. Christ! They would resent our Marines on their soil without their permission. Mayotte is a part of France.'

'No, we've got that under wraps, the French are not about to find out. Our chaps are already winging their way back to the Seychelles.'

'Thank God!' Sir Harry sighed. 'Now, how to stop the next shipment, hey?'

Sir Harry had a file in front of him on the desk. 'This banker, God knows what his name is, he has so many. Who is he?'

'We've been trying to find out. It seems he is the money man, or rather put this way, he sees to it that payment is made to the various suppliers. The bagman, as it were. We know he's been issued a Rhodesian passport, which he uses between South Africa and Rhodesia, but he's not Rhodesian, of that, I'm certain. I actually believe he is South African, but why he's working for the Rhodesians, I don't know.'

Sir Harry leant back. 'Hmm, well, it seems he can be anybody. Gracious me, he's quite a linguist. How many languages does he speak?'

'Four, it seems, and those fluently without a trace of an accent. Maybe his French is not quite up to scratch.'

'Of course, you know we've got to remove him, don't you. He's dangerous, worth his weight in gold to the Rhodesians, I would think.'

'I know,' Seymour replied quietly. Englishman killing Englishman. Why did it always come to this?

It was obvious that Sir Harry had said what he wished to say. It was now his problem.

Seymour returned to his office an hour later. He called his secretary in.

'Find Denton and Strathmore. I need to see them.'

For a moment she stood rooted to the floor, shock registering on her face. She knew who these men were. She loathed them.

CHAPTER 23

Unfortunately, the British were better prepared when the crude oil-laden *Deborah* approached the Mozambique Channel. She flew a Greek flag and was under the command of a Greek captain with a Greek crew. Oosterwijk had been unable to pull off another coup as he done with the *Georgio V*. From the outset, she was under British surveillance and, as she approached the Mozambique Channel, she was shadowed by a British frigate and destroyer. If she ignored a British command to heave to, the British were authorised to open fire. This was a new game. The Greek captain played the same card, as had Captain Le Clercq, insisting that the crude was destined for a Portuguese company in Beira. The British were not buying this; the captain was eventually forced to divert his tanker to Durban in South Africa. All eyes were now on South Africa. It was decided to leave the crude in the tanker, the ship berthed in the tanker dock, a picture of inactivity. The crew was reduced to a few men. It was a waiting game. The British kept it under constant surveillance. The South Africans made no attempt to discharge the crude.

Finally, the Rhodesians, owners of the cargo, realised that they had been thwarted. In turn, the South Africans knew they had no alternative but to obey the United Nations' directive. Months later, the news now old, the South Africans bought the cargo and pumped it to a nearby refinery in the Durban area.

The purchase of the vessel, as well as the buying of the crude on the high seas, had gone well. David and Oosterwijk in the Netherlands had done their job. The British were resolute. The crude never got to Rhodesia but then nor had the *Georgio V*'s crude been pumped through the pipeline to the Rhodesian refinery at Umtali. Rholon's board would not permit this. They had Wilson and the British Government on their necks, the consequences of doing so too risky. After all, they were business executives of the highest standing. Still, Ian Smith had thumbed his nose at Great Britain and got away with it. Captain Le Clercq was a hero and it was only by applying pressure that the more moderate members of the French government were able to keep President de Gaulle from any utterances, which would have only widened the rift between Great Britain and France.

****

David had now spent three months alternating between South Africa and Rhodesia. There were import and the few export transactions requiring his attention, but they were uncomplicated and easy to deal with compared to crude oil and helicopters. Gisela had returned to her ranch where David would occasionally visit. Neither of them had ever raised the question as to where their relationship was heading. It seemed that they agreed that the current situation, and in particular their work, was not an ideal environment to contemplate advancing beyond the relationship they now had.

Gisela spent every available moment on the farm. In fact, there were two farms. The smaller one was situated no more than twenty-five miles out of Salibury in the Sinoia district, given over to tobacco cultivation and dairy farming. The other was just over a hundred miles from Salisbury towards the Mozambique border, it with a herd of over six hundred cattle. The farm was divided into fenced camps to control cattle movement and to optimise grazing. Each camp had its own borehole, reservoir and cattle pens, these really small ranches within a large ranch. The farm was near thirty thousand acres in size and was run by the farm manager and his family, assisted by a number of black employees. Gisela's farmhouse was still the original house first built on the farm, now renovated and enlarged with a veranda along its one length with drop-down canvas awnings. This was generally referred to as the 'owner's house'. An assortment of rattan chairs, couches and matching coffee tables, complete with scatter cushions, transformed the veranda into a friendly, relaxing, family gathering area. A circular driveway bordered by flower and rose beds in full bloom led to the house. Tall trees and lush lawns completed the picture.

The manager's house, sheds and barns, and the other employees' abodes, were a good half a mile away, a stream flowing between them. A winding dirt road joined the two complexes. The employees' houses adjoined the huge cattle pens where the cattle were held awaiting transportation to the railhead and on to the abattoirs. These were practical and unostentatious. Those who occupied them never put down any roots, treating the houses as a place to stay until they moved on.

It was Friday and Gisela had invited him to the ranch for the weekend. He left his offices, which were situated in the Trade and Industry ministry building, and at five drove to the Charles Prince Airport situated on the outskirts of Salisbury. At the flying club, he changed into clothing that was more suitable: shorts and a loose cotton shirt.

He threw his weekend tote bag behind the two seats of the Cessna 150 aircraft, securing it with a strap. Soon the aircraft gained speed down the runway. He gently eased her into the air, the airspeed indicator hovering between sixty and seventy knots as it slowly climbed, pointing the aircraft in the direction of the Centenary area. It had been a hot day and the small aircraft bucked in the near-ground turbulence. He levelled out just a thousand feet above the ground, the aircraft eventually settling down to a smooth flight. Salisbury was surrounded by numerous farms and, from the air, these were a patchwork of squares each dotted with a house and outer buildings, all joined by roads. As the distance from Salisbury increased so did the farms gain in size, the cultivated fields less numerous and the expanses of virgin bush far larger.

The picture tranquillity below belied the murmurs of dissatisfaction and underlying tensions that emanated from the indigenous population. African nationalism was the new catchphrase. To the north and east, the yokes of colonialism had already been cast off. To the east, Bechuanaland was now an independent Botswana; and Northern Rhodesia, an independent Zambia. Freedom was the rallying cry, most believing this to be the road to wealth and prosperity, an opportunity to be the masters of their own destiny. Already the tentacles of fear had invaded the farming community, ever since a ZANU terrorist squad had crossed the border and carried out night attacks on a few homesteads, killing farmers in their beds. The Rhodesian security forces had immediately responded, mounting an extremely successful pursuit-and-destroy operation, but all knew that this would not deter the nationalists, referred to as 'terrs'.

The sun was low on the horizon, casting its last yellow-orange hue over the bush, the shadows long as the aircraft approached the farm strip. The wheels touched with a puff of dust, David taxiing towards the three people waiting for him at the end of the strip where a small corrugated-iron hangar had been built. Gisela was waiting with two servants. They embraced, sharing a short passionate kiss. She had an HK MP-54 submachine gun slung over her shoulder. She ordered the servant to collect his bag while he retrieved his HK from the aircraft's passenger seat. The servants helped push the aircraft into the hangar, securing the sliding doors, after which they all piled into the open Land Rover for the short drive back to the homestead.

She drove at a fair speed, the vehicle trailing a cloud of dust. Although it was now dusk, she had a pair of sunglasses perched on her nose, her now-blonde hair streaming behind her in the wind. The few weeks in the African sun had worked wonders. Her long legs were tanned, as was her bare midriff, the blouse she wore tied in a knot below her breasts. She wore a pair of white shorts, but good sense had prevailed and her feet were shod in a pair of suede leather hiking boots.

'So, how are things?' he asked.

'Great, but better now that you are here,' she half-shouted above the noise of the Land Rover, a naughty grin on her face.

He looked down at the machine pistol.

'The police said we were not to go anywhere without a weapon. I see you have yours as well. That's sensible. Things are a little hairy at the moment,' she said, reading his mind. Of course, he had read and heard about the attacks in the Centenary district.

If the homestead cast an aura of opulence from the outside, this was no match for the interior. The floors of both the lounge and adjoining dining room were of polished teak, as was the heavy and elaborately-carved furniture. Paintings of African bush scenes and the indigenous people adorned the walls. A well-stocked bar took up one wall and, next to it, a cabinet complete with locks and armoured glass contained a variety of exquisite hunting weapons. He knew that these had previously belonged to her husband.

She poured drinks while he freshened up and they retired to the veranda. A black servant already had a fire going in the barbecue built into the wall. Two huge steaks on a board covered by a square of white muslin could be seen. His mouth watering, he realised how hungry he was. He sat down on a sofa, Gisela sitting next to him, snuggling up close, placing a hand on his bare thigh, his leg jerking involuntarily. Both HK's were on the floor next to them.

'Have you heard of any terrorists near the farm?' he asked.

'I hope the police find and kill the whole lot of them.'

He was quite taken aback by the hatred and vehemence she displayed. It seemed abnormal.

'I suppose you're right,' he replied, 'but I must admit that given my intelligence and were I in the same position as these blacks, I'd probably also be hell-bent on killing you. '

Her face registered her surprise. 'Really? Are you suggesting anything else?'

'Not at all, but I think we need to be aware of something. These people are never going to give up. All this talk about Communists, Russians and Chinese, they really have nothing to do with this. They just help and supply weapons. These blacks, like the rest in Africa, just want to be free of the white man. We both know we are not going to stop them. Yes, we may for a while contain the situation, but stop? No, never. It's not just Rhodesia. Watch, the same is going to happen in South Africa.'

They had been up this road before. The argument was going to lead nowhere.

'But you fight them. Why, if that's what you think?'

He couldn't help smiling.

'That's because I'm stupid.'

'What the hell's that suppose to mean?'

'I'm like everybody else here. I don't want to change. I like what I've got.' He then added as an afterthought, 'Change will come at a price. They want what we've got and they will take it. Just as the Russians did when they captured Berlin. '

She thought the comparison strange but knew what he meant. It was a sobering thought.

The sound and smell of seared sizzling meat wafted through the veranda. Dinner was about to be served. Two servants had laid a small table covered by a white linen cloth, complete with wine glasses and candle sticks. An ice bucket containing an ice-cold, dry white wine stood on a small stand next to the table.

'I thought we would have a romantic dinner. Hope you don't mind the white wine. It's too hot for red,' she said, touching his arm and indicating the bucket.

The last remnants of the day disappeared as he sat down. He heard a generator start up in the distance, then the house's security lights suddenly bathed the entire lawn for about a hundred yards in the distance in stark white electric light from its eaves. She saw his surprise.

'I had this done straight after they murdered the Oberholzer family.'

'Do you leave this on all night?'

'No, I can switch it off from the bedroom. There are special motion sensors around the house which, when activated, will start up the generator.'

He nodded.

CHAPTER 24

He lay awake, his eyes open. Something had woken him. He lay naked beneath the bed sheet, as did she. They had fallen asleep after their lovemaking. She still slept. A tiny red light blinked on the bedside table next to her. He listened intently. Something bothered him and then he realised what – the insects in the nearby vicinity of the house were quiet. Had that woken him?

He gently shook her. As she woke, he gently placed his hand over her month issuing a faint 'shh'.

'What is it?'

'I don't know,' he whispered, 'Why is that red light blinking?'

'Jesus, that's an outer perimeter detector. It doesn't activate the generator, but whatever activated it is not small,' she said, already feeling for the machine pistols on the floor next to the bed.

He saw a faint shadow flick across the wall opposite the huge open window, the curtains drawn except for an opening a foot or so wide.

He grabbed her by the arm and dragged her towards him.

'Come. Get out of the room.' They had already had found their weapons. He pulled her as she slid across the bed on her backside, her feet groping for the floor. He realised he must be hurting her, his grip so tight on her arm but he was relentless, dragging her off the bed and through the open door into the passage.

The generator, why had it not started?

Suddenly the curtain billowed inward followed by a loud thump and then the sound of something rolling on the wooden floor. In a flash, he realised what it was.

'Down!' he shouted, dragging her to the floor and flinging himself on top of her.

The explosion was gigantic in the confined space of the bedroom, the shockwave lifting them both off the floor and flinging them back a few feet. The air was knocked from his lungs, his vision and hearing distorted, the dust thick in the passageway. Very faintly, he could hear her say something. His hearing had yet to return. Rifle fire, that's what it was, realising that somebody was spraying the room from the window.

Miraculously still grasping the machine pistol, instinct took over. He slipped the safety and cocked the weapon in one smooth motion while crawling to the door, barely seeing the outline in the dust. The grenade had set something alight in the bedroom. He stuck the muzzle around the corner and pulled the trigger. The HK bucked in his hands as he wildly swept the room with the burst, hardly hearing the racket.

He crawled back to where she lay, reaching out to touch her. The moment his fingers closed on her, she sidled to him. With every second, his hearing improved. Now he could pick up gunfire in the distance followed by another explosion. Suddenly there was light, not much as this appeared to come from outside through the windows. He realised that the generator must have started up, as the security lights were now on. Dust still swirled in the passageway. He looked at Gisela. Although shocked and covered in dust, she appeared unhurt. Both of them were still completely naked. He heard more shots, these single shots fired from an automatic rifle. He also heard the sound of a vehicle engine. From the passage, he ran into an adjoining room to peer over the windowsill. The lawns were bathed in light. It dawned on him that with the security lights on, nobody from outside could look into the house, they would be blinded by the lights. He saw three men standing on the lawn, rifles in their hands. The AKs in their hands confirmed that they had to be terrorists. Gisela now stood next to him, also looking out.

She tapped him on the arm pointing towards the trio.

'Look!' he heard her say.

What's it?' he said, hardly hearing his voice.

'God, it's Jeremiah, the houseboy.'

Gisela grabbed a sheet off the bed in the room and wrapped herself in it. The towels, which had been laid out on the bed, now lay on the floor. He picked up a bath towel and put this round his waist. They had only one HK pistol between them. The other had been lost with the grenade explosion. Gisela disappeared from the room only to appear seconds later clutching a hunting rifle with a fitted telescopic sight. She worked the bolt action and he heard the cartridge slam into the breech.

The vehicle still approached although it was still not in sight. He thought it came from the sprawl of houses occupied by the management. The terrorists also heard the vehicle and took up position behind the trees, their weapons at the ready. Seconds later another two terrorists appeared gesturing to the trio, clearly indicating that the others were to follow. They promptly obeyed, running away from the house. Out of the corner of his eye, he saw Gisela lift the rifle and take aim. With a crack, the rifle jumped in her hands, she immediately worked the bolt action, the spent cartridge spinning into the darkness and clattering to the floor. He saw one of the fleeing men stop and fling both arms into the air and then fall backwards to the ground. By then, the others had disappeared in the darkness. Using the HK at that distance would have been a futile effort.

Gisela's mouth was a thin line and pure hatred burned in her eyes. For a fleeting moment, he saw another person, somebody he did not know at all. Aware of an inner jolt of bewilderment, he did not know this strange woman wrapped in a towel.

'That was Jeremiah, the houseboy. I had to kill the bastard. He was untrustworthy.' She spat and then sunk to the floor turning, her back against the wall below the windowsill, her knees drawn up, her head bent between her legs. She started to cry.

Her revelation shocked him to the core.

A Toyota pickup swung into the driveway, skidding to a halt in front of the entrance to the house. Two men alighted, one black, one white both carrying FN rifles. David recognised them, the white man the farm manager, an Afrikaner named Botha, known as Kallie, and the other was Joseph, his overseer. Kallie saw David at the window and came running over.

'Are you all right?' he asked, taking in the fact that he was half-naked.

'We're all right. The main bedroom's a mess. They tossed a grenade through the window. Fortunately, we were not in the room.'

Kallie stared at him. David began to feel uncomfortable. Eventually, he dropped his eyes and looked towards the lawn seeing the houseboy sprawled on the grass.

'Christ! I see the bastards got Jeremiah.'

'Not true,' David hesitated for a second, 'We did. He was one of them. Have a look, you'll find his AK next to him.'

'Hell, aren't they full of surprises! The houseboy.' Botha shook his head in disbelief, 'He was a new recruit – has only worked here for a few months. He can't be more than seventeen, eighteen.' He turned his face away and spat at the ground, 'It just shows you, you can't trust these buggers – ever. We killed two of them. I reckon there were about twenty.

146

We lost none of our own. This was a real hit-and-run operation, but it seems they were after the owner. The BSAP are already on the way and by first light you'll see the first helicopters and trackers.'

'Where are they going to look for them?'

'Oh, they're running north for the Mozambique border. You can be sure of that. It's not too far, but they'll start here, pick up the spoor. Where's the lady?'

David turned to face the house looking for Gisela but couldn't see her.

'Look, we've had a bad time. Those terrs are not coming back. Mrs Mentz is a little overwrought. I'm going in. I'll see you in the morning,' David replied, suddenly feeling very tired and drained, conscious that he only had a towel wrapped around his waist.

'I understand. I'll keep the generator running till morning. Okay?'

'Fine, I'll see you in the morning.'

The two men climbed into the pickup, which roared off into the night, leaving a cloud of dust hanging in the air.

He returned to the house to find Gisela in the second bedroom still wrapped in the sheet, lying on the bed curled up in a fœtal position. He did not know quite how to handle the situation. She clearly was a woman of many facets and this recent display of unadulterated hatred left him with a feeling of unease. Sure, the terrs were the enemy but the hatred he had seen was an evil thing. It was not something that could ever be tempered, so intense that you could not reason with her. This is how it seemed to him.

He sat next her on the bed. 'Are you all right?' he asked, placing his hand on her shoulder. She jerked away from him and then rolled onto her other side leaving a space between them.

'Please, leave, I need to be alone for a while, she said without looking up, her voice muffled by the sheet, which she had drawn up to her face.

He was bewildered as this was so unlike her. He left the room. The passageway light still worked, providing sufficient light in the destroyed main bedroom enabling him to find most of his clothes and his bag. The grenade had ripped a massive hole into the wall where the window had been. Part of the wooden floor had collapsed, as had the ceiling. It was a mess. Dust covered everything.

He retreated to the lounge, heading straight for the bar where he poured a generous shot of whisky. He swallowed it in one gulp, the raw spirit burning his throat. He followed this with another. This seemed to clear his mind. Deciding it was best to leave her alone he showered and then collapsed onto the bed in the third adjoining bedroom. It took a while before he fell asleep. The last thing he saw was that hatred-distorted look on her face as she pulled the trigger.

He awoke to the *whap-whap* sound of an approaching helicopter. He quickly washed and dressed before stepping out on to the veranda. The helicopter had landed next to a few police vehicles, which had discharged a number of men, some with dogs on leashes. A BSAP police officer approached dressed in civilian clothes, followed by a black man in uniform.

They greeted each other after which the police officer opened with a barrage of questions, making notes in a small notebook. He noticed that the others had picked up the dead houseboy's body and rather unceremoniously loaded it into a closed van.

The men and dogs on the lawn dispersed, all heading in a northerly direction, evident that they had picked up some sort of trail.

'Good morning,' he heard and turned to find Gisela standing behind him dressed in a pair of jeans, which reached to just below her knees, and a light khaki shirt, hanging loosely over them. She had showered and appeared have recovered from the night's mayhem.

They exchanged greetings. She listened to the police officer's questions, letting David do the talking. It was only when the subject of the houseboy came up that she took part.

'Jeremiah, your houseboy, how long was he with you?' the officer asked.

'About three months or so,' she replied.

'Did he come recommended?'

'No, he just turned up here one day looking for work. He had a written reference from another farmer. He wanted to work nearer to his family whom, he said, lived nearby.'

'Presumably you checked?'

'Sorry, I didn't,' she replied, brushing a strand of her away from her face with a hand.

The officer's disappointment was evident. 'We have repeatedly requested that you farmers check and check again. You realise that your houseboy probably provided them with all the intelligence they needed to carry out this raid. You make our job exceedingly difficult,' the officer said, admonishment evident in his voice.

'I'm sorry.'

'Can't be undone. We've got to apprehend them so I'm off. Just keep an eye on things. They won't be back for a while.'

They returned to the helicopter, which took off in a northerly direction.

After the police's departure and notwithstanding the damaged main bedroom, the household returned to a semblance of normality. The house staff cleared the bedroom of everything still usable, after which a gang of workers started to clear the rubble and carry out repairs. They barricaded the end of the passageway, which led to the bedroom and adjoining bathroom, preventing entry from outside.

At about three that afternoon, two trucks and a pickup arrived. About twenty men disembarked, mostly blacks dressed in camouflage fatigues and all heavily armed. They immediately sought shade and water. A few remained with the vehicles. The police officer from the morning approached the porch where David and Gisela met him.

'We were rather successful. We caught up with them a few miles from here. A firefight ensued, most of them were killed. However, I have a few wounded and two uninjured in the truck. We need you to have a look at them and see if you can identify any of them,' he asked Gisela.

'Okay,' she said, nodding her head.

'Mrs Mentz, I need to point out that this is not a pretty sight, but it's necessary. Are you up to this?'

'I'm okay.'

They walked to the high-sided truck, David next to her. They had to climb on the steel structure affixed to the back of the truck that housed the rear lights and to which a huge tow-bar was fitted. They both peered over the top.

Gisela gasped. David winced, gritting his teeth. There were about a dozen bodies in the truck. Most appeared dead. It became clear that those who were bound were alive. They were trussed up with some sort of silver tape, their hands behind them, and their legs together. Their feet were bare. They sat with their backs against the side. They were dirty and covered in dust, their eyes mere black sockets with an occasional flash of white as they furtively looked around. Their expressions radiated abject fear, hardly aware that they were being appraised. The wounded were also bound, their white bandages stark against their black skin. The floor of the truck was smeared with blackened blood where the wounded had been dragged to the side. Attracted by the blood, the first flies buzzed around.

'Jesus Christ!' he exclaimed, his face screwed up in a picture of momentary torment, his teeth clenched.

She had closed her eyes and was looking away. She then faced forward and looked at the men with purpose, staring at each individually.

He was appalled by the carnage in the vehicle. It was clear the medical attention given to the occupants had been minimal. From the manner in which some bodies lay on the truck floor, he realised that the police had callously flung or dragged the dead and living into the truck. Clearly, those alive had been subjected to clubbing and beating, their lips and cheeks swollen, some with blood in their mouths.

'God, did they have to do that to the people?' he said in total disbelief, unable to contain his emotion.

She turned to him, he saw again the hatred in her eyes as he had that night. 'What the hell do you expect? They are murderers – they kill children. They would've killed you and me. These men should have been killed, not taken prisoner. God, I could shoot them myself,' she said, close to incoherent, her fists balled, her arms rigid and her eyes mere slits.

This sudden intense display of hatred that seemed to consume her dismayed him. It frightened him. He had thought he knew her well. Now suddenly, she was somebody he didn't know at all.

Kallie Botha and his overseer had arrived in the pickup, also standing on the bumper looking into the truck.

Unable to restrain himself, David blurted. 'God, they didn't have to treat them like this. We're not bloody animals. This is the type of thing the Nazis did.'

Botha stepped down from the bumper and mumbled something in Afrikaans. David understood.

'Listen to me, I'm not a bloody do-gooder or a kaffir-boetie, but what I am is human and what I just saw shouldn't be allowed to fuckin' happen.' David said, the corners of his mouth white with rage.

'You English are all the same. You just want to kiss their fuckin' arses.' Botha replied, a sneer on his face, unable to hide his contempt. He uttered some expletive in Afrikaans and shook his head in resignation as if to say he thought David beyond hope. There was nothing you could do with such a man. Thereafter Botha pointedly ignored David, as did the police officer. They both walked to one side, turning their backs to the others, talking earnestly. He realised that they had categorised him: no longer was he one of them; not an enemy, but certainly not a follower of the true cause.

Gisela had also stepped off the truck. She looked at him, shaking her head. She turned and retraced her steps to the house.

He was confused. Things had suddenly changed. He realised he was out of step with them. He didn't belong. Sure, he had helped but he was an outsider, not a Rhodesian, and that he would not be able to change no matter what he did. Yes, fundamentally, he thought as they did but somewhere they had crossed a line.

Other than the houseboy, they had recognised none of the dead and injured. A short while later, the police climbed into their vehicles and drove off.

CHAPTER 25

The black man cowered beneath the blackened canopy of the stunted thorn bush. Around him, the ground was burnt black, still smouldering in places. Only the trees revealed any green. Their canopies were out of reach of the flames and too wet to catch fire. As the wall of flame approached, he had been able to find a piece of open ground. He had tried to protect himself, bending over and wrapping his arms around himself. Still, his hands and face were blistered where the flames had touched those parts of his skin that had not been covered.

He still clutched his AK-47 rifle. Two taped-together magazines hung round his neck on a leather thong. Patches of his black hair were singed and a long gash on his forehead showed pink flesh, a bloodied fluid seeping from the wound. He was bewildered, terrified and witless.

When still across the Zambezi River in Zambia at the training camp, it had all sounded so easy. The black Communist instructor, the Komissar, had been adamant that the whites were not expecting any attack. They could literally cross and walk into the country undetected.

The black Rhodesians were relative newcomers to the emerging nationalistic movements and only recently had this begun to take on the form of an armed struggle. Military training was a new concept, the level of which was mediocre or virtually non-existent. Weapons were still difficult to come by and any training with live ammunition was not possible, as there simply was not enough ammunition to go round. Every day, they had simulated battle conditions using wooden rifles or those with rifles would do so without ammunition.

The battle plan was ill-conceived. The whites would not be expecting an attack so near to Salisbury. The farm was not guarded at night. They had crossed the border from Zambia four days ago, moving only at night and sleeping hidden in the densest bush during the day. He, his brother and seventeen others. Some had never even fired their rifles before they set out. In Mozambique at the training camp, no more than a clearing in the bush with a few huts situated in the remotest area of the country's western border, the Komissar had told them that this was their land, not the white man's, and that they needed to take it back. All Africa had awoken and it was just the Boers and the Rhodesians who refused to change.

The Komissar said that many other countries in Africa had been given back to the blacks and that most whites had left. They needed to show the Rhodesians that they could not ignore the black man and continue to treat them no better than slaves.

Jeremiah, his youngest brother, had found a job as a houseboy on the Mentz's farm a few months ago. Over time, he reconnoitred the area and provided them with the necessary information, which enabled them to approach the farm without detection.

He was overcome with grief. He had now lost two brothers, both killed by the whites. His youngest, Jeremiah, had died in sight of the farmhouse, where they were forced to leave him. At the first sign of dawn the pursuit had started. Their trail was only hours old. The white man's dogs had quickly picked up the fresh scent. The police seemed to know in which direction they were heading. Suddenly, they found their flight blocked by a wall of flame. The police had set the bush on fire, the flames driven towards them by the wind. In the ensuing panic, the police emerged from the bush and, finding them, immediately opened fire. Many of his comrades had thrown down their weapons and raised their hands. The police ignored this sign of surrender and, despite the dead on the ground, continued to shoot. He had hidden in a tangle of burnt roots and branches, the fire deadening his scent, the dogs not finding him. He still dare not move, he had to wait for darkness.

The sun was low on the horizon by the time the police seemed to have left. Nor could he hear the helicopter.

CHAPTER 26

It was Sunday. Gisela had persuaded him not to return to Salisbury until Monday morning. He could take off at first light and still arrive in time at his office.

She knew that in the last forty-eight hours their relationship had undergone a subtle change. Yes, she still loved him dearly and wished him continuously close to her but now, when she looked at him, he seemed not to be quite the man she thought she knew. She was vaguely uncomfortable. It was as if something she cherished deeply had been taken from her. The feeling frightened her. She had tried to discuss the episode with the prisoners and Botha's vicious remarks, but he shied away. All he said was that he thought the Rhodesian outlook naïve and that events in the world would overtake them. They needed to realise that they lived in a doomed era. He said he thought it imperative that they prepare for change, in other words, prepare themselves to eventually succumb to majority rule. There was, in his opinion, no other way of putting it. History would repeat itself were his last words. She could not do that. Such a concept was unacceptable. She said so. He just shrugged his shoulders and when she tried to raise the issue of the shooting of the terrorists, he curtly demanded that she leave it alone and walked out of the house.

Tradition had it that the farm manager and his wife joined the owner for dinner every Sunday night. Her late husband had religiously upheld the tradition and, after his death, she continued to do so.

The evenings still warm, they decided to have the dinner at a long table on the porch.

The Bothas arrived in their pickup at seven, He was a big man, broad-shouldered, standing a good six feet three with powerful arms. He arrived dressed in khaki shorts and bush boots, highly polished for the occasion. He was South African born and had grown up in the Western Transvaal, the most conservative of areas with strong Calvinistic traditions and beliefs. He possessed an agricultural degree from the University of Potchefstroom. His dress and attitude belied the fact that he was an intellectual, an educated man, a member of the Afrikaner elite, who had chosen Rhodesia to be his home.

Gisela introduced Botha's wife. Her name was Petronella. She barely spoke English, but told them in English with a strong Afrikaans accent, that she was rapidly learning. She was a beautiful woman, but this was disguised, her dress and makeup subdued as it befitted her background.

The happenings of the previous night and day still tainted the atmosphere around the table, evident in the behaviour of the diners: there was a definite tension. Concerned by the events of the last two days, David had drunk too much and by the time he sat down at the table, he was already on his fifth Black Label and soda. The women merely sipped their wine, talking about those matters that relate mainly to women.

Kallie had a few beers before dinner and once seated settled for a bottle of Beaujolais. The two men had pointedly ignored one another but were now seated opposite each other. With the women earnestly in conversation, they could not continue to do so without drawing attention to it.

Kallie looked up at David.

'Look, I just want to apologise for my remark on Friday. Things were a bit tense out there. I'm sorry.'

David took the cue. 'It's okay. I was also a bit overwrought. Christ, one doesn't get to see death like that. It's a shocker' This sadistic bastard, he thought; does the man think that this was no more than an organised hunt for vermin that plagued the farm? He was not about to forget the blood, gore and broken bodies and how they had been unceremoniously dumped on the truck.

Kallie held up his glass.

For a second he was at loss as to what the man was getting at. Suddenly it dawned on him what the man wanted. What could he do? He raised his, they chinking the glasses together.

'Is alles reg?' Kallie asked in Afrikaans, a questioning look on his face, clear the man wished to make peace.

He had no alternative. He nodded in agreement. Yes, all was well. Maybe there was some good in the gesture. He felt better now that the ice had been broken. This had not gone unnoticed. Both the women saw the exchange. Gisela smiled at David, clearly happy with developments.

'Do you mind talking about this?' the Afrikaner asked.

'Not at all.' What did he want to say now?

'You know I'm Afrikaans and I probably can trace my family back to near the days when Van Riebeeck landed in the Cape in the 1650s.' He hesitated for a moment and then continued, 'Please, I don't want to leave you with any misconceptions. I've nothing against the blacks but, unlike the English, I don't have a home other than this one and you must understand, I just cannot conceive myself just handing this over. Where do I go with my wife and children?'

'You must stay. A new South Africa or Rhodesia will need people like you.'

'That's what they all say. I say, give them the country and they'll force us out,' Kallie replied sceptically, David's remark just washing over him.

David felt that he had to make a point. They needed to know where he stood.

'The situation is difficult and I understand your concerns and those are mine as well. You know I'm also a South African. We are not the problem. The Communists are. The West is reluctant to arm what they conceive to be a terrorist movement. They want to follow the route of diplomacy. However, Russia and China see an opportunity. They exploit these black nationalists, providing them with everything the West won't give them – the ability to make war. They feed them a new ideology, weapons and advisers. That's where the problem lies. The Communists are after an African continent with a distinct Marxist flavour. Christ! Just look at Africa, it's already heading that way.'

'Of course, you know that if Rhodesia goes then there eventually goes South Africa. It cannot stand alone,' Kallie said ruefully.

'Kallie, for God's sake, South Africa will change. Sure, it may take fifty years but change it will. Surely, you must realise this.'

'Well, as long as it doesn't happen in my lifetime,' he replied with the scorn a white man feels for his lesser black minions.

A raw nerve had been touched. Gisela had caught the last part of their conversation.

'Please let's discuss something more pleasant.'

They finished the meal in relative silence, their comments confined to everything but the recent events.

That night, they made love but it seemed that this was borne out of sheer desperation. It was as if they wanted to mend the divide that had crept into their relationship. Still, their passion was physically fierce. Afterwards, they clung to each other, their bodies slick with sweat, their hair damp and

156

they gasping for breath. Not once had he said that he loved her. For the first time, she realised that she did not entirely have him, that some part of him just was not there, and she was excluded from it. It was as if their relationship had become a trial affair. He was no longer committed to the relationship.

CHAPTER 27

This was not a densely populated area, still there was the odd village, at intervals of a few miles, each containing a score or more people. Invariably fires burnt amongst the huts, he was able to see them flickering in the distance. He dared not approach. For hours, he had craved water, his mouth dry, and his tongue sticking to the roof of his mouth. Fortunately, near one of the villages he saw a cattle trough, fed by water from a small spring on a hillock. He climbed some way up the hill, collapsing on the bank of the stream, drawing the fresh cool water into his mouth. He lay there for a while listening to the voices and shouts that drifted up from the village. It sounded tranquil and peaceful. He was acutely aware of the sound of children's happy voices. It was so far removed from his own personal predicament, his brothers being killed and his fleeing for his life. Had he really done the right thing?

He was twenty-three years old. He was born in a small village near Mount Darwin, the eldest of seven children. His father was the village headman, a proud, headstrong member of the Shona tribe. His childhood had not been easy. They existed just above the poverty line, growing their own food, and tending their own livestock, but it had been a happy and carefree life. He had the privilege of being the eldest, supported by a wonderful doting mother and a proud, but stern, father. Their village was situated near the Karanda Mission station run by the Evangelical Alliance Mission. He had attended the missionary school from an early age and was one of the few who graduated, the only black in the district with an A-Level certificate – not the best marks, but they still constituted an acceptable pass. His father's efforts to get him admitted to university had been unsuccessful. His ambition was to be a doctor though this was not to be. They blamed the whites. White school-leavers were freely admitted although their marks were lower than his. It was clear to him that it was the colour of his skin which barred him from a better education. He was disillusioned and embittered. His father saw it differently. This was life. You could not always have what you wanted. These things happened, he had said resignedly on more than one occasion. For Sizwe, this was neither good enough nor acceptable.

He had heard that the emerging black national movements now outlawed from Rhodesia offered a university education to those who possessed the necessary qualifications and who joined their ranks. He had never been political but if he had to be so to further his education, then he would be. He had crossed the border into Zambia and presented himself to the offices of ZANU in Lusaka. He received a warm welcome, this infusing him with a new sense of belonging. Little did he realise that ZANU was about to embark on a rolling subversive military campaign against the Smith government of Rhodesia. All those young men who willingly joined, as well as those press-ganged into the parties ranks, were given very basic military training. Their purpose was to kill the white farmers, mine their roads, blow up bridges and pipelines, and so disrupt the Rhodesian economy. This had been his first incursion into Rhodesia.

He continued along the road, twice having to disappear into the bush at the approach of a vehicle. These were pickup trucks filled with blacks. He never saw any whites or police. He had left his rifle at the scene of the skirmish where he had also disposed of his ration packs and water bottle. To be caught armed could mean torture and death. He was dressed in civilian clothes, which were torn and dirty, although he had tried to clean himself up as best as he could.

The loss of his brothers left him numb and dejected. The emerging hate for the white man and the Ian Smith government threatened to mentally overwhelm him. It was not the manner in which they had died, it was the loss itself. He would have summarily killed any white had they captured them, even if this included women and children. His Komissar was emphatic: all should be killed; no prisoners were to be taken, as this would send a strong message – a bolt of fear through the white population.

The team had agreed on a rendezvous point along the banks of the Zambezi River. It took him four days of walking at night to get there. There was no sign of the police. It seemed they were under the impression that they had killed or captured all the insurgents who had been part of the raid.

He stood on the bank looking down at the body of slow-moving water, the sole survivor. He was weak, having eaten little more than a few raw corn cobs stolen from a village.

They had used wooden flat-bottomed boats to cross the river. The river was not particularly wide at this point, only a hundred yards or so. Huge trees lined the riverbanks, the bush in close proximity to the water, near impenetrable. The boats were pulled up on the riverbank, hidden under cut-down thorn bushes. He found these in the early hour of the morning just as the first light of day began to flood the Bushveld. An attempt to cross the river by day would be foolhardy. He would wait until nightfall.

While he wished to cross the river as soon as possible, he anticipated the eventual confrontation with his ZANU superior with mounting anxiety. They were harsh and cruel people who considered failure traitorous and it was quietly rumoured amongst the comrades that they tortured and killed those who had failed the cause. He was the only survivor. Had he failed the cause?

He was in acute pain. Most of his blisters had burst, now weeping a pink liquid with blood, the first signs of infection visible.

He knew the position of a small base established across the river in Zambia. It was from here that the raid had been launched and orders were that they were to return to that camp. That night he pushed a boat into the water. The task was difficult, the boat heavy and he weak and in excruciating pain. Kneeling in the prow of the boat, he slowly paddled across the dark water.

The boat had barely grounded when men emerged from the thickets. They waded into the water and grabbed the gunwales, dragging the boat up the embankment. Willing hands grabbed him and guided him out of the boat. They placed him on a stretcher and carried him along a trail through the bush. He was hardly aware of his surroundings, exhausted to a near-blackout and in acute pain. Two men walked on each side of him, one holding his hand. An indescribable sense of relief overcame him. He had made it. He had survived.

The hospital facilities at the base camp were primitive, no more than a building constructed of ugly ash brick with a corrugated iron roof. There was no ceiling or windows, just holes in the walls. Only a medical orderly served the medical station. There was no doctor. Nonetheless, the man did the best he could, inserting a saline drip, cleaning the blisters and applying an antibiotic powder. The orderly had also administered an injection to alleviate the pain. By the second day they considered him sufficiently recovered to travel and placed him a on a stretcher which they slid onto the back of a pickup truck. They left for Lusaka with the medical orderly in attendance.

Things were a lot better organised in Lusaka. They summoned a civilian doctor who replaced his dressings and gave him an antibiotic injection. They had assigned a black nurse, presumably one of their own people, to look after him. Once he had settled in, they told him that Joshua Nkomo would see him the next day.

He jerked inwardly at the sound of the name, a feeling of fear washed over him. Nkomo was the current leader of the ZANU movement, an astute man who fearlessly took on the forces of the Rhodesian government. He was the thorn in Ian Smith's side and had repeatedly avoided capture. He had successfully mobilised the black masses against the Smith regime. They said he was ruthless, with little compassion for the weak.

Nkomo was a big man. His face sat on a square neck, as wide as his ample, flabby cheeks. He stood over six feet and weighed well in excess of two hundred pounds. He was dressed in quill khaki trousers with a matching shirt. In his hand, he held an ornate flywhisk made of wood with long ox-tail hairs protruding from the end, which he continuously whisked around him, more out of habit than to dispel any flies. Beady eyes peered through rolls of fat. He perspired profusely, sweat beading visibly on his brow and cheeks, the faint acrid smell discernible through the man's deodorant. He stood next to Sizwe's bed surrounded by two of his aides, the three men towering over the prone man.

'We mourn the loss of your two brothers and the death of the others. They are true heroes of the cause, but you are the first living hero. Your attack has sent a ripple of shock through the white population and awakened a feeling of resolution in our own people. It is in all the newspapers. Our people have realised that we are no longer just a threat. We are now a reality the whites will have to reckon with.' Nkomo paused for a moment, seemingly appraising the young man before him. 'We have no medals to give you and, yes, you are young. Still, what you have done cannot go unrewarded. Be proud, you have just been earmarked for proper officer training. Every Shona and Ndebele salutes you. Thank you.'

Sizwe was flabbergasted, not sure that he heard correctly.

'Thank you,' was all he whispered. A candidate officer, what did that mean?

'Is there anything I can do for you?' Nkomo asked.

'Yes, I'd like to study medicine at a university,' he whispered.

A shadow of annoyance swept over Nkomo's face.

'That later,' he retorted with barely concealed irritation, 'we will look into that, but for now we must fight on and free ourselves from the yoke of colonialism. The whites don't want to do this peacefully, so we have no alternative but to resort to force. For all whites – men, women and children – we must make our country unsafe until they relent and free us or until we overrun the country and take control,' Nkomo said, his vehemence so intense a droplet of spittle appeared at the corner of his mouth.

Sizwe made no reply.

The imposing man seemed to recollect himself. 'Again, we thank you, Comrade Sybonga, our medical people will look after you, and when you have recovered I will call for you.'

CHAPTER 28

David arrived back at the office to find Doyle waiting for him. The mere sight of the man left him with a feeling of foreboding. He was not one to bring glad tidings.

After exchanging perfunctory greetings, David asked, 'What brings you here? I thought you the proverbial "Elusive Pimpernel", never to be seen again, or so at least I hoped!'

Doyle laughed. 'When would I ever go forth and do battle with the English without Lord Tusk at my side?'

His feelings of apprehension were spot on. He looked at the large man in front of him. Christ, he thought, the bastard actually enjoys his job. 'You know my sentiments. I wish I had never met you!'

Again the man laughed, brushing David's protestations aside. He was dressed in a suit, which seemed out of character, most of the men opting for something more comfortable in the oppressive summer heat. 'Come, David,' he beckoned, 'let's find somewhere secure where we can talk. I've others who will be joining us.'

They retired to one of the many mini boardrooms, David ordering coffee from the tea girl on the floor.

Just as they sat down, Anthony Gainsborough entered with John Taylor in tow. David's heart sank. Something big had to be afoot, of that he was certain. Taylor had not changed. He would always remain the bureaucratic lackey that he was, a civil servant to the core, dour and not prone to laughter; everything was serious. In contrast, Tony's face beamed at seeing David. The man had undergone a metamorphism; he radiated a picture of heath. He had gained weight, not fat but muscle tone. The pilot had obviously being doing some serious exercising, David thought.

'Jesus, Tony, who are you trying to emulate? You look a damn sight better than two months ago.'

'Bond, James Bond,' Tony replied jokingly with a smile. 'I've got the job but not yet the physique, but I'm trying.'

Everybody laughed. The latest James Bond film, *Thunderball*, opened almost ten months ago, but Bond's effect on the people was still profound.

163

Hardly had the film had its premiere in Leicester Square, London, when it was showing in Salisbury. Truly, the Rhodesians' ingenuity knew no bounds.

'No, I just gave up drinking, or rather I only do so in moderation, you know, only beer. I've also been exercising.'

'Good for you.'

Everybody sat down, the initial joviality disappearing. 'David, we need you again,' Doyle quietly said.

David shook his head. 'C'mon guys, this is not for me. This is really not my fight. You should know that by now. It's also not my game!'

'Sorry, friend. Nobody speaks the lingo as you do. German, French. You know Europe, you know aircraft, and you are a legitimate foreigner.'

'That means fuck all. I mean, there must be others who fit the bill?' He simply could not dispel the feeling of dread that had manifested itself.

'Christ, David! We need you,' John Taylor said. 'We simply can't do this without you.'

'Why not?'

'We have managed to ship the remaining Alouettes out of France in crates by sea to Lebanon. They can't leave the country before we pay. Hiram has paid the French but we have to pay him. He won't deal with anyone else except you. He's adamant. He's not about to give the Alouettes to us on credit!'

'Listen, I'm not flying any aircraft loaded with these helicopters,' he said with growing frustration.

'No, you don't have to, Tony and his men will do that. Just look after the payment for us. We may have to make two or three payments.'

'Two or three! Christ, that's madness, making just the one is dangerous enough. The Brits have learnt. They're wide-awake now. What's the problem?' David complained.

Doyle fished a packet of cigarettes out of his suit pocket and proceeded to light up. 'Like I said before. We've got a leak. MI6 has descended on Beirut in force. They've got at least ten operatives in the city. I won't say they're all waiting for us, but some must be.'

David sat back in his chair and looked up at the ceiling, his face an expression of resignation. 'What are you sending me on, a suicide mission? Well, that's reason enough not to go there at all.'

'Just hang on,' Doyle interrupted, waving his protestations aside. 'As I said, no flying all over the place, nothing like that. Just meet and pay

Hiram, that's all. I know that this sounds like we are asking you, but actually you're being ordered. You know that anyway,' he said, turning his palms up in a gesture of resignation.

He knew that, strictly speaking, Doyle was right. He was a member of the military and an officer to boot, not that he believed they would ever really order him to do so. They would rather that he 'volunteered'.

'Okay, give me some background. How's this going to be done?' he sighed.

'Good boy. We've still got a whack of German passports, which Mrs Mentz got from God knows where. These haven't been used at all. Secondly, Siemens, you know, the telecommunications people, recently sold a host of new telephone exchanges to the Lebanese government. Apparently they've gone for a total overhaul of the system, a one- to two-year job. You will be a legitimate member of the Siemens task team. So will Mrs Mentz.'

'Gisela is going?' he asked, unable to hide his surprise.

'Yes.'

'In fact, we've gone one better. Siemens took over a hotel on the Beirut beachfront to accommodate their staff. You will have rooms in the hotel. A private French firm is handling the security. No British agent or anybody else is going to simply walk in.'

'What do you know about all these MI6 operatives, why so many?'

'We don't know, but what we do know is that they have Hiram under observation around the clock. He told us himself. He says you need to be careful. It's a "don't call me, I'll call you" situation,' Doyle said.

Nobody said anything. Everyone waited.

Finally, Doyle exhaled. 'Look, man, they may know you're coming but as to what and when they don't know. Not even I know yet.'

David nodded, indicating that he understood.

'Okay,' he said with a long sigh. 'Let me first speak to Gisela.'

Doyle was right. It seemed the only aircraft he would fly on belonged to the airline that flew them to Europe.

Gisela had agreed without any hesitation. He realised that she considered this her patriotic duty, a sentiment he did not share. The wedge that the attack on the farm had driven between them still lingered, but their mutual physical attraction was still strong, he could feel it. They made love whenever the occasion presented itself. However, they never forgot that they did not share the same approach to the situation in Rhodesia and how this unfolded. Her stance was clear-cut. The dissidents were traitors and should be treated accordingly, while his perception was that that they were after what was rightfully theirs, which the white man withheld. At least they agreed that violence was not the answer. Certainly not violence supported by the Communists whose only objective was the spread of the communist ideology, an ideology he vigorously opposed. Certainly, he was opposed to torture and wanton killing.

Doyle had gone to great lengths to ensure that their arrival in Beirut would be as inconspicuous as possible. From Johannesburg, they had flown separately to Rome as South Africans. There they assumed their new identities as a married German couple staying in an obscure hotel on the outskirts of the city going through the normal tourist ritual, speaking only German and visiting the usual sights. After about a week, they boarded an aircraft in the livery of some budget holiday airline and flew to Nicosia, Cyprus, ostensibly for a three-day stay. On landing, they boarded a bus for Larnaca on the coast where they booked into one of the many hotels situated on the Promenade overlooking the yacht basin. The British still maintained a military presence in Cyprus.

He had to hand it to Doyle: the man had devised the most elaborate scheme to hide their true identities. Their arrival in Beirut in such a manner would completely fool the British. As they had been briefed, he and Gisela approached the Harbour Café, a restaurant on the old harbour wall, at just before nine-thirty. He was dressed in shorts and sandals, sporting sunglasses, hats and beach bags. They were the epitome of a German couple on holiday, his copy of the *Frankfurter Allgemeine Zeitung* newspaper under his arm. Already the European noveaux riches were beginning to make their presence felt in Cyprus, if the number of yachts moored in the basin was anything to go by. This attracted tourists from all over Europe. They blended in well with the others, many of whom were German. Who would ever believe that the Germans had just emerged from a world war which had devastated their entire country and economy?

They sauntered into the sidewalk café and took seats at a table that bordered the sidewalk, being as inconspicuous as possible. They ordered the continental breakfast, conversing in German, and then going through the pretence of having to make themselves understood in broken English, the waiter not understanding them at all.

The Harbour Café had been chosen as an ideal place to meet. It was a tourist landmark, many of the tourists from the yachts frequenting it for breakfast, sitting under the large umbrellas on the sidewalk and on the porch with a view over the basin. They were to rendezvous with another German couple. He kept a wary eye open. This was another of Doyle's 'we'll contact you plans'. The less he knew, the better. Or so it seemed.

'Look what we have here, it's the Brendels,' he heard behind him in German. He recognised the name Brendel, their new identity: Mr and Mrs Brendel.

He swung round to be confronted by a couple considerably older than he expected, the man grey and portly, dressed similarly to him, obviously also on holiday, but exuding an aura of wealth. What was remarkable was their tan. They obviously spent a great deal of time in the sun.

They greeted each other as old friends. He had been told that their names were Bernd and Ursula Hacker. She was the typical, slightly overweight, German hausfrau, a round face with rosy cheeks. Clearly, she did not tan easily. Her hair was short and grey. They were German but had lived in South Africa for years, he a successful industrialist who had accumulated a fortune in the structural steel business. Both were ardent yachtsmen and every year spent two to three months of the South African winter in the Mediterranean sailing the Greek islands. To all around, it appeared as if David had invited the couple to join them for breakfast. From the occasional greeting bestowed on the couple, he realised they were known to the locals, even the waiter recognised the newcomers, greeting them by name. The yacht anchored in the basin was their own, a forty-three foot, centre-cockpit rigged sloop – the *Felicity*.

David had wondered how Doyle had persuaded this couple to assist. Actually, they were still German citizens but had permanent South African residence status. From Doyle he had learnt that they had an only son in Bulawayo also with a steel structure business, originally financed by his father. In addition, what the Hackers were about to do was not illegal. All they had to do was keep their mouths shut.

There was nothing elaborate about the plan. They had kept their baggage to a minimum and, after breakfast, their bags were collected from the hotel and brought aboard the *Felicity*, which soon cast off its moorings and headed for the open sea. There was no record that the Hackers had ever left Cyprus. The harbour log would reveal that the yacht would be cruising around the island for a few days.

They arrived in Lebanon two days later in the late afternoon, just as the sun set over the sea. The Beirut harbour authorities had been contacted and had alerted the custom official at the Beirut Yacht Club. Their reception was perfunctory, the official merely glancing at their passports and handing them back noting that their stay in Beirut was for pleasure and that the yacht would depart in a few days' time. To further confuse any would-be followers, which David was sure they did not have, Peter Hacker rented an American Ford sedan in his name, using the vehicle to drive to the Meridian Hotel, which had been taken over by Siemens. Here they presented their Siemens security cards. What was surprising was that their arrival was expected and they were quickly whisked off to their room. It appeared that the Germans were being surprisingly helpful. He wondered whether Gisela had anything to do with this, but chose not to ask.

It was with a sigh of relief that David flung himself on the bed, his hands clasped behind his head looking at Gisela. She was strikingly beautiful, already displaying the first signs of a good tan which she had acquired on the yacht crossing the sea, accentuated by her blonde hair. They had arrived at the hotel in smart casual wear.

'I'm sure we've arrived unannounced. This gives us a distinct advantage,' he said.

'Be careful, they're watching Hiram. That's where the problem lies. If that telephone number you've got is tapped. Well, that's that,' she replied clicking her fingers.

'I can't see the British arranging a wiretap in Beirut,' he replied, dismissing the notion.

Both had refrained from discussing their individual stance on the bush war in Rhodesia. For her, it was no big deal. That he did not entirely share her view never bothered her. She loved him and was appreciative of what he was doing for her new country, which had given her so much, even if this was because of her marriage. She was sure that her late husband would have approved of David, in many ways the two men were similar. For David, it was not that simple. When it came to fighting, there was nothing effeminate about her. The woman was possessed of a degree of bravery and resolve which was astounding. These attributes coupled with her stunning beauty made for a formidable foe, and when she displayed the hate that she felt for her place of birth, East Germany, the Stasi and the Communists, which included the terrorists, this could be frightening and intense. She was Boadicea ready to do battle with the Romans and would spare them no quarter. It was then that he found her a stranger. Yes, the rift had narrowed but it still was ever-present.

David had committed the contact telephone number to memory. His instructions were to phone immediately on arrival and, in French, ask for Monsieur Fabian. He would be told that Mr Fabian was not at that address and he would be given another address. This he had done. He stared at the piece of paper on which he had written the address. He opened the Beirut telephone book and looked at the map in the front, referring to the index to find the street. They had instructed him to report to the house at eight that evening.

The suburb was in the lower foothills of the mountains that overlook Beirut. It was already dark, the street only illuminated by an occasional street light, as they tried to read the numbers off the walls as the headlights fell onto these. There it was, Number 46. He swung into the driveway at the end of which he could see the house with a few windows emitting light. He realised the house was in an affluent area, it being larger than most. As soon as the car stopped, two men appeared out of the shadows, one opening the door for Gisela and then, speaking French, asked that they follow, walking towards the house on the crushed white gravel, which crunched underfoot. He saw two other men. It seemed Hussein Hiram was taking no chances.

Once inside, they were led to a spacious living room with a large, low coffee table at its centre, and surrounded by two couches and two deep lounge chairs. Persian rugs covered the floor and other decorative items lent the room a definite Arab flavour. A few small lamps on ornate tables illuminated the interior.

A few minutes later, two cars stopped in the driveway, four men entering the house. They conversed for a minute or so with the other two, their voices low so that they could not be overheard.

They heard footsteps approaching on the marble-tiled floor. It was Hiram in his usual dark suit, not a hair out of place. He greeted them both.

'Sorry you had to wait, but I had to have my men check that you were not followed although I must say there was little likelihood of that, the British have absolutely no idea that you are here but they're certainly expecting you,' he said with a laugh.

'Well, you've seemed to have gone to elaborate lengths to conceal our arrival,' David ventured.

'In this game, it pays to be careful. I'm told that before we even discuss payment, and how it will be made, I need to prove to you that I have the equipment you're looking for. In fact, it's gathering dust in a warehouse in the dockyards. It is about to be re-crated, the contents disguised as general machinery. We would like to take you there now'

'Sure, I have a copy of the list of items as these were provided to us by the French. I would like to check on a few of these items, you know what I mean, carry out a spot check.'

'Fine. Shall we leave?'

The drive to the warehouse was without incident. They travelled in three cars with Hiram with them in the centre car, the leading and trailing cars keeping a fair distance from them.

It was an old warehouse built directly on the wharf. Opposite the warehouse an old tramp steamer was moored, an old Liberty ship, its high smoke stack towering over them, the hawsers tying it to the quay groaning as the ship moved to the movement of the sea. The warehouse was dirty with junk strewn around and pieces of paper blowing in the breeze. They entered through a small door, one of the men throwing a switch in an electrical switchboard, the warehouse lighting up inside, row upon row of orange mercury-vapour lights revealing a disarray of crates, boxes, steel beams, large rolls of printing papers and a host of other items.

'This way please,' Hiram said.

They followed him down an aisle between stacked items of miscellaneous cargo until he stopped in front of a number of neatly packed crates.

'Here you are,' he said, pointing with an outstretched arm.

David took a bulky envelope from his pocket and removed the contents, which he studied. He then walked along the crates noting that they were sorted in numerical order.

'Can we open this one please?' he asked.

Two of the men stepped forward with crowbars and prised the crate open. Inside was an item wrapped in heavy greaseproof paper. He opened this carefully, revealing a complete turbine engine and gearbox. Methodically, he checked the serial number against the manifest. He nodded his head in satisfaction. This operation was repeated a half dozen times, taking nearly three hours. Everything matched up.

'I'm satisfied,' he said.

'Can we now re-crate?' Hiram asked.

'Yes.'

Whatever happened to the crates after this was not his problem. Nor had Doyle indicated how these were to eventually reach their final destination.

The problem was the near eleven million dollars that had to be paid. What amazed David was that Aerospatiale had shipped these to Lebanon without payment or so he assumed. He could not imagine the French shipping them to a known international arms dealer based on a promised payment. The French were adamant that they wanted no direct financial dealings with the Rhodesian government and therefore the necessity of having to route the transaction through Hiram.

'I propose paying you in three equal amounts simply to reduce the risk in the event MI6 should intervene,' David said. 'If, in any way, they are successful and confiscate the money, the most we could lose would be three million.'

'Makes sense, but how are you going to get the money to me?'

'What I have arranged is that the Byblos Bank delivers the money in cash by bullion van to a bank of your choosing. They check it and hold it, remaining ours until you decide what you propose to do with it. When you are ready, we sign off the release. That means I don't have to actually handle the money and the British won't be able to get access.'

Hiram nodded his head in agreement. 'That sounds acceptable,' he said. 'I need to tell you something. Normally I don't involve myself in matters that really don't concern me. However, perhaps you are somewhat different from the normal type of purchaser I deal with. You appear to have some decency and believe me, in this game, nobody's decent.' He paused and lit a cheroot. 'Obviously, I have quite an extensive intelligence network of my own. It costs millions each year to maintain. I have access to information often classified "Top Secret". If you are who I think you are, then I must tell you, that you are targeted. When I say targeted I'm saying that they won't stop at killing you.'

David felt a chill run down his spine. The man was confirming his worst fears, the British would come after him. The list of dealings which had crossed his desk and which the British considered illegal was nearly endless. He had been both directly or indirectly involved in virtually every item imported or exported from the country. They must surely perceived him to have done them irreparable harm and would continue to do so. He was sure that any such action would include all of his accomplices, which would also place Gisela in danger.

'Where did you hear this?'

'Suffice to say that I know that such a squad is in Beirut looking for you.' He looked at David. 'Is your real name Tusk by any chance?'

His blood ran cold. This was getting worse. There was no doubt the he was the target. It had to be he they were looking for. He didn't respond to the question but it was clear that Hiram knew he was right.

'Be careful, Mr Brendel. Government-backed assassinations are usually successful. Strictly speaking, Britain is on a war footing with your country. You are the enemy and not even in uniform. Nobody out there would think that an attempt on your life was criminal and unjust. Please, you must realise that the British have tacit UN approval. You know what I mean.'

Hiram noted Gisela's expression. She was unfazed, unlike her counterpart.

'We will be careful. I will avoid British-controlled territory like the plague,' he said. What else was there to say?

'I'm not sure that will help. They're looking for you in Beirut at this very moment,' he said. He motioned over one of his men who carried a small satchel. 'I know that you've repeatedly said that you do not want to carry a weapon in a foreign country. Well, I'm now insisting that you both do. These weapons are licensed so if you are caught with them, you could explain your way out. Carry them with you at all time. This also applies to the lady and if need be, please – don't hesitate to use them.'

CHAPTER 29

Christian Seymour had loosened his tie and leant back on the sofa, a whisky soda in his hand. He was not a happy man. He had arrived in Beirut a week ago on his own, his other operatives having arrived a few days earlier. One of the secretaries at the embassy was an undercover MI6 agent and had arranged the use of this house, normally used as a safe house. Other than the housekeeper and the gardener, he was the only occupant. Denton and his crowd were billeted elsewhere and he doubted that their accommodation was as pleasant. Denton's team comprised four men and they had been following every possible lead trying to establish the whereabouts of Tusk. Hiram had been under observation for days, revealing nothing. They had connections with the right people at the airports and border posts and anybody whom they thought remotely suspicious they investigated. Still, they had come up with nothing. He was disgusted. The damn Rhodesians were outsmarting him at every turn. He was sure that the embassy already had a message from Sir Henry that he should contact him urgently. The British knew that the remaining helicopters were in Beirut. Trying to confiscate these could only lead to a diplomatic incident, the documents in no way indicating that these either belonged to the Rhodesians or were about to be shipped there. What they had to do was stop payment and if possible get their hands on the money. Not simple when you did not know neither where the cash was nor the donor.

The phone rang. He picked it up. It was Denton.

'Yes, Denton?' he answered impatiently. 'Have you people not come up with anything?' He listened to what Denton had to say.

'No – well then, you better bloody well keep on trying. The shit's about to hit the fan,' he remarked. 'Listen, I've been thinking. The money is not in British pounds, it's US dollars. No British banks handled it, neither those partially owned nor completely owned. We believe the money will arrive by telegraphic transfer in US dollars. We agree, okay? How many five million plus dollar telegraphic transfers do you think pass through these few banks daily? Not many. We know the transaction originated with the Republic Bank in South Africa. Which bank is their main correspondent bank in the States? Irving Trust Company, New York, right? Find out who Irving Trust Company's correspondent bank is in Beirut and whether they have received any super-large transfers during the past fortnight. Nobody leaves that kind of money lying around for long.'

He then listened to what Denton has to say, frustration clearly etched on his features. Finally, he spoke again his voice heavy with scorn.

'Listen Denton, I know that's a tall order, I don't care. Get cracking.'

Seymour replaced the phone muttering about incompetence and total imbeciles and threw the last of his drink into the back of his throat in disgust.

Tusk was the proverbial thorn in his side. During the last three weeks, he had initiated an in-depth investigation into this man. From South Africa, he had established that the man was a banker who was said to be an expert in foreign-exchange dealings. He was South African by birth and multilingual, speaking English and German without any trace of an accent, as well as Afrikaans. Apparently, his French was not quite fluent but near enough. They said that he had resigned from the South African Air Force, where he served as a lieutenant flying various types of aircraft as well as helicopters. Seymour didn't believe all that. He was sure the man still worked for the Republic Bank and was also in the employ of the Rhodesian intelligence services. Virtually all payments for all international Rhodesian purchases were routed through the Republic Bank; somehow he knew this to be Tusk's domain. What he did know was that since Smith's UDI declaration, Tusk seemed to have disappeared. MI6 also knew that he had travelled to Europe on a German passport. That he was targeting the right man, he did not doubt.

CHAPTER 30

The knockdown helicopters were safe for the moment. Nobody was going to forcefully remove these from Hiram's warehouse. He would vigorously defend what was his property. Some obscure North African rebel group had attempted this before. Suffice to say that everyone knew that Hiram did not shy from violence if the need arose. Anyway, did the British really know where the helicopters were?

Both David and Gisela had integrated well with the other Germans at the hotel. There were a few hundred Siemens personnel coming and going all the time. The hotel was closed to the public. Provided they kept a low profile and, at this stage, did not approach the banks, he was certain MI6 would draw a blank on their whereabouts. Best let them cool their heels for a while, he thought. Hiram agreed, not concerned if payment was delayed for a few weeks.

CHAPTER 31

Denton strode out of the apartment building and walked towards the car waiting at the kerbside. He opened the door and slid in next to his companion behind the wheel. It was hot. He was perspiring profusely, as was his companion. They had days ago decided that wearing suits was not on; very few wore suits in Beirut. Casual was the way to go. They wore slacks and knitted-collared golf shirts.

'I had Seymour on the phone. Well, he's not a happy man. We are going to have to find these people,' he said, taking a little bound notebook from his pocket, which he studied. 'We've drawn a blank at the airport and border posts and I've tried most hotels. Christ, do you know what it costs to bribe these concierges? A damned small fortune!'

'What're you worried about? You're not paying.'

'I know, I know, but still. Our man speaks fluent German, so where would you stay if you wanted to be inconspicuous? What was that hotel's name where all those bloody Jerries are staying, you know, that crowd fixing the telephone exchanges? Well, whatever, that's where we should look.'

The Meridian was a huge hotel built on the beachfront. The car park was full and they were forced to park a fair distance from the hotel, having to walk back in the sweltering heat.

Denton walked up to the reception desk and, as the concierge approached, surreptitiously revealed a large Lebanese banknote in his hand. He saw that two women were assisting, speaking German to each other. This concerned him.

Nothing like being brazen and bold, he thought. 'I'd like to see your register. I'm looking for a recent acquaintance, somebody I met on the flight from Europe, who arrived a few days ago; they could be a couple. I believe they are staying here.'

'And what would the purpose be, Monsieur?' the concierge asked, ignoring the proffered banknote and ratcheting up his hauteur a notch or two.

Denton realised that this was not going to be easy. The bastard was not going to be bought. He wondered whether that was because the two frauleins were assisting.

'Do you have a name, Monsieur?'

'Well, that's the problem, he gave me a business card which I lost, but if I see the name, I'll recognise it,' Denton said, a sheepish grin on his face.

'Very well, Monsieur,' the concierge said, hauling a large register from below the counter. He opened it, simultaneously shooting his hand out and removing the banknote from Denton's hand. The move was slick and unobtrusive.

Denton studied the register; it contained scores of names and address. He immediately realised that he would glean nothing from it. The register would need to be studied carefully and he did not have the time to do so. The concierge was already hovering impatiently. This would need another approach.

He briefly studied the list and then indicated to the concierge that he thought it a futile task. The man was nonplussed.

'Sorry I could not help you, Monsieur.'

Outside he met with his companion.

'That wasn't much help. Christ, there were scores of names and we don't even know what name to look for, but I'm sure we're on the right track. This has got to be the best place to hide for somebody masquerading as a German,' Denton said, lighting a cigarette.

'Well, let's get out of the bloody sun and with that I mean not get in the car!' his companion said.

There was a bar nearby, overlooking the swimming pool. It was open on three sides providing a clear all-round view. There were a few people sitting on barstools at the bar counter. Denton indicated that they should go there.

They ordered two beers. They were ice cold, the condensation pearling on the glasses.

Denton's assistant raised his eyebrows and with a slight jerk of his head indicated towards the right. Denton turned to see what had drawn his attention. He chuckled to himself. A stunning blonde wearing the skimpiest of bikinis lay on a deckchair of which the back had been lowered. A pair of large sunglasses, the lenses reflective, hid her eyes. Her golden tan indicated that she had been here in Beirut a while or had recently acquired this elsewhere. He thought her exquisite, truly a beautiful woman. Ursula

177

Andress, a Nordic bombshell, who had burst on the scene in the first James Bond film, came to mind. His assessment made him smile.

Denton slowly faced his companion. 'Wow, George, that's something all right.'

George was frowning. 'She's familiar.'

Denton smiled.

'With those looks, I would think so. Those images tend to stay. Seeing that you know her, why don't you go up and say hello?' Denton jokingly suggested.

'No, no, I've seen this woman before,' he whispered.

Denton waved his hand dismissively, 'That babe's German and as far as I know, you don't know any beautiful German women.'

'You're probably right. '

Half an hour later, they reluctantly left the hotel and moved on to the next on the list. Both were dejected. This was boring and tiresome and the chance of success was pretty remote. They needed a break, some small thing that would put them on the right track. Somehow or other the opposition always slips up. It's always something small, but enough to point them in the right direction.

That evening from their apartment, Denton phoned Seymour and told him that they had drawn a blank again. He mentioned the register at the Meridian Hotel, saying that he believed that it would be a good idea if they could get hold of it and study it. Seymour said he would think about it but thought it not possible. He insisted that they continue working their way through the hotel list. Denton groaned inwardly.

CHAPTER 32

Gisela was used to men looking at her, but the two at the bar were different. They just didn't fit in. All the guests were German, but these two men dressed in longs and knitted golf shirts sitting at the pool bar, spoke English. She could not ignore a lifetime of training. Something was wrong. She decided that she would ask the concierge who these men were who spoke English. She wondered whether they had made any enquiries regarding the guests. After they left, she donned a long, loose blouse which reached to just above her knees, slipped on her beach sandals and walked to the reception.

The moment the concierge saw her, his demeanour changed. Gone was the stern, reserved look, now replaced with a friendly smile.

'Bonjour, Madame, is there anything I can do?'

She gave him her best smile. 'There are some friends of ours looking for us, two men actually. Did anybody make any enquiries?' she asked.

'Two men were here but did not have a name. They said they had lost the business card. They asked to see the register but did no more than just glance at it,' he replied.

'Were they locals?'

'No, no. They spoke French. Awful French. In fact, they sounded English. '

'Really, well then it couldn't have been us they were looking for. We don't know any Englishmen. But if anybody comes looking for my husband or me, please let us know,' she said with a chuckle, pretending it to be quite funny and incidental. She slipped him a twenty-dollar bill.

'But, of course, Madame,' he replied demurely, the banknote disappearing.

She made her way to the elevators. Not for one moment did she doubt that this had something to do with David. She had no idea whether the British were even aware of her existence. If they were doing the rounds of the hotels then they were still in the dark. This was a consolation, she thought.

David listened carefully to what she had to say. He realised that MI6 had to be on the lookout but if they were going from hotel to hotel in the city of Beirut, well, that could take a while. Still, it was a matter of concern. The thing was to not overreact. Had they associated them with any names? Doubtful, their identities were brand new. No, that was unlikely. On analysis, the only thing he thought the British had was his physical description. Surely, they had that by now. If he kept a low profile, that should keep them at bay, as they would be unable to find any trace of him. The question was how long would MI6 spend on this. Could he outwait them?

CHAPTER 33

It had been a tiring day. He would never have believed there were so many hotels in Beirut. The list was endless. To crown it all, Seymour insisted on meeting with them, probably for no other reason but to aggravate what was already a bad day, Denton thought.

This type of tedious, relentless research was not new to him. He had done this before, many times. Invariably it began with their being handed a confidential folder, which contained everything you needed to know about the victim. This contained such ridiculous information as to what the victim's taste was in food, theatre, women, and anything else that may be unique to an individual. Using this as a basis, they would systematically compartmentalise this information, slowly putting the puzzle together until they knew the man, his description, traits and character. When you set out to get him you knew him intimately, nearly able to guess his every move. Unfortunately, the information on Tusk was sparse, but they knew he was no walkover. The man was resourceful and cunning. He had evaded them before. He would know that what he was doing and would make every endeavour, even if this required force, to evade them. He would be on his guard. As an officer, weapons training would have been thorough and he would know how to use them. He was unique in that he was a pilot and has seen covert military action. He was no newcomer to danger. This was no ordinary adversary. They, too, had to be careful.

Seymour had chosen a supper nightclub to meet, a place called the 'The Super Super Star'. Denton realised that his boss was about to mix business with pleasure – the word 'super' before a bar's name in Lebanon designates a strip club. A second 'super' before the name lends a completely different meaning to the place. This would be a strip club, but also where prostitutes could ply their trade.

As they walked to the club from where they had parked the car, Denton remarked, 'This could get quite interesting. I didn't know Seymour was into this type of thing. I wonder whether Her Majesty's government is paying.' He laughed, giving George a jab in the ribs.

George Berkeley had started his working life off as an English bobby stamping the pavements of London. He had diligently applied his mind to his studies, passing most exams first time. His devotion to duty was soon recognised and, within a few years, he joined the ranks of the detective unit. Shortly thereafter, military intelligence recruited him. He was a tall, well-built man with curly black hair. His complexion bordered on swarthy, a hint of a five o'clock shadow a permanent feature. He jogged every morning and played squash at every available opportunity.

They walked into the club. There was a large bar at one end with a small stage, which took up the wall on the opposite side. The interior lighting was dim, purposely so, to lend the club the right atmosphere and to hide the shabby décor. It was still early, there were few guests although there were quite a number of women standing around, wearing either miniskirts or hot pants and displaying ample cleavage and thigh. Their lipstick was bright and garish as was the makeup and eyeliner. Seymour had already arrived and was seated at the bar with a drink in front of him, looking at a woman on the stage with enormous breasts, which seemed to defy gravity, she gyrating around a pole.

Denton was a little uncomfortable meeting his boss in a strip club. It was as if Seymour was about to lay bare part of himself. It certainly seemed out of character. They were work colleagues, not friends. Still, he wondered about the man, the stiff-upper-lip-crowd was known to have their fair share of sexual deviants.

They had a few drinks, Seymour never once touching on business. He had clearly had a few, now jovial and friendly. The mood relaxed, the men beginning to leer at the passing women who flaunted themselves.

A very attractive blonde woman sauntered up to the bar with an exaggerated sway of the hips and greeted them in French, showing more than a casual interest in George. She certainly was a cut above the rest with a magnificent bosom, giving George every opportunity to stare. He played along. She stayed for a drink and introduced herself, finally leaving with a promise to be back later.

As she left, Seymour patted George on the back. 'Now, that's a beauty, my boy. That's the best I've seen around here and I have been looking.'

They all laughed. They had all been looking.

'Hang on,' Denton said, 'That's nothing … Christ, there was some bird in a bikini at the pool at one of the hotels … ' He rolled his eyes. 'Jesus, I would've given a month's salary.'

Again, the three roared uproariously as the conversation moved into a more conspiratorial phase where talk was laced with those secret sexual innuendoes shared by men as their alcohol intake increased.

'Not a local, I take it?' Seymour asked.

'No. She must've been German. It was at the Meridian, you know, the hotel which the Siemens crowd invaded,' Denton said.

'Oh, what a dish. I'm sure I've seen her before.'

Seymour thought that funny, slapping George on the back. 'Next you'll be telling us more about her ... what?' he said.

'No, seriously, I've seen her before. It's actually bothering me. Usually, I remember these things.'

'Well, it could not have been an exciting encounter. You would've remembered,' Seymour added, permitting himself a jovial grin.

The evening slowly degenerated into a wild party, the three drinking heavily. George and the blonde – her name was Tinky – found themselves mutually attracted, she probably only from a pecuniary point of view, yet she was fun. By two in the morning, the other two having found themselves women of the night, they decided to return to their apartment. Seymour waved them off, saying he was returning to where he stayed, but still had his woman in tow.

Accompanied by the women, Denton and George returned to their apartment and after a few more drinks retired to their bedrooms.

****

'Holy shit!' George shouted, sitting bolt upright in bed. He looked around to find Tinky, the blonde lying next to him, her eyes wide in alarm. Suddenly, he remembered where he was.

'Sorry, it's okay, I just remembered something,' he said, first flinging his bedclothes off, but then grabbing them and covering himself after realising that he was completely naked. He wanted to say something to her, but could not remember her name.

'It is Tinky,' she said, grabbing his arm and twisting it to read his wristwatch. 'Merde!' she shouted, jumping naked out of the bed and scampering towards the bathroom.

He grabbed a pair of shorts, pulled them on, and ran to Denton's room, flinging the door open. The fact that he had stumbled into them in flagrante delicto did not deter him in the least. He shouted, 'Christ, Denton! I remember that bloody bird in the bikini at the swimming pool. I know who

183

she is. She was at that hotel in London. Oh hell, you weren't there. Anyway, I remember her.'

Denton was not happy. With surprising alacrity, he had rolled off the woman, who pulled the sheet up, covering herself.

'For fuck's sake!' Denton shouted, 'Was this bloody necessary?'

'Sorry, sorry, I wasn't thinking. '

'Okay, let's get rid of these women. Get dressed. We'll discuss this. You'd better get hold of Seymour. I'm sure you're onto something here.'

After giving them both a cup of coffee, Denton renegotiated payment with the two women and then paid them. He told them to find themselves a taxi.

'God, I hope Seymour gives me the bloody money back. That was a fortune! And, I've got no fuckin' chits from them,' he muttered, sticking his wallet back into his pocket.

George wasn't listening, he was too excited. He knew that somehow this woman was involved with Tusk. They were together as they had been in London, but MI6 had not then realised that they were a couple. He picked up the phone and dialled Seymour. The housekeeper answered. When she refused to call him to the phone, saying he was still sleeping, he started shouting, demanding to speak to him immediately. A short while later Seymour came onto the line.

He was furious.

'Berkeley, this better be good! Are you bloody insane? Just look at the time.'

'Sir, just let me get to the point,' he said, unable to contain his excitement. 'That woman I saw at the hotel was at the same hotel in London with Tusk, the Belleclaire Hotel. I suddenly remembered, that's where I saw her. I'm absolutely certain.'

'What? Are you sure? That can't be a coincidence?'

'Absolutely not!'

'Okay, just stay there. I'll get back to you in a few minutes. Make sure that Denton gets dressed.'

The three men met at their usual morning haunt, a bistro on the beach road overlooking the sea. The place was renowned for the excellent English breakfasts it served.

The previous night's revelry had taken its toll. Seymour merely picked at his breakfast but was already on his second cup of tea.

'That bastard. If we don't stop him this time, we all land up in the back room doing filing for the rest of our careers. So, anything we come up with had better be good.,' he muttered sourly.

'It's her, I'll stake my reputation on it,' George said, repeating himself for the third time.

'Okay, we can't cock this up. None of us is to go near to the Meridian. We'll get one of our local chaps, somebody who looks and acts like and Arab. May be our local boys can arrange to get somebody attached to the hotel staff or something. I'm going to give that a try. A few photographs of the couple would be a good idea, just in case he has altered his appearance.'

'She's altered hers,' George said.

'Correct, then he probably has done the same,' Denton said.

'All right, agreed. I'll get in touch with the local boys and arrange something. I'll keep you informed.'

CHAPTER 34

She stared at her reflection in the mirror, aware of David on the bed behind her reading a magazine. He was dressed in shorts and a loose top, his feet bare.

'Listen, my dear, two men have been making enquiries.'

'What do you mean?'

She saw him discard the magazine, now staring intently at her reflection in the mirror. She still wore her bikini.

'Who's being making enquiries? About us?'

'Well I presume so. I spoke to Jamal, the concierge. I slipped him twenty. He told me that two men asked to see the register. That was roundabout the same time that I saw two men at the pool bar speaking English. I'm sure they're the same.'

'That's bad,' he said quietly, shocked. He couldn't believe it. Somehow, they must have gotten lucky, but he could not imagine how.

'Actually, I don't think they know anything. Apparently, they merely glanced at the register, it was too complex. They needed more time to study it. The guy never even spent more than fifteen seconds studying it. They can't possibly know that we're here.'

He had to agree. How could they possibly know? He had been extremely careful and made a point of not revealing himself.

The small white bikini was getting to him. It was a tease. It accentuated her every curve, the swell of her breasts and roundness of her derrière. He felt the exhilarating feeling of an arousal. She watched him in the mirror aware of what was happening to him. She felt her own arousal and she shuddered as her need washed over her. He saw the expression on her face change. He knew the new expression, it told him that she was focused inward, taken over by what was happening inside her, concentrating so that she was near oblivious of what was happening around her.

'Come here,' he whispered in a husky voice.

She slid off the stool and knelt over him on the bed, kissing him softly on the lips, her mouth playing over his. He stretched up and undid her bikini, freeing her breasts. They kissed, their tongues exploring each other. She lowered her chest, her breasts brushing his face. He took a now-erect nipple into his mouth and rolled his teeth over it. She moaned.

They made passionate love, until she dug her nails into his back emitting a low keen of pleasure and he exploded inside her.

She stirred beside him. He woke. It was still daylight, just after midday. A cool breeze wafted in through the balcony sliding doors from the sea. She opened her eyes and smiled at him, then put her arms round his neck and said, 'I love you. '

He responded by kissing her.

'A swim sounds like a good idea.'

She agreed.

CHAPTER 35

Working through the embassy and their many informants, they eventually found an undercover candidate who suited their needs perfectly. The man, Baqil Habib, was a young man in his twenties who spoke a little German, which qualified him well for a job at the Meridian. In Lebanese society, friends help friends and Baqil eventually found himself a job as a waiter at the hotel. Fortunately, he had waited on tables before in restaurants in the city, which qualified him well for the job. Seymour made certain that the undercover man knew what was expected of him. He had to focus on the woman and establish who her partner was. They issued him a cigarette lighter, which housed a miniature camera. The lighter was functional. They asked that he try to photograph Tusk.

For two days, Baqil waited on tables not once seeing the woman. He had been told that he would immediately recognise her, the blonde hair and her stunning beauty. During the next two days, she never entered the dining room.

It was particularly hot on the third day. Many of the Germans who were not working congregated at the pool. The poolside bar was hard pressed to serve that many people, the catering manager assigning Baqil and another to assist. The bar was busy, the work uncomfortable in the heat, the two men wearing black trousers and white shirts, the sun beating down relentlessly.

Baqil kept a lookout for the woman and when he saw her there was no mistaking her. Her beauty was truly profound. She had removed a loose white blouse and, after placing a large bath towel on a deck chair, she lay down on her back to catch the full sun. He walked over to her and asked whether there was anything, he could get her. She asked for a large ice-cold Diablo Monte, a refreshing sweet mint drink, an excellent thirst-quencher. He brought this to her, she scribbling a signature on the tab and writing down the room number. He memorised the number, Room 542. This was on the fifth floor.

He was entitled to a smoke break of ten minutes every two hours. During his next break, from a public phone in the foyer he dialled the number he had memorised. Seymour answered. The conversation was brief, Baqil merely conveying the room number.

His duties in the dining room enabled him to be acquainted with a few of the other waiters. On enquiry, it soon emerged that the occupants of Room 542 never visited the dining rooms but, invariably, had all meals brought to the room.

They still had to identify Tusk. Seymour seethed with impatience, afraid that Tusk could just take off again leaving the trail cold. Through London he learnt that, during the period that it was thought that large transfers were made to Lebanon, a large transfer, eleven million dollars exactly, had been paid in New York from the Irving Trust Company to the New York branch of the Byblos Bank S. P. L. This payment was not accompanied by any instructions. This meant nothing as Byblos would already have instructions as to what was to happen on receipt of the transfer. British Intelligence had no means of penetrating the bank's security. However, the other large amounts transferred during the period in question were clear-cut. The transferee, drawee bank, and ultimate recipient were clearly stated. It seemed unlikely that any of these related to the helicopter deal. Seymour was reasonably certain that if Tusk could be stopped, this would impede payment, enabling them to deal with this at a later stage. Clearly, it was imperative to concentrate on Tusk.

CHAPTER 36

David had replaced the rented American sedan with a two-door sports car, a white Mercedes Benz 190 SL, not a particularly fast car, but capable of a hundred miles an hour and possessed of excellent handling characteristics. This he kept parked in a public parking garage a half-mile away. This enabled them to leave the hotel through a rear entrance, their movements not recorded in the foyer. Most evenings they would dine out at unobtrusive restaurants.

He glanced around the restaurant, his hand rubbing the week-old stubble of a beard he was growing. She hated it but he argued that it enabled him to blend in, the Lebanese men prone to beards or only shaving once a week.

'God, sweetheart, I'm bored, impatient and uneasy. Dammit, I can't do this anymore. We've got to pay these people and get out of here,' he said, both irritated and agitated, continuously fidgeting.

She sipped her glass of wine and wiped her lips with the napkin. 'David, you can't do that.' She only used his name when trying to make a point. 'Don't think they haven't checked on the banks. That's the first thing the Stasi would have done if in the same position. I'm sure MI6 has excellent connections in Beirut. They probably could call on the CIA to help. You have to wait. A month or two will make no difference to the helicopter shipment.'

At eleven that night, they took a long detour back to the hotel, driving slowly along the coastal road, the top down, the wind in their faces. It would have been an idyllic holiday were it not for the constant fear of being discovered. Every second day they would hear from Hiram, these messages cryptic and always the same: just wait.

The next morning, he rose early and showered. Just before eight, there was a knock on the door. He looked through the peephole and saw a waiter with a trolley; the man was dressed in black pants and starched white linen jacket, the morning uniform. He could see no one else but then the field of vision was very narrow. He placed the SIG automatic on the table next to the door in easy reach should he need it. He opened the door just a crack.

There was nobody else to be seen in the passageway. He let the man roll the trolley into the room.

'Where is Izaak?' he asked.

'It's his day off,' the new man replied.

The man was in his twenties, a typical Lebanese with a swarthy complexion and curly hair. David indicated that he should put the breakfast on the small dining table in the room. David watched him. Suddenly there was a thump as something fell to the carpet.

'Sorry,' the waiter said, 'My lighter fell out of my pocket.' He smiled obsequiously and retrieved it from the floor.

David merely nodded and when the man finished laying the table, he opened the door for him giving him a Lebanese hundred-pound note as he exited.

CHAPTER 37

It was not the best photograph but it certainly would do. It was Tusk. They were jubilant – they had found him at last. Seymour was insistent that they take action immediately, afraid that Tusk could suddenly disappear, but this was Denton's territory and it required his expertise.

'We've got to get you into the hotel. I suppose you could just walk in. But how are going to get him to open the door?' Seymour asked.

'We get our waiter to go up to the room with you right behind him. He gets Tusk to open up and you step in,' George said to Denton.

'Forget it. He's too wary and as you've just heard, he's armed. The waiter saw the automatic on the table. What about her, she's probably also armed. You don't think he had her accompany him just for fun, do you?'

Seymour smiled. 'Well, isn't that just dandy? Now what?'

'We have to create a diversion, something that will force him to leave the suite. I think I know just how to do it,' Denton said.

Denton never failed to amaze Seymour. The man treated an assassination like any other job: it was work. No doubt, the government paid him handsomely for its dirty work. The man seemed to have no conscience at all. He had never married. Either he spent his off time in his Bayswater flat, its appearance from outside belying the lavish interior, or he was at his local gym pumping iron or instructing others in the art of kung fu. Seymour thought it extraordinary that the man's taste in music was inclined towards the classical. Girl friends he did not have, but did occasionally indulge in the one-night stand. He apparently avoided attachments. A definite loner and deadly dangerous.

CHAPTER 38

The loud, strident ringing of a bell awakened him. He was baffled, not knowing what it meant. A small red flashing light affixed to the wall near the ceiling above the door drew his attention. He groped for the bedside lamp switch. With the light on, he saw a small board with 'FIRE' written on it, which was attached below the light.

'Christ! Gisela, wake up. We've got a fire,' he shouted, jumping out of bed and starting to put his clothes on. She was already out of bed, squeezing into a pair of jeans.

Suddenly there was a pounding on the door and somebody in the passageway shouted, 'Fire, fire! Get out!'

He knew where the fire escape was, his usual exit route from the hotel. He looked up at the ceiling and saw the automatic sprinkler heads. These had not yet been activated. The fire could not be nearby.

'Have you got your gun?' he asked Gisela.

For a second she just stared at him and then removed it from her bedside table. He shoved his own SIG into his belt. A bullet was in the chamber, the gun cocked, the safety on.

At that moment, the room was plunged into darkness. God, he thought, the power's gone.

'Just stay close behind me,' he said, waiting for his eyes to adjust. Being on the fifth floor and free from prying eyes, they left the curtains open to allow the fresh air in. The moonlight from a half-moon was sufficient for him to make out everything in the room. Again, there was a banging on the door, the gap at the bottom revealing a flash of light obviously from a torch. The light then disappeared. He pulled the automatic from his waist and unlocked the door slowly turning the handle, ready to slam it shut at the first sign of danger. There was nothing. An acrid smoke smell assaulted his nostrils. With his free hand, he groped for her hand. When he touched her fingers, they closed over his. He turned left and slowly moved down the passage towards the first escape door at the end, discernible in the dim light from the moonlight streaming through the window at the end. The other occupants seemed to have already fled the building. He didn't know where the fire was. He wondered how serious it was, there not as much smoke as he expected.

As they approached the door, he pulled her forward and pushed her to the front. She opened the door and stepped through, the stairs illuminated by little red emergency lights fitted to the floor against the wall of the stairwell. They made no sound, the floor thickly carpeted. In the corridor, next to the fire escape door, was another door which led to the floor's linen cupboards where the house cleaners kept their equipment. The door was slightly ajar, which escaped his notice. He stepped past the door, automatic held at the ready. Gisela was already on the fire escape steps.

For a brief instant in the moonlight from the window, he caught a silver flash just ahead of his face, jerking his hand up to protect himself. The steel piano wire loop had passed over his head and, as his assailant pulled the handles to close the loop, the wire caught on the bottom of the automatic, which was now pointing towards the roof. The man's strength was incredible, the automatic being pulled against his throat, the only thing preventing his carotid artery from being severed. He pushed his gun hand forward with all his strength, feeling the wire cut into the sides of his neck, just able to breathe. He tried to shout but could only manage a low short croak. His attacker was immensely strong, stubbornly resisting his attempts to free himself. It would be over in seconds. With his free arm, he flayed around, his hand closing over something attached to the wall. He immediately recalled what it was having seen it virtually every day. It was a fire axe clamped to the wall next to the door. He managed to grab the handle and work it loose. He realised that he was close to losing consciousness. The man had planted his feet on the outside of each of David's shoulders, pulling David up in his attempts to close the steel noose. He swung the axe at the man's foot, the blade cutting into the shoe just above the man's toes. There was a loud howl of agony, his assailant's grip loosening. He pushed his gun hand forward with the last vestiges of strength. Again he swung the axe, again making contact with the man's foot, this followed by another scream, the noose loosening further. He managed to push the wire entirely away and up, swinging it back over his head. He swung round staggering back, seeing his assailant for the first time.

He saw the automatic in the man's hand, a silencer screwed to the front of the barrel. He realised that the man would shoot before he could level his own gun. At this range, at just a few feet, he was a dead man.

Something roared next to his ear nearly deafening him. The man staggered back clutching his abdomen, the automatic falling from his fingers bouncing on the carpeted floor. Again a gun roared, the bullet knocking him to the floor. He saw Gisela standing at the top of the landing a foot or two from him, the revolver still in her outstretched arm, her eyes wide and a wild look on her face.

CHAPTER 39

George, standing behind Denton in the linen room, realised that something had gone wrong. The struggle should have been over yet this man still fought on. He could not pass, Denton's huge bulk blocked the doorway. They had decided to avoid the use of guns, if possible. That didn't matter anymore. He would shoot if he could get a shot in.

He saw the axe swing down and virtually lop Denton's toes off, the man's cry of pain reverberating in the linen room. Again, the axe swung followed by another scream. Still, Denton kept the pressure on the garrotte around Tusk's neck.

The sudden roar of the gun took him by surprise, not knowing from where this came. Another shot followed, Denton staggering back against him and falling to the floor. He looked down at his colleague, his gun pointing at the floor. He looked up and stared into the eyes of Tusk, who had his weapon levelled.

'Oh, fuck,' he uttered. The last thing he saw was the blossom of flame that erupted from the barrel.

CHAPTER 40

'Run. Run!' he shouted at Gisela, 'There's got to be more than two of them.'

They ran down the stairs. He realised that there was no fire and that this had been a diversion created by MI6 to enter the hotel unobserved and catch them unawares. The stairwell was still heavy with smoke. They were only able to navigate their way down by following the red lights. As they got lower, the smoke began to dissipate. They burst through the steel fire door into the underground parking garage. David grabbed Gisela by the arm and pulled her along the route he usually followed when leaving the hotel. Once outside they slowed to a walk.

Quite a crowd had gathered on the pavement all looking up to the hotel where smoke billowed from a few windows. Most of those around them spoke German and he realised that these were hotel guests.

'Come on, honey, let's go. It's not safe here,' he said.

'God, you're bleeding badly,' she said.

He put his hand up to his neck, feeling the slick wetness of blood. As he brought his hand away, he saw his wet palm. He was bleeding profusely. The piano wire had cut deeply into the skin on both sides of his neck. He looked down and saw that his shirt was soaked in blood.

They walked away, avoiding any others, keeping a sharp lookout.

Seymour sat in the car with one of his assistants. He had heard the three shots. Smoke still billowed from the windows; he knew that the smoke canisters would work for about three minutes. This was just about up. People had streamed out of the hotel. He had heard the occasional scream of panic. A large crowd now stood outside the hotel on both sides of road, their attention focused on the building.

'There was supposed to be no shooting,' Seymour said, his concern mirrored on his face. He had no way of knowing who had done the shooting. 'Just keep a sharp lookout for our chaps,' he added.

In the distance, they heard the sound of an approaching fire engine, the blast of its klaxon audible. The crowd had grown considerably and a number of police cars had arrived. The fire engine screeched to a halt.

Firefighters, wearing breathing apparatus, jumped off and entered the hotel. The canisters had burnt out and the smoke was rapidly disappearing. After about five minutes, the firefighters emerged from the building. It was clear that something was wrong; they all approached the police, with whom they were now in discussion.

'They've found something,' Seymour commented. 'I hope it's Tusk. Where the hell are our people? They should have been out of the hotel by now.'

'Sir, I think something's wrong. They've been gone too long.'

'I know, let's give it another minute or two. We are not the only car parked in the street. If the police come along, then we'll get out of here,' Seymour replied.

They watched as the police disappeared into the building, which was now smoke-free. A firefighter had come out of the building holding up the two smoke canisters. They then proceeded to allow the guests to return to the hotel. This had all taken about an hour. Neither Denton nor Berkeley made an appearance. Seymour realised that he dare not make any enquiries. Something had happened in the hotel and his people seemed to have disappeared. He instructed his assistant to drive back to the house.

CHAPTER 41

'Other than this damn gun, I've got nothing on me,' David said. He was dressed only in trousers, shirt and slip-on sandals. He needed to clean himself up. He wondered whether his neck wounds would require stitches.

'I'm no better. I've got nothing to give you that you could use to clean yourself. At least I brought my purse, so I've some cash and my credit cards,' she replied, breathing hard from the exertion of their rapid walk to the parking garage.

'Oh, Christ! I forgot the car keys,' he said, patting his trousers.

She opened her bag and withdrew a set of keys, which she dangled in front of him, a mischievous grin on her face. 'Now, what would you do without me?'

He grabbed the keys and they both got into the car. Fortunately, the top was up, which would make them less conspicuous, especially him with his blood-drenched shirt.

'What about our things in the hotel?' she asked.

'Hell, I don't know. Let's think about that later. May be we can salvage the stuff without going there. You seem to be taking what happened there quite well considering that we've just killed two people.'

'I'm still feeling sick, but we had no choice. I had to shoot him, he was about to kill you!'

He reached out a hand and placed it on her knee. 'And thank God you did, I thought I was a goner.'

'Where are you going?' she asked.

'I don't know. I have to get in touch with Hiram. He's the only one who can help now. The Beirut police are going to be all over this. Eventually they will discover that our room is deserted and we are nowhere to be found. They will wonder what happened to us and whether we had anything to do with the killing. That could be a while, I mean our room is far from the fire escape, but get to us they will,' he said.

'You've forgotten the British. They'll really be after us,' she retorted.

'I know.'

'You've got to clean yourself up. You can't let anybody see you like that.'

Everything had happened so fast. Now was the first time he could reflect on what had occurred. He had nearly died and, had it not been for Gisela, well, she had done the only thing she could. The men were dead. Both the police and MI6 would want to apprehend the perpetuators.

He drove to the airport. On the way, he pulled into a roadside garage and disappeared into the public toilet, which was deserted fortunately. He stripped off his shirt and washed his upper torso, removing all the blood. The cuts on his neck had stopped bleeding. He washed the shirt under the tap, wrung it out, and then donned it again. He had been able to wash out most of the blood, leaving only a few dark blotches just discernible. Hopefully, it would soon dry in the heat and the breeze through the car's open windows. By the time they got to the airport, his shirt had partially dried. He was now sufficiently decent to pass scrutiny at a distance. He chose a booth from the bank of public phones in the hall and placed a call to the number Hiram had given him. When the phone was answered, he asked that he be phoned back giving them the booth's phone number.

Within fifteen minutes, Hiram returned his call. Very briefly, in clipped sentences, he told him what had happened. Again, he thanked him for warning them and said that they probably had him to thank for saving their lives. He told him that they had abandoned the hotel and had left all their belongings. Hussein said that he had already heard that there had been a shooting at the hotel and that two men had died. He said he had no idea how the police would interpret the crime but thought that the used smoke canisters would indicate that this had been a planned operation, although they could not know to what end. He suggested that David drive to his lodge in the mountains where he would put them up for a few days until the tumult had died down.

Gisela had curled up in her seat, the full extent of the events only hitting her now, close to shock. He knew her to be a resourceful woman. This was not the first time she had killed. He left her alone.

They arrived at the bungalow. They were expected. They were shown the same room as before. Gisela excused herself saying that she was taking a sedative.

David's mind was in turmoil. The consequences of what MI6 had tried were appalling, although they had only themselves to blame. Eventually, the Lebanese police would piece the puzzle together, two dead men, a blood-smeared garrotte, two used smoke canisters, and two silenced automatics with only the dead men's fingerprints on them. Surely, they would realise that this had to have a political connection? The dead men were British subjects in Her Majesty's employ. Maybe the British government would go cap-in-hand and apologetically tell the Lebanese government all in order to avoid an international incident. Again, the British could hide behind the apron strings of the UN. After all, there was an international embargo in force against Rhodesia. Possibly, they thought their actions justified, although in a foreign country

Gisela and he had nowhere to go. Still clothed, he eventually fell asleep on the bed.

The next morning, Gisela found a first-aid kit in the house. She cleaned and dressed the cuts on his neck. They did not require stitches and a few sticking plasters seemed to do the trick. She seemed to have recovered quite well from their ordeal and he again wondered what true woman lurked in the recesses of her mind. He recalled the flashes of sheer unadulterated hatred she could display. She killed when so required, an extraordinary woman indeed. The Stasi trained their personnel well. He wondered what her field of expertise would have been had she stayed with them.

During the afternoon, Hiram arrived with a number of his men in tow. They deposited their personal belongings from the hotel in the lounge. Hussein had instructed that their hotel suite be cleaned out. Nothing was to be left behind, even the used toiletry items in the bathroom had been retrieved. The fictitious names in the hotel register would lead the police nowhere, nor would their German passport numbers. This information would not help the British either. For the moment, they had simply disappeared.

'The only reason that I have gone out of my way to assist you as I've done is that I need to be paid. This must happen soon before I also compromise my own position,' Hiram said when they were all congregated in the lounge, collecting their belongings.

'I realise that and that's why I think it imperative that you supply banking details so that I can instruct the bank to make payment to your account,' David asked.

'No, as I said before, I can't do that. Ultimately this would be traced,' he replied

'I've another idea. I'll try to persuade the bank to release the funds to you, to be collected by you in person without either of us being present. I could give them the necessary codes telephonically,' David suggested.

'If they agree to that it would be surprising, but try. I certainly will agree to such an arrangement.'

David contacted the bank and, although initially reluctant, they agreed to release the funds to Hussein Hiram in person, provided David and Gisela had signed certain release documentation. The bank also relented and agreed to send such documentation with a bank official to an address nominated by David where it could be signed in the presence of a bank official. The bank's director assured him that this would take place in the strictest of confidence. Hiram, who listened to the conversation, using gestures, indicated to David that the signing should take place at the bungalow.

David was tempted but then said he would get back to the bank director with a time and place.

CHAPTER 42

Seymour sat alone in the office of the First Secretary of the British Embassy in Beirut. The reason he was alone was that he was waiting to be connected on a tested secure line to Sir Henry in London. He was shocked. Matters had gone dismally wrong. The developments of the last forty-eight hours had cast a pall of doubt over the Rhodesian desk's operations in the corridors of the intelligence division in London. Two operatives were dead, 'killed by their own kind' as it had been put by his colleagues or so he had heard said. Everybody seemed to have forgotten or was unaware that the two operatives had themselves set out to wipe out their own kind. Seymour swore to himself, 'Damn the Labour government. They could fuck anything up given half a chance. Christ, Denton of all people, he had been a bloody expert.'

How many so-called enemies of the state had he removed in his lifetime all in the line of duty and now? Then there was Berkeley, this all had been new to him and he too was a victim of incompetence. Now he had to speak to Sir Harry who, no doubt, would lay the blame at his feet.

The phone on the desk rang. He picked it up.

'You're through, sir. Just press the button on the top of the phone. The light will flash indicating that the scrambler is working.'

'Thank you,' he said, pressing the button.

'Seymour, is that you?' he heard the voice of Sir Harry but with a distinct metallic sound.

'Yes, sir.'

'Dreadful, absolutely bloody dreadful. I've just read the telexed report. Not much detail yet. What the hell went wrong? I mean two of our men dead, shot by the Rhodesians. I've still got to tell the Home Secretary.'

Seymour looked up at the ceiling. The bastard's conveniently forgotten what we were trying to do to them, Seymour thought. What did he think, that these people would lie down and die?

'I don't know but it seems Tusk must have been expecting us,' he hesitantly ventured.

'Well, of course he was. Anyway, we've got to put this disaster behind us and stop Tusk and those helicopters. Every time they are mentioned, the PM goes apoplectic. We have confirmation that the money to pay Hiram is already in Beirut and believed to be with the Byblos Bank. Not much we can do about that. Lebanese banks are like the Swiss, they never help. Tusk is still the target. We don't want him doing any more deals, not ever. Do you understand?'

The implications of what he had just said were clear.

'Yes sir. '

'Please, no cock-ups this time.'

This was followed by a click. He could picture Sir Harry slamming the phone down in frustration. The bastard had not offered any replacements for Denton and Berkeley. It was now up to him and his assistants. He had only the four, all relative newcomers. Christ, he thought, I'm not a field man. What did Sir Harry expect?

He walked out of the First Secretary's office down the passage to another office, this one far from opulent, a working man's office, and sat down in front of the desk looking at the man opposite him.

The man waited a few seconds watching the expression on Seymour's face. 'That could not have been very pleasant,' he said.

'No, it wasn't. We're on our own now. I need your help.'

'You know I'll do what I can but there's not much I can do. I'm a desk man, I just collect information and pass it on. I can't help you with the fieldwork. God, I haven't fired a gun in years,' the man replied, leaning back against his chair his hands folded in his lap, clearly indicating that he would live up to what he just said. He would not be taking any chances.

'No, all we want is information. Hiram has to be helping this man. He knows that if anything happens to Tusk he may never be paid. Tusk holds the keys to the kingdom. Remember, we understand from our sources that Hiram has already paid the French. The damn helicopters now belong to him. He needs a buyer.'

'What do you want to know?'

'Hiram has this man and woman holed up somewhere. This has to be in or around Beirut or in the mountains. I need to know where and that soon. I also need to know everything you have on Hiram.'

The man removed a file from his desk's top drawer and placed it front of Seymour.

'Here, read this but you can't remove it from my office, okay?'

Seymour nodded and took the file.

'Meanwhile I'll go and find myself a cup of tea,' the man said and left the office.

It was a thick file. For over an hour, he studied the prodigious contents. Hiram was a very successful gunrunner but had shied away from supplying true terrorist organisations or so it seemed. He chose his clients carefully and had, on a few occasions, whispered in the ears of both the CIA and British intelligence when approached by known terrorist organisations whose deeds were designed to disrupt the Western way of life.

There was no doubt that he was an extremely wealthy man but with the exception that he did not flaunt it, his lifestyle far less flamboyant than that of the many playboys who had made Lebanon their playground. There was nothing ostentatious about him. The man possessed numerous properties, most of these registered in companies of which he or his close family were shareholders. It seemed the man planned for an eventuality, little was in his name. If things went wrong for him, he could still emerge with most of his wealth intact.

Seymour skimmed through the list of properties and addresses. He was sure Hiram would have chosen some out-of-the-way place. He purposely avoided the properties in the city and eventually came up with a list of five properties: three of them were beach properties; the other two in the mountains overlooking the coast. He copied down the addresses.

He thought the property situated high in the Lebanese Alps on the road that passed through Shtawrah and then onto Damascus to be the most likely place Hiram would have chosen. He decided that he would reconnoitre that property first.

CHAPTER 43

Just before dusk, Seymour and another operative left Beirut driving on the Damascus road. As they entered the foothills, the temperature gradually dropped with the increasing height. The road wound its way through the hills penetrating a light mist, which had descended on the slopes of the mountains.

His companion spoke Arabic fluently, his mother a Lebanese who had married an Englishman, born and educated in England and finally graduating from the University of Leicester, majoring in Arabic languages. The intelligence services had snapped him up and after completing the required military combat course – six months of gruelling, exhausting physical and weapons training in all aspects of undercover warfare – he was assigned to the Middle East desk as an operative. He had been seconded to Seymour for the duration of this operation. His name: John Bartlett. He fooled no one. His features were distinctly Arabic.

They easily found the turn-off to the property, the road cutting a swathe through the cedar forest. Seymour pulled the car off onto a sidetrack, penetrating the forest until he was certain it could not be seen from the road. Hiram's property was still at least a mile farther, which would have to be travelled on foot through the forest. They were appropriately dressed, both in black with black balaclavas and hiking boots. Seymour had a compass which he consulted before they took off.

After about forty-five minutes, avoiding trees, thickets and gullies, their progress was stopped by a high steel-mesh fence, the top of which was electrified, the white insulators visible on the fence poles. From the fence, all trees and brush had been cleared, the area flat providing an unrestricted view of the bungalow. It was at quite a distance, the mist hampering their vision. The bungalow glowed in the light mist, the interior lights already on. It was built on the foot of a steep mountain.

From his haversack, Bartlett removed a tripod and attached a powerful night telescope to it. He peered through the instrument for a few minutes, making adjustments. He then drew away indicating the Seymour should look.

'Have a dekko. It's difficult with this fog,' Bartlett said.

Seymour looked and was amazed at the detail the telescope revealed. The scope was powerful, the building now close-up. He ignored the building and swung the telescope round, slowly traversing the entire property. Soon he found what he was looking for. The property was well-guarded, with four men patrolling the house. He knew it would not be possible to approach the house without being observed. This could only give rise to a gun battle, which he knew he had to avoid at all costs and complicated matters. How were they going to get to the couple without being observed? Of course, this was assuming Tusk and the woman were on the property but a nagging feeling told him it was so. The number of guards indicated that the bungalow contained something of importance.

Seymour prepared himself for a long night. He wasn't leaving until he knew the reason for the guards: it had to be Tusk. They would take turns keeping the house under surveillance.

'Have a look at this!' the young man said, his eye glued to the telescope.

Seymour had dozed off. He got to his feet and peered through the scope. The first thing which struck him was that the sliding doors from the lounge to the porch were open, the lights from the interior illuminating the porch. He could dimly discern three people standing outside, one of whom was smoking. He realised that they were two men and a woman. His first reaction was Hiram, Tusk and his woman.

'Christ! It's them,' he said.

'Can you recognise them?' Bartlett asked.

'No, not really, it's too dark, but I'm certain it's them,' Seymour replied excitedly.

Just then, the woman strode back into the lounge. She was briefly illuminated by the inside light as she approached the door. There was no mistaking the blonde hair and the exceptional beauty of the woman.

'Okay, it's them. At least we now know where they are,' Seymour said. 'Let's get out of here before we are discovered. There's only one road that leads to the property. We'll set up a surveillance team. I want it in place before morning with a radio link to the embassy. Everything that comes or goes from here must be reported immediately. I also want a team monitoring the highway from here, that is, the Damascus-to-Beirut highway. They're to position themselves on the outskirts of Beirut just before it enters the built-up area. Get hold of a large truck so that this can be used to block the road. Find an ideal position. This winding road should provide a number of positions.'

Bartlett had removed the telescope and started to collapse the tripod when they suddenly heard the sound of an approaching engine in the distance.

'What's that?' Seymour asked.

'It's a bloody aircraft. It's pretty low,' Bartlett replied, looking up at the night sky.

The mist had lifted and already the first stars could be seen. Suddenly, two strings of blue lights lit up demarcating a short runaway, which started near the fence where the two men were until well past the bungalow. Seymour now realised why the three has come out on to the porch. The aircraft whooshed low over their heads, its landing light stabbing ahead of it, and settled softly onto the ground. It was a four-seater Cessna 180 capable of an extraordinarily low flying speed, an aircraft specifically designed to operate out of short runways. This runway was short, , cut out of the side of the hill below the bungalow.

'Now that complicates matters,' Seymour mused, 'Get the telescope out, I want to see who has arrived.'

Within minutes, the telescope was mounted, Seymour staring through the lens at the two people who had disembarked from the aircraft. They walked to the bungalow and climbed the stairs to the porch.

'One of them is the pilot. The other is in uniform. I don't know what uniform that is but it's naval. He has a number of rings on the wrist. A ship's captain, I think,' Seymour said, 'I wonder what a ship captain is doing here? Memorise that aircraft's registration number, I need to know to whom that aircraft belongs. Okay, I don't think anything else will happen tonight. Let's go'

Seymour did not know that the pilot still sat in the aircraft. The civilian who had exited was not the pilot.

CHAPTER 44

They all sat in the lounge. The bank official had found the flight in a light aircraft at night terrifying and had not quite recovered from the ordeal. He produced a sheaf of documents from his briefcase, which he had handed to David. David perused these and then signed wherever indicated. Once done, he handed these back.

'Is that the lot?' David asked.

'Oui, Monsieur,' replied the clerk, with a slight stammer.

'Well that does it, Hussein, the money is yours,' David said, glad that he no longer needed to concern himself. This was now finalised.

'I have a condition,' Hiram said. All eyes swivelled to rest on him. He addressed the bank official, 'This money is to remain in the account it currently is in until such time that I notify you.'

'But sir, what about the interest? You would stand to lose a large sum of money?' the official stammered.

'Don't let that concern you, I've my reasons. Can this be done?'

'Of course, sir. We will await your instructions.'

Once they were alone, David addressed Hiram, 'Why are you doing this? It doesn't make sense!'

'I'm sure MI6 has inside information on what happens in the banks. Let them think the deal is not yet concluded. They won't dare touch the helicopters and they can't touch the money,' he replied with a mischievous smile.

No matter what, David felt relieved. The money transaction had been concluded.

'You seemed relieved, well that makes two of us. I can't wait to get rid of those crates in my warehouse,' Hiram said. He then called the bank official close, 'Please don't forget to express my thanks to your director for permitting the matter to be settled in such an unorthodox manner.'

'I will, Monsieur,' the man replied.

Hiram turned to the man in uniform who stood to one side, evident that he had no interest in the financial transaction. He was in his late forties, his hair peppered with grey. He had removed his cap, which he now had tucked under his arm.

'Captain, I do believe that at last you can load the crates I have in my warehouse.'

The captain's eyes crinkled as he smiled. 'Thank God, I can't have my ship hanging around in Beirut harbour much longer. I'm running out of excuses. My engineer can't understand why I've wanted to carry out these minor repairs in Beirut and not South Africa. I'll have my ship alongside tomorrow night.'

'Excellent!' Hiram said, taking a sip from his drink and looking at David, 'I take it the papers – the bills of lading, and certificates of origin, and the rest – will be ready by tomorrow night?'

'Yes, the forwarding agents in Beirut will attend to this. They have already been briefed.' He hesitated. 'You're releasing the goods before payment?' David blurted, his surprise evident.

'Don't worry, I'm certainly not concerned.' Hussein gave him a look of appraisal, 'Good, then I suggest that the pilot fly these two gentlemen back to Beirut tonight.'

The bank official paled. 'Tonight?'

''It's perfectly safe, don't concern yourself but it is better that you leave tonight,' Hiram said, no mistaking the finality in his voice.

A half-hour later, the Cessna roared down the short runway and took to the sky.

The two men stood on the porch watching the aircraft disappear.

'What are your plans?' Hiram asked, staring in the darkness.

'I just want to get out of Beirut, for reasons you can imagine. The ship should be alongside tomorrow and I'll visit the warehouse to ensure that the cargo is loaded. The British don't know how we propose to get the helicopters out of Lebanon. They probably don't even know where they are stored. Once I see the last of the crates aboard, my companion and I will wish you au revoir. Only, I don't think we'll be back for a while.' He knew he would not be seeing Hiram again if he could help it. He had killed a man. Admittedly, this may have only been in self-defence. Yet that was enough reason never to return.

'The police could be looking for you, not to mention MI6.'

'We've got new identities which we will assume before we leave. We'll leave during the course of the morning. However, I do have one favour to ask. I need another set of wheels. We can't use the 190SL. The police could be looking for it.'

'No problem. You can use my Mercedes,' Hussein said, flicking his cigarette stub into the garden below.

'Thank you.'

CHAPTER 45

Backed by a first-class communications network, Seymour's men took up their allotted positions placing both the bungalow and the highway under constant surveillance, able to call up assistance at a moment's notice. He wasn't about to take any chances. This time the two were not getting away. No one had slept during the night. Now he allowed his men, one at a time, a short sleep break. Vigilance was constant. One slept in the car the other keeping watch, ready to react immediately.

Although both the British and the Lebanese governments did their utmost to keep the shooting at the hotel under wraps, Britain came forward to give the Lebanese government an explanation as to what had happened. This had created a diplomatic uproar. They were now aware of the two Rhodesian agents, as these were referred to, as well as the fact that payment had been transacted in their country for the purchase of helicopters in defiance of a UN trade embargo. The Lebanese refused to involve themselves in the helicopters or the money exchange as no law appeared to have been broken and therefore, if such a transaction had taken place, it could not be construed as illegal. In addition, they were not about to search warehouses or ships. They would only consider this if the British could provide concrete evidence. The shooting was another matter entirely. Hiram was in the clear, not so David and Gisela. Their description was circulated to the police with instructions that they were to be apprehended but with a request that violence be avoided, if possible.

A South African merchantman had docked alongside the warehouse during the night, moored astern of the old Liberty ship. Instructions had been communicated to other forwarding agents and already other cargo was on its way to Hiram's warehouse where it would assembled, to be loaded together with the knockdown helicopters, designed to look as innocuous as possible.

CHAPTER 46

They rose early, dressing in fresh clothes brought by Hiram's men from the hotel. Breakfast was light, no more than a cup of coffee and a croissant each. David wanted to be on the road as soon as possible. They piled their stuff into the Mercedes' trunk and profusely thanked Marcel, Hiram's right-hand man for their help and hospitality.

They shook hands.

'Please, you must be careful. The police are on the lookout. Try and restrict your driving to a minimum, keep off the main roads,' the man said.

'I will,' David replied taking the proffered car keys from the man.

He was taking no chances. He drove with his automatic resting on his lap while Gisela had placed hers on the seat next to her thigh.

If the police apprehended them, it would be just their bad luck. That they had been targeted was obvious and had merely acted in self-defence. That much must already be clear to the police, based on the evidence they would have found at the hotel and their own enquiries. They both were convinced that the British had not yet finished with them. Why the attempt to kill them? Although he thought it difficult to believe, he thought that MI6 had been cleared to take whatever action they considered appropriate to eliminate him. He played a key role in Rhodesia's sanctions-busting efforts and the British thought it imperative that they be stopped, even if this included murder. By now they would have realised that Gisela was involved, she his operative assistant and, no doubt, if caught in the crossfire they would consider her collateral damage.

Keeping a sharp lookout, he drove slowly along the track, which tunnelled through the tall cedars, suddenly coming on to the main road between Damascus and Beirut. The lodge was near Shtawrah, which was no more than fifteen miles from the Syrian border. He swung right onto the highway and speeded up until the car was moving just above the legal speed limit of 100 kph.

CHAPTER 47

Their departure had not gone unobserved. The surveillance team immediately reported to Seymour who lost no time and departed the embassy with Bartlett in tow, driving to where the planned blockade of the highway was to take place. His men were armed and instructed that in the event of any resistance they were free to fire. The team selected to erect the roadblock were issued with two Heckler & Koch machine pistols. He realised that he was stretching a point and if a gun battle ensued all hell would break loose, giving rise to another diplomatic incident with him in the middle, but instructions were instructions and this was not his concern.

Seymour had chosen the spot to blockade the highway well. It was a cutting through a hill with sheer rock faces on both sides of the road. He proposed to use a truck. The vehicle was a large articulated flat-deck comprising a truck-tractor and flat-deck trailer. This was to be parked across the highway, leaving a small gap between the truck and the rock face of the cutting, which would allow motor vehicles to pass the stalled truck. Any vehicle wanting to pass would have to slow down to a crawl in order to navigate the obstacles. They would delay blocking the road until the last minute and only when David was nearly on them. Seymour hoped that it would take a few minutes before the Lebanese gendarmes responded to any alarms that others might raise. The cutting was in a valley, which ensured that any vehicle coming from the direction of Damascus came upon the truck right after a short rise. He surmised this would give them very little opportunity to U-turn the vehicle before his men could respond. He placed a man at the top of the rise, suitably armed, who was to warn them of David's approach. The police remained a major concern. The area around was populated, a homestead every few hundred yards apart. The populace was bound to hear any gunfire and phone the police.

Seymour brought the Jaguar to halt alongside the truck, which had parked on the verge of the road.

His men were dressed in overalls to avoid raising any suspicion. He and Bartlett had dressed casually with open-necked shirts. The windbreakers were necessary to conceal their weapons.

The man in charge approached Seymour, a hand-held radio at the ready. 'They are about ten minutes away. They're driving a white Mercedes coupe, a 250SE,' the man said, slightly out of breath.

Seymour nodded.

'All right, get the truck started and ready move on my signal,' he barked.

The driver started the engine, revving it to ensure the air pressure remained high so the brakes released when he was required to move the vehicle. The rest of the four took up concealed positions behind two cars and a rock outcrop on the side of the road. All had drawn their weapons.

The man in charge pointed to the top of the hill. 'The man at the top has the car in sight. They'll come over the top any minute now,' he said.

Seymour checked for traffic. There was none.

'Okay, move the truck,' he shouted and walked onto the road indicating where he wanted the truck to stand.

The truck's engine roared as it pulled away from the verge and crossed the road, stopping where indicated with a sharp squeal of brakes. The driver stepped from the cab and got ready to start waving his arms at any oncoming traffic warning them of the danger, this the usual thing to do in the event of a breakdown and hoping that this would not immediately make David suspicious, or so Seymour hoped.

CHAPTER 48

The Mercedes slid over the rise. He saw the truck parked across the road, a man dressed in a blue overall in front of it, waving his arms. He took his foot off the accelerator, allowing the car to coast. He saw two cars parked on the side of the road behind the truck. He decided not to drive right up to the truck. He braked harshly, bringing the car to a stop on the verge, about three hundred yards from the truck.

'Why are you stopping?' Gisela asked.

'I don't know what's going on down there, but I'm not taking a chance. It may be a real breakdown but the spot's well chosen. It blocks the road. I don't like that,' he replied and then looked out to the side to make sure he could make a U-turn.

Before leaving the bungalow, they had studied a road map of Lebanon and acquainted themselves with the various routes that led either to Beirut or to Tyre. Tyre was a port farther south down the coast. If he backtracked, he could turn south at Ain Dara and take an alternative route. There were a number of options, too many to monitor, or so he thought. The British would need a small army of men.

'I'm not waiting to see what happens,' he said, putting the car in drive and making a U-turn, the tyres squealing.

Gisela turned round to stare out of the rear window.

'There are some men. They're getting into the cars,' she shouted excitedly, her concern evident, glancing anxiously at him.

'Jesus Christ! It must be the British.'

He floored the gas pedal, the car rapidly gaining speed as they disappeared over the rise. Gisela kept a sharp lookout behind them.

'There are two cars after us!'

He had also seen them in the rear-view mirror as they topped the rise.

They were in the mountains, the road undulating from one valley to another, twisting and turning as it followed the topographical contours of the terrain. He pushed the car hard, driving as fast as the road permitted, constantly having to slow down for a curve. It was impossible to maintain a constant high speed, occasionally having to slowdown to eighty kph to negotiate a bend, the tyres squealing. The main problem was the trucks, which plied the route to Damascus, most of Syria's imports passing through Beirut, the trucks dominating the road. The road consisted of two lanes only and most trucks were heavily laden, labouring up every incline at low speed, forcing David to stick behind as they approached each blind rise. Their pursuers had to contend with the same problem, sometimes gaining and then falling behind again. The cars appeared to be evenly matched.

'This can't go on. We need to plan something to pre-empt anything going wrong, and at this rate, something will go wrong. We need to do something to give ourselves an advantage,' Gisela said. She turned round to look for the pursuers. They were about half a mile behind.

He had been thinking the same thing. Make a stand at a place of their choosing. Like this, it could only go bad for them.

'I've been racking my brains and I can't come up with a damn thing!'

'Look, we're ten miles from Bhamdoun, it's a small town.' With an outstretched hand, she indicated the signboard that had just flashed by.

'Listen, hon. I've an idea. We have to abandon the car, but we have to find a crowd. Somewhere we can disappear. We leave everything. We only take the guns and what we're wearing. What do you think?'

She was silent for a few moments. It could work.

'We'll only have about thirty seconds to disappear into the crowd, but that should be enough,' she replied. They were casually dressed and could blend easily into the throng. 'We need to find a market or big bazaar. Every town in Lebanon has one,' she added.

The car rapidly approached the outskirts of the town, the traffic increasing, forcing him to slow down. He negotiated a sharp turn in the road, the beginning of an S-turn through the town. On reflex, as the cars behind them disappeared from view, he suddenly swung right into a side street. He now needed to get out of sight. At the next available turn to the left, he skidded around the corner and quickly reduced speed so as not to attract attention. He knew that this would not give him much time. As soon as his pursuers lost him, they would realise that he had swung off the main road. The question was what would they do?

There were quite a few people in the street. Gisela opened her window and asked him to stop. She asked a man close to the car in French where the market was. He understood, pointing further down the road.

'He says the market is a few hundred metres down the road.'

Again, he drove off. The nearer he got to the market, the more people they encountered until they were literally driving at a walking pace through the people who opened up in front of them to allow them passage. The throng then closed behind them.

David looked around for a place to abandon the car. Through the milling people, he glimpsed the first of the market stalls ahead. To the side of these, on an open patch of ground, a number of trucks were parked, these belonging to the farmers who had brought their merchandise into town. He parked behind a large truck, hiding the car from view from the road. He left the keys under the seat. They grabbed their coats and left the car unlocked, the windows up. Eventually, somebody would realise that it had been abandoned and, hopefully, alert the local gendarmerie. Hiram was sure to get his car back.

The market teemed with people, some shouting loudly to each other from stall to stall. Gisela had taken a scarf, which she now put over her head throwing one end of it back over her shoulder. A cursory glance would have left anyone with the impression that she was an Arab woman from a middle-class family. She had also donned her sunglasses. She no longer walked next to him but left a small distance between them so as not to create the impression that they were together.

They came upon an old building that dominated the market ground. This was a huge hall where merchants had erected a multitude of shops separated by partitions, one next to the other, selling goods and food of every description, the owners standing at the entrances calling upon the passers-by to stop and shop.

David had to do something about his appearance. He was far too conspicuous in this crowd, so obviously European. Walking past the shops, mingling with the crowd, he looked out for a shop selling clothing. He found one and entered, noticing that Gisela had entered an adjoining shop to wait there for him. He selected a turban and paid. When he emerged from the shop and mingled again with the crowd, he believed he was no different from any of the many other Arabs in the crowd. Only on close examination would they discover differently. She joined him and they continued as a couple.

'From the map, can you remember if the train station was nearby?' he asked.

'Are there trains running in Lebanon?'

218

'There's a railway line between Damascus and Beirut but whether passenger trains run on the line, I really don't know. We'll have to find out. If there are no trains, we can take a bus,' he replied.

They were not about to ask a gendarme for directions. He espied a small coffee house inside the Arab market, the souk, and led her to a secluded table not visible from the alley. They ordered coffee and flatbread with a bowl of the local lamb stew to share. This they ate with their fingers. It was delicious, they both hungry.

'Great lamb stew,' she said, licking her fingers.

'Probably goat,' he replied mischievously.

He kept a wary eye on the passers-by.

CHAPTER 49

Seymour was frantic. They had outsmarted him, turning either left or right in the town the moment their pursuers were out of sight. Seymour fumed. They had driven past the first intersection and noticing that the Mercedes was missing, he ordered the cars to double back. It took a minute or two before they were able to find a place on the main road to do that.

'For God's sake, hurry!' he shouted, repeating this into the radio for the benefit of the occupants in the other car. Finally, they turned left, following the road that led to the market, looking out for the Mercedes, slowly threading their way through the pedestrians. It took them twenty minutes to find the car, obvious that it had been abandoned.

Bartlett got out of the car, telling the others to do the same and they spread out to start a systematic search. Seymour stopped him.

'Let's not waste our time. The bastard is smarter than that. He's not going to sit around this town. He'll find a way out of here and soon. He's got three options: rail, bus or taxi. Take your pick,' he said. 'Okay, we're six men.' He indicated to two of the men and continued, 'You two take the station. Bartlett and I will tackle the bus terminus and you two get to the taxi rank. We'll all still be in radio range, so don't hesitate to talk to one another if you come up with anything.'

The three groups dispersed.

Seymour pondered the situation. The quickest way out would be the taxis, but Seymour wasn't so sure that's what Tusk would do. C'mon, concentrate. What would the man do? He was sure Tusk would opt for large crowds, making them difficult to find amongst all the people. The town was a major bus terminal with routes running in four directions, to Damascus and Beirut and then north and south. They asked directions and were glad to find that the terminus was no more than two hundred metres away. As they neared the terminus, the crowd seemed to swell. It was as if everybody in the town wanted to catch a bus. They entered the depot. Buses lined up alongside the boards indicating their respective routes, the people boarding while other buses waited their turn. The question was where would they go? Given a choice, he was sure it would be Beirut.

'Find the Beirut bus,' he said to Bartlett.

Oh, they found the Beirut bus or rather busses soon enough. The problem was there were various routes to Beirut. Now, which route to choose?

CHAPTER 50

In the bus depot, Gisela purchased two tickets and, when asked what route, said the shortest.

She emerged from the ticket office with the two tickets in hand. 'It's bus Number Fourteen. It leaves in nine minutes, so the ticket man said. We'd better hurry.'

'Never mind hurry. Watch out for those bastards. They have to be here somewhere. They're not giving up,' he replied, looking furtively around.

They made it to the bus, joining the queue that inched slowly forward as the passengers boarded, the bus driver taking the tickets and punching them before handing them back. During this time, they both kept their backs turned to the direction from which they thought the British would arrive. The British would not recognise them from the back.

'Shit! Something just struck me. When we board, split up. Let's not sit next to each other. Also, keep your face covered until we are sure that none of them have followed us aboard.'

She realised what he was getting at and nodded.

CHAPTER 51

As they boarded, David realised that she had bought tickets from one of the better bus operators. The bus was new with high-backed, cloth-covered seats and the windows had pull-down blinds. At least they would travel in comfort. Still, the bus was crowded, every seat taken. He sat next to a middle-aged, dark-haired man with a large bushy moustache and sideburns. He stank of tobacco smoke and garlic.

The bus started. This was followed by the whoosh of compressed air and hydraulics as the automatic doors closed. The bus jerked into motion pulling away from the kerb.

He had taken a seat near the back of the bus, seated on the aisle. He scrutinised each passenger. Those that looked typically Arab, he ignored, as did he the women. That left him with fifteen men, carefully noting their positions in the bus. How many men were there chasing them? If what he had seen in the valley represented their full complement, he doubted whether they could have more than one or two people on this bus.

For a minute or two, he reflected on his position. The situation was ridiculous. The trip to Lebanon was supposed to have been a simple affair. That the British wanted to kill him was a fact and it was highly probable that Gisela was on their list as well and for no other reason than she was his accomplice. He had not forgotten how close to death he had been in the hotel. They would want to leave no witnesses. It had never occurred to him that they would have set out to kill them. It just seemed so un-British. He was shocked. This whole affair read like the script of a James Bond movie. He recalled his first meeting with the bank's managing director when he was coerced into participating in assisting Rhodesia to fool the British. It had sounded like fun! Killing and death had been furthest from his mind. Now this was a reality. They both could die at any moment at the hands of MI6. He was bewildered. Never would he have volunteered for the job, no matter what rewards were on offer. Had Butler, the minister, not indicated that he stood to make substantial financial gain for assisting them? War was one thing – he had been there and had known what he was letting himself in for – but this undercover stuff, now that death and killing was part of it, and he not even Rhodesian. Well, this was simply was not acceptable. He wanted out.

Nobody seemed to be taking any notice of him. Gisela sat three rows in front of him, also in an aisle seat. She fashioned the scarf into a veil, covering her head and her face from the eyes down. The bus had left the town and was now moving at a fair speed. Some passengers had opened the sliding windows and a cool breeze blew through the bus. He sat with his arms folded, his hand resting on the butt of the automatic under his windbreaker. He wanted to sleep but dared not do so until he was sure that none of the men were British agents.

Lebanon was such a cosmopolitan society: the population was made up of Arabs steeped in the Muslim faith – Sunni and Shia; then there were Eastern Orthodox, Marmite Christians, and Coptics. Their dress was predominantly European except for the die-hard fanatics who stuck to their traditional dress. Without speaking to them, there was no way of knowing which of the men could be the British and of whom he should be suspicious. All they had to do was wait until the bus reached its destination and then apprehend him when he stepped off. He needed to think of something before then.

CHAPTER 52

Seymour was close to panic.

'They are bound to be on the next bus or two due to leave for Beirut. Find those taking the shortest direct route. You take one and I'll take the other,' he said.

'What do I do if I don't have time to get a ticket?' Bartlett said exasperatedly.

'Board anyway. Bribe the driver if you have to. Do anything, I don't give a shit! Offer him anything. Just get on the bus and whatever you do, don't lose them,' Seymour replied with savage irritation.

****

Seymour made it to the bus and managed to find a seat two rows from the front. He wanted to sit further back but had boarded the bus too late, the rear seats already taken. He had immediately seen Tusk seated towards the rear, recognising him from the photograph. He dare not turn round. This would surely give him away. He was sure the man was watching all those passengers who did not appear to be Arabs. He had not recognised Tusk's companion but assumed that she had to be on board, probably disguised, he thought. A few women wore veils which complicated matters. At least he had not lost them. The question was what to do now. He still had the hand-held radio although he had switched it off. He dare not switch it on. This would reveal him. There were two of them and it would be futile to try to do anything while still on the bus. He decided that he would wait until they reached Beirut, but he needed to contact his own people so that they could prepare for the bus' arrival. He hoped Bartlett realised that he must have found them and was now unable to make contact, this being too obvious while on the bus. He wondered whether Bartlett was smart enough to realise this.

****

Bartlett covered every inch of the bus depot. Seymour was not found. He repeatedly called Seymour on the radio, also to no avail as he remained silent. He realised he had to make a decision and could only assume that his boss must have recognised Tusk and boarded the same bus, which would mean that they were on their way to Beirut.

He called the others and conferred with them. They agreed that their targets were on the bus. The men decided to travel as fast as possible to Beirut and intercept the bus at the terminus. Bartlett enquired at the ticket office as to whether that particular bus made any stops on the route. The ticket clerk assured him that it was an express bus. Its next and only stop was Beirut.

The three men climbed into their two cars and sped off in pursuit of the bus planning to overtake it and await its arrival at the terminal. The bus had little start on them and after about twenty kilometres, the first car shot past.

Seymour watched the Jaguar pass. He sighed with relief. At least his men would arrange a reception at the terminus. This time Tusk would not get away.

****

He was not the only one who recognised the car. So had Gisela. She waited for the second car to pass and, when it didn't, she turned round and looked out of the rear window. It was there, about a hundred yards back, keeping pace with the bus. They'll be waiting at the terminus, she thought, while the second car kept a lookout to ensure that they not try and leave while still en route.

CHAPTER 53

The bus was no more than five miles from the Beirut bus terminus and still David had no plan other than hijacking the bus. He had immediately discarded the idea, as this was sure to introduce the police. Although the police may be looking for them, he doubted whether this would result in a murder charge. A hijacking would merely aggravate the situation. How big a reception committee could he expect? Surely, the British agents had radioed ahead. Of course, there was Gisela. He doubted whether she had been recognised.

The last few miles were slow, the traffic congestion in Beirut a continuous nightmare. Driving in Beirut required steel nerves and practised use of the car's horn. The bus was big, which gave the driver a slight advantage, the smaller vehicles giving way.

Finally, the bus terminus came into view. Something was wrong. A huge cloud of smoke billowed from the centre. Police vehicles, fire engines and ambulances surrounded the area. Police and paramedics were everywhere. The police had strung a cordon around the source and all movement into the terminus was being monitored.

As the bus approached, a police officer stepped forward, his hand raised, and halted the bus. The driver leant out of his open window and spoke to the police officer. The driver was being given instructions. The bus moved forward and drove through a gap which had opened in the cordon. It moved slowly towards the bus shelters, all affected by the smoke.

Christ! he thought, it's a bomb. Either a Muslim or a Christian fanatical group trying to send a political message. This is how these fanatics made a point: plant a bomb and then claim responsibility. Tensions between Muslim and Christian had simmered for years and all indications were that this was on the increase.

With a squeal of brakes, the bus came to a halt under a sheltered off-loading point, the pneumatic doors opening with a whoosh. Four police officers, armed with machine pistols, lined the pavement watching as the passengers disembarked. It then struck David. If the British intended to meet him on the bus' arrival this was no longer possible, the police cordon blocking all entry to vehicles and persons other than busses. That meant that he only had to contend with one or two agents and they certainly were hamstrung as long as he remained in sight of the gendarmes. Fortunately, the gendarmes were not subjecting the passengers or their luggage to a search. He stepped down, walking just behind Gisela. The idea was to take a taxi but this was now a restricted area. Taxis were not permitted.

He was about to ask a gendarme when a police officer with a megaphone announced that the passengers were to use the southern exit to leave the depot and that the police would let them through. This was at least two hundred yards away. Fortunately, they were travelling light, not like many others who were loaded down with baggage.

It had been a large bomb. Obviously, a car bomb. The explosion had left a crater in the road. The blast's pressure wave had torn the roofs of the shelters, just leaving the blackened skeletal steel support beams and pillars, the cars adjacent to the blast now no more than smoking blackened hulks. Already forensic experts in white coats were on the scene inspecting the debris. The dead and injured had been removed. It was a gruesome sight.

The passengers formed a scraggy line as they walked towards the exit. He kept right behind Gisela, who ignored him, her face still covered by the veil. He still had no idea which of the men on the bus was the British agent. He knew that they could not make a move. The atmosphere was tense, the police nervous. A bad time to create any type of commotion.

Gisela stopped right next to a gendarme and looked for an available taxi, as did many others. He did not stray more than a yard or two from her and, together with the other passengers, they had formed a small crowd.

He had to speak to her. They had no option. They had to split up.

Pretending to crane forward as if looking for a taxi, she no more than a foot away, he said, 'Meet me at the yacht club.'

She made no sign of recognition, but merely waved her arm indicating that she required a taxi. A French Simca drove up with a taxi sign affixed to the roof. Gisela climbed in and the car sped off. He watched it leave. He saw no other car pull away as if it were in pursuit.

David stepped forward to the kerb, waving his arm trying to draw the attention of a taxi. A black Citroën DS 20 pulled up, this too displaying a taxi sign. As he climbed in, he glanced back and in the distance could see the Jaguar.

'The yacht club on the boat marina, please,' he said to the driver in French. He withdrew fifty dollars from his wallet and waved this at the driver. 'This is yours if you can lose the black Jaguar that will follow us. Can you do it?'

'Of course, Monsieur, I'm the best taxi driver in Beirut!' replied the driver, his eyes twinkling with humour.

He looked at him. From the paraphernalia which hung from the rear-view mirror post on the windscreen roof and the small religious placards stuck to the dashboard it was obvious the man was a Christian, an Eastern Orthodox. He was middle-aged, maybe forty-five, with a swarthy complexion and a huge drooping moustache.

David wondered whether the Citroën was a match for the Jaguar. The Citroën took off, its hydrolastic suspension smoothing out every bump in the road. He noticed that there seemed to be more than the usual complement of gendarmes on the streets, some in cars and on motorcycles, and attributed this to the bomb blast. He kept glancing back. The Jaguar was still there behind them.

'We're going to have to do better than this,' he said to the taxi driver.

'Patience, Monsieur. I have a plan, I've been chased before,' the man replied.

He noticed that they were not travelling in the right direction but refrained from saying anything, hoping that the man knew what he was doing. The driver certainly handled the car superbly considering the amount of traffic and the congestion. In fact, the Jaguar had fallen slightly behind.

He realised that they had entered the old city, the streets narrow. This could be a blessing or a disaster. If anything obstructed their passage, then it was over. The car swayed and bumped over the uneven road, the tyres squealing round every corner they took. Now the streets were even narrower. Suddenly, the car braked hard and swung left. He looked behind, the Jaguar was not yet in sight. The taxi driver stopped the car.

'What the hell are you stopping the car for?'

The driver smiled. 'Don't worry, just watch.'

The Jaguar flashed past behind them. The Citroën reversed harshly backwards into the narrow street, the car now pointing in the same direction they had come.

'Christ! This is a one-way!' David expected a car from the opposite direction at any moment, his face a picture of apprehension.

Fortunately they did not have far to go. At the next intersection, the taxi driver swung right onto a main two-lane road.

'I think we lost them, Monsieur. By the time they find a place to turn their car around, we'll be long gone.'

He allowed himself to relax in the seat. 'Well done, thank you.'

'This is none of my business, Monsieur, but if you ever need my assistance again, please, here is my card,' the driver said, handing him his card.

'I will remember, thank you.'

CHAPTER 54

It was now late afternoon, the sun rapidly slipping towards the horizon. Gisela took a seat at a table in the corner of the La Marina Yacht Club restaurant on the terraced first floor overlooking the protected waters of the yacht basin. There were scores of yachts of every description moored to the jetties jutting out from the quay. The sea beyond was deep blue and a slight breeze blew, perfect weather for yachting. There were still a few boats out at sea. Somewhere amongst these yachts was the *Felicity*. They had never planned to leave Lebanon on board her. This was a last resort, the idea was not to compromise the Hackers in anyway.

Gisela had been fortunate. She had not been recognised. She was concerned for David's safety. They had clearly recognised him. She wondered whether he had been able to give them the slip.

She had mixed feelings about David. Yes, she was deeply in love with him. Certainly, he was a good banker and an expert at circumventing every obstacle the British or the UN could produce to stop Rhodesian imports. The Rhodesian Department of Trade and Industries had the greatest admiration for him and revered the ground he walked on. He was not a Rhodesian and could move freely throughout most of the world. To cap it, he was multilingual, intelligent, and astute. There was no doubt that he would make a caring and loving partner. However, that was where it stopped. He was soft and pliable, his feelings for others sublime. He did not possess the merciless attitude required to be a successful operative. Yes, he did not lack courage and, in fact, was brave to the extreme, but was unable to apply the ruthlessness the job demanded.

Of course, he would tell you that he had never wanted to be an undercover operative and that he was forced into this situation, which may have been true to a degree. Others would say he volunteered. Things had changed, the goalposts had shifted. Both sides no longer shirked from killing. This was war. She now realised that they should have ambushed and killed their pursuers long ago and not have waited to be taken out. She regretted leaving those silenced automatics behind in the hotel. They would've come in handy now.

From her location, she kept the entrance to the marina under observation. All in and outgoing traffic passed through a boomed security area. Various vehicles, including taxis, came and went, but still there was no sign of him. The sun dipped lower as did her confidence. Had something gone wrong?

At that moment a Citroën entered, its lit taxi sign indicating that it was occupied. From below, she heard the crunch of tyres on the chipped stone gravel as it drove under the terrace floor jutting out over the club's main entrance. This was followed by the slam of a car door. She heard David's voice. Her heart lifted, he was safe. She knew that he would not come to the yacht club if he thought he was still being followed.

Each of the jetties that jutted out into the waters of the marina had a security hut at their entrance, manned by uniform security men who controlled access to the yachts. This was the playground of the super-rich, equivalent to the lavishness of the French Riviera, the haunt of millionaires, European aristocrats and Arab princes. It had a mystical atmosphere about it, a legacy from when it originally was mandated to France by the League of Nations. David came into view as he walked towards the nearest security hut and spoke to the guard. The guard came out of his hut and stood on the quayside with David pointing amongst the yachts. David turned to face the yacht club, immediately seeing Gisela on the terrace. He smiled, waved, and then made his way to the entrance disappearing below the canopy. As he appeared on the terrace, she rose and rushed to him. Oblivious of the other guests, she threw her arms around his neck and hugged him, her face resting on his shoulder.

'God, I was so worried,' she whispered, her relief at seeing him evident in her voice.

David told her how he had managed to make his escape, praising the taxi driver. He was confident that he had not been followed.

'What are we going to do know?' she asked.

'Well, I believe the *Felicity* is still here. I suggest we try to find where in this maze of boats and jetties the Hackers are moored. I asked the guard. He wasn't too sure but gave me a vague indication. I hope they can get us out of Lebanon. I certainly don't want us to try any of the airlines.' He remained silent for a moment. 'I'm sure they've got people watching. Christ! I need a stiff drink to settle my jangled nerves. I think we were just fuckin' lucky,' he said, raising his hand to signal a waiter. He ordered a double Black Label, neat, and when placed on the table in front of him, he just threw it back into his mouth. It burnt on the way down, giving his stomach a kick. He felt the coiled tension of the last twenty-four hours in his gut begin to release. He told the waiter to bring another but this time with branch water and ice. Gisela ordered a martini.

The club's restaurant-cum-bar filled rapidly. This was cocktail hour. Many of the crews from the yachts in the marina congregated daily at this watering hole, weather permitting. Dress was casual but smart, the men in white slacks and loafers with open-necked shirts, the women in slacks or shorts and summer blouses.

'Keep a lookout for the Hackers. Knowing Bernd, he's not about to miss this,' he said. Bernd liked his drink.

He had barely spoken when they saw the couple approaching and then disappearing under the canopy. A minute later, they emerged from the stairway. Ursula immediately saw them and her face broke into a smile as she waved to them. The elderly couple approached their table. They greeted, kissing and hugging each other.

'This calls for a celebration. We thought we'd never see you two again. Christ, what a relief,' Bernd said, 'Please, I don't want to know what happened. I'm just happy you are safe.'

David leant back in his chair and closed his eyes for a moment. 'You're right, you don't want to know,' then let out an exaggerated sigh of relief. They all laughed. 'Did anything happen at the marina that was out of the ordinary?' David enquired.

Bernd shook his head. 'Nothing. Nothing at all.'

'I take it we're dining together?' Gisela asked with eyebrows raised.

'But of course, and Bernd and I insist on paying. God, you deserve it!' Ursula said. Again they all laughed.

They started the meal off with grilled calamari. They followed it with tuna steaks caught in the Mediterranean off the Sicilian cost, grilled to perfection, with a butter sauce hinting of garlic. An ice cold and crisp Turkish Semillon wine accompanied the food, with its soft, unique taste. Their drinking a few bottles eventually reflected in their mood.

The waiter removed the plates and served coffee and liqueurs. Bernd produced two cigars, wrapped in cellophane, offering one to David.

'They're Cuban,' he said.

He wasn't really into cigars but then, these were Cuban and this was definitely a special occasion. He took it and watching Bernd, emulated the same elaborate ritual clipping it and lighting up, finally blowing a mouthful of smoke towards the sky.

'Bernd—' David hesitated. Bernd had raised his hand stopping him from finishing the sentence.

'Say no more, I'll take you out of Lebanon tomorrow even if I have to smuggle you out in the bilges,' he whispered, having read the seriousness that had crept into David's voice.

David just nodded. He realised the man knew what was going on.

Bernd had seen the automatic in the shoulder holster under his windbreaker.

The tensions of the last few days had taken their toll. For the first time he felt relatively safe. The feeling was not his alone. Gisela seemed more relaxed and exuded an upbeat mood, enjoying the Hacker's company, talking and laughing and swapping stories about Rhodesia and South Africa.

It did not take long before the cumulative effect of the Black Labels, martinis, wine and then liqueurs finally kicked him in the head. He was drunk, not that the others hadn't had their fair share, but he was streets ahead.

As his head began to droop, Gisela kicked him under the table. 'You're drunk!' she whispered.

''Fraid so,' he replied, his voice close to a slur.

'God, let him be, you've both been through a tough time,' Ursula said consolingly.

'C'mon, let's get him aboard the boat. Christ, just watch that he does not fall off the jetty.' Bernd laughed and rose from his chair. He helped David to his feet. With David's arm over his shoulder, they staggered down the stairs and out of the club, the two women following behind. The La Marina Yacht Club, with a few other restaurants and clubs, represented the epitome of society life in Beirut and as he passed the other tables many cast a reproving glance. Getting fall-down drunk was frowned upon.

The yacht was moored stern-on to the jetty with about three to four feet of gangplank to traverse. Getting David across the gangplank onto the yacht was a hazardous affair, requiring both Bernd and Gisela, they nearly all going into the water. They helped him get his shoes off and then took him through to the for'ard cabin, which was a double two-tier set-up. Gisela eventually got him down to his shorts and let him collapse on the lower bunk. There was little else she could do. He had passed out.

He awoke the next morning at eleven. The porthole curtains were still drawn, the interior dim. He sat up and then dropped back onto the bunk.

His head pounded and his stomach churned. He recalled the previous night's revelry and groaned aloud. He remembered all the different drinks he'd had and groaned again loudly. Today was going to be hell. After five minutes, he gingerly rose, supporting himself on the bunk, and waited for his head to stop spinning. Once his head cleared, he cautiously made his way up on deck. The moment he stepped into the cockpit the stark glare of the sun nearly took his head off. With eyes screwed shut he collapsed on the cockpit seating.

'God, you look terrible,' Gisela said.

'Please, fetch my sunglasses, hurry!' he croaked, his eyes still shut.

She retrieved his sunglasses, which he immediately donned. 'How about coffee?'

'Good God, no, not yet.'

She shook her head and went below.

Slowly, he got his bearings. Bernd and Ursula were busy on the foredeck. Gisela had returned to the galley. He lay back hoping to start a slow recovery to normality.

CHAPTER 55

Seymour's mood was subdued. He had just put the secure phone down after a lengthy conversation with Sir Henry. He was appalled, filled with a feeling of foreboding. To say Sir Henry was unhappy was an understatement. He was furious. He could not understand how Seymour and his men had lost Tusk. He did not consider the fact that a bomb had exploded in the bus depot just before the bus' arrival as an excuse. He told Seymour that the manner in which this operation had been executed bordered on incompetence and insisted that Tusk be found and the matter brought to finality. Intelligence had established that the monies had not yet been paid and therefore Rhodesia still did not own the helicopters. That, in his mind, was the only consolation. Seymour said he needed more men. Sir Henry conceded and agreed to fly another four men out to Beirut.

'Bartlett, get in here!'

Bartlett entered the office. He knew he had to tread carefully. All hell seemed to have broken loose, the expression on Seymour's face said it all; the conversation with Sir Henry could not have gone well at all.

'Yes, sir.' He only used the 'sir' designation with Seymour in times of acute stress. This was one of them.

'Another four operatives are arriving sometime today. I want the group broken into twos and they will thoroughly, and I mean thoroughly, investigate the airport, border posts,and, oh, don't forget the harbour. We have to find these two. Apparently the purchase has not been concluded, so they've got to be around,' Seymour said, pacing the office, his head down, deep in thought.

'Sir, if I may express an opinion, I doubt whether they'll try the airport,' Bartlett ventured.

Seymour looked up. 'You're probably right. Christ, the bastard is like a piece of wet soap.'

'I'd like to try the harbour first. The customs control there is pretty jacked-up because of the threat of arms being smuggled in by the fundamentalists. They keep a record of all movements.'

'Fine, sort the men out. I'll come with you. We'll do the harbour, they can handle the rest,' Seymour replied, dismissing him with a wave of his hand.

Bartlett assigned the two-man groups their various tasks and then informed Seymour that he was ready to leave. They drove out of the embassy and headed for the harbour. They easily gained entrance, using the diplomatic passports they carried. Both realised that this was a blatant misuse of their passports and that they would have to ensure that they caused no diplomatic incidents. Bartlett asked the senior customs official if he would mind assisting them: they were looking for a man and woman, both probably using German passports, who may have passed through during the last twenty-four hours. The official was initially surly but when Seymour withdrew a twenty-dollar note from his wallet, the man's face lit up. He became a lot more accommodating, even smiling. He told the official that he thought they probably would have passed through during the previous early evening. They carefully perused the records and questioned other customs officials. They drew a blank. None could recall a couple matching the description Bartlett had given them.

Demoralised, the two men approached the customs office that served the yacht basin. By then it was already mid-afternoon. Here the officials were more courteous. Dealing with the rich and sometimes famous, being rude and uncooperative usually had serious consequences. They told the two men that, since the previous day, a few boats had left for international waters and certainly nobody who matched the descriptions. However, they were told that papers and passports had only to be produced on a boat's departure and that the people they were looking for could well be on a boat.

Seymour stood on the quay looking at the mass of yachts and boats. Some rode at anchor while others were tied to the jetties in the basin. Not taking his eyes of the boats, he said to Bartlett, 'Just looking at this lot, I'm thinking that this has got to be the best place to hide. Christ, it'll be like a needle in haystack. There must be hundreds of boats. You can't just go tramping on every yacht. But something tells me we're close. Just a feeling I've got.' He pondered the situation for a while, watching the boats and people on the decks and suddenly blurted, 'Shit, we should've thought of this before. Christ, I'm a bloody fool! This bloody lot came to Lebanon on a yacht.'

'You think so?'

'I damn well know so. Pull in one of the other groups. With four we can systematically go through these boats. We can establish which yachts have arrived here in the last seven days or so. Then we can have a good look at each of those boats. Also, we need to speak to each of these jetty supervisors.' A smile touched his lips. 'I believe they're here!'

He grudgingly admired Tusk. The man seemed to slip through every attempt made to seize him.

For the first time that day, Bartlett smiled, taken up with his boss' enthusiasm.

Again, after parting with money – the customs officer did not come cheap – Seymour found success and cajoled a list of all yacht movements covering the last week from him. Surprisingly, the list was not long, only a dozen or so boats appearing on it.

'Okay, which of these has already left?'

Only four had left, leaving fewer than a dozen to investigate. Systematically they worked through the list, asking the supervisors whether these were moored to the jetties and eventually established where is each yacht was positioned in the harbour.

'We're not going to visit each of these boats. What we'll do is book a hotel room with a balcony overlooking the basin and use a powerful telescope. This should enable us to study each yacht carefully. During the day you don't want to be cooped-up below deck, they'll be about on deck. We're bound to spot them,' Seymour said with confidence. 'Bartlett, get a room as close to the marina as possible and quite high up. And oh, by the way, you'd better secure a launch, a sea-going boat, something we can rent for a few days. It just struck me. If we wait until the yacht is beyond the twelve-mile limit, it'll be in international waters. That could save Britain a lot of embarrassment. Piracy on the high seas, something like that.' He chuckled, pleased with his assumption. 'Besides, the Israelis have gunboats patrolling this part of the coast beyond the limit all the time. They could even be lumbered with the blame.'

There now was a bounce in Seymour's step. He was convinced that he was on the right track and that they may just pull the mission off.

They had discarded their suits and now wore casual beach outfits, blending in easily with the many tourists who crowded the hotel, beach and marina. From the balcony, they had an excellent view. The telescope was powerful, able to read the names of the yachts and distinguish the features of the crews. The jetty supervisors were mostly elderly men, each doing an eight-hour shift. Most were uncooperative, morose, and suspicious of Seymour and his men. However, once they realised that there was good money on offer for what was not confidential information, they relented and became willing informants.

By midday the next day, they had whittled the list of potential yachts down to three boats: the *Esmeralda*, the *Felicity*, and *Sea Strike*. These were distributed in the basin. They were unable to observe the *Esmeralda* from the balcony of the hotel as the vision was blocked. There was no alternative but to approach it on foot. The yacht was moored side-on to the jetty about halfway down its length. Seymour and Bartlett, dressed in shorts, T-shirts and moccasins, casually approached, talking, and not appearing to take much interest. The first thing Seymour noticed was the Argentinean flag fluttering from the stern. Four people sat in the cockpit beneath an awning. They were speaking Spanish. One of the crew actually waved as they passed. Although there were two couples, an elderly couple and the other younger, it was obvious that none were Tusk and his accomplice.

'Okay, gents, I think it is the *Felicity*,' Seymour said once they were back at the hotel, 'Those on the *Sea Strike* speak American, a real southern drawl which is just about impossible to imitate. They're Yanks all right. Concentrate on the *Felicity*.'

Bartlett trained the scope on the *Felicity*. He recognised her as a sloop, which he estimated to be about forty feet in length, gleaming white with a centre-cockpit covered by an awning.

'That thing cost a few bob,' he said to Seymour.

He saw movement below the awning and a woman emerged from the cockpit, dressed in a skimpy white bikini.

'Wow, you've got to see this! Now, that's what I call knock 'em dead. What a figure, just look at those tits.'

Seymour pushed Bartlett aside and stuck an eye to the scope. 'I'm telling you, that's her. His woman or whatever. No mistake,' he said, unable to contain his excitement. 'We've found them, thank God.' He stared, making slight adjustments. 'Hey, I can see Tusk. He's just shown up from below dressed in bathing trunks.'

He stepped aside and invited Bartlett to have another look to confirm it was Tusk.

'Okay, see to it that someone keeps the boat under continuous observation while you and I sit down and plan exactly how we are going to go about carrying out this mission from here on. Seriously, a fuck up now will see the end of our careers. Sir Henry says the American press is laughing at us as the Rhodesians run circles around us. Nobody takes this bloody embargo seriously! They're buying and selling stuff all over the world. Tusk and his bank have lot to do with this. Remember, it has to look like an accident. That's the new directive,' he said.

'Fuckin' hell, that's a tall order,' Bartlett responded, clearly unhappy with the new directive.

CHAPTER 56

Gisela changed their identities again, although they remained German nationals. She thought staying German would fit better with both Bernd and Ursula when they cleared customs to leave Lebanon.

'Have you got a suitcase full of these?' he asked, unable to hide his astonishment.

'I've still got a few left,' she giggled.

Bernd decided that they would leave early in the evening of the next day, which would shroud their departure in darkness and, hopefully, they would be unobserved and only known to the harbour master.

David had recovered from his excessive alcohol intake and spent most of the day on deck sunbathing with Gisela and the others. He stuck to beer, avoiding any hard tack.

At about four in the afternoon, he took Gisela's hand. 'Come, all this bare flesh in such close proximity is getting to me. Let's go below,' he said.

She lay with her head on her hands, her face turned sideways. She opened her eyes and looked at him. He looked at her, his face propped up on his elbow, lying on his side. She let her gaze wonder down his body and stared at his crotch.

'Good God! Is it that bad?'

'Damn right it is, c'mon, let's go,' he replied with a leering grin.

Trying to appear as nonchalant as possible, they passed the Hackers sitting in the cockpit and disappeared below.

Gisela was asleep on the bunk opposite him, the bunks too narrow to accommodate them both. Their lovemaking had been intense, she giving herself completely to him, he forgetting his concerns and the world around, loosing himself completely in her. As the euphoria wore off, his mind returned to the problems on hand. He realised that the MI6 operatives would be scouring every exit point in the country looking for them. They were not about to give up. They probably knew that once the pair were back in Rhodesia or South Africa, they would be beyond their reach, still able to buy and sell on the international market with impunity. Leaving

Lebanon on the yacht no longer seemed such a good idea. It narrowed down their options and heightened their vulnerability. The Hackers were no mercenaries, they were elderly folk – retired was the right description. He did not wish to place them in danger and, from experience, he knew that the British were prepared to condone some collateral damage, if the need arose. Yes, they could board the yacht out at sea in international waters and well away from Lebanon. Also, if the British knew of their whereabouts, a sudden change of plan could throw them off the trail. But how else to exit the country? He decided to discuss this with Bernd and swung his legs off the bunk.

'Where you going?' he heard her muffled voice.

'Going up. I need to speak to Bernd.'

'Tell them I'll be up later. They're not to worry about me. I'm taking a nap. '

He stepped into the cockpit to find Bernd and Ursula each with a drink watching the sun set over the sea.

'Gisela?' Ursula asked.

'She'll be up later. She's having a nap,' he replied. He wondered whether they had guessed what had happened below. Probably, but did it really matter?

'Bernd, I don't think it a good idea that we be aboard the yacht when you leave.'

'But I thought we were going to help you escape the country?' he asked, clearly confused.

'Well, who says they haven't found us. I know these bastards. They don't give up. The British never do. They could nab you.'

'Christ! How else are you to get out of Lebanon at such short notice?' Bernd asked, unable to hide his mounting irritation.

'I've an idea, but I need to bounce it off you. It's going to need your cooperation.'

'Okay, go on.'

'I find a motor boat, a large one. You know, a boat that you can take out to sea. Gisela and I use this to leave the harbour and then rendezvous with you once beyond the twelve-mile limit or even further out, out of sight of land.'

'You must assume you are being watched, otherwise why this new elaborate plan?' Bernd asked, still sceptical.

'Precisely, we see you off. Quite openly, that is. If they are watching, they'll see this. Hopefully it will confuse the shit out of them, throw their plans in disarray.'

'Obviously you'll want to do this at night.'

'Of course.'

Bernd chuckled, unable to hide his sarcasm. 'You'll need somebody to operate the launch. Where do you propose finding him?'

'That's why I'm speaking to you. I need some input.'

Bernd didn't reply but got up to pour another drink. It was clear to David that he was mulling over what he had just heard. With a fresh drink in hand, Bernd sat down again.

'Forget the launch. We need a fishing boat. They go out every night, nothing suspicious about that, it's a time-old tradition in these parts. The fishing harbour is no more than a mile away.' He smiled, pleased with himself. 'You're going to have to part with a lot of money,' he added.

'I've enough.'

'Okay, don't you do anything. Be inconspicuous and let me arrange something. I know one or two people who possibly can help or can put me onto the right people.'

'Thanks, I appreciate that. I've quite a stash of US dollars. Can I not give you some?'

'No, we'll work out how you need to pay these people later. God, I don't even know whether they would be prepared to help. But I do know that the whole lot are smugglers. Some small, some in a big way.'

When they came up on deck the next morning, they found only Ursula aboard preparing breakfast. She told them that Bernd had risen early and had left before eight.

It was overcast, the weather slowly building up to a blow. The temperature had also dropped overnight.

'The weather experts say we're in for a storm tonight, probably with some rain. Bernd listens to the weather every morning at seven,' Ursula said.

The weather steadily worsened and, by the time Bernd returned at about four, the wind was blowing near gale strength.

They both stood on the deck looking at the weather.

'Can you go out in this?' David asked.

'Yes, it's not so bad out there.'

'What did you manage?'

'Well, I got an introduction to a fishing boat skipper, Sameh Gamal is his name. He owns a fifty-foot boat and goes out every night, weather permitting, but not Sundays. He's an ardent Catholic, I mean, he's serious. Anyway, he's prepared to take you out and rendezvous with *Felicity*. He has the works on the boat. It may not look like much but there's nothing wrong with the equipment, radio, radar and echo-sounder.'

What does he want?' David asked loudly, grabbing a mast stay as the wind gusted violently.

'Two thousand. Half when you get on the boat, the rest when you jump over. Oh yes, he's also heavily armed. Probably a smuggler. He says if anybody tries anything, he'll shoot. He wants to take you beyond the twelve-mile limit.'

David smiled, this was the best news he had heard today. 'Sounds fantastic. Thank you very much!' he shouted above the wind.

'Hang on. It can't be done tonight. They won't go out in this weather. It'll be tomorrow.'

He shrugged his shoulders. He would have to live with it. What choice did he have? He was reliant on Mr Sameh Gamal, the skipper, to get him out of the country.

'Bernd, listen to me, this is the hard part. We've have to let them realise – that's presuming they're watching – that we've stayed behind while you depart on the yacht. That's relatively easy, do you agree? The hard part is to lose them so that we can make it to the fishing boat without being tailed. Hell, the moment they see we don't board … well, I don't have to tell you the rest.'

'Come on, let's get into the cockpit. I can't hear a bloody thing!'

It certainly was a lot better in the cockpit, the screens down, the wind now partially contained. Bernd rummaged in a locker under the bench seat and withdrew a bottle of Black Label. He took a generous swig and then handed it to David. He too took a generous swallow. It burnt his throat on the way down, its warmth spreading through his stomach.

'If they're watching, it's going to be difficult. They'll be watching from up there.' He indicated the tall hotel building on the opposite side of the beach boulevard overlooking the marina. 'That's where I would be watching from. They probably will have a few men below, just in case you make a smart move. Know what I mean? So, you suddenly make a dash for it, you've a car standing by. Will you get away?'

'Give me that bottle.' David stretched out a hand and took another swig. 'We would have to coordinate that. You have to bring the boat to the club end of the marina, as close to the cars as possible, ostensibly to load something prior to departure. That would not look suspicious. The car would then be nearby. We also buy the gate guard, pay him handsomely. Gisela and I make a dash for the car. Not run and make it obvious, just a quick walk, jump into the car and drive out of the already open gate. That's what the guard has to do, ensure that the gate is open before we get to it. What do you think?'

'Bloody dicey. I can think of a couple of ifs that could go wrong,' Bernd replied sourly.

'Listen, they're not about to shoot in a public place, even with silenced weapons. They've got to catch us on the boat, or somewhere else that's isolated. A deserted road, building or whatever.'

'Okay, I'll have a car delivered by the rental company, something not conspicuous, a Renault or Simca. They can leave the keys under the mat. I mean it will be safe in the car park. Provided we don't go anywhere near, it won't raise any suspicions.'

CHAPTER 57

David applied his mind to the escape, but every option he came up with was fraught with problems. He did not like the car idea with its dash for the fishing harbour. He thought too many things could go wrong. Yes, he believed the British would not start a gun battle in Beirut's streets but still, if what had occurred at the hotel was anything to go by, well, that had to be an indication as to how desperate they were. Better not take a chance.

There was another option that he favoured. A night-time escape. He and Gisela would slip over the hidden side of the yacht, the side that did not face the hotel and harbour. They'd swim along the yachts and, when well away from the *Felicity*, would emerge farther along the jetty or at least to where they would not draw attention. Surely the surveillance was concentrated only on the yacht to see who came and left. It was impossible to watch the whole basin.

He put this to Bernd.

'Forget it. I think they're convinced you'll stick to the yacht. They're not expecting a dash for a car. You'll take them by surprise. Secondly, the guys on the fishing boat won't let the Brits harm you. They'll resist, shoot if necessary, especially if they think they're being shot at. These Lebanese are savagely possessive and don't shirk from a fight,' he retorted.

What could he say, the man was probably right. He harrumphed an okay.

By nine that evening, the wind had whipped up a near gale, the yachts tugging at their moorings. The harbour was filled by a continuous drumming as the sheets on every yacht hammered against the masts. It was too unpleasant atop, even in the cockpit. Dinner was eaten below. After a few drinks, everyone retired early.

David did not sleep well. Every two hours or so he woke up, unable to stop thinking about what had to be done the following night. Could they really do it? Were there no other options?

By the next morning, the storm had passed, leaving a strong breeze at its tail end. The cloud cover had broken up and, already, stabs of sunlight struck the sea. It was turning out to be just another pleasant and probably hot day on the Levant.

Bernd had already left to do some shopping and organise the car. David made a mental note not to forget to reimburse the man for all his expenses. A short while later, both Gisela and Ursula emerged, enjoying their first cup of coffee topside.

After that, David took a stroll to the entrance of the club, ostensibly to purchase a newspaper, the *New York Herald*, from a vendor who had a kiosk just outside the walls, which surrounded the harbour. He wanted to place the men the British would have stationed to watch the entrance. There had to be at least one person with a radio stationed near the entrance, or so he thought. He bought the paper and then looked through the other magazines on the rack while furtively taking in the surroundings. At first, he saw nothing that appeared suspicious. Farther along on the opposite side, he saw only two people: a flower vendor and an underground car-park attendant. Then he saw a solitary panel van parked next to the kerb diagonally across the road. It was one of those strange French vans. It had a near-flat-nosed cab with that slightly corrugated body which only the French build. The vehicles were not renowned for their speed, another consolation. It bore no signage and the driver's seat was empty. It just had to be them, he thought. There was another van, but this one had a driver behind the wheel. He was sure that this would be the vehicle that would pursue them. He saw a slight advantage. To follow them, the driver needed to make a U-turn, which would mean he would have to proceed up the road to the next intersection, it being the first place to afford him the opportunity to reverse direction.

It was agreed that the fishing boat would wait until nine o'clock. The last of the twilight would be between seven to seven-thirty. That gave more than sufficient time to get aboard. Also, the fishing boat would be moored to the fishing jetty as close to the shore as possible.

The car was delivered at noon, driven into the car park, and the driver disappeared into the club. The Brits would have to be clairvoyant if they were to connect the car with the escape. Bernd had chosen the car well. It was a white Mercedes 230, probably the most popular car in Lebanon, certainly amongst taxis. Bernd assured David that it had started at the first turn of the key. They had repeatedly tested it. The car was left unlocked. During the afternoon, they visited the local customs office and filled out a few forms, the customs officer informing the harbour master that the *Felicity*, with a crew of four, would be exiting the harbour around eight that evening.

As soon as the sun disappeared, the temperature dropped. Both Gisela and he wore jeans over which they had donned dark-green waterproof yachting parkas, hoping that the colour would make them less conspicuous. Brilliant orange was out of the question. Bernd and Ursula were similarly dressed, this less likely to raise suspicion.

The auxiliary diesel engine was started and, once this had warmed up, the mooring lines were cast off. The *Felicity* proceeded slowly to the club's main jetty. No yachts were allowed to moor there permanently, large signs in various languages advertising dire consequences for the skipper of any boat infringing the regulation. They had already bid Bernd and Ursula farewell. He had remembered to reimburse Bernd who eventually accepted the money after furious protestations.

Bernd had previously stacked a few boxes containing foodstuffs next to the small office hut on the quayside. He brought the yacht alongside, the engine running. No moorings were thrown out, he using the engine every time the yacht strayed too far from the quay. David and Gisela proceeded to fetch the boxes and carry these to the yacht where Ursula stowed them below. Finally, there were only two boxes left. They both stepped from the yacht walked towards these, within thirty or forty yards of the car.

His apprehension over what was to happen next had further raised his already heightened adrenaline levels. He saw Ursula was just as tense, her face was drawn. The nearest point from which to make a dash for the car was about halfway to the boxes. They carried nothing except their firearms.

'Now!'

They both swung to the right and ran, their feet digging loudly into the gravel. They got to the car, her side being the nearest to them. They both slid into their seats. He lifted the floor mat and groped for the keys, his hand closing over them. The engine caught. He shoved in the clutch and engaged the gears. The wheels spun, throwing gravel and dirt. He turned and steered towards the boom, which miraculously rose. They shot through the gate and swerved onto the boulevard with a squeal of tyres. Only then did he switch the lights on. He glanced into his side mirror and saw the van pull away from the kerb. The pursuit was on!

He quickly ran through the gears, the accelerator floored, the engine protesting loudly.

'Just watch what's going on behind. I saw the bastards pull away. They're after us,' he shouted. His senses were heightened, acutely aware of what was happening around him.

They certainly had a good start on their pursuers who now had to be quite a distance behind them. David passed a number of slower cars, a few hooting at him for driving in this maniacal manner. The panel van would never match this speed.

Soon they approached the entrance to the fishing harbour. It was not manned. He swung through the concrete posts, the car sliding to a halt in the car park. They abandoned the car as close to the main fishing jetty as he could get. They sprinted for the jetty. There were only three boats alongside as the others had already left for the fishing grounds. He recognised the boat, the only one without mooring lines, and the engine thumping in idle.

They both jumped over the gunwales. He heard the throttle open. The boat pulled away, water churning at its stern.

Christ, they had done it! He wrapped his arms around Gisela and hugged her close, the adrenaline still pumping in his veins. They were at least a hundred yards out when they saw headlights in the car park. Two men got out and ran onto the jetty.

'Monsieur, I'm Skipper Gamal,' he heard behind him.

He turned round to face a huge man. What struck him was the man's girth: it was considerable. His features were as dark as the full black beard he sported. He was dressed for the sea in a thick grey woollen pullover and dark trousers stuck into calf-high black rubber gumboots. He took the proffered hand and tried not to wince as his fingers were crushed.

'I'm glad you are safely aboard,' the man said with a twinkle in his eyes and a wide grin.

Of course, the skipper was not entirely in the dark. At their first meeting, Bernd had to divulge the fact that they would probably be pursued. He had even hinted that, once away from the harbour, there was a possibility that they would be followed at sea. The skipper did not appear to be concerned and countered that nobody would interfere with him while in Lebanese waters. A look at the other crew members who watched what was happening indicated that these were men not to be trifled with.

A slight fog began to lift from the sea but visibility was still fair. The boat's appearance belied its performance, its blunt bow cut through the water at a good eight or nine knots. It passed the breakwater into the open sea where it ploughed through the first swell of the open sea, a legacy of the previous night's storm.

'How are you going to find the yacht?' David asked.

'We're both going to hold the same course, which should stop us from drifting more than a mile or two apart. That means we'll be able to see each other. Of course, the other boats out there could confuse us but there won't be many boats. The fish are not in the direction we're sailing, so we should find each other rather quickly,' the skipper replied, making corrections with the helm every time the boat slid over a swell.

David realised that if MI6 had any sense at all they would have found a launch in order to give chase. That's what he would have done.

CHAPTER 58

Bernd's plan had taken the British completely by surprise. The van gave chase but by the time the two men inside turned the vehicle round, David had a good head start. The driver fumed, first having to drive in the wrong direction, find a gap in the road's centre island, and then turn round. The panel van was a bad choice. It was underpowered and clumsy. Those in the hotel had kept track of the Mercedes that had been used to bolt from the marina and radioed its final destination to the van. With the fishing boat disappearing in the darkness, they reluctantly reported to Seymour by radio, explaining what had happened.

This galvanised Seymour into action.

'Jesus Christ! The buggers are on the loose again. Everybody to the launch now!' He grabbed his coat and bolted down the passage to the lift tower, three other operatives following close behind.

Once in the underground parking garage, they sprinted to the black Jaguar. The car roared up the ramp from below so fast it briefly launched and then screeched to a halt behind the boom. Seymour swore at the attendant in French to hurry up, this having the opposite effect, the man stoically taking his time while Seymour raged.

The car tore into the yacht basin, again having to wait for a boom to be lifted, and then swung left to the marina where all motorised launches were moored. Once as close to the launch as he could get, he stopped. They scrambled out of the car leaving the doors open and sprinted to the launch, jumping aboard. Already the engines were started, the diesels bubbling away. The twin diesels roared, the cabin cruiser rapidly leaving the quayside. It climbed onto its plane, half the hull out of the water, rapidly reaching thirty knots.

Seymour went down to the stern to a bundle that lay wrapped in canvas on the deck. He opened it to reveal two MAT-49 machine pistols. Into each, he rammed a magazine, each capable of holding thirty-two 9mm Parabellum rounds, and cocked the weapons. He gave one to Bartlett, keeping the other for himself. Soon they were beyond the breakwater, the hull slamming into the first of the swells. Seymour was nearly thrown off his feet. He quickly grabbed hold of a stay.

He made his way to the wheelhouse and stuck his head into the cabin.

'Head straight out to the twelve-mile limit. That must be about due west,' he shouted at the helmsman above the roar of the engines.

The man at the wheel just nodded to indicate that he understood, visibly concerned at the automatic pistol.

Bartlett had climbed to the top of the flying bridge. At this height from the surface, the boat seemed to pitch and roll more violently. He realised that to accurately fire the machine pistol from the platform would be near impossible.

Seymour stuck his forehead against the rubber hood of the radarscope. The rotating light beam on the oscilloscope enabled him to see about twelve miles. Numerous boats were visible. He had to make a few assumptions. Firstly, he believed the fishing boat would try to put as many miles as possible between them and the Lebanese coast. This meant that they would hold a due west course. Secondly, he believed that the yacht and the fishing boat planned to rendezvous just beyond the limit. The fishing boat's only purpose was to get to the yacht where Tusk and his companion could board the yacht again, but where? The only thing to do was to plot the courses of all small vessels within a few miles radius on the radarscope. There were not that many. He was only interested in those moving westward.

CHAPTER 59

Gisela approached the skipper and asked him in French if his radar could tell them whether another craft had left Beirut yacht basin and was heading westward. Gamal gave the helm to another and manipulated the dials on the radarscope, staring at the oscilloscope.

'Yes,' he said, 'There's another vessel on a course parallel to our own but moving at high speed. It must be a fast motor launch, probably one of those Chris-Craft Cruisers.'

She turned to David. 'That's them, I'm sure.'

He nodded.

God, he thought, this game isn't over yet. Everybody must be staring at their radar sets trying to figure out who was who.

He called Gisela aside. 'Tell him that we think that the fast boat could be after us and if we are seen it could open fire on us. Tell him that they've done it before.'

'You're sure you want to tell him?'

'Yes, tell him! I don't think we have much time,' he said.

Reluctantly she approached Gamal and told him that he could expect the launch to find their boat and approach, quite prepared to open fire.

To her amazement, he uttered a French expletive, the equivalent of 'Fuck them!' and disappeared into the wheelhouse cabin only to emerge again with three brand new AK47's. 'Just let them try. I've wanted to try these out,' he said with a wry smile. He handed a rifle to David and the other to another crewmember speaking to him in Levantine Arabic.

'Where's mine?' she asked.

He studied her for a few seconds and then shrugged his shoulders and disappeared in the cabin again, returning with another rifle.

'Here. I hope you know what to do with it,' he said curtly in French.

'Just keep an eye on the scope. That fast boat could be our problem.'

The skipper gave her a disdainful look. Where he came from women did not instruct men.

****

Seymour looked at the radarscope again. He then walked forward to stand next to the helmsman and shouted above the engines. 'There's a boat about a mile or so on our right. I'm convinced that's the vessel we're looking for. Turn right and put us onto an intercept course. As you get nearer, just slow down and match his speed. Have you got a loudhailer?'

The helmsman rummaged in a large locker above his head and extracted an amplified bullhorn, handing it to Seymour.

'Perfect,' he said, grabbing hold of the console as the boat heeled over into a sharp turn to starboard.

The going was easier, the cruiser now running parallel to the swell, the only distraction the spray that flew diagonally across the prow each time she dug her bow into a trough.

The navigational lights of a boat became visible. The harsh throb of the engines diminished, the cruiser losing speed. The helmsman manœuvred the cruiser until it was running parallel to the fishing boat, matching its speed, the distance between the boats about a hundred yards.

Seymour switched on a searchlight mounted on the top of the wheelhouse, the beam stabbing through the darkness illuminating the fishing boat. He had difficulty keeping the light trained on the fishing boat with the sea that was running.

'That's the boat all right!' Bartlett shouted from the flying bridge.

Seymour grabbed the bullhorn and asked another agent to take over the operation of the searchlight.

'Are we beyond the twelve-mile limit?' he asked the helmsman in French.

'Oui, Monsieur.'

He hefted the bullhorn to his mouth and turned to face the fishing boat. 'We are British intelligence agents. We require that you hand your two passengers over to us.' His French boomed across the water. He saw everyone on the boat's deck look in their direction,

No reply followed. After thirty seconds, he repeated himself.

'We are not obliged to hand anyone over to you. We are in international waters and you have no jurisdiction either here or in Lebanese waters.'

Seymour realised that he would have to be more informative. 'Your passengers are in contravention of international law and thus may be apprehended. Please hand them over. Failing that, we will have no alternative but to use force.'

The agent had difficulty keeping the light on the boat but still there was no mistaking the AKs that suddenly appeared in the hands of the crew.

'Christ, they're not about to let us walk over them,' Bartlett said to Seymour from the flying bridge.

'Oh, they will, I'll make sure of that. Fire a short burst over their heads,' Seymour shouted angrily.

The staccato sound of the MAT machine pistol reverberated through the air. Fire was returned immediately, some shots scoring hits on the cruiser, everybody falling to the deck and taking cover behind the gunwales, the helmsman opening the throttles and swinging the cruiser out of range.

'Bloody hell! That nearly hit me!' Bartlett shouted as he clambered down from the flying bridge.

'Swing back! Swing back!' Seymour ordered.

Again, they came within a hundred yards, the searchlight pointing at the other boat.

He spoke to the helmsman, 'On my command, turn towards the fishing boat aiming ahead of it so that we have a broadside view. Have you got that?'

The man nodded. Seymour put down the bullhorn and lifted the machine pistol.

'Okay, now!'

The cruiser rapidly overtook the boat and then turned slightly right, closing the gap. At about fifty yards away, Seymour gave the signal. He and Bartlett raked the boat from bow to stern with gunfire. Even with continuous motion, at this range it was an easy target. The shots broke off wood splinters, shattered wheelhouse windows and ricocheted off of steel. As soon as they stopped firing, those on the boat who had fallen to the deck for cover rose in unison blasting away with their AKs. The rifles had better range and accuracy and their bullets chewed into the glass fibre structure of the cruiser.

'Goddamn hell,' Seymour shouted, still prone on the deck where he had fallen to take cover, 'I never expected the boat to be carrying an arsenal.'

He instructed the helmsman to circle back but to keep a good distance from the boat. What to do now? Both were evenly matched, they were not about to overpower the fishing boat with only the machine pistols. They needed heavier firepower.

CHAPTER 60

David lay prone on the deck, Gisela next to him as gunfire raked the fishing boat, showering them in wood splinters from the wheelhouse above.

As soon as the shooting stopped, they all rose from the deck with their AKs and fired at the departing cruiser, still well within range of the automatic rifles. They all emptied their magazines.

He tried to ascertain whether anybody had been hit. Miraculously, other than a few cuts from splinters, no one had been killed or injured.

'Ask the skipper if he hasn't got anything else in terms of firepower,' he said to Gisela.

She spoke to Gamal. His face broke into a wide grin and once again he disappeared into the cabin. He soon reappeared with a wooden olive-green crate fitted with two rope handles on each end. He lifted the lid. David stared at the contents. In the box were nestled six hand grenades.

'Jesus wept,' he said, 'Where the hell did he get these from and for what?'

Without giving David's exclamation a thought, she promptly translated. Gamal roared with laughter and started talking.

'You should know, there's forever trouble in Lebanon. Christian, Muslim, Syrian; they can't live together without fighting, so it's good to be prepared. Rest assured the whole population arms itself. I've always been ready. These things are so easy to find in my country,' Gamal replied, gesturing at the box of grenades.

David took one of the grenades and hefted it in his hand.

'Somehow we've got to lure them into a trap. We have to do it soon before they realise that capturing the yacht is the easier option. Without the yacht we're buggered. It would be back to Lebanon for us,' David said.

Again, she translated.

'Let's hope they make another pass,' Gamal said. 'We then slow down and tell them we submit and wish to hand you both over, also that we have injured on board requiring urgent medical attention. As soon as we are in range we open fire and toss two grenades.' He paused and then frowned.

Lowering his voice, he continued, 'The only thing is that this time we may have real casualties, but it is the only option.'

'I agree. How are we going to do this?' David asked.

Gamal removed a hip flask from his back pocket and took a generous swig and then held the flask out to David. David gulped down a mouthful. It was ouzo. The strong aniseed spirit burnt his mouth and throat, he gagged.

Gamal laughed. 'Strong, eh?' he said in broken English. David's eyes watered.

A serious expression returned to Gamal's face. 'We wait until the cruiser comes alongside. When it's about twenty yards from us, we open fire and you and I toss the grenades on deck,' he said.

'Jesus, for us to do that we'll have to expose ourselves completely to their fire,' David retorted, unhappy with the proposal.

Gamal shrugged. 'We must just be sure my people give us covering fire forcing those on the cruiser to take cover.'

The man has a death wish, David thought. He obviously thought nothing of it and really left David no choice but to agree or reveal his anxiety. God, he was terrified! This could go horribly wrong.

Gamal produced a torch and pointed it in the direction of the cruiser, flashing on-off repeatedly.

'I hope this will entice them to return,' he said.

****

'Look at the boat, they're flashing lights at us. What do they want? I wouldn't trust those bastards as far I could throw them,' Bartlett said, sucking on his wrist where a shard of plastic window had cut him.

'Stop the boat,' Seymour shouted.

With the engines now idling, the cruiser gradually slowed until it pitched in the swell.

Seymour fetched a pair of binoculars from the cabin and proceeded to study the now-stationary fishing boat, its crew standing openly on deck staring in the cruiser's direction.

'Let's just watch for a while. I wonder what they are up to,' Seymour mused. 'Somebody's waving. I think they want us to go back.'

'You must be bloody crazy to do that. Never trust a damn Arab,' Bartlett said vehemently.

'I don't agree with you. What can they do? We are just about evenly matched. Let's get nearer so that I can use the hailer. Christ, we can't report another failure to Sir Henry.'

The cruiser started to move, making a wide circle approaching the fishing boat's stern on its port side, stopping about a hundred yards away. All the crew on the fishing boat stood openly on deck, showing no weapons.

A megaphoned voice was heard. 'Ahoy, we have wounded, we require assistance.'

Seymour and Bartlett looked at each other, astounded.

'What the hell?' Seymour uttered.

'Careful, it's a bloody trap!'

Seymour grabbed the bullhorn. 'What about the couple you have aboard?'

'If you come alongside we will hand them over to you but you must undertake to take our wounded. Our engine is misfiring. It was damaged in the attack.'

Bartlett was adamant. It would be foolhardy to get too near to the fishing boat. He reckoned they had half a dozen AK rifles. Seymour heard what Bartlett said, but could not come up with an alternative plan.

'Listen, what if we forced them to stand on deck in full view without weapons, their hands in view as we came alongside. By the time they can make a grab for their weapons, if they planned to do so, we'd have already opened fire with the MATs. They wouldn't stand a chance,' Seymour suggested.

Bartlett reluctantly agreed.

Using the bullhorn the skipper of the fishing boat was told precisely what was expected and that if anyone made a false move, Seymour's men would open fire. The skipper agreed.

'All right, bring the boat slowly alongside. Bartlett, you ensure that the men are ready with the MATs. You open fire at the slightest sign of provocation. You got that?' Seymour asked.

'Yes sir,' he replied, cocking the machine pistol.
****

The fishing boat's engine idled, appearing stationary, its forward motion only sufficient to give it steerage and keep its bow pointed at the incoming swell.

The skipper pointed to the fishing net, a huge rolled-up sausage, which stretched the length of the boat on the port side of the gunwale. This was nearly three feet in diameter.

'No bullet can penetrate that. They come alongside on our port side and, as we said, when five to ten yards away, two of my crew who are concealed below the gunwales, throw the grenades. The moment they do that, everybody on deck drops to the floor behind the net. We don't attempt to shoot back. We let the grenades do their work,' the skipper said to David.

He had to agree. The plan could work and what alternative did they have other than being handed over to the British? He looked at Gisela and shook his head. He still didn't like the idea.

'We're placing all these men's lives in danger. Is that right?' he asked.

'David, you don't have a choice. Besides that, they accepted the payment Bernd offered. If they're all right with it, just leave it, okay?' she whispered.

He never failed to amaze her. He was courageous man but he had this streak of compassion, which could jump to the fore at a moment's notice, at the most inappropriate moment.

'For God's sake, just think of something else,' she muttered.

The AK rifles lay at their feet on the deck. As the cruiser approached and came within range, the crew raised one arm above their heads in a show of surrender, the other also visible, but grasping onto something to steady them against the pitch of the boat.

The cruiser approached slowly. The fishing boat's crew could see the three men with their MAT machine pistols trained on them. Both boats lit each other with their deck lights. The two men with the grenades crouched below the level of the net, ready to extract the pin when the time came. These were shrapnel grenades.

The helmsman on the cruiser expertly approached the fishing boat, it hardly making headway against the swell. This was crunch time. David knew people would die, this could not go smoothly as the firepower involved was enormous. The cruiser was now no more than fifteen yards away. He could see the men on board and the weapons they held.

'Bas!' Gamal shouted.

In unison, everybody dropped below the height of the net. The two crew members stood up and threw the grenades, this movement triggering a volley of fire from the cruiser, the three machine pistols traversing the length of the boat with a fusillade of gunfire. One of the grenade men was struck twice in the chest, he falling back with a scream which cut off as he dropped to the deck. The net shook as it absorbed multiple shots, wood splinters flew, and ricochets zinged off into the darkness.

Suddenly there was a loud explosion. Seconds later, pieces of the boat rained down on the sea and fishing boat. An orange fireball erupted on board the cruiser followed by pall of black smoke.

David looked over the top of the net and was horror-struck by the scene of destruction he beheld. The cruiser was on fire, the flames fed by fuel and burning fibreglass. A figure ran across the foredeck with clothes aflame, jumping overboard into the sea. Another floated in the water. David realised that he must have been blown overboard by the blast. The starboard side of the cruiser had a huge hole in it right down to the waterline. He watched the sea pouring in. Part of the main cabin had disappeared.

Everyone had risen from behind the net, the crew members cheering and slapping each other on the back. The skipper bent over his prone crew member, the man hardly bleeding, the only blood being where the bullets had struck him.

Gamal stood up and made the sign of the cross, the others doing the same. 'He's dead, he died instantly it seems.'

All were silent for a moment.

'Get any survivors out of the water,' Gamal ordered. The men sprang to the task, subdued, the shock of what had occurred still with them. Using boathooks, they helped the two survivors alongside and then hoisted them aboard. Both were burnt, their faces scarred with black and red patches, their hair singed. The one's hands were burnt as well. Both were barely conscious.

The stern of the cruiser was already submerged. It was clear that it would sink within minutes. Gisela demanded the first-aid box and attended to the two injured men, not that there was much she could do except to apply some ointment. She had the men carried inside the cabin and placed on bunks.

David was devastated. This was a catastrophe, something he had never envisaged. Men had died. He did not want to know any names, all because kith was fighting kin. A mad world, he thought. When this was eventually leaked to the press, there would a political uproar.

'Stop standing around! Look for other survivors,' Gamal shouted at his men.

They found no others, only the bodies that they brought aboard which now lay covered on deck by a tarpaulin.

'What are we going to do now?' David asked Gamal.

'What do you mean, "What are we going to do?" We're going to find the yacht, you're going to pay the balance you owe me and you board the yacht. We then say goodbye.'

'But, what about the injured men and your dead crew member? What are you going to tell the police?'

'Leave that to me. I'll dump my dead crew member.' Gamal made the sign of the cross. 'I'll say we saw the cruiser blow up, these two were the only survivors and that my crew member drowned during the rescue attempts. My crew will back me up. I don't think these two Englishman will say anything else. I'm sure they don't want to mention a gun battle.'

'The bullet holes in the boat?'

'Now, that's a problem, but I'll deal with it. Don't forget this is Lebanon, bullet holes are commonplace,' he said, with a sarcastic smile.

David entered the cabin and approached the bunks. Both men were conscious. Gisela was attending to the one whose clothes had been on fire, his arm appearing to be badly burnt. He turned to the other who had been blown overboard. He didn't know what to say.

'That was a bloody mess, wasn't it?' he eventually said.

The man on the bunk looked up at him. 'Mr Tusk, I presume?' he asked, a faint smile on his face.

David nodded.

'This is truly tragic. Like many of my colleagues I would have preferred a more amicable solution, but then I'm not a politician,' the man said.

'I know, neither am I. '

'You're a South African banker, aren't you?'

David did not reply.

'Well, for a banker you're quite a formidable foe and probably will cause me to be transferred to the archives for the rest of my working life.' The man smiled again. 'You bloody Rhodesians are all the same, a bunch of fuckin' diehards.'

David took the man's hand. 'I'm sorry.' He turned round and left the cabin.

Within an hour, they found the yacht, drifting in the sea waiting for them. David paid Gamal the balance, the total amount of four thousand dollars, a small but fair fee for what he and his crew had endured.

They clambered aboard the yacht. Both he and Gisela waved to the crew on the fishing boat as the yacht drew away.

David put his arm round Gisela's waist. 'Christ, I hope I never see Lebanon again.'

She laid her head on his shoulder.

CHAPTER 61

Twelve weeks had passed since Sizwe Sybonga's miraculous escape from Rhodesia. He had adjusted well to the daily rigours of the new training program which he had been subjected.

His instructors were North Koreans who relentlessly drilled and instructed the dozen trainee officers who had been assigned to them, subjecting them to a merciless training schedule. The mornings started at five, driven from their beds onto the parade ground clad only in shorts. Six laps at a fast jog were mandatory. This was followed by gruelling callisthenics, then another four laps. Thereafter, only forty-five minutes were allowed in which to shower, dress, and clean their quarters. Breakfast consisted of maize meal porridge with milk, sugar, and two slices of bread, washed down with coffee.

Classes followed until three in the afternoon, their studies devoted to ambush and battle tactics, incoming intelligence reports, clandestine operational procedures and communist ideology. The rest of the afternoon until seven concentrated on practical weapons and radio training.

He was fortunate. He, because of his escape from Rhodesia, had acquired a degree of respect that bordered on hero-worship. In addition, his academic marks were of the best and no one was in doubt that he would qualify top of his class. In fact, in private, it was rumoured that he was a protégé of Nkomo himself, the self-proclaimed leader of the ZANU movement. He was now proficient in the use of all weapons supplied by the Communist bloc. His marksmanship was excellent. In physical combat, he excelled so that even his instructor was wary to take him on.

****

After fourteen weeks, they held a passing out parade. This may have been low-key and an unpublicised event, but it did much to raise his self-esteem. He never forgot how his brother and the others were killed. Revenge was his ultimate goal. The instructors were right: the whites had taken his land, his freedom, and his family. It was time to take it back.

They promoted him to squad commander and assigned a troop of twelve men to him. The squad practised manoeuvres for two weeks in the Zambian

263

bush, fifty miles from Lusaka, until Sizwe had welded them into a well-coordinated team. He was ready to go back to Rhodesia.

ZANU command decided that his squad should again infiltrate the Centenary area because he was familiar with the district and it was close to Salisbury, the capital. They were convinced that any terror attacks on the capital's doorstep would have a profound effect on the population. A wave of fear rippling through the whites was what they wanted.

Different tactics were to be applied. The last consignment of weapons from the communists included PMN landmines and anti-tank mines. They proposed to lay these beneath the civilian roads in use in Rhodesia and so disrupt civilian traffic. The mines were easy to bury as most roads were gravel. Sizwe's squad was also issued with two RPG-70 rocket launchers to use against large trucks and military vehicles.

Weighed down with all their equipment, they crossed the Mpata Gorge on the Zambezi River below the Kariba Dam at night during a heavy thunderstorm, which they hoped would wash away their tracks. The Rhodesian Security Forces regularly patrolled the riverbank for precisely that reason.

They were a motley band of men. They wore no uniforms but were dressed in an assortment of civilian clothes chosen to camouflage them in the bush – green, beige, and grey – some with hats and others not. If need be, they would be able to assume the disguise of civilians, which was necessary in order to reconnoitre ahead.

Once in Rhodesia and penetrating the initial stages of the Zambezi Escarpment, it was possible to move during the day, the area comprised of virgin bush, wild animals and few humans. The heat was intense. They were plagued by insects and were continuously watchful lest they encounter wild animals. Once beyond the mountains, which were eighty miles from the river where the land was more densely populated, they moved only during the night and then only after the moon had risen. Where possible, they chose to walk on dirt roads. Every time vehicle lights appeared, they hid in the bush that thronged the roads. It was reckoned that vehicles using the road would wipe out any tracks they may leave and that the road was the last place the enemy would look. That was not entirely true. Roads were patrolled but usually any tracks left were obliterated by vehicles before a security patrol happened by.

He made no effort to make contact with the black civilian population. The Rhodesian Security Forces had persuaded many to be informants.

Making contact with the locals was just too risky. As long as their supplies held out, this would be the plan he would follow.

Detection by an informant or any other enemy force would be disastrous. The BSAP and the armed forces would descend on the area, supported by helicopters, and track them down until they were annihilated in a firefight. Those who escaped would remain on the run, forced to abandon equipment, weapons and food to lighten their packs. They would be unable to carry out their assigned tasks.

He planned to mine the main road from Salisbury to Centenary. This was an asphalt road but the last fifteen miles to Centenary were still untarred, with a gravel surface. He proposed to lay the mines early at night and, with many hours of darkness left, walk the few miles to the Mentz farmstead and attack it, using his superior firepower to kill as many as possible.

As they neared Centenary, the going became tougher. They were forced to thread their way carefully through numerous black homesteads each with a two-and-a-half acre plot, usually cultivated with maize. Most homesteads also owned a few head of cattle, belonging to the local blacks. The whites lived in the town in suburban houses. The town was typical of a rural community, the hub of a farming district. It took nine days to reach the hills that overlooked Centenary. They finally sought out a high kopje overlooking the town. The business centre was small and consisted of two banks, a post office, a few department stores, a farmer's cooperative and other small shops and businesses.

These nights, the moon's phase was nearing full. He believed it would rain, in keeping with such a phase during the rainy season. This would provide excellent cover. The thunderstorms usually built up during the late afternoon and evening. He decided to wait it out for a day or two, which would allow his men time to recuperate from their long trek from Zambia.

CHAPTER 62

Bernd took the yacht due west into the Mediterranean, wanting to put as much distance between them and the Lebanese coast, not that he believed that they would be pursued, but it just made him feel that more comfortable. It was clear that the couple had been through a rough ordeal. David's nerves were as taut as a bowstring. He was not up for conversation. She seemed to fare better. It was as if she were better conditioned, obviously having received some training in this type of undercover operation. The first two nights, they both drank heavily and only after they had consumed a fair number of drinks did they unwind and become more talkative and a lot friendlier.

He did not want to set course for Larnaca, Cyprus. Better to let the hubbub die down. The situation between the Lebanese and British governments had to be tense. The Lebanese were certain to object to a British operation resulting in death and the sinking of a Lebanese cabin cruiser being launched from their shores. The police docket mentioned that the cruiser had blown up for unknown reasons, possibly due to a fuel leak. This was also considered as the cause of death, save one man lost at sea attempting to rescue survivors from the cabin cruiser. The Lebanese government never believed the story. They knew that the survivors and the dead were British operatives.

By the third day, fresh air, sufficient sleep, and just lazing in the sun had worked wonders. Both David and Gisela were now more approachable and easier to live with on a small boat. Bernd change course for Larnaca.

The deaths of the men initially weighed heavily on David's conscience. This war of subterfuge and cunning was very different from tactical combat of flying aircraft, with its strafing ground troops and dropping bombs. Certainly, many more had probably died because of his actions but then they were on the ground and he was in the air, never seeing his victims close up. This had been different. He did not want to fight the British and, probably, they did not wish to fight him. Both had been pawns in a conflict about race and supremacy. Gisela's attitude was different. She had taken this in stride. She didn't seem to care – it happened; too bad. He had once remarked that had she been born earlier, she would probably have been a senior officer of the Third Reich administering the women's section of a Nazi death camp. She hadn't spoken to him for two days after that. He was forced to apologise.

On the yacht's arrival in Larnaca, they produced well-worn Austrian passports revealing arrival and departure stamps from various European places and the Mediterranean. David remained baffled as to how Gisela had obtained them, but knew better than to ask. They were now Mr and Mrs Grubner from Vienna. He was an executive of a well-known musical instruments manufacturer, a family business. Such a company did exist, as did the Grubner family. They had merely taken on their identity.

They bade farewell to the Hackers and travelled by road to Nicosia where they boarded a British European Airways Viscount for Frankfurt, where they never left the confines of the international airport, connecting with an Air Afrique flight to Lusaka in Zambia.

CHAPTER 63

It was a cold winter morning when the taxi dropped Seymour at the entrance to Century House in London. Now that he had recovered, he had been summoned by Sir Henry. He dreaded the meeting and the consequences that were sure to follow.

Although he had recovered from his burns, most of these merely superficial, his face was still blotched, those places now a distinct bright pink.

He had to wait twenty minutes before he was asked to enter Sir Henry's office. He entered with a sense of foreboding. He thought it extraordinary that his boss rose from his seat behind the desk and came round to shake his hand. What was more surprising that he was offered a drink, considering the early hour.

Sir Henry carefully studied Seymour's face. 'That's an occupational hazard, I'm afraid,' he said, pointing to his burnt face. He walked to a cabinet, withdrew two glasses, and poured a generous tot in each. He handed Seymour a glass.

'This is a unique single malt whisky, I'm sure you will appreciate it,' Sir Henry said, not returning to his chair but coming to stand next to Seymour in front of his desk, displaying more than his usual friendliness.

Sir Henry raised his glass.

'Here's to the British, Bartlett, and the others. What a tragedy, a waste of good men. May we never fight our own again.' With that, he took a sip and sat in a chair in front of his desk, gesturing to Seymour to do the same.

'Well, Seymour, to put it mildly, that was a fuck-up, wouldn't you say?'

Seymour didn't know how to reply, after all this had been his operation.

'Yes' was all he said.

Sir Henry took another sip. 'Between you and me and these four walls I must confess that I'm not disappointed. Yes, the loss of life I truly regret. Those men should still be with us. This conflict with Rhodesia could have been avoided.' He threw the rest of the whisky down his throat, 'Quite frankly, my attitude is: "Fuck the party and fuck the Prime Minster." Don't blame yourself. Not like us, the Rhodesians are fighting for their very existence, how do you expect them to react?'

He rose from his chair indicating that the meeting was over. 'Incidentally, there will be no enquiry and no blame. Your record is clean.'

He held out his hand, 'Seymour, good day.'

CHAPTER 64

They had to ditch their weapons before boarding the flight from Larnaca. They felt naked without them although they did not believe the British had any idea where they currently were. It would be a while yet before they traced them.

The aircraft landed in Lusaka in the early hour of the morning. They remained in the terminal waiting for a connecting flight to Livingstone, a border town with Rhodesia, a tourist haven for all those visiting the Victoria Falls.

Since Ian Smith's UDI declaration, the relationship between Zambia and Rhodesia had deteriorated. It was difficult to travel between the two countries and hiring a rental car in Livingstone to drive through to Salisbury was out of the question. Gisela had telegraphed her farm manager who had arranged a small charter plane to collect them from Victoria Falls, the town adjoining Livingstone on the Rhodesian side of the border. By two that afternoon, they landed in Salisbury where Kallie Botha, the farmer manager, collected them and drove them back to the farm.

David had decided that he needed time to adjust and would take an unauthorised one-week's leave of absence. Considering the success of the mission, he did not believe that the bank or Rhodesian Government would object. Of course, he would meet with Taylor or Butler in the next few days for a debriefing and update.

They sat on the veranda, he nursing a whisky and she a glass of wine. They had been on the farm for four days now.

'It's a full moon tonight,' he said, glancing up from the newspaper he was reading.

'I know,' she said, 'but I doubt whether you will see much of it, maybe in the early hours of the morning.' She pointed to the north from where a grey band of cloud advanced, already displaying the typical anvil development of a thunderstorm. 'It's going to rain tonight.'

He looked. She was probably right. At least it would break the oppressive heat they were experiencing.

The attack on the farmstead had galvanised everyone into action. A closed-mesh security fence was in the process of being erected but it would still require a week or so. It was eight feet high and strung with razor wire on top. Electric cable had been laid below the ground for security lights to be situated at intervals along the fence. They would be activated from the house in the event of an emergency. David didn't think the terrorists would be fool enough to attack the same farm so soon after the last attack. Nonetheless, he would feel a lot more comfortable once the fence was completed. Like the rest of the white population, nobody went anywhere without a firearm at hand. Every week one heard of sporadic terrorist attacks. Word had it that they could not shoot straight, but he knew that this would soon change as they became better trained. They had also heard that the small police contingent at Centenary had been boosted since the attack.

At times Gisela displayed a cruel and uncompromising attitude, which he had experienced on a number of occasions. Unable to explain it, he related this to the fact that her star sign was Gemini. They were fickle and had split personalities, or so he had read. While he did not consider Geminis cruel, he found them to be difficult. Once, they had light-heartedly discussed personality traits, including their own, and she reluctantly admitted that he had point. However, it was her ability to kill without conscience which he feared.

CHAPTER 65

Sizwe decided tonight would be the right time to attack. The rapid cloud build-up to the north promised rain, exactly what he needed. He decided to change his plan. He would split his troop. He would send three men to the road leading from Salisbury to Centenary. There, they were to mine the road from Centenary to the Mentz farm. Sizwe himself would attack the farm. The owner would call for the BSAP for help and, hopefully, their vehicles would detonate the landmines laid in the road. He would achieve the best kill rate and weaken their ability to pursue him. Yes, the farmstead's defences would be better organised, but the rain would work in his favour.

Already, jagged lightning flashes lit up the sky, the thunder rolling through the hills, as he and his men started their descent from the kopje. They left nothing behind except for two satchels, one with first-aid packs and the other with rations. The lightning allowed them to move briskly in the dark. Soon the first drops fell, splattering on the surroundings rocks. At the hill's base, the troop split. Three moved off to the road while the rest went towards the farm. It took them no more than an hour and half to reach the homestead, now a hundred yards in front of them. The house still showed signs of activity. The generator was running and the lights were on. Not that he could hear the generator with the falling rain.

As they approached the farmstead, he saw that a section of the security fence had still to be erected. He led his troop towards the gap that remained. The man behind him carried the rocket-propelled grenade. The rain fell in waves driven by the wind, drumming on his bush hat. Their feet sloshed through the water as puddles formed. The house had a corrugated iron roof. He knew that the sound of rain would drown out any noises they might make. Seeing the security fence, he realised that they probably had installed motion sensors to trigger the security lights. He hoped that none had been placed around the break in the fence.

They took cover behind a few garden bushes fifty yards from the gap.

He needed to destroy the generator. He knew that it was housed in an outer building behind the house. Hopefully, the rain had forced any dogs either indoors or to take shelter on the veranda. He could not imagine them anywhere outside in the rain.

The three men who had mined the road had now rejoined the group. He gestured to two men and told them that they should penetrate the gap while he and his men would give them covering fire if necessary. They slunk off into the darkness, one carrying a small satchel of WWII surplus explosives. The other two men dropped to the ground at the end of the bushes, ready to open fire while the others advanced.

He estimated the distance to the house to be about eighty yards.

'Remember, the main front door,' he said to the RPG-man. 'Fire when I say so.'

Two or three minutes passed.

A massive explosion rent the air, the ensuing fire lighting up the house. 'Fire!' he shouted.

They stood up as one and ran towards the house. His two men who destroyed the generator plant now concentrated their automatic rifles on the rear entrance to the house, gunfire filling the air. The RPG had penetrated the front door and exploded inside, blasting the entrance and all the glass out of the windows, the curtains all billowing outwards. Two men plunged through the entrance as they fired their rifles. There was a fusillade of bullets and both men crumpled to the floor. Sizwe and the rest of his men threw themselves behind the quarter-wall that surrounded the porch. Gunfire from the rear of the house could still be heard.

****

With the previous attack still foremost in her mind and the security fence still to be completed, Gisela thought it prudent not to sleep in any rooms that bordered on the outer wall of the house. She was well-acquainted with Russian rocket-propelled grenades and the damage these could do. It was the Communist bloc's chosen weapon for house-to-house combat. An armour-piercing round could penetrate an American T14 tank. She had taken the mattress from the master bedroom and placed this on the floor in an anteroom of the house, surrounded by other rooms. They had just retired to bed, both reading.

The generator blast plunged the house into darkness. They scrambled for their clothes and weapons. The RPG attack caught them unawares. The concussion blew out windows and blasted doors open, its shock wave washing over and momentarily stunning them. Strange though it may seem, they quickly collected their wits, having experienced this before.

David figured they would attempt to enter through either the front or the back doors. He chose the front, she the back. With his machine pistol in hand, he flung open the door leading to the main entrance hall. He made out the gaping hole where the entrance had been, it now faintly backlit. The hall smelt strongly of cordite but the smoke was rapidly dissipating.

He discerned two crouched shadows approaching and squeezed the trigger. The machine pistol spewed out fire and death, jumping in his hands as they absorbed the recoil. He saw both shadows crumble. At the same time, he heard the unmistakable sound of Gisela's rifle magazine emptying near the kitchen. He sprinted for the emergency two-way radio mounted on a small table in the corner of the anteroom.

'Centenary, Centenary, this is Woodbrook Farm. We are under attack. Urgently request help.' He repeated this again.

The BSAP must have had somebody operating the radios around the clock. Within seconds they confirmed help was on its way. They requested further details but he ignored them, returning to his previous position, keeping an eye on the entrance.

The front entrance faced in the direction of the management compound. He saw two sets of headlights approaching in the distance. Kallie Botha and his men must be on their way to assist. As they neared, he noticed Kallie wisely had extinguished the pickup's lights, the other doing the same. There was a volley of AK fire followed by a loud noise of wrenching metal. He knew that one of the vehicles must have been hit and crashed. He realised that they were about to be overrun.

'Gisela, grab some ammo and come here quickly!'

Within in seconds she was crouched down next to him, clutching three magazines in her hand.

'Quickly, put on whatever clothes and shoes you have here. We've got to get out now!' He grabbed clothing for himself. 'Come on, Come on!'

He was frantic. He knew that their final charge on the house could only be minutes away. It took no more than minute for both to dress. He led her by the hand down the darkened passage towards the window at the end.

'Wait!' he said and retraced his steps, feeling along the wall in the anteroom for where the keys to the gate hung. His fingers closed over them.

'What happened in the kitchen?'

'There were two, I'm sure one of them is down,' she said with open contempt and unbridled hatred, 'I hope they're both dead. '

He quietly opened the window. They both clambered through and dropped to the lawn below. They crouched low looking out for any movement. Still bent over, he slowly led her along the wall towards the rear gate in the fence. As he peered round the corner of the house, an AK sent concrete splinters flying from the wall. He saw the muzzle flashes. They were no more than twenty yards away. He stepped out and fired a long burst at where he thought the shots emanated. A short scream pierced the air and a body sank to the ground from behind the huge tree which shaded the rear entrance during the day.

'Come on, run!'

They sprinted for the rear gate and slipped through for the maize fields beyond, hoping to lose themselves in the dense rows of corn. A few parting shots whizzed in their direction but in the dark they were not easy targets. Soon they were drenched to the skin. Amongst the corn, they dropped to the ground and stared in the direction of the house. They heard further shots and assumed that Kallie must have arrived on the scene.

****

Sizwe was concerned. Things had not worked out as planned. The reaction of the residents to the attack had been unusually rapid. They were obviously not affected by the RPG blast. Three of his men were dead and one was wounded, whom he doubted would survive. They would have to leave him behind, though he dare not let him be captured alive.

They stormed into the house. It was empty.

'Torch the place,' he shouted.

They heard an enormous explosion, far away, the sound muffled by the rain. He realised that a landmine had exploded. He hoped it was a police vehicle.

The first flames were licking at the curtains and other items that ignited easily. The fire spread rapidly, smoke filling the house.

'Assemble outside at the back,' he ordered, moving in that direction himself. 'Did anyone see were the owners were heading?' he asked.

The one firing the departing shots at the pair raised his hand. 'They went that way towards the maize field,' he said.

'Okay, after them. Be careful, they're armed. We have a while before help arrives. The men's landmines have done their work. The police won't arrive tonight. Let's just get the owners.'

The survivors of his troop spread out and advanced slowly on the maize field. Behind them, the house was now a mass of flame, roaring and crackling, a shower of sparks rising into the sky.

****

'Fuck! The bastards.'

'Oh, my God! My house!' her voice full of anguish.

Silhouetted against the fire, he saw the insurgents advancing on the maize field.

He dragged her to her feet. 'Come on, we've got to get out of here. They're looking for us!'

Drenched from the collected water, they thrashed their way through the leaves from the edge of the field into the eight-foot-tall maize stalks. Their pursuers must have perceived movement as bullets were zipping through the plants. Some were damned close. He wondered whether their progress through the tall, dense maize would leave an easily-read broken path. The fire was casting an eerie yellow light for quite a distance, helping the terrorists.

'We best are careful,' she croaked between gasps, now breathless, 'The next field is an alfalfa field and it's less than a metre high.'

'Let's just get into the field. We can lie down. They'll never find us in the dark,' he replied between pants.

They broke out of the maize, crossed a farm road, no more than a double-wheel track, and plunged into the knee-high alfalfa. This was bordered by a two-foot-wide irrigation ditch. He threw himself down dragging her with him.

It didn't take long before they heard thrashing as the men in the maize field worked their way through the plants to the perimeter. He knew that they would break out onto the road within seconds. He tentatively peered over the top of the alfalfa.

The situation was getting progressively worse. The first man broke out of the maize field directly in front of him, no more than twenty yards away. He was soon followed by the others, quickly forming a line abreast along the road, spaced at intervals of about fifteen yards, their AKs at the ready. They knew that their targets had to be hiding nearby. David realised that the plan was to maintain the line alongside each other and so enter the alfalfa field, giving them the best chance of finding them. The rain had eased to no more than a drizzle. Other than the sound of drops falling on leaves, it was deathly quiet.

An intense, near-paralysing fear gripped him. If the guerrillas stumbled on them, they were dead; they had no chance against five men. He knew the terrorists were desperate. Every second they delayed reduced their chance of escape. They had to be gone before the BSAP arrived. They needed to put as much distance between them and the security forces as soon as possible. If the guerillas did not find them within the next few minutes, they would have to abandon the search.

The black men spoke amongst themselves. He did not understand the language but it seemed that two of them were arguing. Gisela brought her lips right close up to his ear.

'Some don't want to go on, they want to go back. One is saying that if they enter the alfalfa some will surely die. He says we must be hiding in it,' she whispered.

He didn't blame them. They must have realised that in this type of situation he would open fire before they could. It would be foolhardy to wait until they stumbled on them in the dark.

'We must shoot now!' she whispered.

'Okay, the moment any one of them steps forward, we fire. Okay – ready? Then on my mark.'

She nodded her head.

The man who seemed to be in charge shouted at another and then turned away from him. He saw him raise his arm and then with a forward motion indicate that the troop move forward.

'Shoot!' His voice was no more than a hiss.

In unison they rose, pulling the triggers, he spraying shots from right to left and she from the opposite direction, the pattern of shot converging on the middle. Men fell on both sides, those in the middle dropping to the road, theirs AKs spurting flame. A bullet, sounding like a hornet, shot past no more than an inch from David's head. Beside him, Gisela yelped loudly and spun like a top to face in the opposite direction. He knew she had been hit. She collapsed to the ground groaning loudly. He kept the trigger depressed spraying the road with bullets. He felt something tug at his left side, still he kept firing until there was a metallic click, the magazine empty. He looked intently at the road. Nothing moved, but he realised that there were only four shapes on the road. One was missing.

He uttered an expletive and dropped to the ground next to Gisela, she still groaning. Down below the height of the alfalfa the light was particularly bad. He could barely make her out. He could not see where she had been hit.

'Where? Where?' he asked, anxious and concerned.

She groaned again. 'My left shoulder.'

The situation left him terrified. The remaining guerrilla must have seen Gisela go down. What would he do, run for it? He thought not. It was now one on one. The man would come after him. He must be hiding nearby waiting for David to make a move.

'Can you crawl?' he asked, with unconcealed anxiety.

'I think so,' she replied, her voice quivering with suppressed pain.

They crawled through the alfalfa until they had put thirty to forty yards between them and where they had originally lain.

'Okay, we'll stop here,' he whispered.

She did not reply. He knew she was bleeding but had no idea of how badly she was wounded. He let his hand rove over her upper body and soon felt the slick wetness of blood. She had been shot high in the left shoulder. If she did not move he would be able to minimise the blood loss, but first he had to deal with the one missing guerrilla.

****

Sizwe was devastated and in shock. The plan had so drastically misfired. Most of his men were dead. He had been convinced that they would overrun the house and kill the occupants. He had lost virtually his whole troop. He had no idea if anyone survived and, if so, where they were. He was sure the police would have responded with more than one vehicle and twenty or more men. A major pursuit operation was sure to be mounted in the morning. The troop had agreed that if they were separated they would make their way back to the river and rendezvous where the boats were, but he would not leave this district until he avenged the loss of his brother. His killers were still alive and had killed even more.

He knew the man and woman were still out there hiding in the alfalfa. If they had any sense, they would have changed their position, but he was sure the woman had been shot. Maybe they were unable to move far.

As the gunfire had erupted from the alfalfa field and his men were struck down on both sides of him, he had dropped to the ground and returned fire. A bullet had struck him in the left side but it appeared not to have penetrated his ribcage, the slug entering on the edge of his body. He thought it might have ricocheted off a rib-bone, exiting at the back. It burnt like fire and it was excruciating when he moved. Blood trickled down his side into his trousers. The moment the shooting stopped, he rolled into the irrigation ditch, where the water was six inches deep, and crawled along its length until a good distance away. Only then, did he climb out and roll into the adjoining alfalfa field. He estimated that he was no more than seventy yards from where the shoot-out had began. As quietly as he could, he replaced the magazine of his rifle and cocked it. It had begun to drizzle again. The house still burnt, the orange glow discernible against the sky.

****

David racked his brains. He knew that stumbling around in the dark trying to find the lone guerrilla would give the man an advantage. He had to devise some plan which would force the man to reveal himself, hopefully inadvertently so. But what to do? The alternative was a waiting game for daybreak, which was still hours away. He dreaded leaving Gisela unattended until morning. He had no way of establishing how serious her wound was and how much blood she had lost.

Gisela groaned softly next to him.

'Don't worry, you're going to be okay. I'll get you out of this.'

She mumbled but he couldn't understand her.

'Listen, I want you to just stay here and lie still. I'm going to try and divert his attention. I've got to leave you alone for a while.'

'Yes, it's okay, but come back soon,' she said, her voice barely audible.

He had a plan. First, he replaced the spent magazine with his last and then, cradling the weapon in his arms, he crawled towards the irrigation ditch where he slowly lowered himself into the slow-flowing water. The water wasn't cold at all. As quietly as possible, he wormed his way forward in the direction he thought the guerrilla to be. He didn't want to look over the top and instead counted every time he moved an elbow forward, estimating each movement to be about a foot. He stopped on the count of two hundred and lay still for a few minutes, just listening.

He lifted his head to peer over the lip of the ditch. It was slightly higher than the alfalfa field and afforded him better visual perception of the field despite the near darkness being a problem. He saw nothing suspicious. He realised he would have to stage some incident, something that would trigger a reaction from the man, but what?

Over time, the ditch had accumulated a few small stones and rocks, none any larger than half a fist. Clearly, this was cleaned from time to time. Groping around, he soon found a small rock. He realised that he would have to raise his body if he were to throw it. He flung it at an angle into the field, dropping down so only his eyes peered over the top. He distinctly heard the rustle of leaves and a slight thump as the stone fell. He expected a reaction, yet there was none. Surely, the guerrilla must have heard that? The guy's smart, David thought. If he threw another, he would know for sure that this was a ruse. Christ, what was he to do now? Periodically he peeked over the lip. Nothing moved.

Then he heard the sound of a vehicle in the distance. Either it had to be from the management compound or the BSAP had arrived. Again, he looked. He saw headlights flickering through the trees in the distance, the vehicle on a farm road. He hoped they were circling the homestead looking for them. It approached slowly, at times disappearing completely where the bush was thick or it had disappeared behind the maize field. If it continued on this track, it would eventually come along this road.

He still lay still in the ditch. From the sound of the vehicle, he knew it to be nearby, but his adversary would know this as well. What would the man do? David believed that the man would crawl through the alfalfa until he reached the bush and then disappear. To singularly take on those in the vehicle was suicidal. They were probably armed to the teeth just looking for a fight. Still, he chose not to rise but waited until they were close. He saw that those standing on the rear of the pickup had two hand-held hunting lights, with particularly powerful beams, playing them over the terrain to the left and right of the vehicle.

Once the light swept over where he lay he slowly got to his feet, his hands in the air. 'Don't shoot! It's me – Tusk.'

He heard the sound of people jumping off the vehicle onto the road.

'Be careful! There could still be a few of the bastards around,' David shouted.

The armed men who jumped off the vehicle quickly formed a perimeter. It was the chief supervisor, FN rifle in hand, who approached David. He was a large man of mixed blood, a coloured, his father white, his mother black. He was dressed in khaki and wore a slouch hat.

'Boss, you're bleeding,' he said, staring at the blood that seeped through David's wet shirt where the bullet had entered.

'I know, but don't worry about me. Mrs Mentz is wounded. She's lying in the alfalfa. Go and find her. We need to get her medical attention urgently.'

'The terrorists?' the man asked.

'Most are dead and I'm sure the rest have fled. I heard gunfire from the direction of the compound?'

The man shook his head, his facing taking on a distressed expression.

'They ambushed Boss Botha's truck, killing them all. Boss Botha and three of the other workers. The truck smashed into a ditch and overturned, but all were shot. They're all dead.'

'Jesus Christ!' He was appalled. 'Where are the bodies?'

'We took them to Centenary with one of the other pickups.'

They strode into the field with another two armed men following, searching for Gisela, whom they quickly found. They shone a torch on her. She hadn't moved. She was deathly pale, her left shoulder covered in blood glistening in the torchlight. The front and side of her T-shirt was a dark stain. She was hardly aware of them, but managed a weak smile.

'Thank God,' she whispered.

'I don't want to move her but we've got no choice. Let's all join hands underneath her body, two at the front, two in the middle and the other at the feet and carry her to the truck. Just keep her body horizontal,' he said, with evident concern.

They carried her to the pickup and laid her flat on the loading area. All hopped aboard and they drove back to the farmstead where they found a BSAP vehicle waiting with eight men and a sergeant. They learnt that three vehicles had responded to their initial call for help, the leading vehicle triggering an anti-tank mine no more than three miles from the farm. The result was absolute carnage, a massive smoking hole in the road, bits of vehicle and body parts strewn around. It was like a slaughterhouse, the man said. The vehicle was a near-unrecognisable wreck and six of the nine men on the vehicle had been killed by the explosion. They took the three seriously injured men back to Centenary on the other police vehicle.

'Can you take her back to Centenary?' David asked, 'She's in a bad way. Please?'

'Of course, boss. I'll leave immediately.'

'Thank you. Just hurry. I'll follow a little later.'

The supervisor departed with a promise to return in minutes with the pickup, leaving two men with David.

The house was burnt to the ground. Just the walls stood; the corrugated iron roof had collapsed, the sheets now bent and twisted and lying on the floor amongst the walls. Embers still glowed and a few small fires still burnt. There was nothing to salvage. Fortunately, the outer buildings had escaped the inferno. They housed a multiple car garage, workshop, small dairy, laundry and two furnished cottages. The cottages were no more than a bedroom and bathroom each, used by guests or a visiting hunting party. He knew the workshop contained a portable petrol-driven electric welding plant on wheels. It could also serve as a standby generator with enough power for a small household. The men pulled it to where the generating plant had been. The workers traced the wiring and connected the welding machine to the interface that fed the outer building annex. They started the generator. They had light.

He broke the lock on one of the rooms and went into the bathroom. The mirror was small but still enough for him to realise he was a mess. He lifted his shirt to look at the wound. The bullet had entered his left side above the hip. It seeped blood. He thought it might have nicked his kidney. The pain was excruciating whereas before he was unaware of even having been hit. He needed medical attention soon. As he urinated into the white toilet bowl, he saw signs of blood. This was serious. He went to the garage and painfully climbed into a Wolseley Westminster, Gisela's best car, and beckoned one of the workers to bring his rifle and join him. They drove to Centenary.

CHAPTER 66

His plan had fallen apart. He hoped that those who had set the mines had escaped unscathed. His ribcage was on fire and he thought he might have a broken rib or two. He needed medical attention, but from where? Blood still seeped from both the entry and exit wounds. He knew the white man was somewhere in the alfalfa field waiting for him to make a move. They were too close together. Both could easily die in an exchange of fire. Still, the operation had been a success. The farmhouse was destroyed, a BSAP vehicle blew up full of police officers, the farm vehicle ambushed and men shot and killed. It would make the headlines in Salisbury and Bulawayo.

He had dozed off but something had woken him, his ears tuned to hear any strange sounds. What could it have been? If he was being stalked, he was not fool enough to raise his head. If the man nearly stumbled on him, he would shoot him from his prone position. The idiot would be silhouetted against the night sky. The clouds had disappeared and he could see the stars.

He heard the approaching vehicle, realising that it was coming down the road next to the irrigation ditch. It was sure to have a number of armed men aboard. Probably BSAP, he thought. Best stay undercover. It stopped, a light sweeping over the alfalfa, probing the most likely places. He did not move, flattening himself to the ground. There were voices and movement in the field. He daren't look. He was so close, he overheard their discussion. From it, he gathered that some had remained behind and that the vehicle would return.

After fifteen minutes the vehicle returned, only to drive right off again. He waited another half hour, every now and then peeping over the top of the field. Nothing moved. Slowly he rose, taking in the surroundings. There was nothing suspicious. Dawn was not far away, he had to move. He filled his canteen from the water in the irrigation ditch and slowly walked along the road towards the kopje. As soon as he was beyond the fields, he changed direction cutting across the virgin bush.

He realised that he would never make the border in the state he was. He would need to get help or hole up for a week or two until the wound had healed and, if he could blend in with the local black population, he could still deal with the man and the Mentz woman. But for now, the top of the kopje was the best place.

CHAPTER 67

The first thing David did on arrival at the hospital was to check on Gisela. This was a small country hospital served by two doctors. He told the nurse at reception who he was. She was rather dubious at first, looking at him suspiciously. He was covered in blood on the one side and dirty from head to foot. She looked at the machine pistol clasped in his hand.

'Is that a gunshot wound?' she asked, not in the least surprised. Nobody went anywhere without a weapon.

'Yes,' he said.'

'Please just wait here, I'll be back in a second,' she said and disappeared through a set of swing doors that led down a passage. He desperately needed something to alleviate the pain, all he wanted was an injection, and now he had to run into a possessive, matronly woman who, notwithstanding his appearance, blood and all, asked him to wait!

The door swung open again and a tall elderly man with a shock of white hair and a pair of half-glasses perched on his nose strode into the reception area, followed by the nurse.

'Good God, you're a mess!' the man exclaimed. 'I'm Doctor Howard and I'm in charge here. What happened to you?'

'I've been shot,' he croaked.

'That's obvious, let me take a look.' He turned to the nurse. 'Get Sister Wainwright. I want this man on a gurney and brought into casualty immediately. Before I examine him, I need him cleaned up.' The doctor walked up to him and bent down to inspect his wound. 'Not too bad. You'll live.'

'Thanks doc, but what I'd really like to know is how is Mrs Mentz? Is she okay?'

The doctor's face took on a sombre expression, hesitating before replying.

'Unfortunately, I have to tell you that her condition is not good at all. She's lost a great deal of blood. We are giving her a transfusion now. Fortunately, we have all her details on file. It seems the gunshot didn't damage any vital organs, but it did damage certain muscles and ligaments.

She is also in deep shock. They got her here just in time, but it will be a while before she'll be mobile again. The next twenty-four hours will be critical. I'll need to operate.'

'I'd like to see her,' he said.

'I'm afraid you can't. Anyway, she's unconscious and sedated,' the doctor replied. 'Besides, I need to attend to you.'

He realised that the doctor's word was final and reluctantly climbed on to the gurney they had brought and allowed them to wheel him down the passageway.

In the casualty ward they removed his clothing. He lay stark naked on the examination table while two junior nurses washed him. They then covered him with a sheet and waited for the doctor who soon arrived.

The doctor examined him thoroughly.

'You're bloody lucky. It's really no more than a flesh wound. Yes, it has just nicked your kidney, but only just, and there's no reason to put you under the knife. You're tough. You'll survive,' he said, a slight smile on his face.

'Doc, please do something about the fuckin' pain!'

'Of course, I'll give you an injection now,' he said and turned to the nurse indicating that she could proceed with the injection.

The feeling of relief and the immediate release from pain was heaven.

'You don't want to get used to that stuff,' the doctor warned with a chuckle. He got to work on the wound.

David woke up in a single ward, his side bandaged and stiff. It was already past midday. He was ravenous. He rang the bell above the bed. The day nurse arrived within minutes, giving him a friendly smile. She was young with a bob of short blonde hair beneath her nurse's cap. Her body was trim, clothed in the starched nurse's uniform. Fortunately in the tropics they did not have to wear stockings, only the white shoes.

'Good morning, I'm Sister Wiggin,' she said giving him her best smile, white teeth flashing. Already she had the clipboard and a thermometer in hand.

'All I want is breakfast,' he said.

'All in good time, but first your temperature, blood pressure and a bed-wash.'

He groaned in despair.

After breakfast, the doctor visited while doing his rounds. He examined him and proclaimed himself satisfied with David's progress. He probed the doctor concerning Gisela.

'The good news is that she's out of danger. The operation was a success and she's sleeping off the anaesthetic. She did ask about you during one of her lucid moments. I think you can go and say hello. It may be a good idea.'

The doctor left. The nurse told him that Gisela was on the same floor in the opposite wing. It was not far as this was a small hospital. He rolled out of bed and stood next to it for a minute or so waiting for his head to stop spinning, holding onto the bed with one hand. Eventually the room righted itself and he started walking. With every step, he felt better. By the time he got to her ward all that remained of his ordeal was the stiffness. He was sure that this would also loosen up in time.

He stood next to her bed looking down at her, deeply regretting that she had had to endure the terrifying moments they had experienced during the last two days. His heart went out to her. She was asleep, still pale. He stayed there with her for a while and then quietly left.

During the afternoon, he heard the sound of helicopters passing overhead and, around five that evening, a warrant officer of the BSAP visited him requesting that he carefully relate the sequence of events as these had taken place from the moment of attack until his arrival at the hospital. The man confirmed the tragic news of the loss of the police officers in the landmine explosion as well as the death of Kallie Botha and his men on the pickup.

'Have you been able to track the terrorists?' David asked.

'Yes, we picked up their trail and are in hot pursuit. They won't get away,' the warrant officer said. David believed him and was sure there weren't going to be any survivors. It was that kind of war.

'What about the survivors Mrs Mentz and I fought in the alfalfa?'

'Ha! There was only one survivor. In daylight, it was easy to read what had happened. Both of you did a brilliant job. There were five, you killed four. The last was wounded. We found his track and saw the blood. He's smart. He lost us, but don't fear, we'll still pick him up,' the warrant officer replied with confidence.

David wasn't so sure. This one was a lot smarter than that.

'Do you know where to start looking?' he asked.

'Sure, they always make for the border.'

'I wouldn't be so sure about this one,' David said.

The warrant officer did not reply, he merely sniffed, leaving David with the impression that he thought David was wrong.

The warrant officer bade him goodbye and left.

Ignoring the protests of both the nurses and doctor, David discharged himself. He had phoned the farm's office in the management compound and asked them to scrounge some clothes and fetch him.

Before leaving Centenary, they stopped at the bank. Although the manager was sympathetic, it still took a good hour before he had gone through the process of having himself identified and verified, they phoning numerous people to confirm his bona fides, but eventually the bank released three thousand Rhodesian dollars in cash against his signature. He then entered a men's outfitter and bought two sets of outdoor clothing and shoes. Next, he called on the cooperative and bought essentials in order to convert the laundry in the outer building into a makeshift kitchen. This included a refrigerator, a gas stove, crockery, cutlery, pots and pans. Finally, he bought foodstuffs from the supermarket. They arrived back at the farm in the early evening. Five of the black staff helped him offload and setup the kitchen.

He felt sad and depressed when he drove the pickup to the management compound and stopped in front of the Botha's house. This was large, similar to the main house, also with a veranda that stretched the length of the one side of the house. Cane chairs with cushions and tables were scattered on the veranda. Obviously, this the family's chosen spot where they spent their leisure time in the evenings and weekends.

Petronella, Kallie's now-widowed wife, stepped out onto the porch from the house dressed as she normally would be on any working day on the farm except for a small triangle of black cloth pinned to her left upper arm sleeve, a sign of mourning. Yes, she looked haggard and her eyes were red, yet she still held her head high, clearly a strong woman. She was an Afrikaner, proud of her heritage and ancestors, many of whom had perished when fighting the blacks. She felt compelled to show no weakness, he thought.

'Petronella,' he said, taking hold of her hand and holding her palm in his, 'I'm truly very sorry and my deepest sympathies.'

She merely nodded looking him in the eye, her lower lip quivering.

'It is God's will,' she whispered.

He didn't know what to say.

'Are you all right? What about the children?' he asked.

'They are too young to understand. We will manage.' Tears began to run down her cheeks.

'Is there anything I can do?' he asked.

'Just go, please! Leave now. We'll be fine.'

He left and returned to the farmstead.

CHAPTER 68

By the time Sizwe got to the foot of the kopje, dawn was already a smudge on the eastern horizon. As he started to climb, the light improved and he was able to pick his way through the rock outcroppings. It took him nearly an hour to reach the recess in the face not easily seen from below which they had used as a layover site. The last part of the climb was in broad daylight and he hoped nobody detected any unusual movement on the slope.

He was utterly exhausted and slightly woozy from the blood he had lost. His ribcage burnt. He stripped off his clothes and rummaged in the packs they had hidden until he found a field first-aid kit. He cleaned the wound as best he could, applied disinfectant and then strapped his ribs up with wide adhesive bandage tape. He tore open a ration package, some goo to which you merely added water, and presto! It tasted horrible. He washed this down with a few gulps of water. He then lay down under the rock overhang. Within a minute, he lapsed into a sleep of exhaustion, oblivious of the hard ground which was his bed.

He had planned starting that night for the border but realised he needed another day or two to recuperate. Water was a problem but it had rained the previous night. He hoped to find a rock pool amongst the outcrops. He would do so at first light the next morning. He still had sufficient water for another day.

The next morning, still stiff and sore, he scoured the rocks and found two rock pools, the water clean and fresh. He slaked his thirst and then filled two canteens. By that afternoon, his side felt better. He decided he would be able to move out the following night and scout around. He had the names of a few Shona families who lived in this area and who were believed to be sympathetic to the cause. At the moment, the best thing to do would be to remain where he was. After a few days, he could start to try to make contact with one of those families. The search was still on. He occasionally heard the Alouette helicopters of the Special Forces.

In one of the rucksacks left behind on the kopje, he found a shirt and shorts, which he donned. He would have to go barefoot, the combat boots he wore a definite giveaway. Many blacks in the area still went barefoot and by doing so he would not be conspicuous. They had spent no money since crossing the border from Zambia. He still had nearly two hundred dollars, considered a considerable sum amongst blacks. He descended the kopje in the dark hours of the morning and slowly made his way into town mingling with the others who walked to work.

Once the shops opened, he entered a 'native' shop. This was how the whites referred to it. It was actually a general trading store frequented by blacks. He bought a pair of sandals, shirt, belt, hat and underwear. His side still ached. He could live with it, but certain movements he still had to avoid, as they were too painful. He found a deserted building with an entrance to the back. He changed his clothes and dumped his old set in a large dumpster in the alley. He now felt a lot more presentable. Near the railway station he found an African eating-house, where he ate an enormous lunch of maize meal, beef stew and a salad of chopped onions, tomatoes and chillies. It was superb, he thought. He followed this with two cups of sweetened coffee. He perked up now, feeling more confident.

The information that he had been given for those who might help him was vague to the extreme. All he had was the man's name and what he did for a living. Simon Thakanda owned a butchery situated near the entrance to the black township bordering Centenary. The township was fed by one single main road. He thought he would try that first; at least it indicated a place.

The butchery wasn't difficult to find. He was surprised how modern it was with refrigerated counters containing pre-packed meats of every description right down to cowheels, black tripe, and offal. The shop was busy, at least four people serving from behind the glass counters filled with various cuts of meat. The owner, or at least the person Sizwe presumed to be the owner, was immediately recognisable. His attire was different from the others and his appearance more that of a man serving behind the counter of an upmarket butchery in an affluent white area. He was dressed in white with a white cap and a striped blue apron. Queues had formed, each being served by one of the butchers behind the counter. He joined the queue of the flamboyantly dressed individual.

He stepped forward when it was his turn and greeted the butcher in the traditional manner.

'What will it be?' the man behind the counter asked impatiently.

'I bring greetings from Mr Nkomo. He recommends you. He says your meat is of the finest,' Sizwe said, carefully watching the man's face for a reaction.

The man never batted an eyelid, but merely smiled.

'Our meat is the best in Centenary,' the man replied.

This was the coded reply he was to expect. A thrill of apprehension ran down his spine; he had found help at last! Sizwe chose two different cuts of meat from the display, which the man wrapped in brown paper. The butcher scribbled on the paper and then handed the parcel to him telling him to pay at the cashier at the door. Once outside and seated where he was alone Sizwe inspected the parcel. On the outside, the price had been written and on the inside of the folded flap was an address, just a street and number, and a time – 7 p.m.

He spent the rest of the day in town, remaining with the crowds, arousing no suspicion. He even found a group of young men who had lit their own private barbecue. When he asked, they let him fry his meat, which he shared as there was too much for one man.

In the late afternoon, he entered the township and asked directions to the street. The address was easy to find. It was nearly dark when he approached the house. A pickup stood in the driveway, the butchery's name stencilled on it. It was clear that, by African standards, the owner was a wealthy man. This also reflected in the house, larger than most with a porch and well-kept garden.

It was now dark. He tentatively knocked on the door. It was immediately opened by the butcher, now dressed in shorts with sandals, his sport shirt hanging over his pants. The man beckoned Sizwe inside and, once the door closed, grabbed his hand.

'I'm Thakanda,' he said, 'Please come in. It's wonderful to meet one of you. What happened at the Mentz farm is great news to us. It's just such a pity that you lost so many men. But we understand, you did account well for yourselves. It's terrific news, the whites in town are worried. You can actually feel their fear. '

'Thank you,' he replied.

'What can I do for you?'

'I need a place to hide and I need food. Also, I need medical attention, I've been wounded, not seriously, but I don't want it to get infected. Can you help?'

The butcher's face broke into a smile. 'But of course. I have quarters behind the house, servants quarters actually,' he said with a laugh. 'You can stay there, nobody will see you. We'll bring you food. You are not to leave the room. There are far too many informers, understand?'

Sizwe nodded.

'Medical attention could be a problem, but I'll see what I can do. I presume your weapons are hidden?'

'That's correct.'

'Come, let me take you to your room straight away. I don't want you in the house. It's too dangerous.'

The room was spartan but clean.

'This will be fine,' he said, 'but before you go I want to ask whether it is possible for you to obtain information for me about the Mentz Farm. I want to know whether Mrs Mentz survived the attack and whether the man living with her is still there. I don't know his name, but he may have been wounded in the attack.'

'I'll see what I can do. Give me a day or two. '

It took three days before Thandaka got back to him with the information he wanted. Both the whites on the farm had been wounded but Tusk and his mistress, the Mentz woman, were already up and about again. Mrs Mentz had undergone an operation and was still in the Centenary hospital but would be discharged in a few days time and would probably return to the farm.

Sizwe would wait.

CHAPTER 69

After five days, the hospital discharged Gisela. She had made a remarkable recovery although her shoulder was still strapped up and virtually immobile. David collected her with the Wolseley and, as they swept into the drive towards the house, she saw the devastation and ruin. He expected a show of anguish and sorrow. That did not happen. She clenched her jaw, her eyes narrowed and she grabbed his arm with her good hand, her fingers digging into his flesh.

'The fuckin' bastards,' she hissed, 'If they think I'm going to give this up, they're mistaken. I will rebuild this house. They won't stop me! It will look like it used to, believe me, they don't know me yet! I will stay here in those rooms you have converted into our living quarters until the job is done The farm will continue as before. I'm truly sorry about Kallie. Petronella can stay for as long as she wishes, their house is hers to use, but I'll get a new manager. You just wait and see!' she said, her voice full of venom and hatred.

He was taken aback by her outburst but agreed with her. This was not the time to throw in the towel. He had his own vendetta. He wanted the bastard who had led the terrorist group.

In view of his gunshot wound and Gisela still recuperating, he took an indefinite leave of absence. He assumed the role of manager, running the farm with Gisela overseeing him. The confines of the living quarters did wonders for their relationship. There was no place to hide and continuous interaction between them on a daily basis. Her convalescence was miraculous. Within three weeks, she no longer needed the sling although her arm was still stiff. Yes, he loved her. If he had any doubts before, these had evaporated. Still the intense, uncontrolled hatred she harboured towards the terrorists, which seemed to simmer just below the surface and periodically came to the fore, still concerned him. It unnerved him, leaving him with the feeling that during such a moment she could lose total control and could be capable of anything, even cold-blooded murder.

He found that he actually enjoyed farming, the sun, being out in the open, the bellowing of cattle, the ceaseless humour of the blacks and watching things materialise before his eyes. The building of the new house, the ploughing of a field, and the sunset after a hard day's physical work imbued him with a new sense of belonging.

It had been weeks since he had made love to her. Yes, he had hugged and kissed her, but he had been told that while her shoulder mended and the tendons knitted again she was not to move it. After three weeks, he was so consumed by his need for her that he saw something erotic in most things she did.

Eventually she was allowed to remove the sling. He was already in bed when she exited the bathroom. Only the bedside lights were on, casting a pool of light on each side of the bed, enough to read by. She stood at the foot of the bed in the flimsiest of negligées, reaching to just below her crotch. He just stared, she giggled.

'God, what it takes to turn you on!'

'You were in a sling and I thought—'

'Stop making excuses. Just watch.'

She took the hem of her negligée and slowly lifted it, pulling it over the top of her head until she was naked. She dropped the garment to the floor, lifted her arms above her head and slowly pirouetted. At that moment, he thought her the most beautiful woman in the world. He let his eyes slowly rove over her, her sex, her beautiful firm breasts that seemed to defy gravity, the aroused nipples, the cascade of blonde hair, the thin waist, and the long legs.

'My God! You're beautiful. Come here,' he whispered, aware of his wanton arousal, aching for her.

She slowly walked to his side of the bed and stood in front of him. He grabbed her by the buttocks and drew her to him. He let his lips slide over her stomach, kissed her inner thighs and then her pubes. She threw her head back and emitted a low moan of pleasure and expectation.

'Oh Christ!' she moaned, 'Oh yes! Please ...'

He felt her fingers tremble. He slid over to make room for her and drew her into the bed, she lying down on her back. She reached out her hand and let her fingers glide over his stomach and then took him in her hand. He gasped as her fingers closed on him.

He moved on top of her and with his knees parted her legs. He kissed her nipples and buried his face in her neck. He felt her tremble again.

'Please, do it now.'

As he slid inside her, she gasped in his ear.

He made love to her with both her hands clenched in his, pressed into the bed behind her head.

Soon she heaved and then keened as he, with a shudder, exploded inside her.

CHAPTER 70

Frustration gnawed at Sizwe. He could not leave the room during the day and even at night, it was dangerous. Thandeka had told him that it seemed the Special Forces no longer concentrated on the Centenary area, probably having assumed that he had escaped. There was no news about his three comrades. Every evening after ten, Thandeka would slip into the room and they would talk. The butcher complained about the laws that prohibited him from buying property where he wished, from obtaining a licence to sell liquor and doing business as a free man. The white man's laws were designed to stifle the black man's business and political ambitions. He admitted he had many white friends but they all saw him as inferior, always evident whenever they met. Some would subconsciously lapse into English tinged with a black man's accent when speaking to him. It was as if they were lowering themselves to his level. It hurt and was an insult. He was adamant that the white man had to be driven from his land. He wanted to be master of his own destiny.

'I have found someone to assist you,' Thandeka said one evening during their discussions.

Sizwe was immediately wary. This is how you were caught or killed, he thought.

'Who is he?'

'He was a policeman until about a year ago when he was booted out of the BSAP.'

'What for?'

'He struck an officer. They jailed him for a few months and after his release chucked him out. He has now got a job at the local municipal stores and vehicle pool as a security guard,' the butcher said.

'He knows weapons?'

Thandeka nodded and added. 'Look, he's reliable. I would trust him with my life. He hates the white man.'

The man came the next evening. His name was Michael. He was thin and tall but all muscle and sinew like a long distance runner, with a narrow face, a long jaw and flat ears.

'I don't have a weapon for you,' Thandeka said.

'Don't worry. I've my own. It's an FN2 rifle and I've got about fifty rounds of ammunition for it.'

'That's enough. '

From Thandeka's sources amongst the locals, they learnt that the erection of the security fence at the farmstead had been temporary halted, the workers concentrating on clearing the debris and rubble. Additional labour had also been recruited to help rebuild the house. There were now also two armed guards who patrolled the property at night. They had learnt that the outer building had been converted into living quarters, both Mrs Mentz and Tusk staying there. They and the farm supervisors carried weapons at all times, FN rifles and machine pistols. A small contingent of Special Forces troops were now billeted in the town in support of the BSAP stationed there.

'What's the plan?' the newcomer asked.

'It's difficult. Those on the farm have re-installed the radio rapid-response system. The moment the farm has the slightest perception that we're around, they'll call for help, as will any other farmers in the district. So we have to get to their sleeping quarters without being seen.'

'That's not possible. If the police are guarding the property you won't be able to get near. The locals will alert the police of any unknowns,' Michael said.

All three pondered the problem until Thandeka spoke up.

'I've an idea,' he said hesitantly. 'They've employed additional people on the building site. I believe we need to get you two employed by the group that's rebuilding the house. I have a connection in the group who can assist. You work there for a week or two until those at the site are familiar with you so that you can move around without suspicion. I'm sure that a few of the builders stay there overnight, not wanting to travel back and forth everyday. I mean it's inconvenient. That would put you close to the outer buildings. Of course, you're going to have to smuggle your weapons in.'

A slight smile crossed Sizwe's face. 'That's brilliant,' he said, looking at Michael for a response. Michael nodded his approval.

'Can you get us into the building team?' Sizwe asked dubiously.

'I can only try,' Thandeka responded. He raised a hand and waved a finger at them. 'But, be sure, I don't want to attract any attention to myself or my family. Don't put me or my family in danger.'

He refused to assist them in any other way and once they left his house, they were not to return.

Thandeka never told them how he managed to get them included in the group that travelled to work on the farm every day. Two days later, he told them that they were to report to the assembly point in town near the main bus stop at six in the morning where they were to ask for Paul, who was one of the foremen. He would tell them what they would earn and what their duties were. Under no circumstances was anybody to be brought into their confidence. They all boarded a large truck, which drove them to the farm, the same vehicle returning them in the evening. Michael had given Sizwe temporary accommodation.

Paul was just what Thandeka had said he was, a foreman. It was evident that if they intended to keep their cover they would have to work as labourers. He was clear on that, those that shirked were fired.

For a few days the two men mixed cement, pushed wheelbarrows filled with bricks or sand, and did other menial jobs they were given. Sizwe enjoyed the work. It helped him get back into physical shape again. He also had time to study the farmstead complex and the habits of those they had targeted. He regularly saw Mrs Mentz, who took a keen interest in the rebuilding process, and often she had the man she called David at her side. Each time Sizwe saw them an intense hatred consumed him, whilst he pretended to carry on his work lest he become obvious and draw attention. They were always armed, at least with automatics strapped to their sides and even at times carrying automatic machine pistols. Fortunately, both Michael and Sizwe were Ndebele and mixed easily with the others, readily accepted as the others were also Ndebele. No one was suspicious.

There was no work on Sundays. Sizwe had moved in with Michael, who shared a large shack with others in Centenary. The accommodation was primitive. He shared a room with four others. During the night of the first Sunday, Sizwe returned to the kopje. He dismantled his rifle, putting the pieces into a gunnysack with the ammunition and two hand grenades. Once at the bottom of the kopje, he slung it over his shoulder and carried it back to Centenary. A man with a sack over his shoulder would not be seen to be unusual. He had also added a pair of boots, clothes and a water bottle. His concern was that he would be asked about its contents, but he had seen others boarding the vehicle with toolboxes and bags and hoped no-one would think his carrying a bag unusual. Similarly, Michael had also smuggled his weapon onto the farm.

The travelling back and forth to Centenary was tedious and, after a week or so, some of the workers decided to ask permission to stay overnight on the building site, which Gisela allowed. The men were unarmed and there was no reason to be suspicious. Michael and Sizwe joined the small group, sleeping in the half-erected house, lighting a wood fire on the ground. They had also built a crude shelter in the event of rain. For this, they used the twisted and burnt corrugated iron roof sheets.

The security fence had remained untouched, all work still concentrated on the house, the work progressing rapidly. In the early evenings, they were free to walk round. The guards would always arrive just before sunset and after a while no longer concerned themselves with the workers, knowing most of them by name. Sometimes the workers would even share their food with the guards, developing a degree of camaraderie between them.

They stopped work for an hour at one in the afternoon, the hottest time of the day. The two men lay down in the shade.

'We do it tonight,' Sizwe said.

Michael jerked out of his half-sleep. 'Why tonight?'

Sizwe pointed to the northwest. 'Look at the clouds. It will be overcast tonight, it might even rain.'

'You're right. We'll wait until about midnight.'

Their biggest concern was the two guards. They dare not shoot. From steel reinforcing rod used to rebuild the house, Sizwe had fashioned two nearly two-feet-long pointed spikes, with a wooden handle on the end. Both also had knives honed until razor-sharp.

As Sizwe had predicted, and so typical of Africa, by ten that evening the clouds blotted out the moon. The first jagged lightning flashes and rolls of thunder heralded the coming rain. Everyone sought shelter in the lean-to they had erected, all cramming into it. When Sizwe said that he and Michael would look for shelter elsewhere, none objected. They sprinted to the other side of the building site and clambered beneath the new corrugated sheets, which were raised above the ground lying flat on wooden trestles. It was primitive but effective. It started to rain before midnight.

From where they were, they could see over the expanse of lawn in front of the house. The two security guards had taken shelter under an enormous plane tree that dominated the front of the house, the thick foliage providing excellent cover. At intervals, one would patrol around the house, the other remaining in the front. The area around the house was littered with all sorts of building paraphernalia: cement mixers, shuttering, bundles of wooden boards, wheelbarrows and stacks of cement bags, the latter covered by corrugated iron sheets to protect them from the rain. The guard would invariably make his way clockwise round the house and outer buildings, winding his way through the building site.

Sizwe sought a site to ambush him that was as far away as possible from the outer annex and the large tree. The rain would cloak most sound but not a piercing death scream. That had to be avoided at all costs. The area where the cement bags were stacked was ideal. Sizwe had placed a few wheelbarrows in the passageway, not quite blocking it, but forcing anybody passing through to move to the left, nearer to the stacked bags.

He waited in the rain behind the bags, Michael next to him. Half an hour passed. The guard was reluctant to leave the shelter of the tree but eventually he started his perimeter patrol, a small slicker draped over his shoulders to protect him from the rain. He wore a slouch hat, the brim pulled down to protect his face.

As the guard stepped past where he was concealed, Sizwe stepped out from behind the bags, clamped one hand over the man's mouth and, with all his strength, drew the man's head back, trying to slit his throat with the knife. Meanwhile, Michael moved up in front and drove the steel rod into the man's heart. Blood spurted, a bubbling sound coming from the guard's throat as he dropped his weapon, both hands trying to clasp his slit throat. The man slid to the ground, his heels drumming on the dirt in his final death throes. Sizwe grabbed the man by the collar and dragged him behind the cement bags while Michael picked up his FN rifle and hat.

'Okay, I'm going to take up position behind these bags. As we discussed, you go and beckon the other guard to come and look at something on this side of the house. Tell him his partner sent you. Let's hope this works. He'll probably make you walk in front of him. Just be prepared for anything, I don't know what he's going to do,' Sizwe said.

It was still raining lightly. Michael walked towards the front, making sure that there was nothing suspicious in his actions, appearing unconcerned and relaxed. Once he rounded the corner of the building and the security guard was no more than twenty yards from him, he stopped and called, beckoning with his hand.

'Your partner wants you to come and look at something on the other side of the house. He asked me to call you,' he said loudly above the sound of the light rain.

The guard seemed to think nothing of it. He took his rifle and slung it over his shoulder, clearly indicating to Michael the man was unconcerned. 'What's wrong?' he asked as he got to Michael.

'I really don't know. Something at the fence on the other side. He asked me to call you.'

He led the way with the guard following behind him. As they passed the stacked bags, Sizwe stepped out from behind and swung a piece of four-by-four timber at the guard's head, striking him from behind with a loud thunk. The guard fell to the ground. Michael turned round and drove the oversized ice pick into the man's temple. The man had died soundlessly. His body was also dragged behind the cement.

Both men quickly returned to where they had hidden their weapons, which they retrieved along with the hand grenades, water bottles and other items they would need.

'Now to get near to the outside rooms without alerting those ridgebacks,' Sizwe said.

During the past week, they had befriended the dogs, giving them scraps from their meals. However, they knew that dogs were unpredictable, especially ridgebacks. During the day they could be your friend while at night the only friend they had was their master, which meant that, whilst they may not physically attack, they would bark and possibly try a mock charge. This was bound to arouse everybody. He wondered whether the rain had driven the dogs indoors. They were house pets, Mrs Mentz allowing them free rein in the house.

Sizwe peered around the corner of the half-erected house and slowly examined the yard between the house and the outer buildings. Everything appeared normal. The dogs were not to be seen. However, in the dark, they would not be discernible if they had taken shelter. He looked at the room which the couple used as their sleeping quarters. The wooden door was closed, as was the outer security grille door. He knew it was a large room, having walked past it a few times during the last week. He had seen a large double bed at the one end of the room and a couch and two easy chairs in front of the bed with a small coffee table in between. He had hoped that he could toss a grenade through the bars of the grille door. This was not possible as both the grille door and the window were protected by a layer of closed-mesh steel wire. All he could do was throw a grenade at the foot of the door, which would probably take out both doors, but would not kill the occupants as they were too far from the door. That would mean that he would have to step inside and finish them off. They were sure to have their weapons near at hand. Would the concussion from the grenade leave them incapable of retaliating for a few moments?

CHAPTER 71

David woke up to find Gisela shaking him.

'David, wake up!' There's something outside, the dogs are growling.'

'The fuckin' dogs growl at anything,' he retorted, swinging his legs over the side of the bed, clearly irritated.

He moved towards the switch next to the bed against the wall. If activated, this started the generator. Suddenly he heard something heavy strike the steel mesh of the grille door and drop to ground with a heavy metallic sound. He immediately realised what it was.

'Grenade! Take cover! Get down!' he shouted, pure reflex, simultaneously depressing the switch and dropping to the floor.

The next moment the grenade exploded, the force slamming him into the bedside table driving the wind from his lungs, the blast deafening him. The doors were torn from their hinges, rushing into the room. Seconds later the outside security lights bathed the yard in light as the generator caught. Acrid smoke and dust filled the room, blinding him. David fought to recollect himself. He was sure that that they would charge the room or throw another grenade through the door. Although deafened, he could faintly hear the yelping of a dog. He knew he had to stop anybody getting near the doorway and groped around on the floor looking for his machine pistol. Where the hell were the security guards? There had been no shooting. It would've woken him. Were the guards still alive?

His fingers closed over the barrel of the gun. The doorway was illuminated by the outside lighting. He aimed the gun in that direction and let off a short burst to discourage anyone contemplating an entry.

'Gisela! Are you all right?' He shouted. He could now vaguely make out the interior of the room, lit up by the light outside.

'I'm okay,' she said. Her head appeared over the side of the bed where she had been thrown by the blast. A large mahogany hope chest at the end of the bed, about three feet in height, had absorbed most of the explosion.

The two dogs lay sprawled on the floor. They both appeared dead.

'Just stay where you are,' he said to Gisela and ran to the window.

The glass had been blow out and lay collected on the sill behind the mesh. He stared out into the yard, which was brightly lit. The start-up of the generator and the lights must have caught the terrorists by surprise, he thought. They were out there somewhere. He was sure they were waiting for him to make a move.

He turned around and looked at Gisela, still dressed in her negligée, staring at him, her expression registering shock. 'Snap out of it. Get yourself some shoes and clothes and then bring your weapon. I want you to come here and keep a lookout while I get dressed.' His ears rang and he hoped she could hear him. Worse, he wasn't sure how loud his voice was.

About a minute later, she joined him at the window.

'If you see anything just fire a burst in their general direction,' he said and went back to find his things.

He returned, properly dressed, and brought three additional magazines for the MP4s.

'I'm surprised they hit this place so soon again. Especially with two trained security guards around,' he said. 'We can only assume that they somehow overwhelmed the guards. They should have responded long ago,' he said, unable to disguise his concern.

Gisela heard what he said but did not respond, still staring out into the yard.

Suddenly the throb of the generator slowed and then stopped, the light from the security lights fading out. The yard plunged into darkness again.

'Come on, let's get out here.'

He grabbed her by the arm and ran out of the broken entrance, nearly tripping over some rubble. They skirted along the wall of the outer building in the opposite direction of the generator plant, hoping that none of the killers were in that direction. Once away from the building, he stepped into some shrubbery and sank to his haunches, pulling her down next to him. He had to wait until his eyes adjusted properly to the darkness. He had one concern. The break in the fence was behind the property, which meant that to exit the compound the terrorists would have to pass this way. How many were there?

Slowly his surroundings began to take shape. He was now able to see the outer building and the yard. Nothing moved. They must have remained hunkered down for about five minutes when suddenly there was the sound of an object falling to the concrete floor of the yard. Quickly, he placed a restraining hand on Gisela, not wanting her to open fire.

'Don't shoot until we see something,' he whispered.

They stared intently at the yard. The building cast a shadow in the moonlight, half the yard in total blackness.

He drew her close to him and whispered in her ear. 'There's only one thing to do. I'm going to make a run for the tractor.' He pointed to where it was parked under a huge tree about twenty yards away. 'They're bound to open fire. The moment you see their muzzle flashes, fire a short burst in their direction and then fall flat as you can. Do you understand?'

'Yes. Be careful!'

Bent over double, he broke out of the shrubbery. Immediately, there was the unmistakable of chatter an FN rifle on automatic, the bullets whipping past him like bees. Gisela opened up with a short burst. The FN fire ceased, David making it unscathed to the cover the tractor provided. He had seen where from the gunfire had originated. Behind the cover of the tractor, he lifted the machine pistol and sprayed a few shots in that direction, hoping that they would be forced out of the courtyard.

In the distance, he heard the sound of an approaching vehicle from the direction of the manager's compound. The terrorists would have heard the same, he knew. This would force them to make their escape in his and Gisela's direction. How many were there? he wondered.

Suddenly two rifles opened fire from different directions. Somehow, one of them had managed to flank him. He was now the target of a fusillade of shots. Something slammed into his right thigh pulling his leg from under him, sending him crashing to the ground. He heard an MP4 open up, followed by a loud cry.

Other than the sound of the vehicle, it was now deathly quiet. David could feel the blood pumping out of the wound. He was going to need urgent attention. He pulled his belt from his pants and fashioned a tourniquet, using the barrel of his automatic to twist the belt and stem the flow of blood.

'Don't shoot! Please don't shoot! I'm coming out with my hands in the air.'

This came from the direction of the courtyard. David crawled from behind the tractor wheel and peered around the corner. A man stood in the moonlight with his hands raised.

'Don't move. Gisela, shoot him if he even twitches.' Then he shouted at the man. 'How many are you?'

'Two of us.'

'Where is the other?' David shouted again. He could hear the vehicle stop on the other side of the house.

'Over to your right. I think he's dead.'

David crawled slowly with the machine pistol at the ready, emerging from cover. He heard a groan. It seemed to emanate from behind a concrete stand with a thick, flat concrete slab table used to butcher game after a hunting trip. He approached, keeping the stand between him and whoever lay behind it.

'Throw your gun out where I can see it, together with any pistols or grenades,' he said.

There was a faint rustle of clothing and then the rifle emerged, pushed out along the ground. David bent forward and grabbed it.

'There is nothing else,' a voice croaked.

Still on his stomach, he slowly peered around the corner. The black man sat behind the slab leaning against the cement. He raised one arm, the other lay useless in his lap, the gunshot wound and blood visible on his right shoulder. He heard running footsteps.

'Over here,' he heard Gisela shout. 'Go and help Mr Tusk over at the butcher block!'

The farm supervisor joined David, cradling his automatic rifle in front of his chest.

'Boss, are you okay?' the concerned supervisor asked.

'I've been better, I'm bleeding like a pig. You're going to have to get me to a hospital pretty quickly,' he replied in an attempt at humour. Nobody laughed.

Another farmhand approached the intruder still standing with his hands in the air. He clubbed him with the rifle butt, the man falling to the ground. The generator started up again, flooding the yard with light.

'Don't do that!' David shouted.

Gisela emerged from the shrubbery, the MP4 clutched in one hand, a SIG automatic in the other. She stopped in front of the fallen man, lifted the barrel of the automatic until it pointed at the fallen man's head and pulled off two shots in succession, the man's head jerking as the bullets impacted.

'Jesus Christ!' David screamed, 'Are you fuckin' insane!' He was revolted and numb with shock. He simply could not comprehend what she had done. Her face was a mask of sheer hatred. She turned and walked in David's direction, clear what her intentions were.

'Fuck you, don't! Gisela. I warn you, we're not fuckin' murderers,' he shouted at her, raising the MP4 until it pointed at her.

'The bastards, they're the murderers, they kill innocent people, women and children and now you want to protect them. Suddenly, you're a man of principle,' she screamed, nearly incoherent.

'Please Gisela, please! Calm down, you can't do this,' he said, trying to keep his voice level. He could feel himself weakening, the loss of blood beginning to tell. More armed men now surrounded the terrorist.

Gisela began to sob – huge racking sobs, which shook her body.

'Why are we fighting this war?' she cried in anguish. 'Why?' She sank to ground next to him. She suddenly saw the blood on his leg. Her hand flew to her mouth.

'My God, you're shot,' she said.

'I know,' he said, 'You have to get me to hospital.'

'Bring the pickup,' she shouted.

The truck was driven from the other side of the house and David, together with Siwze, were loaded onto the loading bay, the two men lying side by side, an armed farmhand at one end and the supervisor at the other. Gisela climbed in the front with the driver. The pickup drove off.

'You shot me,' David said.

There was a moment's silence.

'But you shot me!'

'In self-defence. Do you really believe this is necessary?' David said.

'Do you think we have a choice? You grab our land, the best land. You treat us like slaves without a say in our own country. We want it back, so we have to fight. Even if this takes forever. We'll fight you.'

There was a moment of silence.

'So, there's no chance of peace?'

'Never!'

What's your name?'

'Sizwe.'

****

The BSAP was waiting as the pickup arrived at the local hospital in Centenary, immediately taking control of the wounded prisoner. David was wheeled into casualty, the resident doctor attending to his wound.

He woke up in the same ward where he had previously lain. When he opened his eyes, Gisela was standing next to him. He realised that his leg was encased in a cast of plaster of Paris to keep it rigid.

'Hi!' he said, a faint smile on his lips.

'Hi, yourself,' she whispered, taking his hand.

'Promise me you'll never do that again. You have to promise me that, sweetheart. I love you, but I can't stay if you hate and kill like that.'

She started to cry. 'Do you know how sorry I now am for what I did?' she sobbed. 'I promise.'

'Thank you.'

She squeezed his hand. 'You can't ever leave me now. You and I are stuck with each other. I'm pregnant.'

'Oh, God!' he said smiling, elated with the latest development.

'You know we'll never stop them. We can shoot them, the government can hang them, but it won't help. They will never stop fighting. Africa has changed: this will happen in Angola, Mozambique, and South Africa. One day we'll have to give in to them,' he said.

'I never believed this before, but now I know you're right.'

'Can you live here knowing this?' he asked.

She never hesitated. 'Yes, I can.'

About the author

Peter Vollmer is the grandson of German colonists who settled in the German colony of South West Africa in the late 19th century. After living and studying in Namibia, France and England, Peter returned to his native South Africa. He was involved in assisting then Rhodesia when it declared UDI and assisted in breaking the embargo set by the United Nations.

His other novels include *The Gunrunners, Diamonds Are But Stone, Per Fine Ounce* and *Left for Dead.*

Printed in Great Britain
by Amazon